P9-DMU-643

The Way It Wasn't

*Great Science Fiction Stories of
Alternate History*

Compiled by Martin Greenberg
with an Introduction by Robert Silverberg

A Citadel Twilight Book
Published by Carol Publishing Group

Flagstaff Public Library
Flagstaff, Arizona

Copyright © 1996 by Martin Greenberg
All rights reserved. No part of this book may be reproduced in any
form, except by a newspaper or magazine reviewer who wishes to quote
brief passages in connection with a review.

A Citadel Twilight Book
Published by Carol Publishing Group
Citadel Twilight is a registered trademark of Carol Communications, Inc.
Editorial Offices: 600 Madison Avenue, New York, N.Y. 10022
Sales and Distribution Offices: 120 Enterprise Avenue, Secaucus, N.J.
   07094
In Canada: Canadian Manda Group, One Atlantic Avenue, Suite 105,
   Toronto, Ontario M6K 3E7
Queries regarding rights and permissions should be addressed to Carol
Publishing Group, 600 Madison Avenue, New York, N.Y. 10022

Carol Publishing Group books are available at special discounts for bulk
purchases, sales promotion, fund-raising, or educational purposes.
Special editions can be created to specifications. For details, contact:
Special Sales Department, Carol Publishing Group, 120 Enterprise
Avenue, Secaucus, N.J. 07094

Manufactured in the United States of America
10   9   8   7   6   5   4   3   2   1

Library of Congress Cataloging-in-Publication Data

The way it wasn't: great stories of alternate history / edited by
   Martin Greenberg; introduction by Robert Silverberg.
        p.   cm.
     "A Citadel Twilight book."
     ISBN 0–8065–1769–7 (pbk.)
     1. Fantastic fiction, American.   2. Historical fiction, American.
   3. Imaginary histories.   I. Greenberg, Martin Harry.
   PS648.F3W39   1996
   813′.08708—dc20   95–49287
                                                         CIP

S-F
WAY IT
WASN'T

Contents

Introduction

by Robert Silverberg

Science fiction is a literature of infinite possibilities; and the subgenre of alternate-timetrack fiction is one of its most infinite compartments. To ask oneself, "What if history had not taken the course we know?" is a delicious liberation of the writer's imagination. Inventing the future can become a stale business to someone like me, whose profession it has been for many decades; but reinventing the past holds endless and irresistible fascinations. What if Napoleon had died in infancy, or the Thirteen Colonies had lost the American Revolution, or the Roman Empire had lasted another thousand years? The writer makes his one basic history-changing assumption; then he plunges his characters into a world that never was, and investigates all the imaginable consequences of that world's divergence from the "real" time-line. The result, if the work is done intelligently and perceptively, is an excursion into speculative history that is both amusing and intellectually stimulating.

I have been tempted again and again into this kind of thought experiment. More than thirty years ago I wrote a novel called *The Gate of Worlds*, in which I postulate that the Black Death of 1348 had killed so much of Europe's population that the expansionist Western Europe of the Renaissance did not emerge and thus the European conquest of the Americas and Africa never took place. That left the Aztec and Incan empires intact in the New World of the twentieth century, and the great black kingdoms of Africa still in power there. (I return to this notion a quarter of a century later in the novella "Lion Time in Timbuctoo," which is included in the present volume.)

In a story called "Trips" I take my protagonist through a dozen or more alternate Earths in the course of about ten thousand words—one in which the Axis had won World War II, one in which John F. Kennedy had not been assassinated in 1963, one that found the hordes of Genghis Khan in possession of twentieth-century California, and so on in rapid succession. More recently, I have written a whole series of stories dealing with my imagined unfallen Roman Empire ("Via Roma," "To the Promised Land," to name just two), and one in which wandering Crusaders bring Christianity to Florida long before the voyage of Columbus ("Looking for the Fountain,") and several more in a similar vein. It is an infinitely seductive theme, for every moment of our lives is a convergence of potential infinities, and every trifling decision we make sends a billion billion unborn worlds into oblivion: And so any moment at all in the world's history can give rise to a quite literal infinity of possible stories as the writer recaptures some of those lost possibilities.

The theme can be handled in many ways. The writer may suppose that an infinite number of possible worlds exist simultaneously, as parallel universes, each unaware of the others. One of them is our world. In the world immediately adjacent, perhaps, the atomic bomb was never successfully invented, though all other details of history were identical up until 1945. In the world beyond that, electricity is unknown. In the one beyond that, the steam engine proved too much for the ingenuity of James Watt. And in the world somewhere beyond that, mankind itself never evolved. So on and so on, ad infinitum, with the characters employing some device allowing them to step from world to world as the plot dictates, as in "Trips."

Contrariwise, the writer may want to assume that only one "real" world can exist at a time, which is our own; but that it is possible somehow to enter the past and make some alteration—as small as catching a butterfly, as large as assassinating a key historical figure—that will throw the entire history of our world into some alternate probability-track from the point of the alteration on. (Poul Anderson's classic Time Patrol series, in which special agents rove all eternity to prevent such changes from happening, is one of the best examples of this approach. Alfred Bester's "The Men Who Murdered Mohammed" is an uproariously funny and equally valid refutation of the whole possibility of changing the world in this way.)

Just when the first what-might-have-been story of this kind was written is difficult to say. Plenty of speculations on alternative possibilities of history have been offered over the centuries, at least as far back as Plato's account of Atlantis, but they do not quite fit the fictional format we are concerned with here. Perhaps the first example of the modern genre is Louis-Napoleon Geoffroy-Chateau's *Napoleon and the Conquest of the World, 1812–1823*, published in 1836, which showed Napoleon calling a halt to his ill-fated invasion of Russia just ahead of the onset of the winter that would, in fact, destroy his army, and going on to create a world empire.

Another Frenchman, Charles Renouvier, offered *Uchronie* in 1857, a book in which the Roman Empire survives by keeping Christianity in check. (My own variant on this, "To the Promised Land," eliminates Christianity from the equation altogether by having the Biblical Exodus fail, thus keeping the Jews in Egypt and entirely subverting the birth of any charismatic Jewish prophets in Palestine later on.)

Shortly after Renouvier, another French writer, Louis-Auguste Blanqui, became the apparent inventor of the multiple-time-track story with his *Eternity Through the Stars*

(1871), giving us duplicate Earths with duplicate individuals living variant lives in each version of our world.

The first known English-language alternate-history story seems to be Edward Everett Hale's "Hands Off," published in *Harper's Magazine* in 1881. This curious theological fantasy assumes that Joseph, the son of Jacob, was *not* sold into slavery in Egypt but instead escaped the slave-traders and returned to his father's camp in the desert—whereupon, without the shrewd mind of Joseph to guide Pharaoh's government, Egypt was conquered by Canaanite barbarians who went on to engulf the rest of the ancient world. Judaism died out, the great culture of Greece never had a chance to emerge, Rome was crushed, and a reign of "lust, brutality, terror, cruelty, carnage, famine, agony, horror" descended on humanity, until, after a series of hideous wars, civilization perished entirely.

An extraordinary volume called *If It Had Happened Otherwise: Lapses Into Imaginary History,* edited by J. C. Squire (1931), offers an entire anthology of dazzling alternate-world speculations by such famous writers as G. K. Chesterton, Winston Churchill, Hilaire Belloc, and André Maurois. This is not exactly a work of science fiction, since most of its eleven contributions are in the form of historical essays rather than stories; but each of the distinguished contributors supplies a fascinating and challenging exploration of a world of possibility. Churchill's, with characteristic brilliance, is called "If Lee Had Not Won the Battle of Gettysburg," thereby providing a dizzying double layer of parallel-world conceptualization. Two other chapters are "If Napoleon Had Escaped to America" and "If Booth Had Missed Lincoln."

When science fiction became a genre of American popular fiction after the founding of Hugo Gernsback's *Amazing Stories* in 1926, parallel-world stories quickly established themselves as staples of the form. One of the first was Nat

Schachner's "Ancestral Voices," in *Astounding Stories* (1933), in which the killing of a fifth-century Hun removes Hitler, among others, from the time stream. Murray Leinster's "Sidewise in Time," published in *Astounding* the following year, provides a number of alternate time-tracks, a theme successfully explored soon after by Stanley Weinbaum in "The Worlds of If" and David Daniels in "The Branches of Time" in the same 1935 issue of *Wonder Stories*.

Since those early days of magazine science fiction, the multiple realities of alternate history have been examined with great success by such genre novelists as L. Sprague de Camp, whose *Wheels of If* (1940) shows Norsemen ruling the New World in the twentieth century, and whose *Lest Darkness Fall* (1939) sends a twentieth-century time-traveler back to the Dark Ages to attempt to keep the flame of civilization burning; Ward Moore, who depicts a world in which the South won the Civil War in *Bring the Jubilee* (1952); and Philip K. Dick, whose *The Man in the High Castle* (1962); unforgettably demonstrates the United States as it exists after the Axis victory in World War II. Keith Roberts's *Pavane* (1968) makes its point of departure the assassination of Queen Elizabeth I, leading to a victory for the Spanish Armada and a vastly altered modern England untouched by the Industrial Revolution.

Randall Garrett's *Too Many Magicians* (1966) and the associated Lord Darcy group of stories are set in a very different version of twentieth-century England that traces its course of development back to Richard the Lion-Hearted (who in Garrett's universe lived long, ruled wisely, and built a great thirteenth-century empire dominating Western Europe and the Americas.)

And I could list dozens more, both novels and short stories. It is an inexhaustible theme. There is no event, great or small, in the long span of human history that would not be usable as the springboard for alternate-world fiction. Martin H. Greenberg has gathered in this collection some of the best short work in this genre of the past ten or fifteen years; but for each story included here, there are five or six equally worthy ones that had to be omitted. Perhaps, in some alternate world of publishing, they have already found a collection of their own in which to assemble.

The Way It Wasn't

Robert Silverberg

Lion Time in Timbuctoo

INTRODUCTION

There's one tricky aspect about writing alternate-history stories, which is what "Lion Time in Timbuctoo" is: how to let the reader know the point at which your imaginary world's history diverges from our reality. Sometimes the writer can drag in soothsayers, visions, dreams, or the clever speculation of some smarty-pants character to communicate necessary information. Sometimes the writer simply cheats, by sticking the information in as exposition. ("Whereas in our world, where France actually did have a revolution in 1789...") Sometimes it's absolutely obvious from the context that the story is set in an alternate world. ("One sunny day in 1978, as former President John F. Kennedy opened his morning newspaper...") And sometimes the writer just has to write a preface to spell things out. Which is what I'm doing right now.

"Lion Time in Timbuctoo" is related, in a way, to an alternate-universe novel I wrote many years ago called "The Gate of Worlds," in which I used the device of a soothsayer to make my divergence point clear. It didn't seem cricket to do that again. What I postulated, in that earlier story (which takes place in an alternate 1963, in a New World ruled by Aztecs and Incas) is that the Black Death of 1349 was far more virulent than it had been in our reality, and wiped out three quarters of the population of Western Europe, instead of the one quarter it

actually killed. Which left Europe shattered and defenseless against the imperial-minded Turks, who conquered everything in their way, right up to and including England. Thus the Renaissance never happened, nor did the exploration of the New World, or the European colonial expansion. The black kingdoms of Africa and the Mesoamerican empires of the New World remained independent. Technology was slow to develop. The Turks imposed Islam and the Turkish language on most of Europe.

And now it's the twentieth century in that other world. The Turkish empire is starting to break up. England has already regained its independence; other nations are pulling away. Meanwhile, in the ancient and great African kingdom of Songhay...

—R.S.

In the dry stifling days of early summer, the Emir lay dying, the king, the imam, Big Father of the Songhay, in his cool, dark mud-walled palace in the Sankore quarter of Old Timbuctoo. The city seemed frozen, strange though it was to think of freezing in this season of killing heat that fell upon you like a wall of hot iron. There was a vast stasis, as though everything were entombed in ice. The river was low and sluggish, moving almost imperceptibly in its bed with scarcely more vigor than a sick, weary crocodile. No one went out of doors, no one moved indoors, everyone sat still, waiting for the old man's death and praying that it would bring the cooling rains.

In his own very much lesser palace alongside the Emir's, Little Father sat still like all the rest, watching and waiting. His time was coming now at last. That was a sobering thought. How long had he been the prince of the realm?

Twenty years? Thirty? He had lost count. And now finally to rule, now to be the one who cast the omens and uttered the decrees and welcomed the caravans and took the high seat in the Great Mosque. So much toil, so much responsibility: but the Emir was not yet dead. Not yet. Not quite.

"Little Father, the ambassadors are arriving."

In the arched doorway stood Ali Pasha, bowing, smiling. The vizier's face, black as ebony, gleamed with sweat, a dark moon shining against the lighter darkness of the vestibule. Despite his name, Ali Pasha was pure Songhay, black as sorrow, blacker by far than Little Father, whose blood was mixed with that of would-be conquerors of years gone by. The aura of the power that soon would be his was glistening and crackling around Ali Pasha's head like midwinter lightning: for Ali Pasha was the future Grand Vizier, no question of it. When Little Father became king, the old Emir's officers would resign and retire. An Emir's ministers did not hold office beyond his reign. In an earlier time they would have been lucky to survive the old Emir's death at all.

Little Father, fanning himself sullenly, looked up to meet his vizier's insolent grin.

"Which ambassadors, Ali Pasha?"

"The special ones, here to attend Big Father's funeral. A Turkish. A Mexican. A Russian. And an English."

"An English? Why an English?"

"They are a very proud people, now. Since their independence. How could they stay away? This is a very important death, Little Father."

"Ah. Ah, of course." Little Father contemplated the fine wooden Moorish grillwork that bedecked the doorway. "Not a Peruvian?"

"A Peruvian will very likely come on the next riverboat, Little Father. And a Maori one, and they say a Chinese. There will probably be others also. By the end of the week the city will be filled with dignitaries. This is the most important death in some years."

"A Chinese," Little Father repeated softly, as though Ali Pasha had said an ambassador from the Moon was coming. A Chinese! But yes, yes this was a very important death. The Songhay Empire was no minor nation. Songhay controlled the crossroads of Africa; all caravans journeying between desert north and tropical south must pass through Songhay. The Emir of Songhay was one of the grand kings of the world.

Ali Pasha said acidly, "The Peruvian hopes that Big Father will last until the rains come, I suppose. And so he takes his time getting here. They are people of a high country, these Peruvians. They aren't accustomed to our heat."

"And if he misses the funeral entirely, waiting for the rains to come?"

Ali Pasha shrugged. "Then he'll learn what heat really is, eh, Little Father? When he goes home to his mountains and tells the Grand Inca that he didn't get here soon enough, eh?" He made a sound that was something like a laugh, and Little Father, experienced in his vizier's sounds, responded with a gloomy smile.

"Where are these ambassadors now?"

"At Kabara, at the port hostelry. Their riverboat has just come in. We've sent the royal barges to bring them here."

"Ah. And where will they stay?"

"Each at his country's embassy, Little Father."

"Of course. Of course. So no action is needed from me at this time concerning these ambassadors, eh, Ali Pasha?"

"None, Little Father." After a pause the vizier said, "The Turk has brought his daughter. She is very handsome." This with a rolling of the eyes, a baring of the teeth. Little Father felt a pang of appetite, as Ali Pasha had surely intended. The vizier knew his prince very well, too. "Very handsome, Little Father! In a white way, you understand."

"I understand. The English, did he bring a daughter too?"

"Only the Turk," said Ali Pasha.

"Do you remember the Englishwoman who came here once?" Little Father asked.

"How could I forget? The hair like strands of fine gold. The breasts like milk. The pale pink nipples. The belly-hair down below, like fine gold also."

Little Father frowned. He had spoken often enough to Ali Pasha about the Englishwoman's milky breasts and pale pink nipples. But he had no recollection of having described to him or to anyone else the golden hair down below. A rare moment of carelessness, then, on Ali Pasha's part; or else a bit of deliberate malice, perhaps a way of testing Little Father. There were risks in that for Ali Pasha, but surely Ali Pasha knew that. At any rate it was a point Little Father chose not to pursue just now. He sank back into silence, fanning himself more briskly.

Ali Pasha showed no sign of leaving. So there must be other news.

The vizier's glistening eyes narrowed. "I hear they will be starting the dancing in the marketplace very shortly."

Little Father blinked. Was there some crisis in the king's condition, then? Which everyone knew about but him?

"The death dance, do you mean?"

"That would be premature, Little Father," said Ali Pasha unctuously. "It is the life dance, of course."

"Of course. I should go to it, in that case."

"In half an hour. They are only now assembling the formations. You should go to your father, first."

"Yes. So I should. To the Emir, first, to ask his blessing; and then to the dance."

Little Father rose.

"The Turkish girl," he said. "How old is she, Ali Pasha?"

"She might be eighteen. She might be twenty."

"And handsome, you say?"

"Oh, yes. Yes, very handsome, Little Father!"

There was an underground passageway connecting Little Father's palace to that of Big Father; but suddenly, whimsically, Little Father chose to go there by the out-of-doors way. He had not been out of doors in two or three days, since the worst of the heat had descended on the city. Now he felt the outside air hit him like the blast of a furnace as he crossed the courtyard and stepped into the open. The whole city was like a smithy these days, and would be for weeks and weeks more, until the rains came. He was used to it, of course, but he had never come to like it. No one ever came to like it except the deranged and the very holy, if indeed there was any difference between the one and the other.

Emerging onto the portico of his palace, Little Father looked out on the skyline of flat mud roofs before him, the labyrinth of alleys and connecting passageways, the towers of the mosques, the walled mansions of the nobility. In the hazy distance rose the huge modern buildings of the New City. It was late afternoon, but that brought no relief from the heat. The air was heavy, stagnant, shimmering. It vibrated like a live thing. All day long the myriad whitewashed walls had been soaking up the heat, and now they were beginning to give it back.

Atop the vibration of the air lay a second and almost tangible vibration, the tinny quivering sound of the musicians tuning up for the dance in the marketplace. The life dance, Ali Pasha had said. Perhaps so; but Little Father would not be surprised to find some of the people dancing the death dance as well, and still others dancing the dance of the changing of the king. There was little linearity of time in Old Timbuctoo; everything tended to happen at once. The death of the old king and the ascent of the new one were simultaneous affairs, after all: they were one event. In some countries, Little Father knew, they used to kill the king when he grew sick and feeble, simply to hurry things along. Not here, though. Here they danced him out, danced the new king in. This was a civilized land. An ancient kingdom, a mighty power in the world. He stood for a time, listening to the music in the marketplace, wondering if his father in his sickbed could hear it, and what he might be thinking, if he could. And he wondered too how it would feel when his own time came to lie abed listening to them tuning up in the market for the death dance. But then Little Father's face wrinkled in annoyance at his own foolishness. He would rule for many years; and when the time came to do the death dance for him out there he would not care at all. He might even be eager for it.

Big Father's palace rose before him like a mountain. Level upon level sprang upward, presenting a dazzling white façade broken only by the dark butts of the wooden beams jutting through the plaster and the occasional grillwork of a window. His own palace was a hut compared with that of the Emir. Implacable blue-veiled Tuareg guards stood in the main doorway. Their eyes and foreheads, all that was visible of their coffee-colored faces, registered surprise as they saw Little Father approaching, alone and on foot, out of the aching sunblink of the afternoon; but they stepped aside. Within, everything was silent and dark. Elderly officials of the almost-late Emir lined the hallways, grieving soundlessly, huddling into their own self-pity. They looked toward Little Father without warmth, without hope, as he moved past them. In a short while he would be king, and they would be nothing. But he wasted no energy on pitying them. It wasn't as though they would be fed to the royal lions in the imperial pleasure-ground, after all, when they stepped down from office. Soft retirements awaited them. They had had their greedy years at the public trough; when the time came for them to go, they would move along to villas in Spain, in Greece, in the south of France, in chilly remote Russia, even, and live comfortably on the fortunes they had embezzled during Big Father's lengthy reign. Whereas he, he, he, he was doomed to spend all his days in this wretched blazing city of mud, scarcely even daring ever to go abroad for fear they would take his throne from him while he was gone.

The Grand Vizier, looking twenty years older than he had seemed when Little Father had last seen him a few days before, greeted him formally at the head of the Stairs of Allah and said, "The imam your father is resting on the porch, Little Father. Three saints and one of the Tijani are with him."

"*Three* saints? He must be very near the end, then!"

"On the contrary. We think he is rallying."

"Allah let it be so," said Little Father.

Servants and ministers were everywhere. The place reeked of incense. All the lamps were lit, and they were flickering wildly in the conflicting currents of the air within the palace, heat from outside meeting the cool of the interior in gusting wafts. The old Emir had never cared much for electricity.

Little Father passed through the huge, musty, empty throne room, bedecked with his father's hunting trophies, the twenty-foot-long crocodile skin, the superb white oryx head with horns like scimitars, the hippo skulls, the vast puzzled-looking giraffe. The rich gifts from foreign monarchs were arrayed here, too, the hideous Aztec idol that King Moctezuma had sent a year or two ago, the brilliant feather cloaks from the Capac Yupanqui of Peru, the immense triple-paneled gilded painting of some stiff-jointed Christian holy men with which the Czar Vladimir had paid his respects during a visit of state a decade back, and the great sphere of ivory from China on which some master craftsman had carved a detailed map of the world, and much more, enough to fill half a storehouse. Little Father wondered if he would be able to clear all this stuff out when he became Emir.

In his lifetime Big Father had always preferred to hold court on his upstairs porch, rather than in this dark, cluttered, and somehow sinister throne room; and now he was doing his dying on the porch as well. It was a broad square platform, open to the skies but hidden from the populace below, for it was at the back of the palace facing toward the distant river and no one in the city could look into it.

The dying king lay swaddled, despite the great heat, in a tangle of brilliant blankets of scarlet and turquoise and lemon-colored silk on a rumpled divan to Little Father's left. He was barely visible, a pale sweaty wizened face and nothing more, amid the rumpled bedclothes. To the right was the royal roof-garden, a mysterious collection of fragrant exotic trees and shrubs planted in huge square porcelain vessels from Japan, another gift of the bountiful Czar. The dark earth that filled those blue-and-white tubs had been carried in panniers by donkeys from the banks of the Niger, and the plants were watered every evening at sunset by prisoners, who had to haul great leather sacks of immense weight to this place and were forbidden by the palace guards to stumble or complain. Between the garden and the divan was the royal viewing-pavilion, a low structure of rare satin-smooth woods upon which the Emir in better days would sit for hours, staring out at the barren sun-hammered sandy plain, the pale tormented sky, the occasional wandering camel or hyena, the gnarled scrubby bush that marked the path of the river, six or seven miles away. The cowrie-studded ebony scepter of high office was lying abandoned on the floor of the pavilion, as though nothing more than a cast-off toy.

Four curious figures stood now at the foot of the Emir's divan. One was the Tijani, a member of the city's chief fraternity of religious laymen. He was a man of marked Arab features, dressed in a long white robe over droopy yellow pantaloons, a red turban, a dozen or so strings of amber beads. Probably he was a well-to-do merchant or shopkeeper in daily life. He was wholly absorbed in his orisons, rocking back and forth in place, crooning indefatigably to his hundred-beaded rosary, working hard to efface the Emir's sins and make him fit for Paradise. His voice was thin as feathers from overuse, a low eroded murmur which scarcely halted even for breath. He acknowledged Little Father's arrival with the merest flick of an eyebrow, without pausing in his toil.

The other three holy men were marabouts, living saints, two black Songhay and a man of mixed blood. They were weighted down with leather packets of grigri charms hanging in thick mounds around their necks and girded by other charms by the dozen around their wrists and hips, and they had the proper crazy glittering saint-look in their eyes, the true holy baraka. It was said that saints could fly, could raise the dead, could make the rains come and the rivers rise. Little Father doubted all of that, but he was one who tended to keep his doubts to himself. In any case the city was full of such miracle-workers, dozens of them, and the tombs of hundreds more were objects of veneration in the poorer districts. Little Father recognized all three of these: he had seen them now and then hovering around the Sankore Mosque or sometimes the other and greater one at Dyingerey Ber, striking saint-poses on one leg or with arms outflung, muttering saint-gibberish, giving passersby the saint-stare. Now they stood lined up in grim silence before the Emir, making cryptic gestures with their fingers. Even before Big Father had fallen ill, these three had gone about declaring that he was doomed shortly to be taken by a vampire, as various recent omens indisputably proved—a flight of owls by day, a flight of vultures by night, the death of a sacred dove that lived on the minaret of the Great Mosque. For them to be in the palace at all was remarkable; for them to be in the presence of the king was astounding. Someone in the royal entourage must be at the point of desperation, Little Father concluded.

He knelt at the bedside.

"Father?"

The Emir's eyes were glassy. Perhaps he was becoming a saint too.

"Father, it's me. They said you were rallying. I know you're going to be all right soon."

Was that a smile? Was that any sort of reaction at all?

"Father, it'll be cooler in just a few weeks. The rains are already on the way. Everybody's saying so. You'll feel better when the rains come."

The old man's cheeks were like parchment. His bones were showing through. He was eighty years old and he had been Emir of Songhay for fifty of those years. Electricity hadn't even been invented when he became king, nor the motorcar. Even the railroad had been something new and startling.

There was a claw-like hand suddenly jutting out of the blankets. Little Father touched it. It was like touching a piece of worn leather. By the time the rains had reached Timbuctoo, Big Father would have made the trip by ceremonial barge to the old capital of Gao, two hundred miles down the Niger, to take his place in the royal cemetery of the Kings of Songhay.

Little Father went on murmuring encouragement for another few moments, but it was apparent that the Emir wasn't listening. A stray burst of breeze brought the sound of the marketplace music, growing louder now. Could he hear that? Could he hear anything? Did he care? After a time Little Father rose, and went quickly from the palace.

In the marketplace the dancing had already begun. They had shoved aside the booths of the basket-weavers and the barbers and the slippermakers and the charm-peddlers, the dealers in salt and fruit and donkeys and rice and tobacco and meat, and a frenetic procession of dancers was weaving swiftly back and forth across the central square from the place of the milk vendors at the south end to the place of the wood vendors at the north when Little Father and Ali Pasha arrived.

"You see?" Ali Pasha asked. "The life dance. They bring the energy down from the skies to fill your father's veins."

There was tremendous energy in it, all right. The dancers pounded the sandy earth with their bare feet, they clapped their hands, they shouted quick sharp punctuations of word-less sound, they made butting gestures with their outflung elbows, they shook their beads convulsively and sent rivers of sweat flying through the air. The heat seemed to mean nothing to them. Their skins gleamed. Their eyes were bright as new coins. They made rhythmic grunting noises, oom oom oom, and the whole city seemed to shake beneath their tread.

To Little Father it looked more like the death dance than the dance of life. There was the frenzied stomp of mourning about it. But he was no expert on these things. The people had all sorts of beliefs that were mysteries to him, and which he hoped would melt away like snowflakes during his coming reign. Did they still put pressure on Allah to bring the rains by staking small children out in the blazing sun for days at a time outside the tombs of saints? Did they still practice alchemy on one another, turning wrapping paper into bank-notes by means of spells? Did they continue to fret about vampires and djinn? It was all very embarrassing. Songhay was a modern state; and yet there was all this medieval nonsense still going on. Very likely the old Emir had liked it that way. But soon things would change.

The close formation of the dancers opened abruptly, and to his horror Little Father saw a group of foreigners standing in a little knot at the far side of the marketplace. He had only a glimpse of them; then the dance closed again and the foreigners were blocked from view. He touched Ali Pasha's arm.

"Did you see them?"

"Oh, yes. Yes!"

"Who are they, do you think?"

The vizier stared off intently toward the other side of the marketplace, as though his eyes were capable of seeing through the knot of dancers.

"Embassy people, Little Father. Some Mexicans, I believe, and perhaps the Turks. And those fair-haired people must be the English."

Here to gape at the quaint tribal dances, enjoying the fine barbaric show in the extravagant alien heat.

"You said they were coming by barge. How'd they get here so fast?"

Ali Pasha shook his head.

"They must have taken the motorboat instead, I suppose."

"I can't receive them here, like this. I never would have come here if I had known that they'd be here."

"Of course not, Little Father."

"You should have told me!"

"I had no way of knowing," said Ali Pasha, and for once he sounded sincere, even distressed. "There will be punishments for this. But come, Little Father. Come: to your palace. As you say, they ought not find you here this way, without a retinue, without your regalia. This evening you can receive them properly."

Very likely the newly arrived diplomats at the upper end

of the marketplace had no idea that they had been for a few moments in the presence of the heir to the throne, the future Emir of Songhay, one of the six or seven most powerful men in Africa. If they had noticed anyone at all across the way, they would simply have seen a slender, supple, just-barely-still-youngish man with Moorish features, wearing a simple white robe and a flat red skullcap, standing beside a tall, powerfully built black man clad in an ornately brocaded robe of purple and yellow. The black man might have seemed more important to them in the Timbuctoo scheme of things than the Moorish-looking one, though they would have been wrong about that.

But probably they hadn't been looking toward Little Father and Ali Pasha at all. Their attention was on the dancers. That was why they had halted here, en route from the river landing to their various embassies.

"How tireless they are!" Prince Itzcoatl said. The Mexican envoy, King Moctezuma's brother. "Why don't their bones melt in this heat?" He was a compact copper-colored man decked out grandly in an Aztec feather cape, golden anklets and wristlets, a gold headband studded with brilliant feathers, golden ear-plugs and nose-plugs. "You'd think they were glad their king is dying, seeing them jump around like that."

"Perhaps they are," observed the Turk, Ismet Akif.

He laughed in a mild, sad way. Everything about him seemed to be like that, mild and sad: his droopy-lidded melancholic eyes, his fleshy downcurved lips, his sloping shoulders, even the curiously stodgy and inappropriate European-style clothes that he had chosen to wear in this impossible climate, the dark heavy woolen suit, the narrow grey necktie. But wide cheekbones and a broad, authoritative forehead indicated his true strength to those with the ability to see such things. He too was of royal blood, Sultan Osman's third son. There was something about him that managed to be taut and slack both at once, no easy task. His posture, his expression, the tone of his voice, all conveyed the anomalous sense of self that came from being the official delegate of a vast empire which—as all the world knew—had passed the peak of its greatness some time back and was launched on a long irreversible decline. To the diminutive Englishman at his side he said, "How does it seem to you, Sir Anthony? Are they grieving or celebrating?"

Everyone in the group understood the great cost of the compliment Ismet Akif was paying by amiably addressing his question to the English ambassador, just as if they were equals. It was high courtesy: it was grace in defeat.

Turkey still ruled a domain spanning thousands of miles. England was an insignificant island kingdom. Worse yet, England had been a Turkish province from medieval times onward, until only sixty years before. The exasperated English, weary of hundreds of years of speaking Turkish and bowing to Mecca, finally had chased out their Ottoman masters in the first year of what by English reckoning was the twentieth century, thus becoming the first of all the European peoples to regain their independence. There were no Spaniards here today, no Italians, no Portuguese, and no reason why there should be, for their countries all still were Turkish provinces. Perhaps envoys from those lands would show up later to pay homage to the dead Emir, if only to make some pathetic display of tattered sovereignty; but it would not matter to anyone else, one way or the other. The English, though, were beginning once again to make their way in the world, a little tentatively but nevertheless visibly. And so Ismet Akif had had to accommodate himself to the presence of an English diplomat on the slow journey upriver from the coast to the Songhay capital, and everyone agreed he had managed it very well.

Sir Anthony said, "Both celebrating *and* grieving, I'd

imagine." He was a precise, fastidious little man with icy blue eyes, an angular bony face, a tight cap of red curls beginning to shade now into gray. "The king is dead, long live the king—that sort of thing."

"*Almost* dead," Prince Itzcoatl reminded him.

"Quite. Terribly awkward, our getting here before the fact. Or *are* we here before the fact?" Sir Anthony glanced toward his young chargé d'affaires. "Have you heard anything, Michael? Is the old Emir still alive, do you know?"

Michael was long-legged, earnest, milky-skinned, very fair. In the merciless Timbuctoo sunlight his golden hair seemed almost white. The first blush of what was likely to be a very bad sunburn was spreading over his cheeks and forehead. He was twenty-four and this was his first notable diplomatic journey.

He indicated the flagpole at the eastern end of the plaza, where the black and red Songhay flag hung like a dead thing high overhead.

"They'd have lowered the flag if he'd died, Sir Anthony."

"Quite. Quite. They do that sort of thing here, do they?"

"I'd rather expect so, sir."

"And then what? The whole town plunged into mourning? Drums, chanting? The new Emir paraded in the streets? Everyone would head for the mosques, I suppose." Sir Anthony glanced at Ismet Akif. "We would too, eh? Well, I could stand to go into a mosque one more time, I suppose."

After the Conquest, when London had become New Istanbul, the worship of Allah had been imposed by law. Westminster Abbey had been turned into a mosque, and the high pashas of the occupation forces were buried in it alongside the Plantagenet kings. Later the Turks had built the great golden-domed Mosque of Ali on the Strand, opposite the Grand Palace of Sultan Mahmud. To this day perhaps half the English still embraced Islam, out of force of habit if nothing else, and Turkish was still heard in the streets nearly as much as English. The conquerors had had five hundred years to put their mark on England, and that could not be undone overnight. But Christianity was fashionable again among the English well-to-do, and had never really been relinquished by the poor, who had kept their underground chapels through the worst of the Islamic persecutions. And it was obligatory for the members of the governing class.

"It would have been better for us all," said Ismet Akif gravely, "if we had not had to set out so early that we would arrive here before the Emir's death. But of course the distances are so great, and travel is so very slow—"

"And the situation so explosive," Prince Itzcoatl said.

Unexpectedly Ismet Akif's bright-eyed daughter Selima, who was soft-spoken and delicate-looking and was not thought to be particularly forward, said, "Are you talking about the possibility that King Suleiyman of Mali might send an invasion force into Songhay when the old man finally dies?"

Everyone swung about to look at her. Someone gasped and someone else choked back shocked laughter. She was extremely young and of course she was female, but even so the remark was exceedingly tactless, exceedingly embarrassing. The girl had not come to Songhay in any official capacity, merely as her father's traveling companion, for he was a widower. The whole trip was purely an adventure for her. All the same, a diplomat's child should have had more sense. Ismet Akif turned his eyes inward and looked as though he would like to sink into the earth. But Selima's dark eyes glittered with something very much like mischief. She seemed to be enjoying herself. She stood her ground.

"No," she said. "We can't pretend it isn't likely. There's Mali, right next door, controlling the coast. It stands to reason that they'd like to have the inland territory too, and take total control of West African trade. King Suleiyman could argue that Songhay would be better off as part of Mali than it is this way, a landlocked country."

"My dear—"

"And the prince," she went on imperturbably, "is supposed to be just an idler, isn't he, a silly dissolute playboy who's spent so many years waiting around to become Emir that he's gone completely to ruin. Letting him take the throne would be a mistake for everybody. So this is the best possible time for Mali to move in and consolidate the two countries. You all see that. That's why we're here, aren't we, to stare the Malians down and keep them from trying it? Because they'd be too strong for the other powers' comfort if they got together with the Songhayans. And it's all too likely to happen. After all, Mali and Songhay have been consolidated before."

"Hundreds of years ago," said Michael gently. He gave her a great soft blue-eyed stare of admiration and despair. "The principle that the separation of Mali and Songhay is desirable and necessary has been understood internationally since—"

"Please," Ismet Akif said. "This is an unfortunate discussion. My dear, we ought not indulge in such speculations in a place of this sort, or anywhere else, let me say. Perhaps it's time to continue on to our lodgings, do you not all agree?"

"A good idea. The dancing is becoming a little repetitious," Prince Itzcoatl said.

"And the heat—" Sir Anthony said. "This unthinkable diabolical heat—"

The looked at each other. The shook their heads and exchanged small smiles.

Prince Itzcoatl said quietly to Sir Anthony, "An unfortunate discussion, yes."

"Very unfortunate."

Then they all moved on, in groups of two and three, their porters trailing a short distance behind bowed under the great mounds of luggage. Michael stood for a moment or two peering after the retreating form of Selima Akif in an agony of longing and chagrin. Her movements seemed magical. They were as subtle as Oriental music: an exquisite semitonal slither, an enchanting harmonious twang.

The love he felt for her had surprised and mortified him when it had first blossomed on the riverboat as it came interminably up the Niger from the coast, and here in his first hour in Timbuctoo he felt it almost as a crucifixion. There was no worse damage he could do to himself than to fall in love with a Turk. For an Englishman it was virtual treason. His diplomatic career would be ruined before it had barely begun. He would be laughed out of court. He might just as well convert to Islam, paint his face brown, and undertake the pilgrimage to Mecca. And live thereafter as an anchorite in some desert cave, imploring the favor of the Prophet.

"Michael?" Sir Anthony called. "Is anything wrong?"

"Coming, sir. Coming!"

The reception hall was long and dark and cavernous, lit only by wax tapers that emitted a smoky amber light and a peculiar odor, something like that of leaves decomposing on a forest floor. Along the walls were bowers of interwoven ostrich and peacock plumes, and great elephant tusks set on brass pedestals rose from the earthen floor like obelisks at seemingly random intervals. Songhayans who might have been servants or just as easily high officials of the court moved among the visiting diplomats bearing trays of cool lime-flavored drinks, musty wine, and little delicacies fashioned from a bittersweet red nut.

The prince, in whose name the invitations had gone forth, was nowhere in sight so far as any of the foreigners could tell. The apparent host of the reception was a burly jet-black man of regal bearing clad in a splendid tawny robe that might actually have been made of woven lionskins. He had introduced himself as Ali Pasha, vizier to the prince. The prince, he explained, was at his father's bedside, but would be there shortly. The prince was deeply devoted to his father, said Ali Pasha; he visited the failing Emir constantly.

"I saw that man in the marketplace this afternoon," Selima said. "He was wearing a purple and yellow robe then. Down at the far side, beyond the dancers, for just a moment. He was looking at us. I thought he was magnificent, somebody of great importance. And he is."

A little indignantly Michael said, "These blacks all look alike to me. How can you be sure that's the one you saw?"

"Because I'm sure. Do all Turks look alike to you too?"

"I didn't mean—"

"All English look alike to us, you know. We can just about distinguish between the red-haired ones and the yellow-haired ones. And that's as far as it goes."

"You aren't serious, Selima."

"No. No, I'm not. I actually can tell one of you from another most of the time. At least I can tell the handsome ones from the ugly ones."

Michael flushed violently, so that his already sunburned face turned flaming scarlet and emanated great waves of heat. Everyone had been telling him how handsome he was since his boyhood. It was as if there was nothing to him at all except regularly formed features and pale flawless skin and long athletic limbs. The notion made him profoundly uncomfortable.

She laughed. "You should cover your face when you're out in the sun. You're starting to get cooked. Does it hurt very much?"

"Not at all. Can I get you a drink?"

"You know that alcohol is forbidden to—"

"The other kind, I mean. The green soda. It's very good, actually. Boy! Boy!"

"I'd rather have the nut thing," she said. She stretched forth one hand—her hand was very small, and the fingers were pale and perfect—and made the tiniest of languid gestures. Two of the black men with trays came toward her at once, and, laughing prettily, she scooped a couple of the nut-cakes from the nearer of the trays. She handed one to Michael, who fumbled it and let it fall. Calmly she gave him the other. He looked at it as though she handed him an asp.

"Are you afraid I've arranged to have you poisoned?" she asked. "Go on. Eat it! It's good! Oh, you're so absurd, Michael! But I do like you."

"We aren't supposed to like each other, you know," he said bleakly.

"I know that. We're enemies, aren't we?"

"Not any more, actually. Not officially."

"Yes, I know. The Empire recognized English independence a good many years ago."

The way she said it, it was like a slap. Michael's reddened cheeks blazed fiercely.

In anguish he crammed the nut-cake into his mouth with both hands.

She went on, "I can remember the time when I was a girl and King Richard came to Istanbul to sign the treaty with the Sultan. There was a parade."

"Yes. Yes. A great occasion."

"But there's still bad blood between the Empire and England. We haven't forgiven you for some of the things you did to our people in your country in Sultan Abdul's time, when we were evacuating."

"*You* haven't forgiven *us*—?"

"When you burned the bazaar. When you bombed that

mosque. The broken shop windows. We were going away voluntarily, you know. You were much more violent toward us than you had any right to be."

"You speak very directly, don't you?"

"There were atrocities. I studied them in school."

"And when you people conquered us in 1490? Were you gentle then?" For a moment Michael's eyes were hot with fury, the easily triggered anger of the good Englishman for the bestial Turk. Appalled, he tried to stem the rising surge of patriotic fervor before it ruined everything. He signaled frantically to one of the tray-wielders, as though another round of nut-cakes might serve to get the conversation into a less disagreeable track. "But never mind all that, Selima. We mustn't be quarreling over ancient history like this." Somehow he mastered himself, swallowing, breathing deeply, managing an earnest smile "You say you like me."

"Yes. And you like me. I can tell."

"Is that all right?"

"Of course it is, silly. Although I shouldn't allow it. We don't even think of you English as completely civilized." Her eyes glowed. He began to tremble, and tried to conceal it from her. She was playing with him, he knew, playing a game whose rules she herself had defined and would not share with him. "Are you a Christian?" she asked.

"You know I am."

"Yes, you must be. You used the Christian date for the year of the conquest of England. But your ancestors were Moslem, right?"

"Outwardly, during the time of the occupation. Most of us were. But for all those centuries we secretly continued to maintain our faith in—" She was definitely going to get him going again. Already his head was beginning to pound. Her beauty was unnerving enough; but this roguishness was more than he could take. He wondered how old she was. Eighteen?

Nineteen? No more than that, surely. Very likely she had a fiancé back in Istanbul, some swarthy mustachioed fez-wearing Ottoman princeling, with whom she indulged in unimaginable Oriental perversions and to whom she confessed every little flirtation she undertook while traveling with her father. It was humiliating to think of becoming an item of gossip in some perfumed boudoir on the banks of the Bosporus. A sigh escaped him. She gave him a startled look, as though he had mooed at her. Perhaps he had. Desperately he sought for something, anything, that would rescue him from this increasingly tortured moment of impossible intimacy; and, looking across the room, he was astounded to find his eyes suddenly locked on those of the heir apparent to the throne of Songhay. "Ah, there he is," Michael said in vast relief. "The prince has arrived."

"Which one? Where?"

"The slender man. The red velvet tunic."

"Oh. Oh, yes. *Him.* I saw him in the marketplace too, with Ali Pasha. Now I understand. They came to check us out before we knew who they were." Selima smiled disingenuously. "He's very attractive, isn't he? Rather like an Arab, I'd say. And not nearly as dissolute-looking as I was led to expect. Is it all right if I go over and say hello to him? Or should I wait for a proper diplomatic introduction? I'll ask my father, I think. Do you see him? Oh, yes, there he is over there, talking to Prince Itzcoatl—" She began to move away without a backward look.

Michael felt a sword probing in his vitals.

"Boy!" he called, and one of the blacks turned to him with a somber grin. "Some of that wine, if you please!"

On the far side of the room Little Father smiled and signaled for a drink also—not the miserable palm wine, which he abhorred and which as a good Moslem he should abjure anyway, but the clear fiery brandy that the caravans brought him from Tunis, and which to an outsider's eyes would appear to be mere water. His personal cupbearer, who served no one else in the room, poured until he nodded, and slipped back into the shadows to await the prince's next call.

In the first moments of his presence at the reception Little Father had taken in the entire scene, sorting and analyzing and comprehending. The Turkish ambassador's daughter was even more beautiful than Ali Pasha had led him to think, and there was an agreeable slyness about her that Little Father was able to detect even at a distance. Lust awoke in him at once and he allowed himself a little smile as he savored its familiar throbbing along the insides of his thighs. The Turkish girl was very fine. The tall fair-haired young man, probably some sort of subsidiary English official, was obviously and stupidly in love with her. He should be advised to keep out of the sun. The Aztec prince, all done up in feathers and gold, was arrogant and brutal and smart, as Aztecs usually were. The Turk, the girl's father, looked soft and effete and decadent, which he probably found to be a useful pose. The older Englishman, the little one with the red hair who most likely was the official envoy, seemed tough and dangerous. And over there was another one who hadn't been at the marketplace to see the dancing, the Russian, no doubt, a big man, strong and haughty, flat face and flat sea-green eyes and a dense little black beard through which a glint of gold teeth occasionally showed. He too seemed dangerous, physically dangerous, a man who might pick things up and smash them for amusement, but in him all the danger was on the outside, and with the little Englishman it was the other way around. Little Father wondered how much trouble these people would manage to create for him before the funeral was over and done with. It was every nation's ambition to create trouble in the empires of Africa, after all: there was too much cheap labor here, too much in the way of raw

materials, for the pale jealous folk of the overseas lands to
ignore, and they were forever dreaming dreams of conquest.
But no one had ever managed it. Africa had kept itself
independent of the great overseas powers. The Pasha of
Egypt still held his place by the Nile, in the far south the
Mambo of Zimbabwe maintained his domain amidst enough
gold to make even an Aztec feel envy, and the Bey of
Marrakesh was unchallenged in the north. And the strong
western empires flourished as ever, Ghana, Mali, Kongo,
Songhay—no, no, Africa had never let itself be eaten by
Turks or Russians or even the Moors, though they had all
given it a good try. Nor would it ever. Still, as he wandered
among these outlanders Little Father felt contempt for him
and his people drifting through the air about him like smoke.
He wished that he could have made a properly royal entrance, coming upon the foreigners in style, with drums and
trumpets and bugles. Preceded as he entered by musicians
carrying gold and silver guitars, and followed by a hundred
armed slaves. But those were royal prerogatives, and he was
not yet Emir. Besides, this was a solemn time in Songhay, and
such pomp was unbefitting. And the foreigners would very
likely look upon it as the vulgarity of a barbarian, anyway, or
the quaint grandiosity of a primitive.

Little Father downed his brandy in three quick gulps and
held out the cup for more. It was beginning to restore his
spirit. He felt a sense of deep well-being, of ease and
assurance.

But just then came a stir and a hubbub at the north door of
the reception hall. In amazement and fury he saw Serene
Glory entering, Big Father's main wife, surrounded by her full
retinue. Her hair was done up in the elaborate great curving
horns of the scorpion style, and she wore astonishing festoons
of jewelry, necklaces of gold and amber, bracelets of silver and
ebony and beads, rings of stone, earrings of shining ivory.

To Ali Pasha the prince said, hissing, "What's *she* doing here?"

"You invited her yourself, Little Father."

Little Father stared into his cup.

"I did?"

"There is no question of that, sir."

"Yes. Yes, I did." Little Father shook his head. "I must have been drunk. What was I thinking of?" Big Father's main wife was young and beautiful, younger, indeed, than Little Father himself, and she was an immense annoyance. Big Father had had six wives in his time, or possibly seven—Little Father was not sure, and he had never dared to ask—of whom all of the earliest ones were now dead, including Little Father's own mother. Of the three that remained, one was an elderly woman who lived in retirement in Gao, and one was a mere child, the old man's final toy; and then there was this one, this witch, this vampire, who placed no bounds on her ambitions. Only six months before, when Big Father had still been more or less healthy, Serene Glory had dared to offer herself to Little Father as they returned together from the Great Mosque. Of course he desired her; who would not desire her? But the idea was monstrous. Little Father would no more lay a hand on one of Big Father's wives than he would lie down with a crocodile. Clearly this woman, suspecting that the father was approaching his end, had had some dream of beguiling the son. That would not happen. Once Big Father was safely interred in the royal cemetery Serene Glory would go into chaste retirement, however beautiful she might be.

"Get her out of here, fast!" Little Father whispered.

"But she has every right—she is the wife of the Emir—"

"Then keep her away from me, at least. If she comes within five feet of me tonight, you'll be tending camels tomorrow, do you hear? Within *ten* feet. See to it.

"She will come nowhere near you, Little Father."

There was an odd look on Ali Pasha's face.

"Why are you smiling?" Little Father asked.

"Smiling? I am not smiling, Little Father."

"No. No, of course not."

Little Father made a gesture of dismissal and walked toward the platform of audience. A reception line began to form. The Russian was the first to present his greetings to the prince, and then the Aztec, and then the Englishman. There were ceremonial exchanges of gifts. At last it was the turn of the Turk. He had brought a splendid set of ornate daggers, inlaid with jewels. Little Father received them politely and, as he had with the other ambassadors, he bestowed an elaborately carved segment of ivory tusk upon Ismet Akif. The girl stood shyly to one side.

"May I present also my daughter Selima," said Ismet Akif.

She was well trained. She made a quick little ceremonial bow, and as she straightened her eyes met Little Father's, only for a moment, and it was enough. Warmth traveled beneath his skin nearly the entire length of his body, a signal he knew well. He smiled at her. The smile was a communicative one, and was understood and reciprocated. Even in that busy room those smiles had the force of thunderclaps. Everyone had been watching. Quickly Little Father's gaze traversed the reception hall, and in a fraction of an instant he took in the sudden flicker of rage on the face of Serene Glory, the sudden knowing look on Ali Pasha's, the sudden anguished comprehension on that of the tall young Englishman. Only Ismet Akif remained impassive; and yet Little Father had little doubt that he too was in on the transaction. In the wars of love there are rarely any secrets amongst those on the field of combat.

Every day there was dancing in the marketplace. Some days the dancers kept their heads motionless and put everything else into motion; other days they let their heads oscillate like independent creatures, while scarcely moving a limb. There were days of shouting dances and days of silent dances. Sometimes brilliant robes were worn and sometimes the dancers were all but naked.

In the beginning the foreign ambassadors went regularly to watch the show. But as time went on and the Emir continued not to die, and the intensity of the heat grew and grew, going beyond the uncomfortable into the implausible and then beyond that to the unimaginable, they tended to stay within the relative coolness of their own compounds despite the temptations of the daily show in the plaza. New ambassadors arrived daily, from the Maori Confederation, from China, from Peru finally, from lesser lands like Korea and Ind and the Teutonic States, and for a time the new-comers went to see the dancing with the same eagerness as their predecessors. Then they too stopped attending.

The Emir's longevity was becoming an embarrassment. Weeks were going by and the daily bulletins were a monotonous succession of medical ups and downs, with no clear pattern. The special ambassadors, unexpectedly snared in an ungratifying city at a disagreeable time of year, could not leave, but were beginning to find it an agony to stay on. It was evident to everyone now that the news of Big Father's imminent demise had gone forth to the world in a vastly overanticipatory way.

"If only the old bastard would simply get up and step out on his balcony and tell us he's healthy again, and let us all go home," Sir Anthony said. "Or succumb at last, one or the other. But this suspension, this indefiniteness—"

"Perhaps the prince will grow weary of the waiting and have him smothered in a pillow," Prince Itzcoatl suggested.

The Englishman shook his head. "He'd have done that ten years ago, if he had it in him at all. The time's long past for him to murder his father."

They were on the covered terrace of the Mexican embassy. In the dreadful heat-stricken silence of the day the foreign dignitaries, as they awaited the intolerably deferred news of the Emir's death, moved in formal rotation from one embassy to another, making ceremonial calls in accordance with strict rules of seniority and precedence.

"His Excellency the Grand Duke Alexander Petrovitch," the Aztec major domo announced. The foreign embassies were all in the same quarter of New Timbuctoo, along the grand boulevard known as The Street of All Nations. In the old days the foreigners had lived in the center of the Old Town, in fine houses in the best native style, palaces of stone and brick covered with mauve or orange clay. But Big Father had persuaded them one by one to move to the New City. It was undignified and uncomfortable, he insisted, for the representatives of the great overseas powers to live in mud houses with earthen floors.

Having all the foreigners' dwellings lined up in a row along a single street made it much simpler to keep watch over them, and, in case international difficulties should arise, it would be ever so much more easy to round them all up at once under the guise of "protecting" them. But Big Father had not taken into account that it was also very much easier for the foreigners to mingle with each other, which was not necessarily a good idea. It facilitated conspiracy as well as surveillance.

"We are discussing our impatience," Prince Itzcoatl told the Russian, who was the cousin of the Czar. "Sir Anthony is weary of Timbuctoo."

"Nor am I the only one," said the Englishman. "Did you hear that Maori ranting and raving yesterday at the Peruvian party? But what can we do? What can we do?"

"We could to Egypt go while we wait, perhaps," said the Grand Duke. "The Pyramids, the Sphinx, the temples of Karkak!"

"Karnak," Sir Anthony said. "But what if the old bugger dies while we're gone? We'd never get back in time for the funeral. What a black eye for us!"

"And how troublesome for our plans," said the Aztec.

"Mansa Suleiyman would never forgive us," said Sir Anthony.

"Mansa Suleiyman! Mansa Suleiyman!" Alexander Petrovich spat. "Let the black brigand do his own dirty work, then. Brothers, let us go to Egypt. If the Emir dies while we are away, will not the prince be removed whether or not we happen to be in attendance at the funeral?"

"Should we be speaking of this here?" Prince Itzcoatl asked, plucking in displeasure at his earplugs.

"Why not? There is no danger. These people are like children. They would never suspect—"

"Even so—"

But the Russian would not be deterred. Bull-like, he said, "It will all go well whether we are here or not. Believe me. It is all arranged, I remind you. So let us go to Egypt, then, before we bake to death. Before we choke on the sand that blows through these miserable streets."

"Egypt's not a great deal cooler than Songhay right now," Prince Itzcoatl pointed out. "And sand is not unknown there either."

The Grand Duke's massive shoulders moved in a ponderous shrugging gesture.

"To the south, then, to the Great Waterfalls. It is winter in that part of Africa, such winter as they have. Or to the Islands of the Canaries. Anywhere, anywhere at all, to escape from this Timbuctoo. I fry here. I sizzle here. I remind you that I am Russian, my friends. This is no climate for Russians."

Sir Anthony stared suspiciously into the sea-green eyes. "Are you the weak link in our little affair, my dear Duke Alexander? Have we made a mistake by asking you to join us?"

"Does it seem so to you? Am I untrustworthy, do you think?"

"The Emir could die at any moment. Probably will. Despite what's been happening, or not happening, it's clear that he can't last very much longer. The removal of the prince on the day of the funeral, as you have just observed, has been arranged. But how can we dare risk being elsewhere on that day? How can we even *think* of such a thing?" Sir Anthony's lean face grew florid; his tight mat of graying red hair began to rise and crackle with inner electricity; his chilly blue eyes became utterly arctic. "It is *essential* that in the moment of chaos that follows, the great-power triumvirate we represent—the troika, as you say—be on hand here to invite King Suleiyman of Mali to take charge of the country. I repeat, your excellency: *essential*. The time factor is critical. If we are off on holiday in Egypt, or anywhere else—if we are so much as a day too late getting back here—"

Prince Itzcoatl said, "I think the Grand Duke understands that point, Sir Anthony."

"Ah, but does he? Does he?"

"I think so." The Aztec drew in his breath sharply and let his gleaming obsidian eyes meet those of the Russian. "Certainly he sees that we're all in it too deep to back out, and that therefore he has to abide by the plan as drawn, however inconvenient he may find it personally."

The Grand Duke, sounding a little nettled, said, "We are traveling too swiftly here, I think. I tell you, I hate this filthy place, I hate its impossible heat, I hate its blowing sand, I hate its undying Emir, I hate its slippery lecherous prince. I hate the smell of the air, even. It is the smell of camel shit, the smell of old mud. But I am your partner in this undertaking to the end. I will not fail you, believe me." His great shoulders stirred like boulders rumbling down a slope. "The consolidation of Mali and Songhay would be displeasing to the Sultan, and therefore it is pleasing to the Czar. I will assist you in making it happen, knowing that such a consolidation has value for your own nations as well, which also is pleasing to my royal cousin. By the Russian Empire from the plan there will be no withdrawal. Of such a possibility let there be no more talk."

"Of holidays in Egypt let there be no more talk either," said Prince Itzcoatl. "Agreed? None of us likes being here, Duke Alexander. But here we have to stay, like it or not, until everything is brought to completion."

"Agreed. Agreed." The Russian snapped his fingers. "I did not come here to bicker. I have hospitality for you, waiting outside. Will you share vodka with me?" An attaché of the Russian Embassy entered, bearing a crystal beaker in a bowl of ice. "This arrived today, by the riverboat, and I have brought it to offer to my beloved friends of England and Mexico. Unfortunately of caviar there is none, though there should be. This heat! This heat! Caviar, in this heat— impossible!" The Grand Duke laughed. "To our great countries! To international amity! To a swift and peaceful end to the Emir's terrible sufferings! To your healths, gentlemen! To your healths!"

"To Mansa Suleiyman, King of Mali and Songhay," Prince Itzcoatl said. "Mansa Suleiyman, yes."

"Mansa Suleiyman!"

"What splendid stuff," said Sir Anthony. He held forth his glass, and the Russian attaché filled it yet again. "There are other and perhaps more deserving monarchs to toast. To His Majesty King Richard the Fifth!"

"King Richard, yes!"

"And His Imperial Majesty Vladimir the Ninth!"

"Czar Vladimir! Czar Vladimir!"

"Let us not overlook His Highness Moctezuma the Twelfth!"

"King Moctezuma! King Moctezuma!"

"Shall we drink to cooler weather and happier days, gentlemen?"

"Cooler weather! Happier days! —And the Emir of Songhay, may he soon rest in peace at last!"

"And to his eldest son, the prince of the realm. May he also soon be at rest," said Prince Itzcoatl.

Selima said, "I hear you have vampires here, and djinn. I want to know all about them."

Little Father was aghast. She would say anything, anything at all.

"Who's been feeding you nonsense like that? There aren't any vampires. There aren't any djinni either. These things are purely mythical."

"There's a tree south of the city where vampires hold meetings at midnight to choose their victims. Isn't that so? The tree is half white and half red. When you first become a vampire you have to bring one of your male cousins to the meeting for the others to feast on."

"Some of the common people may believe such stuff. But do you think *I* do? Do you think we're all a bunch of ignorant savages here, girl?"

"There's a charm that can be worn to keep vampires from creeping into your bedroom at night and sucking your blood. I want you to get me one."

"I tell you, there aren't any vamp—"

"Or, there's a special prayer you can say. And while you say it you spit in four directions, and that traps the vampire in your house so he can be arrested. Tell me what it is. And the charm for making the vampire give back the blood he's drunk. I want to know that, too."

They were on the private upstairs porch of Little Father's palace. The night was bright with moonlight, and the air was as hot as wet velvet. Selima was wearing a long silken robe, very sheer. He could see the shadow of her breasts through it when she turned at an angle to the moon.

"Are you always like this?" he asked, beginning to feel a little irritable. "Or are you just trying to torment me?"

"What's the point of traveling if you don't bother to learn anything about local customs?"

"You do think we're savages."

"Maybe I do. Africa is the dark continent. Black skins, black souls."

"My skin isn't black. It's practically as light as yours. But even if it were—"

"You're black inside. Your blood is African blood, and Africa is the strangest place in the world. The fierce animals you have, gorillas and hippos running around everywhere, giraffes, tigers—the masks, the nightmare carvings—the witchcraft, the drums, the chanting of the high priests—"

"Please," Little Father said. "You're starting to drive me crazy. I'm not responsible for what goes on in the jungle of the tropics. This is Songhay. Do we seem uncivilized to you? We were a great empire when you Ottomans were still herding goats on the steppes. The only giraffe you'll see in this city is the stuffed one in my father's throne room. There aren't any gorillas in Songhay, and tigers come from Asia, and if you see a hippo running, here or anywhere, please tell the newspaper right away." Then he began to laugh. "Look, Selima, this is a modern country. We have motorcars here. We have a stock exchange. There's a famous university in Timbuctoo, six hundred years old. I don't bow down to tribal idols. We are an Islamic people, you know."

It was lunacy to have let her force him onto the defensive like this. But she wouldn't stop her attack.

"Djinn are Islamic. The Koran talks about them. The Arabs believe in djinn."

Little Father struggled for patience. "Perhaps they did

five hundred years ago, but what's that to us? In any case we aren't Arabs."

"But there are djinn here, plenty of them. My head porter told me. A djinn will appear as a small black spot on the ground and will grow until he's as big as a house. He might change into a sheep or a dog or a cat, and then he'll disappear. The porter said that one time he was at the edge of town in Kabara, and he was surrounded by giants in white turbans that made a weird sucking noise at him."

"What is this man's name? He has no right filling your head with this trash. I'll have him fed to the lions."

"Really?" Her eyes were sparkling. "Would you? What lions? Where?"

"My father keeps them as pets, in a pit. No one is looking after them these days. They must be getting very hungry."

"Oh, you *are* a savage! You are!"

Little Father grinned lopsidedly. He was regaining some of the advantage, he felt. "Lions need to be fed now and then. There's nothing savage about that. Not feeding them, that would be savage."

"But to feed a servant to them—"

"If he speaks idiotic nonsense to a visitor, yes. Especially when the visitor is an impressionable young girl."

Her eyes flashed quick lightning, sudden pique. "You think I'm impressionable? You think I'm silly?"

"I think you are young."

"And I think you're a savage underneath it all. Even savages can start a stock exchange. But they're still savages."

"Very well," Little Father said, putting an ominous throb into his tone. "I admit it. I am the child of darkness. I am the pagan prince." He pointed to the moon, full and swollen, hanging just above them like a plummeting polished shield. "You think that is a dead planet up there? It is alive, it is a land of djinn. And it must be nourished. So when it is full like this, the king of this land must appear beneath its face and make offerings of energy to it."

"Energy?"

"Sexual energy," he said portentously. "Atop the great phallic altar, beneath which we keep the dried umbilicus of each of our dead kings. First there is a procession, the phallic figures carried through the streets. And then—"

"The sacrifice of a virgin?" Selima asked.

"What's wrong with you? We are good Moslems here. We don't countenance murder."

"But you countenance phallic rites at the full moon?"

He couldn't tell whether she was taking him seriously or not.

"We maintain certain pre-Islamic customs," he said. "It is folly to cut oneself off from one's origins."

"Absolutely. Tell me what you do on the night the moon is full."

"First, the king coats his entire body in rancid butter—"

"I don't think I like that!"

"Then the chosen bride of the moon is led forth—"

"The fair-skinned bride."

"Fair-skinned?" he said. She saw it was a game, he realized. She was getting into it. "Why fair-skinned?"

"Because she'd be more like the moon than a black woman would. Her energy would rise into the sky more easily. So each month a white woman is stolen and brought to the king to take part in the rite."

Little Father gave her a curious stare. "What a ferocious child you are!"

"I'm not a child. You do prefer white women, don't you? One thing you regret is that I'm not white enough for you."

"You seem very white to me," said Little Father. She was at the edge of the porch now, looking outward over the sleeping city. Idly he watched her shoulder blades moving beneath her sheer gown. Then suddenly the garment began to slide downward, and he realized she had unfastened it at the throat and cast it off. She had worn nothing underneath it. Her waist was very narrow, her hips broad, her buttocks smooth and full, with a pair of deep dimples at the place where they curved outward from her back. His lips were beginning to feel very dry, and he licked them thoughtfully.

She said, "What you really want is an Englishwoman, with skin like milk, and pink nipples, and golden hair down below."

Damn Ali Pasha! Was he out of his mind, telling such stuff to her? He'd go to the lions first thing tomorrow!

Amazed, he cried, "What are you talking about? What sort of madness is this?"

"That is what you want, isn't it? A nice juicy golden-haired one. All of you Africans secretly want one. Some of you not so secretly. I know all about it."

No, it was inconceivable. Ali Pasha was tricky, but he wasn't insane. This was mere coincidence.

"Have you ever had an Englishwoman, prince? A true pink and gold one?"

Little Father let out a sigh of relief. It was only another of her games, then. The girl was all mischief, and it came bubbling out randomly, spontaneously. Truly, she would say anything to anyone. Anything.

"Once," he said, a little vindictively. "She was writing a book on the African empires and she came here to do some research at our university. Our simple barbaric university. One night she interviewed me, on this very porch, a night almost as warm as this one. Her name was—ah—Elizabeth. Elizabeth, yes." Little Father's gaze continued to rest on Selima's bare back. She seemed much more frail above the waist than below. Below the waist she was solid, splendidly fleshly, a commanding woman, no girl at all. Languidly he said, "Skin like milk, indeed. And rosy nipples. I had never even imagined that nipples could be like that. And her hair—"

Selima turned to face him. "My nipples are dark."

"Yes, of course. You're a Turk. But Elizabeth—"

"I don't want to hear any more about Elizabeth. Kiss me." Her nipples *were* dark, yes, and very small, almost like a boy's, tiny dusky targets on the roundness of her breasts. Her thighs were surprisingly full. She looked far more voluptuous naked than when she was clothed. He hadn't expected that. The heavy thatch at the base of her belly was jet black.

He said, "We don't care for kissing in Songhay. It's one of our quaint tribal taboos. The mouth is for eating, not for making love."

"Every part of the body is for making love. Kiss me."

"You Europeans!"

"I'm not European. I'm a Turk. You do it in some peculiar way here, don't you? Side by side. Back to back."

"No," he said. "Not back to back. Never like that, not even when we feel like reverting to tribal barbarism."

Her perfume drifted toward him, falling over him like a veil. Little Father went to her and she rose up out of the night to him, and they laughed. He kissed her. It was a lie, the thing he had told her, that Songhayans did not like to kiss. Songhayans liked to do everything: at least this Songhayan did. She slipped downward to the swirl of silken pillows on the floor, and he joined her there and covered her body with his own. As he embraced her he felt the moonlight on his back like the touch of a goddess' fingertips, cool, delicate, terrifying.

On the horizon a sharp dawn-line of pale lavender appeared, cutting between the curving grayness above and the flat grayness below. It was like a preliminary announcement by the oboes or the French horns, soon to be transformed into the full overwhelming trumpetblast of morning. Michael, who had been wandering through Old Timbuctoo all night, stared eastward uneasily as if he expected the sky to burst into flame when the sun came into view.

Sleep had been impossible. Only his face and hands were actually sunburned, but his whole body throbbed with discomfort, as though the African sun had reached him even through his clothing. He felt the glow of it behind his knees, in the small of his back, on the soles of his feet.

Nor was there any way to escape the heat, even when the terrible glaring sun had left the sky. The nights were as warm as the days. The motionless air lay on you like burning fur. When you drew a breath you could trace its path all the way down, past your nostrils, past your throat, a trickle of molten lead descending the forking paths into your lungs and spreading out to weigh upon every individual air-sac inside you. Now and then came a breeze, but it only made things worse: it gave you no more comfort than a shower of hot ashes might have afforded. So Michael had risen after a few hours of tossing and turning and gone out unnoticed to wander under the weird and cheerless brilliance of the overhanging moon, down from the posh Embassy district into the Old Town somehow, and then from street to street, from quarter to quarter, no destination in mind, no purpose, seeking only to obliterate the gloom and misery of the night.

He was lost, of course—the Old Town was complex enough to negotiate in daylight, impossible in the dark—but that didn't matter. He was somewhere on the western side of town, that was all he knew. The moon was long gone from the sky, as if it had been devoured, though he had not noticed it setting. Before him the ancient metropolis of mud walls and low square flat-roofed buildings lay humped in the thinning darkness, a gigantic weary beast slowly beginning to stir. The thing was to keep on walking, through the night and into the dawn, distracting himself from the physical discomfort and the other, deeper agony that had wrapped itself like some voracious starfish around his soul.

By the faint light he saw that he had reached a sort of large pond. Its water looked to be a flat metallic green. Around its perimeter crouched a shadowy horde of water-carriers, crouching to scoop the green water into goatskin bags, spooning it in with gourds. Then they straightened, with the full bags—they must have weighed a hundred pounds—balanced on their heads, and went jogging off into the dawn to deliver their merchandise at the homes of the wealthy. Little ragged girls were there, too, seven or eight years old, filling jugs and tins to bring to their mothers. Some of them waded right into the pool to get what they wanted. A glowering black man in the uniform of the Emirate sat to one side, jotting down notations on a sheet of yellow paper. So this was probably the Old Town's municipal reservoir. Michael shuddered and turned away, back into the city proper. Into the labyrinth once more.

A gray, sandy light was in the sky now. It showed him narrow dusty thoroughfares, blind walls, curving alleyways leading into dark cul-de-sacs. Entire rows of houses seemed to be crumbling away, though they were obviously still inhabited. Underfoot everything was sand, making a treacherous footing. In places the entrances to buildings were half choked by the drifts. Camels, donkeys, horses wandered about on their own. The city's mixed population—veiled Tuaregs, black Sudanese, aloof and lofty Moors, heavy-bearded Syrian traders, the whole West African racial goulash—was coming forth into the day. Who were all these people? Tailors, moneylenders, scribes, camel-breeders, masons, charm-sellers, weavers, bakers—necromancers, sages, warlocks, perhaps a few vampires on their way home from their night's toil—Michael looked around, bewildered, trapped within his skull by the barriers of language and his own disordered mental state. He felt as though he were moving about under the surface of the sea, in a medium where he did not belong and could neither breathe nor think.

"Selima?" he said suddenly, blinking in astonishment.

His voice was voiceless. His lips moved, but no sound had come forth.

Apparition? Hallucination? No, no, she was really there. Selima glowed just across the way like a second sun suddenly rising over the city.

Michael shrank back against an immense buttress of mud brick. She had stepped out of a doorway in a smooth gray wall that surrounded what appeared to be one of the palaces of the nobility. The building, partly visible above the wall, was coated in orange clay and had elaborate Moorish windows of dark wood. He trembled. The girl wore only a flimsy white gown, so thin that he could make out the dark-tipped spheres of her breasts moving beneath it, and the dark triangle at her thighs. He wanted to cry. Had she no shame? No. No. She was indifferent to the display, and to everything around her; she would have walked completely naked through this little plaza just as casually as she strode through in this one thin garment.

"Selima, where have you spent this night? Whose palace is this?" His words were air. No one heard them. She moved serenely onward. A motorcar appeared from somewhere, one of the five or six that Michael had seen so far in this city. A black plume of smoke rose from the vent of its coal-burning engine, and its two huge rear wheels slipped and slid about on the sandy track. Selima jumped up onto the open seat behind the driver, and with great booming exhalations the vehicle made its way through an arched passageway and disappeared into the maze of the town.

An embassy car, no doubt. Waiting here for her all night?

His soul ached. He had never felt so young, so foolish, so vulnerable, so wounded.

"Effendi?" a voice asked. "You wish a camel, effendi?"

"Thank you, no."

"Nice hotel? Bath? Woman to massage you? Boy to massage you?"

"Please. No."

"Some charms, maybe? Good grigri. Souvenir of Timbuctoo."

Michael groaned. He turned away and looked back at the house of infamy from which Selima had emerged.

"That building—what is it?"

"That? Is palace of Little Father. And look, look there, effendi—Little Father himself coming out for a walk."

The prince himself, yes. Of course. Who else would she have spent the night with, here in the Old Town? Michael was engulfed by loathing and despair. Instantly a swarm of eager citizens had surrounded the prince, clustering about him to beg favors the moment he showed himself. But he seemed to move through them with the sort of divine indifference that Selima, in her all-but-nakedness, had displayed. He appeared to be enclosed in an impenetrable bubble of self-concern. He was frowning, he looked troubled, not at all like a man who had just known the favors of the most desirable woman in five hundred miles. His lean sharp-angled face, which had been so animated at the official reception, now had a curiously stunned, immobile look about it, as though he had been struck on the head from behind a short while before and the impact was gradually sinking in.

Michael flattened himself against the buttress. He could not bear the thought of being seen by the prince now, here, as if he had been haunting the palace all night, spying on Selima. He put his arm across his face in a frantic attempt to hide himself, he whose western clothes and long legs and white skin made him stand out like a meteor. But the prince wasn't coming toward him. Nodding in an abstracted way, he turned quickly, passed through the throng of chattering petitioners as if they were ghosts, disappeared in a flurry of white fabric.

Michael looked about for his sudden friend, the man who had wanted to sell him camels, massages, souvenirs. What he wanted now was a guide to get him out of the Old Town and back to the residence of the English ambassador. But the man was gone.

"Pardon me—" Michael said to someone who looked almost like the first one. Then he realized that he had spoken in English. Useless. He tried in Turkish and in Arabic. A few people stared at him. They seemed to be laughing. He felt transparent to them. They could see his sorrow, his heart-ache, his anguish, as easily as his sunburn.

Like the good young diplomat he was, he had learned a little Songhay, too, the indigenous language. "Town talk," they called it. But the few words he had seemed all to have fled. He stood alone and helpless in the plaza, scuffing angrily at the sand, as the sun broke above the mud rooftops like the sword of an avenging angel and the full blast of morning struck him. Michael felt blisters starting to rise on his cheeks. Agitated flies began to buzz around his eyes. A camel, passing by just then, dropped half a dozen hot green turds right at his feet. He snatched one out of the sand and hurled it with all his strength at the bland blank mud-colored wall of Little Father's palace.

Big Father was sitting up on his divan. His silken blankets were knotted around his waist in chaotic strands, and his bare torso rose above the chaos, gleaming as though it had been oiled. His arms were like sticks and his skin was three shades paler than it once had been and cascades of loose flesh hung like wattles from his neck, but there was the brilliance of black diamonds in his glittering little eyes.

"Not dead yet, you see? You see?" His voice was a cracked wailing screech, but the old authoritative thunder was still somewhere behind it. "Back from the edge of the grave, boy! Allah walks with me yet!"

Little Father was numb with chagrin. All the joy of his night with Selima had vanished in a moment when word had arrived of his father's miraculous recovery. He had just been getting accustomed to the idea that he soon would be king, too. His first misgivings about the work involved in it had begun to ebb; he rather liked the idea of ruling, now. The crown was descending on him like a splendid gift. And here was Big Father sitting up, grinning, waving his arms around in manic glee. Taking back his gift. Deciding to live after all.

What about the funeral plans? What about the special ambassadors who had traveled so far, in such discomfort, to pay homage to the late venerable Emir of Songhay and strike their various deals with his successor?

Big Father had had his head freshly shaved and his beard had been trimmed. He looked like a gnome, ablaze with demonic energies. Off in the corner of the porch, next to the potted trees, the three marabouts stood in a circle, making sacred gestures at each other with lunatic vigor, each seeking to demonstrate superior fervor.

Hoarsely Little Father said, "Your majesty, the news astonishes and delights me. When the messenger came, telling of your miraculous recovery, I leaped from my bed and gave thanks to the All-Merciful in a voice so loud you must have heard it here."

"Was there a woman with you, boy?"

"Father—"

"I hope you bathed before you came here. You come forth

without bathing after you've lain with a woman and the djinn will make you die an awful death, do you realize that?"

"Father, I wouldn't think of—"

"Frothing at the mouth, falling down in the street, that's what'll happen to you. Who was she? Some nobleman's wife as usual, I suppose. Well, never mind. As long as she wasn't mine. Come closer to me, boy."

"Father, you shouldn't tire yourself by talking so much."

"Closer!"

A wizened claw reached for him. Little Father approached and the claw seized him. There was frightening strength in the old man still.

Big Father said, "I'll be up and around in two days. I want the Great Mosque made ready for the ceremony of thanksgiving. And I'll sacrifice to all the prophets and saints." A fit of coughing overcame him for a space, and he pounded his fist furiously against the side of the divan. When he spoke again, his voice seemed weaker, but still determined. "There was a vampire upon me, boy! Each night she came in here and drank from me."

"She?"

"With dark hair and pale foreign skin, and eyes that eat you alive. Every night. Stood above me, and laughed, and took my blood. But she's gone now. These three have imprisoned her and carried her off to the Eleventh Hell." He gestured toward the marabouts. "My saints. My heroes. I want them rewarded beyond all reckoning."

"As you say, father, so will I do."

The old man nodded. "You were getting my funeral ready, weren't you?"

"The prognosis was very dark. Certain preparations seemed advisable when we heard—"

"Cancel them!"

"Of course." Then, uncertainly: "Father, special envoys

have come from many lands. The Czar's cousin is here, and the brother of Moctezuma, and a son of the late Sultan, and also—"

"I'll hold an audience for them all," said Big Father in great satisfaction. "They'll have gifts beyond anything they can imagine. Instead of a funeral, boy, we'll have a jubilee! A celebration of life. Moctezuma's brother, you say? And who did the Inca send?" Big Father laughed raucously. "All of them clustering around to see me put away underground!" He jabbed a finger against Little Father's breast. It felt like a spear of bone. "And in Mali they're dancing in the streets, aren't they? Can't contain themselves for glee. But they'll dance a different dance now." Big Father's eyes grew somber. "You know, boy, when I really do die, whenever that is, they'll try to take you out too, and Mali will invade us. Guard yourself. Guard the nation. Those bastards on the coast hunger to control our caravan routes. They're probably already scheming now with the foreigners to swallow us the instant I'm gone, but you mustn't allow them to—ah—ah—"

"Father?"

Abruptly the Emir's shriveled face crumpled in a frenzy of coughing. He hammered against his thighs with clenched fists. An attendant came running, bearing a beaker of water, and Big Father drank until he had drained it all. Then he tossed the beaker aside as though it were nothing. He was shivering. He looked glassy-eyed and confused. His shoulders slumped, his whole posture slackened. Perhaps his "recovery" had been merely the sudden final upsurge of a dying fire.

"You should rest, majesty," said a new voice from the doorway to the porch. It was Serene Glory's ringing contralto. "You overtax yourself, I think, in the first hours of this miracle."

Big Father's main wife had arrived, entourage and all. In the warmth of the morning she had outfitted herself in a startling robe of purple satin, over which she wore the finest jewels of the kingdom. Little Father remembered that his own mother had worn some of those necklaces and bracelets.

He was unmoved by Serene Glory's beauty, impressive though it was. How could Serene Glory matter to him with the memory, scarcely two hours old, of Selima's full breasts and agile thighs still glistening in his mind? But he could not fail to detect Serene Glory's anger. It surrounded her like a radiant aura. Tension sparkled in her kohl-bedecked eyes.

Perhaps she was still smoldering over Little Father's deft rejection of her advances as they were riding side by side back from the Great Mosque that day six months earlier. Or perhaps it was Big Father's unexpected return from the brink that annoyed her. Anyone with half a mind realized that Serene Glory dreamed of putting her own insipid brother on the throne in Little Father's place the moment the old Emir was gone, and thus maintaining and even extending her position at the summit of power. Quite likely she, like Little Father, had by now grown accustomed to the idea of Big Father's death and was having difficulty accepting the news that it would be somewhat postponed.

To Little Father she said, "Our prayers have been answered, all glory to Allah! But you mustn't put a strain on the Emir's energies in this time of recovery. Perhaps you ought to go."

"I was summoned, lady."

"Of course. Quite rightly. And now you should go to the mosque and give thanks for what has been granted us all."

Her gaze was imperious and unanswerable. In one sentence Serene Glory had demoted him from imminent king to wastrel prince once again. He admired her gall. She was three years younger than Little Father, and here she was ordering him out of the royal presence as though he were a child. But of course she had had practice at ordering people around: her father was one of the greatest landlords of the eastern province. She had moved amidst power all her life, albeit power of a provincial sort. Little Father wondered how many noblemen of that province had spent time between the legs of Serene Glory before she had ascended to her present high position.

He said, "If my royal father grants me leave to go—"

The Emir was coughing again. He looked terrible.

Serene Glory went to him and bent close over him, so the old man could smell the fragrance rising from her breasts, and instantly Big Father relaxed. The coughing ceased and he sat up again, almost as vigorous as before. Little Father admired that maneuver too. Serene Glory was a worthy adversary. Probably her people were already spreading the word in the city that it was the power of her love for the Emir, and not the prayers of the three saints, that had brought him back from the edge of death.

"How cool it is in here," Big Father said. "The wind is rising. Will it rain today? The rains are due, aren't they? Let me see the sky. What color is the sky?" He looked upward in an odd straining way, as though the sky had risen to such a height that it could no longer be seen.

"Father," Little Father said softly.

The old man glared. "You heard her, didn't you? To the mosque! To the mosque and give thanks! Do you want Allah to think you're an ingrate, boy?" He started coughing once again. Once again he began visibly to descend the curve of his precarious vitality. His withered cheeks began to grow mottled. There was a feeling of impending death in the air.

Servants and ministers and the three marabouts gathered by his side, alarmed.

"Big Father! Big Father!"

And then once more he was all right again, just as abruptly. He gestured fiercely, an unmistakable dismissal.

The woman in purple gave Little Father a dark grin of triumph. Little Father nodded to her gallantly: this round was hers. He knelt at the Emir's side, kissed his royal ring. It slipped about loosely on his shrunken finger. Little Father, thinking of nothing but the pressure of Selima's dark, hard little nipples against the palms of his hands two hours before, made the prostration of filial devotion to his father and, with ferocious irony, to his stepmother, and backed quickly away from the royal presence.

Michael said, distraught, "I couldn't sleep, sir. I went out for a walk."

"And you walked *the whole night long?*" Sir Anthony asked, in a voice like a flail.

"I didn't really notice the time. I just kept walking, and by and by the sun came up and I realized that the night was gone."

"It's your mind that's gone, I think." Sir Anthony, crooking his neck upward to Michael's much greater height, gave him a whip-crack glare. "What kind of calf are you, anyway? Haven't you any sense at all?"

"Sir Anthony, I don't underst—"

"Are you in *love*? With the Turkish girl?"

Michael clapped his hand over his mouth in dismay.

"You know about that?" he said lamely, after a moment.

"One doesn't have to be a mind-reader to see it, lad. Every camel in Timbuctoo knows it. The pathetic look on your face whenever she comes within fifty feet of you—the clownish way you shuffle your feet around, and hang your head— those occasional little groans of deepest melancholy—" The envoy glowered. He made no attempt to hide his anger, or his contempt. "By heaven, *I'd* like to hang your head, and all the rest of you as well. Have you no sense? Have you no sense whatsoever?"

Everything was lost, so what did anything matter? Defiantly Michael said, "Have you never fallen unexpectedly in love, Sir Anthony?"

"With a *Turk?*"

"Unexpectedly, I said. These things don't necessarily happen with one's political convenience in mind."

"And she reciprocates your love, I suppose? That's why you were out walking like a moon-calf in this miserable parched mudhole of a city all night long?"

"She spent the night with the crown prince," Michael blurted in misery.

"Ah. Ah, now it comes out!" Sir Anthony was silent for a while. Then he glanced up sharply, his eyes bright with skepticism. "But how do you know that?"

"I saw her leaving his palace at dawn, sir."

"Spying on her, were you?

"I just happened to be there. I didn't even know it was his palace, until I asked. He came out himself a few minutes later, and went quickly off somewhere. He looked very troubled."

"He should have looked troubled. He'd just found out that he might not get to be king as quickly as he'd like to be."

"I don't understand, please, sir."

"There's word going around town this morning that the Emir has recovered. And had sent for his son to let him know that he wasn't quite as moribund as was generally believed."

Michael recoiled in surprise.

"Recovered? Is it true?"

Sir Anthony offered him a benign, patronizing smile.

"So they say. But the Emir's doctors assure us that it's nothing more than a brief rally in an inevitable descent. The old wolf will be dead within the week. Still, it's rather a setback for Little Father's immediate plans. The news of the

Emir's unanticipated awakening from his coma must rather have spoiled his morning for him."

"Good," said Michael vindictively.

Sir Anthony laughed.

"You hate him, do you?"

"I despise him. I loathe him. I have nothing but the greatest detestation for him. He's a cynical amoral voluptuary and nothing more. He doesn't deserve to be a king."

"Well, if it's any comfort to you, lad, he's not going to live long enough to become one."

"What?"

"His untimely demise has been arranged. His stepmother is going to poison him at the funeral of the old Emir, if the old Emir ever has the good grace to finish dying."

"What? What?"

Sir Anthony smiled.

"This is quite confidential, you understand. Perhaps I shouldn't be entrusting you with it just yet. But you'd have needed to find out sooner or later. We've organized a little coup d'état."

"What? What? What?" said Michael helplessly.

"Her Highness the Lady Serene Glory would like to put her brother on the throne instead of the prince. The brother is worthless, of course. So is the prince, of course, but at least he does happen to be the rightful heir. We don't want to see either of them have it, actually. What we'd prefer is to have the Mansa of Mali declare that the unstable conditions in Songhay following the death of the old Emir have created a danger to the security of all of West Africa that can be put to rest only by an amalgamation of the kingdoms of Mali and Songhay under a single ruler. Who would be, of course, the Mansa of Mali, precisely as your lady so baldly suggested the other day. And that is what we intend to achieve. The Grand

Duke and Prince Itzcoatl and I. As representatives of the powers whom we serve."

Michael stared. He rubbed his cheeks as if to assure himself that this was no dream. He found himself unable to utter a sound.

Sir Anthony went on, clearly and calmly. "And so Serene Glory gives Little Father the deadly cup, and then the Mansa's troops cross the border, and we, on behalf of our governments, immediately recognize the new combined government. Which makes everyone happy except, I suppose, the Sultan, who has such good trade relationships with Songhay and is on such poor terms with the Mansa of Mali. But we hardly shed tears for the Sultan's distress, do we, boy? Do we? The distress of the Turks is no concern of ours. Quite the contrary, in fact, is that not so?" Sir Anthony clapped his hand to Michael's shoulder. It was an obvious strain for him, reaching so high. The fingers clamping into Michael's tender sunburned skin were agony. "So let's see no more mooning over this alluring Ottoman goddess of yours, eh, lad? It's inappropriate for a lovely blond English boy like yourself to be lusting after a Turk, as you know very well. She's nothing but a little slut, however she may seem to your infatuated eyes. And you needn't take the trouble to expend any energy loathing the prince, either. His days are numbered. He won't survive his evil old father by so much as a week. It's all arranged."

Michael's jaw gaped. A glazed look of disbelief appeared in his eyes. His face was burning fiercely, not from the sunburn now, but from the intensity of his confusion.

"But sir—sir—"

"Get yourself some sleep, boy."

"*Sir!*"

"Shocked, are you? Well, you shouldn't be. There's nothing shocking about assassinating an inconvenient king.

What's shocking to me is a grown man with pure English blood in his veins spending the night creeping pitifully around after his dissolute little Turkish inamorata as she makes her way to the bed of her African lover. And then telling me how heartsore and miserable he is. Get yourself some sleep, boy. Get yourself some sleep!"

In the midst of the uncertainty over the Emir's impending death the semi-annual salt caravan from the north arrived in Timbuctoo. It was a great, if somewhat unexpected, spectacle, and all the foreign ambassadors, restless and by now passionately in need of diversion, turned out despite the heat to watch its entry into the city.

There was tremendous clamor. The heavy metal-studded gates of the city were thrown open and the armed escort entered first, a platoon of magnificent black warriors armed both with rifles and with scimitars. Trumpets brayed, drums pounded. A band of fierce-looking hawk-nosed, fiery-eyed country chieftains in flamboyant robes came next, marching in phalanx like conquerors. And then came the salt-laden camels, an endless stream of them, a tawny river, strutting absurdly along in grotesque self-important grandeur with their heads held high and their sleepy eyes indifferent to the throngs of excited spectators. Strapped to each camel's back were two or three huge flat slabs of salt, looking much like broad blocks of marble.

"There are said to be seven hundred of the beasts," murmured the Chinese ambassador, Li Hsiao-ssu.

"One thousand eight hundred," said the Grand Duke Alexander sternly. He glowered at Li Hsiao-ssu, a small, fastidious-looking man with drooping mustachios and gleaming porcelain skin, who seemed a mere doll beside the bulky Russian. There was little love lost between the Grand Duke and the Chinese envoy. Evidently the Grand Duke thought it was presumptuous that China, as a client state of the Russian Empire, as a mere vassal, in truth, had sent an ambassador at all. "One thousand eight hundred. That is the number I was told, and it is reliable. I assure you that it is reliable."

The Chinese shrugged. "Seven hundred, three thousand, what difference is there? Either way, that's too many camels to have in one place at one time."

"Yes, what ugly things they are!" said the Peruvian, Manco Roca. "Such stupid faces, such an ungainly stride! Perhaps we should do these Africans a favor and let them have a few herds of llamas."

Coolly Prince Itzcoatl said, "Your llamas, brother, are no more fit for the deserts of this continent than these camels would be in the passes of the Andes. Let them keep their beasts, and be thankful that you have handsomer ones for your own use."

"Such stupid faces," the Peruvian said once more.

Timbuctoo was the center of distribution for salt throughout the whole of West Africa. The salt mines were hundreds of miles away, in the center of the Sahara. Twice a year the desert traders made the twelve-day journey to the capital, where they exchanged their salt for the dried fish, grain, rice, and other produce that came up the Niger from the agricultural districts to the south and east. The arrival of the caravan was the occasion for feasting and revelry, a time of wild big-city gaiety for the visitors from such remote and placid rural outposts.

But the Emir of Songhay was dying. This was no time for a festival. The appearance of the caravan at such a moment was evidently a great embarrassment to the city officials, a mark of bad management as well as bad taste.

"They could have sent messengers upcountry to turn them back," Michael said. "Why didn't they, I wonder?"

"Blacks," said Manco Roca morosely. "What can you expect from blacks."

"Yes, of course," Sir Anthony said, giving the Peruvian a disdainful look. "We understand that they aren't Incas. Yet despite that shortcoming they've somehow managed to keep control of most of this enormous continent for thousands of years."

"But their colossal administrative incompetence, my dear Sir Anthony—as we see here, letting a circus like this one come into town while their king lies dying—"

"Perhaps it's deliberate," Ismet Akif suggested. "A much needed distraction. The city is tense. The Emir's been too long about his dying; it's driving everyone crazy. So they decided to let the caravan come marching in."

"I think not," said Li Hsiao-ssu. "Do you see those municipal officials there? I detect signs of deep humiliation on their faces."

"And who would be able to detect such things more acutely than you?" asked the Grand Duke.

The Chinese envoy stared at the Russian as though unsure whether he was being praised or mocked. For a moment his elegant face was dusky with blood. The other diplomats gathered close, making ready to defuse the situation. Politeness was ever a necessity in such a group.

Then the envoy from the Teutonic States said, "Is that not the prince arriving now?"

"Where?" Michael demanded in a tight-strung voice. "Where is he?"

Sir Anthony's hand shot out to seize Michael's wrist. He squeezed it unsparingly.

In a low tone he said, "You will cause no difficulties, young sir. Remember that you are English. Your breeding must rule your passions."

Michael, glaring toward Little Father as the prince approached the city gate, sullenly pulled his arm free of Sir Anthony's grasp and amazed himself by uttering a strange low growling sound, like that of a cat announcing a challenge. Unfamiliar hormones flooded the channels of his body. He could feel the individual bones of his cheeks and forehead moving apart from one another; he was aware of the tensing and coiling of muscles great and small. He wondered if he was losing his mind. Then the moment passed and he let out his breath in a long dismal exhalation.

Little Father wore flowing green pantaloons, a striped robe wide enough to cover his arms, and an intricately deployed white turban with brilliant feathers of some exotic sort jutting from it. An entourage of eight or ten men surrounded him, carrying iron-shafted lances. The prince strode forward so briskly that his bodyguard was hard pressed to keep up with him.

Michael, watching Selima out of the corner of his eye, murmured to Sir Anthony, "I'm terribly sorry, sir. But if he so much as glances at her you'll have to restrain me."

"If you so much as flicker a nostril I'll have you billeted in our Siberian consulate for the rest of your career," Sir Anthony replied, barely moving his lips as he spoke.

But Little Father had no time to flirt with Selima now. He barely acknowledged the presence of the ambassadors at all. A stiff formal nod, and then he moved on, into the midst of the group of caravan leaders. They clustered about him like a convocation of eagles. Among those suncrisped swarthy upright chieftains the prince seemed soft, frail, overly citified, a dabbler confronting serious men.

Some ritual of greeting seemed to be going on. Little Father touched his forehead, extended his open palm, closed his hand with a snap, presented his palm again with a flourish. The desert men responded with equally stylized maneuvers.

When Little Father spoke, it was in Songhay, a sharp outpouring of liquid incomprehensibilities.

"What was that? What was that?" asked the ambassadors of one another. Turkish was the international language of diplomacy, even in Africa; the native tongues of the dark continent were mysteries to outsiders.

Sir Anthony, though, said softly, "He's angry. He says the city's closed on account of the Emir's illness and the caravan was supposed to have waited at Kabara for further instructions. They seem surprised. Someone must have missed a signal."

"You speak Songhay, sir?" Michael asked.

"I was posted in Mali for seven years," Sir Anthony muttered. "It was before you were born, boy."

"So I was right," cried Manco Roca. "The caravan should never have been allowed to enter the city at all. Incompetence! Incompetence!"

"Is he telling them to leave?" Ismet Akif wanted to know.

"I can't tell. They're all talking at once. I think they're saying that their camels need fodder. And he's telling them that there's no merchandise for them to buy, that the goods from upriver were held back because of the Emir's illness."

"What an awful jumble," Selima said.

It was the first thing she had said all morning. Michael, who had been trying to pay no attention to her, looked toward her now in agitation. She was dressed chastely enough, in a red blouse and flaring black skirt, but in his inflamed mind she stood revealed suddenly nude, with the marks of Little Father's caresses flaring like stigmata on her breasts and thighs. Michael sucked in his breath and held himself stiffly erect, trembling like a drawn bowstring. A sound midway between a sigh and a groan escaped him. Sir Anthony kicked his ankle sharply.

Some sort of negotiation appeared to be going on. Little

Father gesticulated rapidly, grinned, did the open-close-open gesture with his hand again, tapped his chest and his forehead and his left elbow. The apparent leader of the traders matched him, gesture for gesture. Postures began to change. The tensions were easing. Evidently the caravan would be admitted to the city.

Little Father was smiling, after a fashion. His forehead glistened with sweat; he seemed to have come through a difficult moment well, but he looked tired.

The trumpets sounded again. The camel-drovers regained the attention of their indifferent beasts and nudged them forward.

There was new commotion from the other side of the plaza.

"What's this, now?" Prince Itzcoatl said.

A runner clad only in a loincloth appeared, coming from the direction of the city center, clutching a scroll. He was moving fast, loping in a strange lurching way. In the stupefying heat he seemed to be in peril of imminent collapse. But he staggered up to Little Father and put the scroll in his hand.

Little Father unrolled it quickly and scanned it. He nodded somberly and turned to his vizier, who stood just to his left. They spoke briefly in low whispers. Sir Anthony, straining, was unable to make out a word.

A single chopping gesture from Little Father was enough to halt the resumption of the caravan's advance into the city. The prince beckoned the leaders of the traders to his side and conferred with them a moment or two, this time without ceremonial gesticulations. The desert men exchanged glances with one another. Then they barked rough commands. The whole vast caravan began to reverse itself.

Little Father's motorcar was waiting a hundred paces away. He went to it now, and it headed cityward, emitting belching bursts of black smoke and loud intermittent thunderclaps of inadequate combustion.

The prince's entourage, left behind in the suddenness, milled about aimlessly. The vizier, making shooing gestures, ordered them in some annoyance to follow their master on foot toward town. He himself held his place, watching the departure of the caravaneers.

"Ali Pasha!" Sir Anthony called. "Can you tell us what's happened? Is there bad news?"

The vizier turned. He seemed radiant with self-importance.

"The Emir has taken a turn for the worse. They think he'll be with Allah within the hour."

"But he was supposed to be recovering," Michael protested.

Indifferently, Ali Pasha said, "That was earlier. This is now." The vizier seemed not to be deeply moved by the news. If anything his smugness seemed to have been enhanced by it. Perhaps it was something he had been very eager to hear. "The caravan must camp outside the city walls until the funeral. There is nothing more to be seen here today. You should all go back to your residences."

The ambassadors began to look around for their drivers.

Michael, who had come out here with Sir Anthony in the embassy motorcar, was disconcerted to discover that the envoy had already vanished, slipping away in the uproar without waiting for him. Well, it wasn't an impossible walk back to town. He had walked five times as far in his night of no sleep.

"Michael?"

Selima was calling to him. He looked toward her, appalled.

"Walk with me," she said. "I have a parasol. You can't let yourself get any more sun on your face."

"That's very kind of you," he said mechanically, while lunatic jealousy and anger roiled him within. Searing contemptuous epithets came to his lips and died there, unspoken. To him she was ineluctably soiled by the presumed embraces of that night of shame. How could she have done it? The prince had wiggled his finger at her, and she had run to him without a moment's hesitation. Once more unwanted images surged through his mind: Selima and the prince entwined on a leopardskin rug; the prince mounting Selima in some unthinkable bestial African position of love; Selima, giggling girlishly, instructing the prince afterward in the no doubt equally depraved sexual customs of the land of the Sultan. Michael understood that he was being foolish; that Selima was free to do as she pleased in this loathsome land; that he himself had never staked any claim on her attention more significant than a few callow lovesick stares, so why should she have felt any compunctions about amusing herself with the prince if the prince offered amusement? "Very kind," he said. She handed the parasol up to him and he took it from her with a rigid nerveless hand. They began to walk side by side in the direction of town, close together under the narrow, precisely defined shadow of the parasol beneath the unsparing eye of the noonday sun.

She said, "Poor Michael. I've upset you terribly, haven't I?"

"Upset me? How have you possibly upset me?"

"You know."

"No. No, really."

His legs were leaden. The sun was hammering the top of his brain through the parasol, through his wide-brimmed topee, through his skull itself. He could not imagine how he would find the strength to walk all the way back to town with her.

"I've been very mischievous," she said.

"Have you?"

He wished he were a million miles away.

"By visiting the prince in his palace that night."

"Please, Selima."

"I saw you, you know. Early in the morning, when I was leaving. You ducked out of sight, but not quite fast enough."

"Selima—"

"I couldn't help myself. Going there, I mean. I wanted to see what his palace looked like. I wanted to get to know him a little better. He's very nice, you know. No, nice isn't quite the word. He's shrewd, and part of being shrewd is knowing how to seem nice. I don't really think he's nice at all. He's quite sophisticated—quite subtle."

She was flaying him, inch by inch. Another word out of her and he'd drop the parasol and run.

"The thing is, Michael, he enjoys pretending to be some sort of a primitive, a barbarian, a jungle prince. But it's only a pretense. And why shouldn't it be? These are ancient kingdoms here in Africa. This isn't any jungle land with tigers sleeping behind every palm tree. They've got laws and culture, they've got courts, they have a university. And they've had centuries to develop a real aristocracy. They're just as complicated and cunning as we are. Maybe more so. I was glad to get to know the man behind the façade, a little. He was fascinating, in his way, but—" She smiled brightly. "But I have to tell you, Michael: he's not my type at all."

That startled him, and awakened sudden new hope. Perhaps he never actually touched her, Michael told himself. Perhaps they had simply talked all night. Played little sly verbal games of oneupmanship, teasing each other, vying with each other to be sly and cruel and playful. Showing each other how complicated and cunning they could really be. Demonstrating the virtues of hundreds of years of aristocratic inbreeding. Perhaps they were too well bred to think of doing anything so commonplace as—as—

"What is your type, then?" he asked, willy-nilly.

"I prefer men who are a little shy. Men who can sometimes be foolish, even." There was unanticipated softness in her voice, conveying a sincerity that Michael prayed was real. "I hate the kind who are always calculating, calculating, calculating. There's something very appealing to me about English men, I have to tell you, precisely because they *don't* seem so dark and devious inside—not that I've met very many of them before this trip, you understand, but—oh, Michael, Michael, you're terribly angry with me, I know, but you shouldn't be! What happened between me and the prince was nothing. Nothing! And now that he'll be preoccupied with the funeral, perhaps there'll be a chance for you and me to get to know each other a little better—to slip off, for a day, let's say, while all the others are busy with the pomp and circumstance—"

She gave him a melting look. He thought for one astounded moment that she actually might mean what she was telling him.

"They're going to assassinate him," he suddenly heard his own voice saying, "right at the funeral."

"What?"

"It's all set up." The words came rolling from him spontaneously, unstoppably, like the flow of a river. "His stepmother, the old king's young wife—she's going to slip him a cup of poisoned wine, or something, during one of the funeral rituals. What she wants is to make her stupid brother king in the prince's place, and rule the country as the power behind the throne."

Selima made a little gasping sound and stepped away from him, out from under the shelter of the parasol. She stood staring at him as though he had been transformed in the last moment or two into a hippopotamus, or a rock, or a tree.

It took her a little while to find her voice.

"Are you serious? How do you know?"

"Sir Anthony told me."

"Sir Anthony?"

"He's behind it. He and the Russian and Prince Itzcoatl. Once the prince is out of the way, they're going to invite the King of Mali to step in and take over."

Her gaze grew very hard. Her silence was inscrutable, painfully so.

Then, totally regaining her composure with what must have been an extraordinary act of inner discipline, she said, "I think this is all very unlikely."

She might have been responding to a statement that snow would soon begin falling in the streets of Timbuctoo.

"You think so?"

"Why should Sir Anthony support this assassination? England has nothing to gain from destabilizing West Africa. England is a minor power still struggling to establish its plausibility in the world as an independent state. Why should it risk angering a powerful African empire like Songhay by meddling in its internal affairs?"

Michael let the slight to his country pass unchallenged, possibly because it seemed less like a slight to him than a statement of the mere reality. He searched instead for some reason of state that would make what he had asserted seem sensible.

After a moment he said, "Mali and Songhay together would be far more powerful than either one alone. If England plays an instrumental role in delivering the throne of Songhay up to Mali, England will surely be given a preferential role by the Mansa of Songhay in future West African trade."

Selima nodded. "Perhaps."

"And the Russians—you know how they feel about the Ottoman Empire. Your people are closely allied with Songhay and don't get along well with Mali. A coup d'état here would virtually eliminate Turkey as a commercial force in West Africa."

"Very likely."

She was so cool, so terribly calm.

"As for the Aztec role in this—" Michael shook his head. "God knows. But the Mexicans are always scheming around in things. Maybe they see some way of hurting Peru. There's a lot of sea trade, you know, between Mali and Peru—it's an amazingly short hop across the ocean from West Africa to Peru's eastern provinces in Brazil—and the Mexicans may believe they could divert some of that trade to themselves by winning the Mansa's favor by helping him gain possession of—"

He faltered to a halt. Something was happening. Her expression was starting to change. Her façade of detached skepticism was visibly collapsing, slowly but irreversibly, like a brick wall undermined by a great earthquake.

"Yes. Yes, I see. There are substantial reasons for such a scheme. And so they will kill the prince," Selima said.

"Have him killed, rather."

"It's the same thing! The very same thing!"

Her eyes began to glisten. She drew even further back from him and turned her head away, and he realized that she was trying to conceal tears from him. But she couldn't hide the sobs that racked her.

He suspected that she was one who cried very rarely, if at all. Seeing her weep now in this uncontrollable way plunged him into an abyss of dejection.

She was making no attempt to hide her love of the prince from him. That was the only explanation for these tears.

"Selima—please, Selima—"

He felt useless.

He realized, also, that he had destroyed himself.

He had committed this monstrous breach of security, he saw now, purely in the hope of insinuating himself into her confidence, to bind her to him in a union that proceeded from shared possession of an immense secret. He had taken her words at face value when she had told him that the prince was nothing to her.

That had been a serious error. He had thought he was making a declaration of love; but all he had done was to reveal a state secret to England's ancient enemy.

He waited, feeling huge and clumsy and impossibly naïve.

Then, abruptly, her sobbing stopped and she looked toward him, a little puffy-eyed now, but otherwise as inscrutable as before.

"I'm not going to say anything about this to anyone."

"What?"

"Not to him, not to my father, not to anyone."

He was mystified. As usual.

"But—Selima—"

"I told you. The prince is nothing to me. And this is only a crazy rumor. How do I know it's true? How do *you* know it's true?"

"Sir Anthony—"

"Sir Anthony! Sir Anthony! For all I know, he's floated this whole thing simply to ensnare my father in some enormous embarrassment. I tell my father there's going to be an assassination and my father tells the prince, as he'd feel obligated to do. And then the prince arrests and expels the ambassadors of England and Russia and Mexico? But where's the proof? There isn't any. It's all a Turkish invention, they say. A scandal. My father is sent home in disgrace. His career is shattered. Songhay breaks off diplomatic relations with the Empire. No, no, don't you see, I can't say a thing."

"But the prince—"

"His stepmother hates him. If he's idiotic enough to let

her hand him a cup of something without having it tested, he deserves to be poisoned. What is that to me? He's only a savage. Hold the parasol closer, Michael, and let's get back to town. Oh, this heat! This unending heat! Do you think it'll ever rain here?" Her face now showed no sign of tears at all. Wearily Michael lowered the parasol. Selima utterly baffled him. She was an exhausting person. His head was aching. For a shilling he'd be glad to resign his post and take up sheep farming somewhere in the north of England. It was getting very obvious to him and probably to everyone else that he had no serious future in the diplomatic corps.

Little Father, emerging from the tunnel that led from the Emir's palace to his own, found Ali Pasha waiting in the little colonnaded gallery known as the Promenade of Askia Mohammed. The prince was surprised to see a string charm of braided black, red, and yellow cords dangling around the vizier's neck. Ali Pasha had never been one for wearing grigri before; but no doubt the imminent death of the Emir was unsettling everyone, even a piece of tough leather like Ali Pasha.

The vizier offered a grand salaam. "Your royal father, may Allah embrace him, sir—"

"My royal father is still breathing, thank you. It looks now as if he'll last until morning." Little Father glanced around, a little wildly, peering into the courtyard of his palace. "Somehow we've left too much for the last minute. The lady Serene Glory is arranging for the washing of the body. It's too late to do anything about that, but we can supply the graveclothes, at least. Get the very finest white silks; the royal burial shroud should be something out of the Thousand and One Nights; and I want rubies in the turban. Actual rubies, no damned imitations. And after that I want you to set up the procession to the Great Mosque—I'll be one of the pallbearers, of course, and we'll ask the Mansa of Mali to be another—he's arrived by now, hasn't he?—and let's have the King of Benin as the third one, and for the fourth, well, either the Asante of Ghana or the Grand Fon of Dahomey, whichever one shows up here first. The important thing is that all four of the pallbearers should be kings, because Serene Glory wants to push her brother forward to be one, and I can't allow that. She won't be able to argue precedence for him if the pallbearers are all kings, when all he is is a provincial cadi. Behind the bier we'll have the overseas ambassadors marching five abreast—put the Turk and the Russian in the front row, the Maori, too, and the Aztec and the Inca on the outside edges to keep them as far apart as we can, and the order of importance after that is up to you, only be sure that little countries like England and the Teutonic States don't wind up too close to the major powers, and that the various vassal nations like China and Korea and Ind are in the back. Now, as far as the decorations on the barge that'll be taking my father downriver to the burial place at Gao—"

"Little Father," the Vizier said, as the prince paused for breath, "the Turkish woman is waiting upstairs."

Little Father gave him a startled look.

"I don't remember asking her to come here."

"She didn't say you had. But she asked for an urgent audience, and I thought—" Ali Pasha favored Little Father with an obscenely knowing smile. "It seemed reasonable to admit her."

"She knows that my father is dying, and that I'm tremendously busy?"

"I told her what was taking place, majesty," said Ali Pasha unctuously.

"Don't call me 'majesty' yet!"

"A thousand pardons, Little Father. But she is aware of the nature of the crisis, no question of that. Nevertheless, she insisted on—"

"Oh, damn. Damn! But I suppose I can give her two or three minutes. Stop smiling like that, damn you! I'll feed you to the lions if you don't! What do you think I am, a mountain of lechery? This is a busy moment. When I say two or three minutes, two or three minutes is what I mean."

Selima was pacing about on the porch where she and Little Father had spent their night of love. No filmy robes today, no seductively visible breasts bobbing about beneath, this time. She was dressed simply, in European clothes. She seemed all business.

"The Emir is in his last hours," Little Father said. "The whole funeral has to be arranged very quickly."

"I won't take up much of your time, then." Her tone was cool. There was a distinct edge on it. Perhaps he had been too brusque with her. That night on the porch *had* been a wonderful one, after all. She said, "I just have one question. Is there some sort of ritual at a royal funeral where you're given a cup of wine to drink?"

"You know that the Koran doesn't permit the drinking of—"

"Yes, yes, I know that. A cup of *something*, then."

Little Father studied her carefully. "This is anthropological research? The sort of thing the golden-haired woman from England came here to do? Why does this matter to you, Selima?"

"Never mind that. It matters."

He sighed. She *seemed* so gentle and retiring, until she opened her mouth.

"There's a cup ceremony, yes. It isn't wine or anything else alcoholic. It's an aromatic potion, brewed from various spices and honeys and such, very disagreeably sweet, my father once told me. Drinking it symbolizes the passage of royal power from one generation to the next."

"And who is supposed to hand you the cup?"

"May I ask why at this particularly hectic time you need to know these details?"

"Please," she said.

There was an odd urgency in her voice.

"The former queen, the mother of the heir of the throne, is the one who hands the new Emir the cup."

"But your mother is dead. Therefore your stepmother, Serene Glory will hand it to you."

"That's correct." Little Father glanced at his watch. "Selima, you don't seem to understand. I need to finish working out the funeral arrangements and then get back to my father's bedside before he dies. If you don't mind—"

"There's going to be poison in the cup."

"This is no time for romantic fantasies."

"It isn't a fantasy. She's going to slip you a cup of poison, and you won't be able to tell that the poison is there because what you drink is so heavily spiced anyway. And when you keel over in the mosque her brother's going to leap forward in the moment of general shock and tell everyone that he's in charge."

The day had been one long disorderly swirl. But suddenly now the world stood still, as though there had been an unscheduled eclipse of the sun. For a moment he had difficulty simply seeing her.

"What are you saying, Selima?"

"Do you want me to repeat it all, or is that just something you're saying as a manner of speaking because you're so astonished?"

He could see and think again. He examined her closely. She was unreadable, as she usually was. Now that the first shock of her bland statement was past, this all was starting to seem to him like fantastic nonsense; and yet, and yet, it certainly wasn't beyond Serene Glory's capabilities to have hatched such a scheme.

How, though, could the Turkish girl possibly know anything about it? How did she even know about the ritual of the cup?

"If we were in bed together right now," he said, "and you were in my arms and right on the edge of the big moment, and I stopped moving and asked you right then and there what proof you had of this story, I'd probably believe whatever you told me. I think people tend to be honest at such moments. Even you would speak the truth. But we have no time for that now. The kingship will change hands in a few hours, and I'm exceedingly busy. I need you to cast away all of your fondness for manipulative amusements and give me straight answers."

Her dark eyes flared. "I should simply have let them poison you."

"Do you mean that?"

"What you just said was insufferable."

"If I was too blunt, I ask you to forgive me. I'm under great strain today and if what you've told me is any sort of joke, I don't need it. If this isn't a joke, you damned well can't withhold any of the details."

"I've given you the details."

"Not all. Who'd you hear all this from?"

She sighed and placed one wrist across the other.

"Michael. The tall Englishman."

"That adolescent?"

"He's a little on the innocent side, especially for a diplomat, yes. But I don't think he's as big a fool as he's been letting himself appear lately. He heard it from Sir Anthony."

"So this is an English plot?"

"English and Russian and Mexican."

"All three." Little Father digested that. "What's the purpose of assassinating me?"

"To make Serene Glory's brother Emir of Songhay."

"And serve as their puppet, I suppose?"

Selima shook her head. "Serene Glory and her brother are only the ignorant instruments of their real plan. They'll simply be brushed aside when the time comes. What the plotters are really intending to do, in the confusion following your death, is ask the Mansa of Mali to seize control of Songhay. They'll put the support of their countries behind him."

"Ah," Little Father said. And after a moment, again, "Ah."

"Mali-Songhay would favor the Czar instead of the Sultan. So the Russians like the idea. What injures the Sultan is good for the English. So they're in on it. As for the Aztecs—"

Little Father shrugged and gestured to her to stop. Already he could taste the poison in his gut, burning through his flesh. Already he could see the green-clad troops of Mali parading in the streets of Timbuctoo and Gao, where kings of Mali had been hailed as supreme monarchs once before, hundreds of years ago.

"Look at me," he said. "You swear that you're practicing no deception, Selima?"

"I swear it by—by the things we said to each other the night we lay together."

He considered that. Had she fallen in love with him in the midst of all her game-playing? So it might seem. Could he trust what she was saying, therefore? He believed he could. Indeed the oath she had just proposed might have more plausibility than any sort of oath she might have sworn on a Koran.

"Come here," he said.

She approached him. Little Father swept her up against him, holding her tightly, and ran his hands down her back to her buttocks. She pressed her hips forward. He covered her mouth with his and jammed down hard, not a subtle kiss but one that would put to rest forever, if that were needed, the bit of fake anthropology he had given to her earlier, about the supposed distaste of Songhayans for the act of kissing. After a time he released her. Her eyes were a little glazed, her breasts were rising and falling swiftly.

He said, "I'm grateful for what you've told me. I'll take the appropriate steps, and thank you."

"I had to let you know. I was going just to sit back and let whatever happened happen. But then I saw I couldn't conceal such a thing from you."

"Of course not, Selima."

Her look was a soft and eager one. She was ready to run off to the bedchamber with him, or so it seemed. But not now, not on this day of all days. That would be a singularly bad idea.

"On the other hand," he said, "if it turns out that there's no truth to any of this, that it's all some private amusement of your own or some intricate deception being practiced on me by the Sultan for who knows what unfathomable reason, you can be quite certain that I'll avenge myself in a remarkably vindictive way once the excitements of the funeral and the coronation are over."

The softness vanished at once. The hatred that came into her eyes was extraordinary.

"You black bastard," she said.

"Only partly black. There is much Moorish blood in the veins of the nobility of Songhay." He met her seething gaze with tranquility. "In the old days we believed in absorbing those who attempt to conquer us. These days we still do, something that the Mansa of Mali ought to keep in mind. He's got a fine harem, I understand."

"Did you *have* to throw cold water on me like that? Everything I told you was the truth."

"I hope and believe it is. I think there was love between us that night on the porch, and I wouldn't like to think that you'd betray someone you love. The question, I suppose, is whether the Englishman was telling *you* the truth. Which still remains to be seen." He took her hand and kissed it lightly, in the European manner. "As I said before, I'm very grateful, Selima. And hope to continue to be. If I may, now—"

She gave him one final glare and took her leave of him. Little Father walked quickly to the edge of the porch, spun about, walked quickly back. For an instant or two he stood in the doorway like his own statue. But his mind was in motion, and moving very swiftly.

He peered down the stairs to the courtyard below.

"Ali Pasha!"

The vizier came running.

"What the woman wanted to tell me," Little Father said, "is that there is a plot against my life."

The look that appeared on the vizier's face was one of total shock and indignation.

"You believe her?"

"Unfortunately I think I do."

Ali Pasha began to quiver with wrath. His broad glossy cheeks grew congested, his eyes bulged. Little Father thought the man was in danger of exploding.

"Who are the plotters, Little Father? I'll have them rounded up within the hour."

"The Russian ambassador, apparently. The Aztec one. And the little Englishman, Sir Anthony."

"To the lions with them! They'll be in the pit before night comes!"

Little Father managed an approximation of a smile.

"Surely you recall the concept of diplomatic immunity, Ali Pasha?"

"But—a conspiracy against your majesty's life—!"

"Not yet my majesty, Ali Pasha."

"Your pardon." Ali Pasha struggled with confusion. "You must take steps to protect yourself, Little Father. Did she tell you what the plan is supposed to be?"

Little Father nodded. "When Serene Glory hands me the coronation cup at the funeral service, there will be poison in the drink."

"Poison!"

"Yes. I fall down dead. Serene Glory turns to her miserable brother and offers him the crown on the spot. But no, the three ambassadors have other ideas. They'll ask Mansa Suleiyman to proclaim himself king, in the name of the general safety. In that moment Songhay will come under the rule of Mali."

"Never! To the lions with Mansa Suleiyman too, majesty!"

"No one goes to the lions, Ali Pasha. And stop calling me majesty. We'll deal with this in a calm and civilized way, is that understood?"

"I am completely at your command, sir. As always."

Little Father nodded. He felt his strength rising, moment by moment. His mind was wondrously clear. He asked himself if that was what it felt like to be a king. Though he had spent so much time being a prince, he had in fact given too little thought to what the actual sensations and processes of being a king might be, he realized now. His royal father had held the kingdom entirely in his own hands throughout all his long reign. But something must be changing now.

He went unhurriedly to the edge of the porch, and stared out into the distance. To his surprise, there was a dark orange cloud on the horizon, sharply defined against the sky.

"Look there, Ali Pasha. The rains are coming!"

"The first cloud, yes. There it is!" And he began to finger the woven charm that hung about his neck.

It was always startling when the annual change came, after so many months of unbroken hot dry weather. Even after a lifetime of watching the shift occur, no one in Songhay was unmoved by the approach of the first cloud, for it was a powerful omen of transition and culmination, removing a great element of uncertainty and fear from the minds of the citizens; for until the change finally arrived, there was always the chance that it might never come, that this time the summer would last forever and the world would burn to a parched crisp.

Little Father said, "I should go to my father without any further delay. Certainly this means that his hour has come."

"Yes. Yes."

The orange cloud was sweeping toward the city with amazing rapidity. In another few minutes all Timbuctoo would be enveloped in blackness as a whirling veil of fine sand whipped down over it. Little Father felt the air grow moist. There would be a brief spell of intolerable humidity, now, so heavy that breathing itself would be a vast effort. And then, abruptly, the temperature would drop, the chill rain would descend, rivers would run in the sandy streets, the marketplace would become a lake.

He raced indoors, with Ali Pasha following along helter-skelter behind him.

"The plotters, sir—" the vizier gasped.

Little Father smiled. "I'll invite Serene Glory to share the cup with me. We'll see what she does then. Just be ready to act when I give the orders."

There was darkness at every window. The sandstorm was at hand. Trillions of tiny particles beat insistently at every surface, setting up a steady drumming that grew and grew and grew in intensity. The air had turned sticky, almost viscous: it was hard work to force oneself forward through it.

Gasping for breath, Little Father moved as quickly as he was able down the subterranean passageway that linked his palace with the much greater one that shortly would be his.

The ministers and functionaries of the royal court were wailing and weeping. The Grand Vizier of the realm, waiting formally at the head of the Stairs of Allah, glared at Little Father as though he were the Angel of Death himself.

"There is not much more time, Little Father."

"So I understand."

He rushed out onto his father's porch. There had been no opportunity to bring the Emir indoors. The old man lay amidst his dazzling blankets with his eyes open and one hand upraised. He was in the correct position in which a Moslem should pass from this world to the next, his head to the south, his face turned toward the east. The sky was black with sand, and it came cascading down with unremitting force. The three saintly marabouts who had attended Big Father throughout his final illness stood above him, shielding the Emir from the shower of tiny abrasive particles with an improvised canopy, an outstretched bolt of satin.

"Father! Father!"

The Emir tried to sit up. He looked a thousand years old. His eyes glittered like lightning-bolts, and he said something, three or four congested syllables. Little Father was unable to understand a thing. The old man was already speaking the language of the dead.

There was a clap of thunder. The Emir fell back against his pillows.

The sky opened and the first rain of the year came down in implacable torrents, in such abundance as had not been seen in a thousand years.

In the three days since the old Emir's death Little Father had lived through this scene three thousand times in his imagination. But now it was actually occurring. They were in the Great Mosque; the mourners, great and simple, were clustered elbow to elbow; the corpse of Big Father, embalmed so that it could endure the slow journey downriver to the royal burial grounds, lay in splendor atop its magnificent bier. Any ordinary citizen of Songhay would have gone from his deathbed to his grave in two hours, or less; but kings were exempt from the ordinary customs.

They were done at last with the chanting of the prayer for the dead. Now they were doing the prayer for the welfare of the kingdom. Little Father held his body rigid, barely troubling to breathe. He saw before him the grand nobles of the realm, the kings of the adjacent countries, the envoys of the overseas lands, all staring, all maintaining a mien of the deepest solemnity, even those who could not comprehend a word of what was being said.

And here was Serene Glory now, coming forth bearing the cup that would make him Emir of Songhay, Great Imam, master of the nation, successor to all the great lords who had led the empire in grandeur for a thousand years.

She looked magnificent, truly queenly, more beautiful in her simple funeral robe and unadorned hair than she could ever have looked in all her finery. The cup, a stark bowl of lustrous chalcedony, so translucent that the dark liquor that would make him king was plainly visible through its thin walls, was resting lightly on her upturned palms.

He searched her for a sign of tremor and saw none. She was utterly calm. He felt a disturbing moment of doubt.

She handed him the cup, and spoke the words of succession, clearly, unhesitatingly, omitting not the smallest syllable. She was in full control of herself.

When he lifted the cup to his lips, though, he heard the sharp unmistakable sound of her suddenly indrawn breath, and all hestitation went from him.

"Mother," he said.

The unexpected word reverberated through the white-washed alcoves of the Great Mosque. They must all be looking at him in bewilderment.

"Mother, in this solemn moment of the passing of the kingship, I beg you share my ascension with me. Drink with me, mother. Drink. Drink."

He held the untouched cup out toward the woman who had just handed it to him.

Her eyes were bright with horror.

"Drink with me, mother," he said again.

"No—no—"

She backed a step or two away from him, making sounds like gravel in her throat.

"Mother—lady, dear lady—"

He held the cup out, insistently. He moved closer to her. She seemed frozen. The truth was emblazoned on her face. Rage rose like a fountain in him, and for an instant he thought he was going to hurl the drink in her face; but then he regained his poise. Her hand was pressed against her lips in terror. She moved back, back, back.

And then she was running toward the door of the mosque; and abruptly the Grand Duke Alexander Petrovich, his face erupting with red blotches of panic, was running also, and also Prince Itzcoatl of Mexico.

"No! Fools!" a voice cried out, and the echoes hammered at the ancient walls.

Little Father looked toward the foreign ambassadors. Sir Anthony stood out as though in a spotlight, his cheeks blazing, his eyes popping, his fingers exploring his lips as though he could not believe they had actually uttered that outcry.

There was complete confusion in the mosque. Everyone was rushing about, everyone was bellowing. But Little Father was quite calm. Carefully he set the cup down, untouched, at his feet. Ali Pasha came to his side at once.

"Round them up quickly," he told the vizier. "The three ambassadors are persona non grata. They're to leave Songhay by the next riverboat. Escort Mansa Suleiyman back to the Embassy of Mali and put armed guards around the building—for purely protective purposes, of course. And also the embassies of Ghana, Dahomey, Benin, and the rest, for good measure—and as window-dressing."

"It will be done, majesty."

"Very good." He indicated the chalcedony cup. "As for this stuff, give it to a dog to drink, and let's see what happens."

Ali Pasha nodded and touched his forehead.

"And the lady Serene Glory, and her brother?"

"Take them into custody. If the dog dies, throw them both to the lions."

"Your majesty—!"

"To the lions, Ali Pasha."

"But you said—"

"To the lions, Ali Pasha."

"I hear and obey, majesty."

"You'd better." Little Father grinned. He was Little Father no longer, he realized. "I like the way you say it: *Majesty.* You put just the right amount of awe into it."

"Yes, majesty. Is there anything else, majesty?"

"I want an escort, too, to take me to my palace. Say, fifty men. No, make it a hundred. Just in case there are any surprises waiting for us outside."

"To your old palace, majesty?"

The question caught him unprepared. "No," he said after a moment's reflection. "Of course not. To my new palace. To the palace of the Emir."

Selima came hesitantly forward into the throne room, which was one of the largest, most forbidding rooms she had ever entered. Not even the Sultan's treasure house at the Topkapi Palace had any chamber to match this one for sheer dismal mustiness, for clutter, or for the eerie hodgepodge of its contents. She found the new Emir standing beneath a stuffed giraffe, examining an ivory globe twice the size of a man's head that was mounted on an intricately carved spiral pedestal.

"You sent for me, your highness?"

"Yes. Yes, I did. It's all calm outside there, now, I take it?"

"Very calm. Very calm."

"Good. And the weather's still cool?"

"Quite cool, your majesty."

"But not raining again yet?"

"No, not raining."

"Good." Idly he fondled the globe. "The whole world is here, do you know that? Right under my hand. Here's Africa, here's Europe, here's Russia. This is the Empire, here." He brushed his hand across the globe from Istanbul to Madrid. "There's still plenty of it, eh?" He spun the ivory sphere easily on its pedestal. "And this, the New World. Such emptiness there. The Incas down here in the southern continent, the Aztecs here in the middle, and a lot of nothing up here in the north. I once asked my father, do you know, if I could pay a visit to those empty lands. So cool there, I hear. So green, and almost empty. Just the redskinned people, and not very many of them. Are they really red, do you think? I've never seen one." He looked closely at her. "Have you ever thought of leaving Turkey, I wonder, and taking up a new life for yourself in those wild lands across the ocean?"

"Never, your majesty."

She was trembling a little.

"You should think of it. We all should. Our countries are all too old. The land is tired. The air is tired. The rivers move slowly. We should go somewhere where things are fresh." She made no reply. After a moment's silence he said, "Do you love that tall gawky pink-faced Englishman, Selima?"

"Love?"

"Love, yes. Do you have any kind of fondness for him? Do you care for him at all? If love is too strong a word for you, would you say at least that you enjoy his company, that you see a certain charm in him, that—well, surely you understand what I'm saying."

She seemed flustered. "I'm not sure that I do."

"It appears to me that you feel attracted to him. God knows he feels attracted to you. He can't go back to England, you realize. He's compromised himself fifty different ways. Even after we patch up this conspiracy thing, and we certainly will, one way or another, the fact still remains that he's guilty of treason. He has to go somewhere. He can't stay here—the heat will kill him fast, if his own foolishness doesn't. Are you starting to get my drift, Selima?"

Her eyes rose to meet his. Some of her old self-assurance was returning to them now. "I think I am. And I think that I like it."

"Very good," he said. "I'll give him to you, then. For a toy, if you like." He clapped his hands. A functionary poked his head into the room.

"Send in the Englishman."

Michael entered. He walked with the precarious stride of someone who has been decapitated but thinks there might be some chance of keeping his head on his shoulders if only he moves carefully enough. The only traces of sunburn that remained now were great peeling patches on his cheeks and forehead.

He looked toward the new Emir and murmured a barely audible courtly greeting. He seemed to have trouble looking in Selima's direction.

"Sir?" Michael asked finally.

The Emir smiled warmly. "Has Sir Anthony left yet?"

"This morning, sir. I didn't speak with him."

"No. No, I imagine you wouldn't care to. It's a mess, isn't it, Michael? You can't really go home."

"I understand that, sir."

"But obviously you can't stay here. This is no climate for the likes of you."

"I suppose not, sir."

The Emir nodded. He reached about behind him and lifted a book from a stand. "During my years as prince I had plenty of leisure to read. This is one of my favorites. Do you happen to know which book it is?"

"No, sir."

"The collected plays of one of your great English writers, as a matter of fact. The greatest, so I'm told. Shakespeare's his name. You know his work, do you?"

Michael blinked. "Of course, sir. Everyone knows—"

"Good. And you know his play *Alexius and Khurrem*, naturally?"

"Yes, sir." The Emir turned to Selima. "And do you?"

"Well—"

"It's quite relevant to the case, I assure you. It takes place in Istanbul, not long after the Ottoman Conquest. Khurrem is a beautiful young woman from one of the high Turkish families. Alexius is an exiled Byzantine prince who has slipped back into the capital to try to rescue some of his family's treasures from the grasp of the detested conqueror. He disguises himself as a Turk and meets Khurrem at a banquet, and of course they fall in love. It's an impossible romance—a Turk and a Greek." He opened the book. "Let me read a little. It's amazing that an Englishman could write such eloquent Turkish poetry, isn't it?"

From forth the fatal loins of these two foes
  A pair of star-cross'd lovers take their life;
Whose misadventur'd piteous overthrows
  Do with their death bury their parents' strife—

The Emir glanced up. "'Star-cross'd lovers.' That's what you are, you know." He laughed. "It all ends terribly for poor Khurrem and Alexius, but that's because they were such hasty children. With better planning they could have slipped away to the countryside and lived to a ripe old age, but Shakespeare tangles them up in a scheme of sleeping potions and crossed messages and they both die at the end, even though well-intentioned friends were trying to help them. But of course that's drama for you. It's a lovely play. I hope to be able to see it performed some day."

He put the book aside. They both were staring at him.

To Michael he said, "I've arranged for you to defect to Turkey. Ismet Akif will give you a writ of political asylum. What happens between you and Selima is of course entirely up to you and Selima, but in the name of Allah I implore you not to make as much of a shambles of it as Khurrem and Alexius did. Istanbul's not such a bad place to live, you know. No, don't look at me like that! If she can put up with a ninny like you, you can manage to get over your prejudices against Turks. You asked for all this, you know. You didn't *have* to fall in love with her."

"Sir, I—I—"

Michael's voice trailed away.

The Emir said, "Take him out of here, will you, Selima?"

"Come," she said. "We need to talk, I think."

"I—I—"

The Emir gestured impatiently. Selima's hand was on

Michael's wrist now. She tugged, and he followed. The Emir looked after them until they had gone down the stairs.

Then he clapped his hands.

"Ali Pasha!"

The vizier appeared so quickly that there could be no doubt he had been lurking just beyond the ornate doorway.

"Majesty?"

"We have to clear this place out a little," the Emir said. "This crocodile—this absurd giraffe—find an appropriate charity and donate them, fast. And these hippo skulls, too. And this, and this, and this—"

"At once, majesty. A clean sweep."

"A clean sweep, yes."

A cool wind was blowing through the palace now, after the rains. He felt young, strong, vigorous. Life was just beginning, finally. Later in the day he would visit the lions at their pit.

Howard Waldrop

Ike at the Mike

Ambassador Pratt leaned over toward Senator Presley.

"My mother's ancestors don't like to admit it," he said, "but they all came to the island from the Carpathians two centuries ago. Their name then was something like Karloff." He smiled, then laughed through his silver mustache.

"Hell," said Presley, with the tinge of the drawl which came to his speech when he was excited, as he was tonight. "My folks been dirt farmers all the way back to Adam. They don't even remember coming from anywhere. That don't mean they ain't wonderful folks, though."

"Of course not," said Pratt. "My father was a shopkeeper. He worked to send all my older brothers into the Foreign Service. But when my time came, I thought I had another choice. I wanted to run off to Canada or Australia, perhaps try my hand at acting. (I was in several local dramatic clubs, you know?) My father took me aside before my service exams. The day before, I remember quite distinctly. He said, 'William' (he was the only member of the family who used my full name), 'William,' he said, 'actors do not get paid the last workday of each and every month.' Well, I thought about it awhile, and next day passed my exams with absolute top grades."

Pratt smiled once more an ingratiating smile. There was something a little scary about it, thought Presley, sort of like Raymond Massey's smile in *Arsenic and Old Lace*. But the smile had gotten Pratt through sixty years of government service. It had been a smile which made the leaders of small countries grin back as Kings George, number after number, took yet more of their lands. It was a good smile; it made everyone remember his grandfather. Even Presley.

"Folks is funny," said Presley. "God knows I used to get up at barn dances and sing myself silly. I was just a kid, playing around."

"My childhood is so far behind me," said Ambassador Pratt. "I hardly remember it. I was small, then I had the talk with my father, and went to Service school, then found myself in Turkey. Which at that time owned a large portion of the globe. The Sick Man of Europe, it was called. You know I met Lawrence, of Arabia, don't you? Before the Great War. He was an archaeologist then. Came to us to get the Ottomans to give him permission to dig up Petra. They thought him to be a fool. Wanted the standard 90 percent share of everything, just the same."

"You've seen a lot of the world change," said Senator E. Aaron Presley. He took a sip of wine. "I've had trouble enough keeping up with it since I was elected congressman six years ago. I almost lost touch during my senatorial campaign, and I'll be damned if everything hadn't changed again by the time I got back here."

Pratt laughed. He was eighty years old, far past retirement age, still bouncing around like a man of sixty. He had alternately retired and had every British P.M. since Churchill call him out of seclusion to patch up relations with this or that nation.

Presley was thirty-three, the youngest senator in the country for a long time. The U.S. was in bad shape, and he was one of the symbols of the new hope. There was talk of revolution, several cities had been burned, there was a war on in South America (again). Social change, lifestyle readjustment, call it what they would. The people of Mississippi had elected Presley senator after five years as representative, as a sign of renewed hope. At the same time they had passed a tough new wiretap act, and had turned out for massive Christian revivalist meetings.

Nineteen sixty-eight looked to be the toughest year yet for America.

But there were still things that made it all worth living. Nights like tonight. A huge appreciation dinner, with the absolute top of Washington society turned out in its gaudiness. Most of Congress, President Kennedy. Vice President Shriver. Plus the usual hangers-on.

Presley watched them. Old Dick Nixon, once a senator from California. He came back to Washington to be near the action, though he'd lost his last election in '58.

The President was there, of course, looking as young as he had when he was reelected in 1964, the first two-term president since Huey "Kingfish" Long, Jr., thought Presley. He was a hell of a good man in his Yankee way. His three young brothers were in the audience somewhere, representatives from two states.

Waiters hustled in and out of the huge banquet room. Presley watched the sequined gowns and the feathers on the women: the spectacular pumpkin-blaze of a neon orange suit of some hotshot Washington lawyer. The lady across the table had engaged Pratt in conversation about Wales. The ambassador was explaining that he had seen Wales once, back in 1923 on holiday, but that he didn't think it had changed much since then.

E. Aaron studied the table where the guests of honor sat—The President and First Lady, the veep and his wife, and Armstrong and Eisenhower, with their spouses.

Armstrong and Eisenhower. Two of the finest citizens of the land. Armstrong, the younger, in his sixty-eighth year, getting a little jowly. Born with the century, thought Presley. Symbol of his race and of his time. A man deserving of honor and respect.

But Eisenhower. Eisenhower was Presley's man. The senator had read the biographies, reread all the old newspaper files, listened to him every chance he got.

If Presley had an ideal, it was Eisenhower. As both a leader and a person. A little too liberal, maybe, in his personal opinions, but that was the only possible drawback the man had. When it came time for action, Eisenhower, the "Ike" of the popular press, came through.

Senator Presley tried to catch his eye. He was only three tables away, and could see Ike through the hazy pall of smoke from after-dinner cigarettes and pipes. It was no use, though.

Eisenhower looked worried, distracted. He wasn't used to testimonials. He'd come out of semiretirement to attend, only because Armstrong had convinced him to do it. They were both getting presidential medals.

But it wasn't for the awards that all the other people were here, or the speeches that would follow, it...

Pratt turned to him.

"I've noticed his preoccupation, too," he said.

Presley was a little taken aback. But Pratt is a sharp old cookie, and had been around god knows how many people through wars, floods, conference tables. He'd probably drunk enough tea in his life to float the Battleship *Kropotkin*.

"Quite a man," said Presley, afraid to let his true misty-eyed feelings show themselves. "Pretty much man of the century, far as I'm concerned."

"I've been with Churchill, and Lenin and Chiang," said Ambassador Pratt, "but they were just cagey, politicians, movers of men and material, as far as I'm concerned. I saw him once before, early on, must have been '38. Nineteen thirty-eight. I was very, very impressed then. Time has done nothing to change that."

"He's just not used to this kind of thing," said Presley.

"Perhaps it was that Patton fellow."

"Wild George? That who you mean?"

"Oh, didn't you hear?" asked Pratt, eyes all concern.

"I was in committee most of the week. If it wasn't about the new drug bill, I didn't hear about it."

"Oh. Of course. This Patton fellow died a few days ago, it seems. Circumstances rather sad, I think. Eisenhower and Mr. Armstrong just returned from his funeral this afternoon."

"Gee, that's too bad. You know they worked together, Patton and Ike, for thirty years or so—"

The toastmaster, one of those boisterous, bald-headed, abrasive California types, rose. People began to applaud and stub out their cigarettes. Waiters disappeared as if a magic wand had been waved.

Well, thought Presley, an hour of pure boredom coming up, as he and Pratt applauded also. Some jokes, the President, the awarding of the medals, the obligatory standing ovation (though all of the senator's feelings were going to be in his part of it, anyway). Then the entertainment.

Ah, thought Presley. The thing everybody has come for.

Because, after the ceremony, they were going to bring out the band. Armstrong's band. Not just the one he toured with, but what was left of the old guys. *The* Armstrong Band, and they were going to rip the joint.

But also, also...

For the first time in twenty years, since Presley had been a boy, a kid in his teens...

Eisenhower was going to break his vow. Eisenhower was going to dust off that clarinet.

For two hours. Ike was going to play with Armstrong, just like in the old days.

"Cheer up," said gravelly-voiced Pops, while the President was making his way to the rostrum. Armstrong smiled at Eisenhower. "You're gonna blow 'em right outta the grooves."

"All reet," said Ike.

The thunderous applause was dying down. Backstage, Ike handed the box with the Presidential medal to his wife of twenty years, Helen Forrest, the singer. "Here goes, honey," he said. "Come out when you feel like it."

They were in the outer hall back of the platform set up behind the head tables. Some group of young folksingers, very nervous but very good, were out there killing time while Armstrong's band set up.

"Hey, hey," said Pops. He'd pinned the Presidential medal, ribbon and all, to the front of his jacket through the boutonniere hole. "Wouldn't old Jelly Roll like to have seen me now?"

"Hey, hey," yelled some of the band right back.

"Quiet, quiet!" yelled Pops. "Let them kids out there sing. They're good. Listen to 'em. Reminds me of me when I was young."

Ike had been licking his reed and doing tongue exercises. "You never were young, Pops," he said. "You were born older than me."

"That's a lie!" said Pops. "You could be my father."

"Maybe he is!" yelled Perkins, the guitar man.

Ike nearly swallowed his mouthpiece. The drummer did a paradiddle.

"Hush, hush, you clowns!" yelled Pops.

Ike smiled and looked up at the drummer, a young kid. But he'd been with Pop's new band for a couple of years, so he must be all right.

Eisenhower heaved a sigh when no one was looking. He had to get the tightness out of his chest. It had started at George S.'s funeral, a pain crying did not relieve. No one but he and Helen knew that he had had two mild heart attacks in the last six years. Hell, he thought. I'm almost eighty years old. I'm entitled to a few heart attacks. But not here, not tonight.

They dimmed the work lights. Pops had run into the back kitchen and blown a few screaming notes which they had heard through two concrete walls. He was ready.

"When you gonna quit playing, Pops?" asked Ike.

"Man, I ain't ever gonna quit. They're gonna have to dig me up three weeks after I die and break this horn to stop the noise comin' outta the ground." He looked at the lights. "Ease on off to the left there, Ike. Let us get them all ready for you. Come in on the chorus of the third song."

"Which one's that?" asked Ike, looking for his play sheet.

"You'll know it when you hear it," said Pops. He took out his handkerchief. "You taught it to me."

Ike went into the wings.

The crowd was tasteful, expectant.

The band hit the music hard, from the opening, and Armstrong led off with the "King Porter Stomp." His horn was flashing sparks, and the medal on his jacket front caught the spotlight like a big golden eye.

Then they launched into "Basin Street Blues," the horn sweet and slow and mellow, the band doing nothing but carrying a light line behind. Armstrong was totally in his music, staring not at the audience but down and at his horn.

He had come a long way since he used to haul coal from the back of a wagon; since he was thrown in the Colored Waifs Home in New Orleans for firing off a pistol on New Year's Eve, 1913. One noise more or less shouldn't have mattered on that night, but it did, and the cops caught him. It was those music lessons at the Home that started him on the way, through New Orleans and Memphis and Chicago to the world beyond.

Armstrong might have been a criminal, he might have been a bum, he might have been killed unknown and unmourned in some war somewhere. But he wasn't: He was born to play that music. It wouldn't have mattered what world he would have been born into. As soon as his fingers closed around the cornet, music was changed forever.

The audience applauded wildly, but they weren't there just for Armstrong. They were waiting. And they got him.

The band hit up something that began nondescriptly—a slow blues beginning with the drummer heavy on his brushes.

The tune began to change, and as it changed, a pure sweet clarinet began to play above the other instruments, and Ike walked onstage playing his theme song, "Don't You Know What It Means to Miss New Orleans?"

His clarinet soared above the audience. Presley wasn't the only one who got chill bumps all the way down the backs of his ankles.

Ike and Armstrong traded off slow, pure verses of the song; Ike's the sweet music of a craftsman, Armstrong's the heartfelt remembrance of things as they were. Ike never saw Storyville; Armstrong had to leave it when the Navy closed it down.

Together they built to a moving finale, and descended into a silence like the dimming of lights, with Ike's clarinet the last one to wink out.

The cream of Washington betrayed its origins with applause.

And before they knew what to do, the tune was the opening screech of "Mississippi Mud."

Ike and Armstrong traded licks, running on and off the

melody. Pops wiped his face with his handkerchief; his face seemed all teeth and sweat. Ike's bald head shone, the freckles standing out above the wisps of white hair on his temples.

They played and played.

Ike's boyhood had been on the flat pan of Kansas, small-town church. America at the turn of the century. A town full of laborers and businessmen, barbershops, milliners and ice cream parlors.

He had done all the usual things—swum naked in the creek, run through town finding things to build up or tear down. He had hunted and fished and gone to services on Sunday; he had camped out overnight or for days at a time with his brothers, made fun of his girl cousins, stolen watermelons.

He first heard recorded music on an old Edison cylinder machine at the age of eight, long-hair music and opera his aunt collected.

There was a firehouse band which played each Wednesday night in the park, across the street from the station. There were real band concerts on Sunday, mostly military music, marches and the instrumental parts of ballads, on the courthouse lawn.

Eisenhower heard it all. Music was part of his background, and he didn't think much of it. His brother had taken piano lessons for a while, but gave it up as, in his words, "sissy."

So Ike grew up in Kansas, where the music was as flat as the land.

Daniel Louis Armstrong was rared back, tooting out some wild lines of "Night and Day." In the old days it didn't matter how well you played; it was the angle of your back and the tilt of your horn. The band was really tight; they were playing for their lives.

The trombone player came out of his seat, jumped down onto the stage on his knees and matched Armstrong for a few bars.

The audience yelled.

Eisenhower tapped his foot and smiled, watching Armstrong and the trombone man.

The drummer was giving a lot of rim shots. The whole ballroom sounded like the overtaxed heart of a bird ready to fly away to meet Jesus.

Ike took off his coat and unknotted his tie down to the first button.

The crowd went wild.

Late August 1908.

The train was late. Young Dwight David Eisenhower hurried across the endless steel grid of the Kansas City rail yards. He was catching the train to New York City. There he would board another bound for West Point.

He carried his admission papers, a congratulatory letter from his congressman (gotten after some complicated negotiations—it looked for a while like he would be Midshipman Eisenhower), his train ticket and twenty-one dollars emergency money in his jacket.

He'd asked the porter for the track number. It was next to the station proper. A spur track confused him. He looked down the tracks, couldn't see a number (trains waited all around, ready to hurl themselves toward distant cities...) and went to the station entrance.

Four black men, ragged of dress, were smiling and playing near the door. What they played young David had never heard before—it was syncopated music, but not like a rag, not a march, something in between, something like nothing else. Ike had never heard polyrhythms like them before—they stopped him dead.

The four had a banjo, a cornet, a violin, and a clarinet. They played, smiled, danced a little for the two or three people watching them. A hat lay on the ground before them. In it were a few, dimes, pennies, and a single new half-dime.

They finished the song. A couple of people said, "Very nice, very nice" and added a few, cents to the hat. They walked away.

The four men started to talk among themselves. "What was that song?" asked young David.

The man with the cornet looked at him through large horn-rimmed spectacles. "That song was called 'Struttin' with Some Barbecue,' young sir," he said.

Dwight David reached into his pocket and took out a shiny one-dollar gold piece.

"Play it again," he said.

They nearly killed themselves this time, running through it. It was great art, it was on the street, and they were getting a whole dollar for it. David watched them, especially the clarinet player, who made his instrument soar above the others. They finished the number and all tipped their hats to him.

"Is that hard to learn to play?" he asked the man of the clarinet.

"For some it is," he answered.

"Could you teach me?" asked David.

The black man looked away; they were no help at all. "Let me see your fingers," he said.

Eisenhower held out his hands, wrists up, then down.

"I could probably teach you to play in six weeks," he said. "I don't know if I could teach you to play like that. You've got to feel that music." He was trying not to say that Eisenhower was white.

"Wait right here," said Ike.

He went inside the depot and cashed in his ticket. He sent two telegrams, one home and one to the Army. He was back outside in fifteen minutes, with thirty-three dollars in his pocket, total.

"Let's go find me a clarinet," he said to the black man.

He knew he would not sleep well that night, and neither would anybody back on the farm. He probably wouldn't sleep good for weeks. But he sure knew what he wanted.

Armstrong smiled, wiped his face and blew the opening notes of "When It's Sleepy Time Down South."

Ike joined in.

Then they went into "Just a Closer Walk with Thee," quiet, restrained, the horn and clarinet becoming one instrument for a while, then Ike bent his notes around Armstrong's, then Pops lifted Eisenhower up, then the instruments walked arm in arm toward Heaven.

Ike listened to the drummer as he played. He sure missed Wild George.

The first time they had met, Ike was the new kid in town, just another guy with a clarinet that some gangster had hired to fill in with a band sometime in 1911.

He didn't say much. He was working his way south from KC, toward Memphis, toward New Orleans (which he would never see until after New Orleans didn't mean the same anymore).

Ike could cook anyone with his clarinet—horn player, banjo man, even drummers. They might make more noise but when they ran out of things to do, Ike was just starting. He'd begun at the saloon filling in, but the bandleader soon had sense enough to put him out front. They took breaks leaving just him and the drummer up there, and the crowds never noticed. Ike was hot before there was hot music.

Till one night a guy came in—a new drummer. He was a crazy man. "My name is Wild George S. Patton," he said before the first set.

"What's the S. stand for?" asked Ike.

"Shitkicker!" said the drummer.

Ike didn't say anything.

That night they tried to cut each other, chop each other off the stage. Patton was doing two-hand cymbal shots, paradiddles, and flails. His bass-foot never stopped. Ike wasn't a show-off, but this guy drove him to it. He blew notes that killed mice for three square blocks. Patton ended up by kicking a hole through the bass drum and ramming his sticks through his snare like he was opening a can of beans with them.

The bandleader fired Patton on the spot and threatened to call the cops. The crowd nearly lynched the manager for it.

As soon as the hubbub died, Patton said to Ike, "The S. stands for Smith," and shook his hand.

He and Ike took off that night to start up their own band.

And were together for almost thirty years.

Armstrong blew "Dry Bones."

Ike did "St. Louis Blues."

They had never done either better. This Washington audience loved them.

So had another, long ago.

The first time he and Armstrong had met had been in Washington, too. A hot bleak July day in 1932.

The Bonus Army had come to the capital, asking their congressmen and their nation for some relief in this third year of the Depression. President Al Smith was powerless; he had a Republican Congress under him.

The bill granting the veterans of the Great War their bonus, due in 1945, had been passed back in the twenties. All the vets wanted was it to be paid immediately. It had been sitting in the Treasury, gaining interest, and was already part of the budget. The vote was coming up soon.

Thousands, dubbed the B.E.F., had poured into Washington, camping on Anacostia Flats, in tin boxes, towns of shanties dubbed "Smithvilles," or under the rain and stars.

Homeless men who had slogged through the mud of Europe, been gassed and shelled, and who had lived with rats in the trenches for democracy, now they found themselves back in the mud again.

This time they were out of money, out of work, out of luck.

The faces of the men were tired. Soup kitchens had been set up. They tried to keep their humor. It was all they had left. May dragged by, then June, then July. The vote was taken in Congress on the twelfth.

Congress said no.

They accused the Bonus Marchers of being Reds. They said they were armed rabble. Rumors ran wild. Such financial largesse, said Congress, could not be afforded.

Twenty thousand of the thirty thousand men tried to find some way back home, out of the city, back to No Place, U.S.A.

Ten thousand stayed, hoping for something to happen. Anything.

Ike went down to play for them. So did Armstrong. They ran into each other in town, got together their bands and equipment. They set up a stage in the middle of the Smithville, now a forlorn-looking bunch of mud-strewn shacks.

About five thousand of the jobless men came to hear them play. They were in a holiday mood. They sat on the ground, in the mud. They didn't much care anymore.

Armstrong and Ike had begun to play that day. Half the band, including Wild George, had hangovers. They had drunk with the Bonus Marchers the night before, and well into the morning before the noon concert.

They played great jazz that day anyway. A cloud of smoke had risen up from some of the abandoned warehouses the veterans had been living in, just before the music began. There was some commotion from over toward the Potomac. The band just played louder and wilder.

The marchers clapped along. Wild George smiled a bleary-eyed smile toward the crowd. They were doing half his job.

Automatic rifle fire rang out, causing heads to turn.

The Army was coming. Sons and nephews of some of the Bonus Marchers there were coming toward them on orders from Douglas MacArthur, the Chief of Staff. He had orders to clear them out.

The men came to their feet, picking up rocks and bottles.

Marching lines of soldiers came into view, bayonets fixed. Small two-man tanks, armed with machine guns, rolled between the soldiers. The lines stopped. The soldiers put on gas masks.

The Bonus Marchers, who remembered phosgene and the trenches, drew back.

"Keep playing!" said Ike.

"Keep goin'. Let it roll!" said Armstrong.

Tear gas grenades flew toward the Bonus Marchers. Rocks and bottles sailed toward the soldiers in their masks. There was a real explosion a block away.

The troops came in.

The gas rolled toward the marchers. Some picked up the spewing canisters to throw them back, fell coughing to the ground, overcome.

The tanks and bayonets came forward in a line.

The marchers broke and ran.

Their shacks and tents were set afire by chemical corpsmen behind the tanks.

"Let it roll! Let it roll!" said Armstrong, and they played "Didn't He Ramble" and the gas cloud hit them, and the music died in chokes and vomiting.

That night the Bonus Marchers were loaded on Army trucks, taken fifty miles due west and led out on the sides of the roads.

Ike and Louis went up before the Washington magistrate, paid ten dollars each fine for them and their band members, and took trains to New York City.

The last time he had seen Wild George alive was two years ago. Patton had been found by somebody who'd known him in the old days.

He'd been in four bad marriages, his only kid died in the taking of the Japanese Home Islands in early '47, and he'd lost one of his arms in a car wreck in '55. He had been in a flophouse when the guy found him. They'd put him in a nursing home and paid the bills.

Ike had gone to visit. The last time they had seen each other in those intervening twenty-odd years had been the day of the fistfight in 1943, just before the Second World War broke out. Patton had joined the Miller band for a while, but was too much for them. He'd gone from band to band and marriage to marriage to oblivion.

He was old, old. Wild George was only five years older than Ike. He looked a hundred. One eye was almost gone. He had no teeth. He was drying out in the nursing home, turning brittle as last winter's leaves.

"Hello, George," said Ike, shaking his only hand.

"I knew you'd come first," said Patton.

"You should have let somebody know."

"What's to know? One old musician lives, another one dies."

"George, I'm sorry. The way things have turned out."

"I've been thinking it over, about that fight we had." Patton stopped to cough up some bloody spittle into a basin Ike held for him.

"God, oh, jees. If I could only have a drink." He stared into Ike's eyes. Then he said:

"About that fight. You were still wrong."

Ike was crying as they went into the final number. He stepped forward to the mike Helen had used when she came out to sing with them for the last three numbers.

"This song is for the memory of George Smith Patton," he said.

They played "The Old, Rugged Cross." Ike, nor anybody else, had ever played it just like that before.

Ike broke down halfway through. He waved to the crowd, took his mouthpiece off, and walked into the wings.

Pops kept playing. He tried to motion Ike back. Helen was hugging him. He waved and brushed the tears away.

Armstrong finished the song.

The audience tore the place apart. They were on their feet and stamping, screaming, applauding.

Presley, out there, sat in his chair.

He was crying too, but quickly stood up and cheered.

Then the whole thing was over.

At home, later, in Georgetown, Senator Presley was lying in bed beside his wife Muffy. They had made love. They had both been excited. It had been terrific.

Now Muffy was asleep.

Presley got up and went to the bathroom. Then he went to the kitchen, poured himself a Scotch, and stood with his naked butt against the countertop.

It was a cold night. Through the half curtains on the window he saw stars over the city. If you could call this a city.

He went into the den. The servants would be asleep.

He turned the power on the stereo, took down four or five of his Eisenhower records, looked through them. He put on *Ike at the Mike*, a four-record set made for RCA in 1947, toward the end of the last war.

Ike was playing "No Love, No Nothing," a song his wife had made famous three years before. She wasn't on this record, though. This was all Ike and his band.

Presley got the bottle from the kitchen, sat back down, poured himself another drink. Tomorrow was more hearings. And the day after.

Someday, he thought, someday, E. Aaron Presley will be President of these here United States. Serves them right.

Ike was playing "All God's Chillun Got Shoes."

I didn't even get to shake his hand, thought Presley.

I'd give it all away to be like him, he thought.

He went to sleep sitting up.

Mike Resnick

Over There

I respectfully ask permission immediately to raise two divisions for immediate service at the front under the bill which has just become law, and hold myself read to raise four divisions, if you so direct. I respectfully refer for details to my last letters to the Secretary of War.

—Theodore Roosevelt
telegram to President Woodrow
Wilson, May 18, 1917

I very much regret that I cannot comply with the request in your telegram of yesterday. The reasons I have stated in a public statement made this morning, and I need not assure you that my conclusions were based upon imperative considerations of public policy and not upon personal or private choice.

—Woodrow Wilson,
telegram to Theodore Roosevelt,
May 19, 1917

The date was May 22, 1917.

Woodrow Wilson looked up at the burly man standing impatiently before his desk.

"This will necessarily have to be an extremely brief meeting, Mr. Roosevelt," he said wearily. "I have consented to it only out of respect for the fact that you formerly held the office that I am now privileged to hold."

"I appreciate that, Mr. President," said Theodore Roosevelt, shifting his weight anxiously from one leg to the other.

"Well, then?" said Wilson.

"You know why I'm here," said Roosevelt bluntly. "I want your permission to reassemble my Rough Riders and take them over to Europe."

"As I keep telling you, Mr. Roosevelt—that's out of the question."

"You haven't told *me* anything!" snapped Roosevelt. "And I have no interest in what you tell the press."

"Then I'm telling you now," said Wilson firmly. "I can't just let any man who wants to gather up a regiment to fight in the war. We have procedures, and chains of command, and—"

"I'm not just *any* man." said Roosevelt. "And I have every intention of honoring our procedures and chain of command." He glared at the president. "I created many of those procedures myself."

Wilson stared at his visitor for a long moment. "Why are you so anxious to go to war, Mr. Roosevelt? Does violence hold so much fascination for you?"

"I abhor violence and bloodshed," answered Roosevelt. "I believe that war should never be resorted to when it is honorably possible to avoid it. But once war has begun, then the only thing to do is win it as swiftly and decisively as possible. I believe that I can help to accomplish that end."

"Mr. Roosevelt, may I point out that you are fifty-eight years old, and according to my reports you have been in poor health ever since returning from Brazil three years ago?"

"Nonsense!" said Roosevelt defensively. "I feel as fit as a bull moose!"

"A one-eyed bull moose," replied Wilson dryly. Roosevelt seemed about to protest, but Wilson raised a hand to silence him. "Yes, Mr. Roosevelt, I know that you lost the vision in your left eye during a boxing match while you were president." He couldn't quite keep the distaste for such juvenile and adventurous escapades out of his voice.

"I'm not here to discuss my health," answered Roosevelt gruffly, "but the reactivation of my commission as a colonel in the United States Army."

Wilson shook his head. "You have my answer. You've told me nothing that might change my mind."

"I'm about to."

"Oh?"

"Let's be perfectly honest, Mr. President. The Republican nomination is mine for the asking, and however the war turns out, the Democrats will be sitting ducks. Half the people hate you for entering the war so late, and the other half hate you for entering it at all." Roosevelt paused. "If you will return me to active duty and allow me to organize my Rough Riders, I will give you my personal pledge that I will neither seek nor accept the Republican nomination in 1920."

"It means that much to you?" asked Wilson, arching a thin eyebrow.

"It does, sir."

"I'm impressed by your passion, and I don't doubt your sincerity, Mr. Roosevelt," said Wilson. "But my answer must still be no. I am serving my second term. I have no intention of running again in 1920, I do not need your political support, and I will not be a party to such a deal."

"Then you are a fool, Mr. President," said Roosevelt. "Because I am going anyway, and you have thrown away your only opportunity, slim as it may be, to keep the Republicans out of the White House."

"I will not reactivate your commission, Mr. Roosevelt.

Roosevelt pulled two neatly folded letters out of his lapel pocket and placed them on the president's desk.

"What are these?" asked Wilson, staring at them as if they might bite him at any moment.

"Letters from the British and the French, offering me commissions in their armies.'" Roosevelt paused. "I am first, foremost, and always an American, Mr. President, and I had entertained no higher hopes than leading my men into battle under the Stars and Stripes—but I am going to participate in this war, and you are not going to stop me." And now, for the first time, he displayed the famed Roosevelt grin. "I have some thirty reporters waiting for me on the lawn of the White House. Shall I tell them that I am fighting for the country that I love, or shall I tell them that our European allies are more concerned with winning this damnable war than our own president?"

"This is blackmail, Mr. Roosevelt!" said Wilson, outraged.

"I believe that is the word for it," said Roosevelt, still grinning. "I would like you to direct Captain Frank McCoy to leave his current unit and report to me. I'll handle the rest of the details myself." He paused again. "The press is waiting, Mr. President. What shall I tell them?"

"Tell them anything you want," muttered Wilson furiously. "Only get out of this office."

"Thank you, Sir," said Roosevelt, turning on his heel and marching out with an energetic bounce to his stride.

Wilson waited a moment, then spoke aloud. "You can come in now, Joseph."

Joseph Tummulty, his personal secretary, entered the Oval Office.

"Were you listening?" asked Wilson.

"Yes, Sir."

"Is there any way out of it?"

"Not without getting a black eye in the press."

"That's what I was afraid of," said Wilson.

"He's got you over a barrel, Mr. President."

"I wonder what he's really after?" mused Wilson thoughtfully. "He's been a governor, an explorer, a war hero, a police commissioner, an author, a big-game hunter, and a president." He paused, mystified. "What more can he want from life?"

"Personally, sir," said Tummulty, making no attempt to hide the contempt in his voice, "I think that damned cowboy is looking to charge up one more San Juan Hill."

Roosevelt stood before his troops, as motley an assortment of warriors as had been assembled since the last incarnation of the Rough Riders. There were military men and cowboys, professional athletes and adventurers, hunters and ranchers, barroom brawlers and Indians, tennis players and wrestlers, even a trio of Masai *elmoran* he had met on safari in Africa.

"Some of 'em look a little long in the tooth, Colonel," remarked Frank McCoy, his second-in-command.

"Some of us are a little long in the tooth, too, Frank," said Roosevelt with a smile.

"And some of 'em haven't started shaving yet," continued McCoy wryly.

"Well, there's nothing like a war to grow them up in a hurry."

Roosevelt turned away from McCoy and faced his men, waiting briefly until he had their attention. He paused for a moment to make sure that the journalists who were traveling with the regiment had their pencils and notebooks out, and then spoke.

"Gentlemen," he said, "we are about to embark upon a great adventure. We are privileged to be present at a crucial point in the history of the world. In the terrible whirlwind of war, all the great nations of the world are facing the supreme test of their courage and dedication. All the alluring but fertile theories of the pacifists have vanished at the first sound of gunfire."

Roosevelt paused to clear his throat, then continued in his surprisingly high-pitched voice. "This war is the greatest the world has ever seen. The vast size of the armies, the tremendous slaughter, the loftiness of the heroism shown and the hideous horror of the brutalities committed, the valor of the fighting men and the extraordinary ingenuity of those who have designed and built the fighting machines, the burning patriotism of the peoples who defend their homelands and the far-reaching complexity of the plans of the leaders—all are on a scale so huge that nothing in history can compare with them.

"The issues at stake are fundamental. The free peoples of the world have banded together against tyrannous militarism, and it is not too much to say that the outcome will largely determine, for those of us who love liberty above all else, whether or not life remains worth living."

He paused again, and stared up and down the ranks of his men.

"Against such a vast and complex array of forces, it may seem to you that we will just be another cog in the military machine of the allies, that one regiment cannot possibly make a difference." Roosevelt's chin jutted forward pugnaciously. "I say to you that this is rubbish! We represent a society dedicated to the proposition that every free man makes a difference. And I give you my solemn pledge that the Rough Riders will make a difference in the fighting to come!"

It was possible that his speech wasn't finished, that he still had more to say...but if he did, it was drowned out beneath the wild and raucous cheering of his men.

One hour later they boarded the ship to Europe.

* * *

Roosevelt summoned a corporal and handed him a hand-written letter. The man saluted and left, and Roosevelt returned to his chair in front of his tent. He was about to pick up a book when McCoy approached him.

"Your daily dispatch to General Pershing?" he asked dryly.

"Yes," answered Roosevelt. "I can't understand what is wrong with the man. Here we are, primed and ready to fight, and he's kept us well behind the front for the better part of two months!"

"I know, Colonel."

"It just doesn't make any sense! Doesn't he know what the Rough Riders did at San Juan Hill?"

"That was a long time ago, sir," said McCoy.

"I tell you, Frank, these men are the elite—the cream of the crop! They weren't drafted by lottery. Every one of them volunteered, and every one was approved personally by you or by me. Why are we being wasted here? There's a war to be won!"

"Pershing's got a lot to consider, Colonel," said McCoy. "He's got half a million American troops to disperse, he's got to act in concert with the French and the British, he's got to consider his lines of supply, he's—"

"Don't patronize me, Frank!" snapped Roosevelt. "We've assembled a brilliant fighting machine here, and he's ignoring us. There has to be a reason. I want to know what it is!"

McCoy shrugged helplessly. "I have no answer, sir."

"Well, I'd better get one soon from Pershing!" muttered Roosevelt. "We didn't come all this way to help in some mopping-up operation after the battle's been won." He stared at the horizon. "There's a glorious crusade being fought in the name of liberty, and I plan to be a part of it."

He continued staring off into the distance long after McCoy had left him.

* * *

A private approached Roosevelt as the former president was eating lunch with his officers.

"Dispatch from General Pershing, sir," said the private, handing him an envelope with a snappy salute.

"Thank you," said Roosevelt. He opened the envelope, read the message, and frowned.

"Bad news, Colonel?" asked McCoy.

"He says to be patient," replied Roosevelt. "Patient?" he repeated furiously. "By God, I've been patient long enough! Jake—saddle my horse!"

"What are you going to do, Colonel?" asked one of his lieutenants.

"I'm going to go meet face-to-face with Pershing," said Roosevelt, getting to his feet. "This is intolerable!"

"We don't even know where he is, sir."

"I'll find him," replied Roosevelt confidently.

"You're more likely to get lost or shot," said McCoy, the only man who dared to speak to him so bluntly.

"Runs With Deer! Matupu!" shouted Roosevelt. "Saddle your horses!"

A burly Indian and a tall Masai immediately got to their feet and went to the stable area.

Roosevelt turned back to McCoy. "I'm taking the two best trackers in the regiment. Does that satisfy you, Mr. McCoy?"

"It does not," said McCoy. "I'm coming along, too."

Roosevelt shook his head. "You're in command of the regiment in my absence. You're staying here."

"But—"

"That's an order," said Roosevelt firmly.

"Will you at least take along a squad of sharpshooters, Colonel?" persisted McCoy.

"Frank, we're forty miles behind the front, and I'm just going to talk to Pershing, not shoot him."

"We don't even know where the front is," said McCoy.

"It's where we're *not*," said Roosevelt grimly. "And that's what I'm going to change."

He left the mess tent without another word.

The first four French villages they passed were deserted, and consisted of nothing but the burned skeletons of houses and shops. The fifth had two buildings still standing—a manor house and a church—and they had been turned into Allied hospitals. Soldiers with missing limbs, soldiers with faces swatched in filthy bandages, soldiers with gaping holes in their bodies lay on cots and floors, shivering in the cold damp air, while an undermanned and harassed medical team did their best to keep them alive.

Roosevelt stopped long enough to determine General Pershing's whereabouts, then walked among the wounded to offer words of encouragement while trying to ignore the unmistakable stench of gangrene and the stinging scent of disinfectant. Finally he remounted his horse and joined his two trackers.

They passed a number of corpses on their way to the front. Most had been plundered of their weapons, and one, lying upon its back, displayed a gruesome, toothless smile.

"Shameful!" muttered Roosevelt as he looked down at the grinning body.

"Why?" asked Runs With Deer.

"It's obvious that the man had gold teeth, and they have been removed."

"It is honorable to take trophies of the enemy," asserted the Indian.

"The Germans have never advanced this far south," said Roosevelt. "This man's teeth were taken by his companions." He shook his head. "Shameful!"

Matupu the Masai merely shrugged. "Perhaps this is not an honorable war."

"We are fighting for an honorable principle," stated Roosevelt. "That makes it an honorable war."

"Then it is an honorable war being waged by dishonorable men," said Matupu.

"Do the Masai not take trophies?" asked Runs With Deer.

"We take cows and goats and women," answered Matupu. "We do not plunder the dead." He paused. "We do not take scalps."

"There was a time when *we* did not, either," said Runs With Deer. "We were taught to, by the French."

"And we are in France now," said Matupu with some satisfaction, as if everything now made sense to him.

They dismounted after two more hours and walked their horses for the rest of the day, then spent the night in a bombed-out farmhouse. The next morning they were mounted and riding again, and they came to General Pershing's field headquarters just before noon. There were thousands of soldiers bustling about, couriers bringing in hourly reports from the trenches, weapons and tanks being dispatched, convoys of trucks filled with food and water slowly working their way into supply lines.

Roosevelt was stopped a few yards into the camp by a young lieutenant.

"May I ask your business here, sir?"

"I'm here to see General Pershing," answered Roosevelt.

"Just like that?" said the soldier with a smile.

"Son," said Roosevelt, taking off his hat and leaning over the lieutenant, "take a good look at my face." He paused for a moment. "Now go tell General Pershing that Teddy Roosevelt is here to see him."

The lieutenant's eyes widened. "By God, you *are* Teddy Roosevelt!" he exclaimed. Suddenly he reached his hand out.

"May I shake your hand first, Mr. President? I just want to be able to tell my parents I did it."

Roosevelt grinned and took the young man's hand in his own, then waited astride his horse while the lieutenant went off to Pershing's quarters. He gazed around the camp: There were ramshackle buildings and ramshackle soldiers, each of which had seen too much action and too little glory. The men's faces were haggard, their eyes haunted, their bodies stooped with exhaustion. The main paths through the camp had turned to mud, and the constant drizzle brought rust, rot, and disease with an equal lack of cosmic concern.

The lieutenant approached Roosevelt, his feet sinking inches into the mud with each step.

"If you'll follow me, Mr. President, he'll see you immediately."

"Thank you," said Roosevelt.

"Watch yourself, Mr. President," said the lieutenant as Roosevelt dismounted. "I have a feeling he's not happy about meeting with you."

"He'll be a damned sight less happy when I'm through with him," said Roosevelt firmly. He turned to his companions. "See to the needs of the horses."

"Yes, sir," said Runs With Deer. "We'll be waiting for you right here."

"How is the battle going?" Roosevelt asked as he and the lieutenant began walking through the mud toward Pershing's quarters. "My Rough Riders have been practically incommunicado since we arrived."

The lieutenant shrugged. "Who knows? All we hear are rumors. The enemy is retreating, the enemy is advancing, we've killed thousands of them, they've killed thousands of us. Maybe the general will tell you; he certainly hasn't seen fit to tell *us*."

They reached the entrance to Pershing's quarters.

"I'll wait here for you, sir," said the lieutenant.

"You're sure you don't mind?" asked Roosevelt. "You can find some orderly to escort me back if it will be a problem."

"No, sir," said the young man earnestly. "It'll be an honor, Mr. President."

"Well, thank you, son," said Roosevelt. He shook the lieutenant's hand again, then walked through the doorway and found himself facing General John J. Pershing.

"Good afternoon, Jack," said Roosevelt, extending his hand.

Pershing looked at Roosevelt's outstretched hand for a moment, then took it.

"Have a seat, Mr. President," he said, indicating a chair.

"Thank you," said Roosevelt, pulling up a chair as Pershing seated himself behind a desk that was covered with maps.

"I mean no disrespect, Mr. President," said Pershing, "but exactly who gave you permission to leave your troops and come here?"

"No one," answered Roosevelt.

"Then why did you do it?" asked Pershing. "I'm told you were accompanied only by a red Indian and a black savage. That's hardly a safe way to travel in a war zone.

"I came here to find out why you have consistently refused my requests to have my Rough Riders moved to the front."

Pershing lit a cigar and offered one to Roosevelt, who refused it.

"There are proper channels for such a request," said the general at last. "You yourself helped create them."

"And I have been using them for almost two months, to no avail."

Pershing sighed. "I *have* been a little busy conducting this damned war."

"I'm sure you have," said Roosevelt. "And I have assembled a regiment of the finest fighting men to be found in America, which I am placing at your disposal."

"For which I thank you, Mr. President."

"I don't want you to thank me!" snapped Roosevelt. "I want you to unleash me!"

"When the time is right, your Rough Riders will be brought into the conflict," said Pershing.

"When the time is right?" repeated Roosevelt. "Your men are dying like flies! Every village I've passed has become a bombed-out ghost town! You needed us two months ago, Jack!"

"Mr. President, I've got half a million men to maneuver. I'll decide when and where I need your regiment."

"When?" persisted Roosevelt.

"You'll be the first to know."

"That's not good enough!"

"It will have to be."

"You listen to me, Jack Pershing!" said Roosevelt heatedly. "I *made* you a general! I think the very least you owe me is an answer. When will my men be brought into the conflict?"

Pershing stared at him from beneath shaggy black eyebrows for a long moment. "What the hell did you have to come here for, anyway?" he said at last.

"I told you: to get an answer."

"I don't mean to my headquarters," said Pershing. "I mean what is a fifty-eight-year-old man with a blind eye and a game leg doing in the middle of a war?"

"This is the greatest conflict in history, and it's being fought over principles that every free man holds dear. How could I not take part in it?"

"You could have just stayed home and made speeches and raised funds."

"And you could have retired after Mexico and spent the

rest of your life playing golf," Roosevelt shot back. "But you didn't, and I didn't, because neither of us is that kind of man. Damn it, Jack—I've assembled a regiment the likes of which hasn't been seen in almost twenty years, and if you've any sense at all, you'll make use of us. Our horses and our training give us an enormous advantage on this terrain. We can mobilize and strike at the enemy as easily as this fellow Lawrence seems to be doing in the Arabian desert."

Pershing stared at him for a long moment, then sighed deeply.

"I can't do it, Mr. President" said Pershing.

"Why not?" demanded Roosevelt.

"The truth? Because of you, sir."

"What are you talking about?"

"You've made my position damnably awkward," said Pershing bitterly. "You are an authentic American hero, possibly the first since Abraham Lincoln. You are as close to being worshiped as a man can be." He paused. "You're a goddamned icon, Mr. Roosevelt."

"What has *that* got to do with anything?"

"I am under direct orders not to allow you to participate in any action that might result in your death." He glared at Roosevelt across the desk. "*Now* do you understand? If I move you to the front, I'll have to surround you with at least three divisions to make sure nothing happens to you—and I'm in no position to spare that many men."

"Who issued that order, Jack?"

"My commander-in-chief

"Woodrow Wilson?"

"That's right. And I'd no more disobey him than I would disobey you if you still held that office." He paused. then spoke again more gently. "You're an old man, sir. Not old by your standards, but too damned old to be leading charges against the Germans. You should be home writing your memoirs and giving speeches and rallying the people to our cause, Mr. President."

"I'm not ready to retire to Sagamore Hill and have my face carved on Mount Rushmore yet," said Roosevelt. "There are battles to be fought and a war to be won."

"Not by you, Mr. President," answered Pershing. "When the enemy is beaten and on the run, I'll bring your regiment up. The press can go crazy photographing you chasing the few German stragglers back to Berlin. But I cannot and will not disobey a direct order from my commander-in-chief. Until I can guarantee your safety, you'll stay where you are."

"I see," said Roosevelt after a moment's silence. "And what if I relinquish my command? Will you utilize my Rough Riders then?"

Pershing shook his head. "I have no use for a bunch of tennis players and college professors who think they can storm across the trenches on their polo ponies," he said firmly. "The only men you have with battle experience are as old as you are." He paused. "Your regiment might be effective if the Apaches ever leave the reservation, but they are ill-prepared for a modern, mechanized war. I hate to be so blunt, but it's the truth, sir."

"You're making a huge mistake, Jack."

"You're the one who made the mistake, sir, by coming here. It's my job to see that you don't die because of it."

"Damn it, Jack, we could make a difference!"

Pershing paused and stared, not without sympathy, at Roosevelt. "War has changed, Mr. President," he said at last. "No one regiment can make a difference any longer. It's been a long time since Achilles fought Hector outside Troy."

An orderly entered with a dispatch, and Pershing read and initialed it.

"I don't mean to rush you, sir," he said, getting to his feet, "but I have an urgent meeting to attend."

Roosevelt stood up. "I'm sorry to have bothered you, General."

"I'm still Jack to you, Mr. President," said Pershing. "And it's as your friend Jack that I want to give you one final word of advice."

"Yes?"

"Please, for your own sake and the sake of your men, don't do anything rash."

"Why would I do something rash?" asked Roosevelt innocently.

"Because you wouldn't be Teddy Roosevelt if the thought of ignoring your orders hadn't already crossed your mind," said Pershing.

Roosevelt fought back a grin, shook Pershing's hand, and left without saying another word. The young lieutenant was just outside the door, and escorted him back to where Runs with Deer and Matupu were waiting with the horses.

"Bad news?" asked Runs With Deer as he studied Roosevelt's face.

"No worse than I had expected."

"Where do we go now?" asked the Indian.

"Back to camp," said Roosevelt firmly. "There's a war to be won, and no college professor from New Jersey is going to keep me from helping to win it!"

"Well, that's the story," said Roosevelt to his assembled officers after be had laid out the situation to them in the large tent he had reserved for strategy sessions. "Even if I resign my commission and return to America, there is no way that General Pershing will allow you to see any action."

"I knew Black Jack Pershing when he was just a captain," growled Buck O'Neill, one of the original Rough Riders. "Just who the hell does he think he is?"

"He's the supreme commander of the American forces," answered Roosevelt wryly.

"What are we going to do, sir?" asked McCoy. "Surely you don't plan just to sit back here and then let Pershing move us up when all the fighting's done with?"

"No, I don't," said Roosevelt.

"Let's hear what you got to say, Teddy," said O'Neill.

"The issues at stake in this war haven't changed since I went to see the general," answered Roosevelt. "I plan to harass and harry the enemy to the best of our ability. If need be we will live off the land while utilizing our superior mobility in a number of tactical strikes, and we will do our valiant best to bring this conflict to a successful conclusion."

He paused and looked around at his officers. "I realize that in doing this I am violating my orders, but there are greater principles at stake here. I am flattered that the president thinks I am indispensable to the American public, but our nation is based on the principle that no one man deserves any rights or privileges not offered to all men." He took a deep breath and cleared his throat. "However, since I *am* contravening a direct order, I believe that not only each one of you, but every one of the men as well, should be given the opportunity to withdraw from the Rough Riders. I will force no man to ride against his conscience and his beliefs. I would like you to go out now and put the question to the men; I will wait here for your answer."

To nobody's great surprise, the regiment voted unanimously to ride to glory with Teddy Roosevelt.

3 August, 1917
My Dearest Edith:

As strange as this may seem to you (and it seems surpassingly strange to me), I will soon be a fugitive from justice, opposed not only by the German army but quite possibly by the U.S. military as well.

My Rough Riders have embarked upon a bold adventure, contrary to both the wishes and the direct orders of the president of the United States. When I think back to the day he finally approved my request to reassemble the regiment, I cringe with chagrin at my innocence and naïveté; he sent us here only so that I would not have access to the press and he would no longer have to listen to my demands. Far from being permitted to play a leading role in this noblest of battles, my men have been held far behind the front, and Jack Pershing was under orders from Wilson himself not to allow any harm to come to us.

When I learned of this, I put a proposition to my men, and I am extremely proud of their response. To a one, they voted to break camp and ride to the front so as to strike at the heart of the German military machine. By doing so, I am disobeying the orders of my commander-in-chief, and because of this somewhat peculiar situation, I doubt that I shall be able to send too many more letters to you until I have helped to end this war. At that tine, I shall turn myself over to Pershing, or whoever is in charge, and argue my case before whatever tribunal is deemed proper.

However, before that moment occurs, we shall finally see action, bearing the glorious banner of the Stars and Stripes. My men are a finely-tuned fighting machine, and I daresay that they will give a splendid account of themselves before the conflict is over. We have not made contact with the enemy yet, nor can I guess where we shall finally meet, but we are primed and eager for our first taste of battle. Our spirit is high, and many of the old-timers spend their hours singing the old battle songs from Cuba. We are all looking forward to a bully battle, and we plan to teach the Hun a lesson he won't soon forget.

Give my love to the children, and when you write to Kermit and Quentin, tell them that their father has every intention of reaching Berlin before they do!

> *All my love,*
> *Theodore*

Roosevelt, who had been busily writing an article on ornithology, looked up from his desk as McCoy entered his tent.

"Well?"

"We think we've found what we've been looking for, Mr. President," said McCoy.

"Excellent!" said Roosevelt, carefully closing his notebook. "Tell me about it."

McCoy spread a map out on the desk.

"Well, the front lines, as you know, are *here*, about fifteen miles to the north of us. The Germans are entrenched *here*. And we haven't been able to move them for almost three weeks." McCoy paused. "The word I get from my old outfit is that the Americans are planning a major push on the German left, right about *here*."

"When?" demanded Roosevelt.

"At sunrise tomorrow morning."

"Bully!" said Roosevelt. He studied the map for a moment, then looked up. "Where is Jack Pershing?"

"Almost ten miles west and eight miles north of us," answered McCoy. "He's dug in, and from what I hear, he came under pretty heavy mortar fire today. He'll have his hands full without worrying about where an extra regiment of American troops came from."

"Better and better," said Roosevelt. "We not only get to fight, but we may even pull Jack's chestnuts out of the fire." He turned his attention back to the map. "All right," he said, "the Americans will advance along this line. What would you say will be their major obstacle?"

"You mean besides the mud and the Germans and the mustard gas?" asked McCoy wryly.

"You know what I mean, Frank."

"Well," said McCoy, "there's a small rise here—I'd hardly call it a hill, certainly not like the one we took in Cuba—but it's manned by four machine guns, and it gives the Germans an excellent view of the territory the Americans have got to cross."

"Then that's our objective," said Roosevelt decisively. "If we can capture that hill and knock out the machine guns, we'll have made a positive contribution to the battle that even Woodrow Wilson will be forced to acknowledge." The famed Roosevelt grin spread across his face. "We'll show him that the dodo may be dead, but the Rough Riders are very much alive." He paused. "Gather the men, Frank. I want to speak to them before we leave."

McCoy did as he was told, and Roosevelt emerged from his tent some ten minutes later to address the assembled Rough Riders.

"Gentlemen," he said, "tomorrow morning we will meet the enemy on the battlefield."

A cheer arose from the ranks.

"It has been suggested that modern warfare deals only in masses and logistics, that there is no room left for heroism, that the only glory remaining to men of action is upon the sporting fields. I tell you that this is a lie. *We matter!* Honor and courage are not outmoded virtues, but are the very ideals that make us great as individuals and as a nation. Tomorrow we will prove it in terms that our detractors and our enemies will both understand." He paused, then saluted them. "Saddle up—and may God be with us!"

They reached the outskirts of the battlefield, moving silently with hooves and harnesses muffled, just before sunrise. Even McCoy, who had seen action in Mexico, was unprepared for the sight that awaited them.

The mud was littered with corpses as far as the eye could see in the dim light of the false dawn. The odor of death and decay permeated the moist, cold morning air. Thousands of bodies lay there in the pouring rain, many of them grotesquely swollen. Here and there they had virtually exploded, either when punctured by bullets or when the walls of the abdominal cavities collapsed. Attempts had been made during the previous month to drag them back off the battlefield, but there was simply no place left to put them. There was almost total silence as the men in both trenches began preparing for another day of bloodletting.

Roosevelt reined his horse to a halt and surveyed the carnage. Still more corpses were hung up on barbed wire, and more than a handful of bodies attached to the wire still moved feebly. The rain pelted down, turning the plain between the enemy trenches into a brown, gooey slop.

"My God, Frank!" murmured Roosevelt.

"It's pretty awful," agreed McCoy.

"This is not what civilized men do to each other," said Roosevelt, stunned by the sight before his eyes. "This isn't war, Frank—it's butchery!"

"It's what war has become."

"How long have these two lines been facing each other?"

"More than a month, sir."

Roosevelt stared, transfixed, at the sea of mud.

"A month to cross a quarter mile of *this*?"

"That's correct, sir."

"How many lives have been lost trying to cross this strip of land?"

McCoy shrugged. "I don't know. Maybe eighty thousand, maybe a little more."

Roosevelt shook his head. "Why, in God's name? Who

cares about it? What purpose does it serve?"

McCoy had no answer, and the two men sat in silence for another moment, surveying the battlefield.

"Madness!" said Roosevelt at last. "Why doesn't Pershing simply march around it?"

"That's a question for a general to answer, Mr. President," said McCoy. "Me, I'm just a captain."

We can't continue to lose American boys for *this!*" said Roosevelt furiously. "Where is that machine-gun encampment, Frank?"

McCoy pointed to a small rise about three hundred yards distant.

"And the main German lines?"

"Their first row of trenches are in line with the hill."

"Have we tried to take the hill before?"

"I can't imagine that we haven't, sir," said McCoy. "As long as they control it, they'll mow our men down like sitting ducks in a shooting gallery." He paused. "The problem is the mud. The average infantryman can't reach the hill in less than two minutes, probably closer to three—and until you've seen them in action, you can't believe the damage these guns can do in that amount of time."

"So as long as the hill remains in German hands, this is a war of attrition."

McCoy sighed. "It's been a war of attrition for three years, sir."

Roosevelt sat and stared at the hill for another few minutes, then turned back to McCoy.

"What are our chances, Frank?"

McCoy shrugged. "If it was dry, I'd say we had a chance to take them out—"

"But it's not."

"No, it's not," echoed McCoy.

"Can we do it?"

"I don't know, sir. Certainly not without heavy casualties."

"How heavy?"

"*Very* heavy."

"I need a number," said Roosevelt.

McCoy looked him in the eye. "Ninety percent—if we're lucky."

Roosevelt stared at the hill again. "They predicted fifty percent casualties at San Juan Hill," he said. "We had to charge up a much steeper slope in the face of enemy machine-gun fire. Nobody thought we had a chance—but I did it, Frank, and I did it alone. I charged up that hill and knocked out the machine-gun nest myself, and then the rest of my men followed me."

"The circumstances were different then, Mr. President," said McCoy. "The terrain offered cover and solid footing, and you were facing Cuban peasants who had been conscripted into service, not battle-hardened professional German soldiers."

"I know, I know," said Roosevelt. "But if we knock those machine guns out, how many American lives can we save today?"

"I don't know," admitted McCoy. "Maybe ten thousand, maybe none. It's possible that the Germans are dug in so securely that they can beat back any American charge even without the use of those machine guns."

"But at least it would prolong some American lives," persisted Roosevelt.

"By a couple of minutes."

"It would give them a *chance* to reach the German bunkers."

"I don't know."

"More of a chance than if they had to face machine-gun fire from the hill."

"What do you want me to say, Mr. President?" asked

McCoy. "That if we throw away our lives charging the hill that we'll have done something glorious and affected the outcome of the battle? I just don't know!"

"We came here to help win a war, Frank. Before I send my men into battle, I have to know that it will make a difference."

"I can't give you any guarantees, sir. We came to fight a war, all right. But look around you, Mr. President—*this* isn't the war we came to fight. They've changed the rules on us."

"There are hundreds of thousands of American boys in trenches who didn't come to fight this kind of war," answered Roosevelt. "In less than an hour, most of them are going to charge across the sea of mud into a barrage of machine-gun fire. If we can't shorten the war, then perhaps we can at least lengthen their lives."

"At the cost of our own."

"We are idealists and adventurers, Frank—perhaps the last this world will ever see. We knew what we were coming here to do." He paused. "Those boys are here because of speeches and decisions that politicians have made, myself included. Left to their own devices, they'd be with their families. Left to ours, we'd find another cause to fight for."

"This isn't a cause, Mr. President," said McCoy. "It's a slaughter."

"Then maybe this is where men who want to prevent slaughter belong," said Roosevelt. He looked up at the sky. "They'll be mobilizing in another half hour, Frank."

"I know, Mr. President."

"If we leave now, if we don't try to take that hill, then Wilson and Pershing were right and I was wrong. The time for heroes is past, and I *am* an anachronism who should be sitting at home in a rocking chair, writing memoirs and exhorting younger men to go to war." He, paused, staring at the hill once more. "If we don't do what's required of us this day, we are agreeing with them that we don't matter, that men of courage and ideals can't make a difference. If that's true, there's no sense waiting for a more equitable battle, Frank—we might as well ride south and catch the first boat home."

"That's your decision, Mr. President?" asked McCoy.

"Was there really ever any other option?" replied Roosevelt wryly.

"No, sir," said McCoy. "Not for men like us."

"Thank you for your support, Frank," said Roosevelt, reaching out and laying a heavy hand on McCoy's shoulder. "Prepare the men."

"Yes, sir," said McCoy, saluting and riding back to the main body of the Rough Riders.

"Madness!" muttered Roosevelt, looking out at the bloated corpses. "Utter madness!"

McCoy returned a moment later.

"The men are awaiting your signal, sir," he said.

"Tell them to follow me," said Roosevelt.

"Sir..." said McCoy.

"Yes?"

"We would prefer you not lead the charge. The first ranks will face the heaviest bombardment, not only from the hill but also from the cannons behind the bunkers."

"I can't ask my men to do what I myself won't do," said Roosevelt.

"You are too valuable to lose, sir. We plan to attack in three waves. You belong at the back of the third wave, Mr. President."

Roosevelt shook his head. "There's nothing up ahead except bullets, Hank, and I've faced bullets before—in the Dakota Bad Lands, in Cuba, in Milwaukee. But if I hang back, if I send my men to do a job I was afraid to do, then I've have to face myself—and as any Democrat will tell you, I'm a lot tougher than any bullet ever made."

"You won't reconsider?" asked McCoy.

"Would you have left your unit and joined the Rough Riders if you thought I might?" asked Roosevelt with a smile.

"No, sir," admitted McCoy. "No, sir, I probably wouldn't have."

Roosevelt shook his hand. "You're a good man, Frank."

"Thank you, Mr. President."

"Are the men ready?"

"Yes, sir."

"Then," said Roosevelt, turning his horse toward the small rise, "let's do what must be done."

He pulled his rifle out, unlatched the safety catch, and dug his heels into his horse's sides.

Suddenly he was surrounded by the first wave of his own men, all screaming their various war cries in the face of the enemy.

For just a moment there was no response. Then the machine guns began their sweeping fire across the muddy plain. Buck O'Neill was the first to fall, his body riddled with bullets. An instant later Runs With Deer screamed in agony as his arm was blown away. Horses had their legs shot from under them, men were blown out of their saddles, limbs flew crazily through the wet morning air, and still the charge continued.

Roosevelt had crossed half the distance when Matupu fell directly in front of him, his head smashed to a pulp. He heard McCoy groan as half a dozen bullets thudded home in his chest, but looked neither right nor left as his horse leaped over the fallen Masai's bloody body.

Bullets and cannonballs flew to the right and left of him, in front and behind, and yet miraculously he was unscathed as he reached the final hundred yards. He dared a quick glance around and saw that he was the sole survivor from the first wave, then heard the screams of the second wave as the machine guns turned on them.

Now he was seventy yards away, now fifty. He yelled a challenge to the Germans, and as he looked into the blinking eye of a machine gun, for one brief, final, glorious instant it was San Juan Hill all over again.

18 September 1917
Dispatch from General John J. Pershing to Commander-in-Chief, President Woodrow Wilson

Sir:

I regret to inform you that Theodore Roosevelt died last Tuesday of wounds received in battle. He had disobeyed orders, and led his men in a futile charge against an entrenched German position. His entire regiment, the so-called Rough Riders, was lost. His death was almost certainly instantaneous, although it was two days before his body could be retrieved from the battlefield.

I shall keep the news of Mr. Roosevelt's death from the press until receiving instructions from you. It is true that he was an anachronism, that he belonged more to the nineteenth century than the twentieth, and yet it is entirely possible that he was the last authentic hero our country shall ever produce. The charge he led was ill-conceived and foolhardy in the extreme, nor did it diminish the length of the conflict by a single day, yet I cannot help but believe that if I had fifty thousand men with his courage and spirit, I could bring this war to a swift and satisfactory conclusion by the end of the year.

That Theodore Roosevelt died the death of a fool is beyond question, but I am certain in my heart that with his dying breath he felt he was dying the death of a hero. I await your instructions, and will release whatever version of his death you choose upon hearing from you.

General John J. Pershing

* * *

22 September 1917
Dispatch from President Woodrow Wilson to General John J.
Pershing, Commander of American Forces in Europe.

John:

   That man continues to harass me from the grave.

   *Still, we have had more than enough fools in our history.
Therefore, he died a hero.*

   *Just between you and me, the time for heroes is past. I hope with
all my heart that he was our last.*

Woodrow Wilson

And he was.

Susan Shwartz

Suppose They Gave a Peace

Twenty-five years after the war, and my damned sixth sense about the phone still wakes me up at 3:00 A.M. Just as well. All Margaret needs is for me to snap awake, shout, and jump out of bed, grabbing for my pants and my .45. I don't have it anymore. She made me sell it as soon as the kids were old enough to poke into the big chest of drawers. I don't interfere when she makes decisions like that. The way things are going to the dogs, though, I'd feel a whole lot better about her safety if I had the gun.

So I stuck my feet into my slippers—the trench foot still itches—and snuck downstairs. If Margaret woke up, she'd think I was raiding the icebox and go back to sleep. I like being up and alone in my house, kind of guard duty. I don't do much. I straighten towels or put books back the shelves—though with Steff gone, that's not a problem anymore. I don't like seeing the kids' rooms so bare.

Barry's models and football are all lined up, and Margaret dusts them. No problem telling the boys from the girls in our family. Barry's room is red and navy, and Steff's is all blue and purply, soft-like, with ruffles and a dressing table she designed herself. Now that she's at school, we don't trip on clothes all over the place. And I keep reminding myself we ought to yank out the Princess phone she got when she turned thirteen. Light on the dial's burned out, anyway.

I wish she hadn't taken down the crewelwork she did her

freshman year. The flower baskets were a whole lot prettier than these "Suppose They Gave A War And Nobody Came" posters. But that's better than the picture of that bearded Che-guy. I put my foot down about that thing, I can tell you. Not in *my* house, I said.

I'm proud of our house: two-floor brick Tudor with white walls and gold carpet and a big ticking grandfather's clock in the hall. Classy taste, my wife has. Who'd have thought she'd look at someone like me?

Besides, dinner was pretty good. Some of that deli rye and that leftover steak...

As the light from the icebox slid across the wall phone it went off, almost like it had been alerted. I grabbed it before it could ring twice.

"Yeah?" I snapped the way I used to in Germany, and my gut froze. My son Barry's in Saigon. If anything goes wrong, they send a telegram. No. That was last war. Now they send a car. God forbid.

But Steff, my crazy daughter—every time the phone rings at night I'm scared. Maybe she's got herself arrested in one of her goddamn causes and I'm going to have to bail her out like I did in Chicago. Or it could be worse. Two years ago this month, some kids were in the wrong place at the wrong time up at Kent. Damn shame about them and the National Guard; it'll take us years to live it down. Hell of a thing to happen in Ohio.

I thought my kid was going to lose her mind about it. The schools shut down all over the place, all that tuition money pissed away, and God only knows what she got into.

Not just God. Margaret. Steff would call up, say "put Mom on," and Margaret would cry and turn into the phone so I couldn't hear what she was saying. I think she sent money on the sly-like, so I wouldn't make an issue of it. You don't send kids to college so they can get shot at. Steff would say you don't send anyone anywhere so they can get shot at. She's just a kid, you know. She doesn't really believe all that stuff. The kids shouldn't have been there. Anyone could tell you that.

"Hey, that you, Joey?" The voice on the other end was thick with booze. "It's Al. Remember me?"

"You son of a bitch, what're you doing calling this hour of night?" I started to bellow, then piped down, "You wanna wake up my whole damn family?"

"Thought you'd be up, Joey. Like we were...the time when..."

"Yeah...yeah..." Sure I remembered. Too well. So did Al, my old army buddy. It happens from time to time. One of us gets to remembering, gets the booze out—Scotch for me these days now that my practice is finally paying off—then picks up the phone. Margaret calls it "going visiting" and "telephonitis" and only gets mad at the end of the month when the bills come in.

But Al wasn't from my outfit at the Battle of the Bulge. Weren't many of them left. Not many had been real close friends to start with: when you run away from home and lie about your age so you can go fight, you're sort of out of place, soldier or not.

Damn near broke my own dad's heart; he'd wanted me to follow him into school and law school and partnership. So I did that on GI bills when I got out. Got married and then there was Korea. I went back in, and that's where I met Al.

"Remember? We'd run out of fuel for the tank and were burning grain alcohol...rather drink torpedo juice, wouldn't you? And pushing that thing south to the 38th parallel, scared shitless the North Koreans'd get us if the engine fused..."

"Yeah..." How far was Korea from Saigon? My son, the lance corporal had wangled himself a choice slot as Marine guard. I guess all Margaret's nagging about posture and manners had paid off. Almost the only time it had with the Bear. God, you know you'd shed blood so your kids don't turn out as big damn fools as you. I'd of sent Barry through school, any school. But he wanted the service. Not Army, either, but the Marines. Well, Paris Island did what I couldn't do, and now he was "yes sir"-ing a lot of fancypants like Ambassador Bunker over in Vietnam. At least he wasn't a chicken or a runaway...

"You there, Joey?" I was staring at the receiver. "I asked you, how's your family?"

"M'wife's fine," I said. How long had it been since Al and I spoke—three years? Five? "So're the kids. Barry's in the Marines. My son the corporal. Stationed in Saigon. The Embassy, no less." I could feel my chest puffing out even though I was tired and it was the middle of the night.

Car lights shone outside. I stiffened. What if...The lights passed. All's quiet on the Western Front. Thank God.

Al and the beer hooted approvingly.

"And Steffie's in college. Some damn radical Quaker place. I wanted her to stay in Ohio, be a nurse or a teacher, something practical in case, God forbid, she ever has to work, but my wife wanted her near her own people."

"She getting plenty of crazy ideas at that school?"

"Steff's a good kid, Al. Looks like a real lady now."

What do you expect me to say? That after a year of looking and acting like the big-shot debs my wife admires in the *New York Times*, my Steffie's decided to hate everything her dad fought for? Sometimes I think she's majoring in revolution. It wasn't enough she got arrested in 1968 campaigning for McCarthy—clean up for Gene, they called it. Clean? I never saw a scruffier bunch of kids till I saw the ones she's taken up with now. Long hair, dirty—and the language? Worse than an army barracks.

She's got another campaign now. This McGovern. I don't see what they have against President Nixon or what they see in this McGovern character. Senator from South Dakota, and I tell you, he's enough to make Mount Rushmore cry. I swear to God, the way these friends of Steff's love unearthing and spreading nasty stories—this Ellsberg character Steff admires, you'd think he was a hero instead of some nutcase who spilled his guts in a shrink's office, so help me. Or this My Lai business: things like that happen in war. You just don't talk about them. Still, what do you expect of a bunch of kids? We made it too easy.

I keep hoping. She's such a good girl, such a pretty girl; one of these days, she'll come around and say "Daddy, I was wrong. I'm sorry."

Never mind that.

Al had got onto the subject of *jo-sans*. Cripes, I hadn't even thought of some of them for twenty years, being an old married man and all. What if Margaret had walked in? I'd of been dead. Sure, I laughed over old times, but I was relieved when he switched to "who's doing what" and "who's died," and then onto current events. We played armchair general, and I tell you, if the Pentagon would listen to us, we'd win this turkey and have the boys home so damned fast...

About the time we'd agreed that this Kissinger was a slippery so-and-so and that bombing Haiphong was one of the best things we could have done, only we should have done it a whole lot earlier...hell of a way to fight a war, tying General Westmoreland's hands, I heard footsteps on the stairs.

"Do you have any idea what time it is?" Margaret asked me.

I gestured *he called me!* at the phone, feeling like a kid with his hand in the cookie jar. My wife laughed. "Going visiting, is he? Well, let his wife give him aspirin for the hangover I bet he's going to have. You have to go to the office tomorrow and…" she paused for emphasis like I was six years old, "you need your sleep."

She disappeared back up the stairs, sure that I'd follow.

"That was the wife," I told Al, my old good buddy. "Gotta go. Hey, don't wait five years to call again. And if you're ever in town, come on over for dinner!"

God, I hope she hadn't heard that stuff about the *jo-sans*. Or the dinner invitation. We'd eat cold shoulder and crow, that was for sure.

Fall of '72, we kept hearing stories. That Harvard guy that Kissinger was meeting with Le Duc Tho in Paris, and he was encouraged, but then they backed down: back and forth, back and forth till you were ready to scream. "Peace is at hand," he says, and they say it in Hanoi, too. I mean what's the good of it when the commies and your own leaders agree, and the army doesn't? No news out of Radio Hanoi can be any good. And the boys are still coming home in bags, dammit.

Meanwhile, as I hear from Margaret, Stephanie is doing well in her classes. The ones she attends in between campaigning for this McGovern. At first I thought he was just a nuisance candidate. You know, like Stassen runs each time? Then, when they unearthed that stuff about Eagleton, and they changed VP candidates, I thought he was dead in the water for sure. But Shriver's been a good choice: drawn in even more of the young, responsible folk and the people who respect what he did in the Peace Corps. But the real reason McGovern's moving way up in the polls is that more and more people get sick and tired of the war. We just don't believe we can win it, anymore. And that hurts.

I get letters from Barry, too. He's good at that. Writes each one of us. I think he's having a good time in Saigon. I hope he's careful. *You* know what I mean.

Barry says he's got a lot of respect for Ambassador Bunker. Says he was cool as any Marine during Tet, when the VC attacked the Embassy. Says the Ambassador's spoken to him a couple of times, asked him what he wants to do when he gets out of the service. Imagine: My boy, talking to a big shot like that.

And Margaret sent Stephanie a plane ticket home in time for the election. Sure, she could vote at school, but "my vote will make more of a difference in Ohio," she said to me. She was getting a fancy accent.

"You gonna cancel out my vote, baby?" I asked her.

"I sure am, Dad. D'you mind?"

"Hey, kid, what am I working for if it isn't for you and your mom? Sure, come on home and give your fascist old dad a run for his money."

That got kind of a watery laugh from her. We both remembered the time she went to Washington for that big march in '69. I hit the ceiling and Margaret talked me down. "She didn't have to tell us, Joe," she reminded me.

No, she didn't. But she had. Just in case something happened, she admitted that Thanksgiving when she came home from school.

I didn't like the idea of my girl near tear gas and cops with nightsticks when I wasn't around, so I pulled a few strings and sent her Congressman Kirwan's card. *Mike,* the Congressman says I should call him when he comes to the lawyers' table at the Ohio Hotel. And I wrote down on it the home phone number of Miss Messer, his assistant. If anything goes wrong, I told her, she should call there. And I drew a peace sign and signed the letter, "Love and peace, your fascist father."

She says I drew it upside down. Well, what do you expect? Never drew one before.

Anyhow, she'll be home for Election Day, and Barry'll

vote by absentee ballot. I'm proud that both my kids take voting seriously. Maybe that school of hers hasn't been a total waste: Steff still takes her responsibilities as a citizen very seriously.

Meanwhile, things—talking and fighting both—slowed down in Paris and Saigon. I remember after Kennedy won the election, Khrushchev wouldn't talk to President Eisenhower's people because Ike was a lame duck. As if he weren't one of the greatest generals we ever had. I tried to listen to some of the speeches by this McGovern Stephanie was wild for. Mostly, I thought he promised pie-in-the-sky. Our boys home by June, everyone working hard and off welfare—not that I'd mind, but I just didn't set how he was going to pull any of it off. I really wanted to ask Barry what he thought, but I didn't. Might be bad for morale.

Then things started to get worse. They stepped up the bombing. Tried to burn off the jungle, too. And the pictures ...Dammit, I wish I could forget the one of that little girl running down the road with no clothes on screaming in pain. Sometimes at night, it gets messed up in my mind with that thing from Kent, with the girl kneeling and crying over that boy's body. Damn things leap out at you from the newspaper or the news, but I can't just stick my head in the sand.

Maybe the kids...maybe this McGovern...I've *been* under attack, and I tell you, there comes a time when you just want it to *stop*. Never mind what it costs you. You've already paid enough. I think the whole country's reached that point, and so McGovern's moving way up in the polls.

Election Day started out really well. The day before, letters had come from Barry. One for me. One for his mother. And even one for Stephanie. I suppose she'd told him she was going to be home, and APO delivery to the Embassy in Saigon is pretty regular. We all sort of went off by ourselves to read our letters. Then Margaret and I traded. I hoped Stephanie would offer to show us hers, too, but she didn't. So we didn't push.

You don't push, not if you want your kids to trust you. Besides, my son and daughter have always had something special between them. He's a good foot taller than she is, but she always looked out for her "baby brother" in school. He never minded that she was the bright one, the leader. Not till he decided not to go to college, and he overheard one of the family saying that Stephanie should have been the boy. So our Bear joined up, not waiting for the draft or anything. I expected Stephanie to throw a fit—Margaret certainly did, but all my girl said was, "He needs to win at something of his own."

I wouldn't have expected her to understand what that means to a boy. Maybe she's growing up.

But it's still all I can do to keep a decent tongue in my head toward my brother-in-law with the big fat mouth.

Election Day, it's a family tradition that everyone comes over to watch the returns on TV. There were going to be some hot words over the cold cuts, if things ran true to speed. And I couldn't see Steff sitting in the kitchen putting things on trays and talking girl talk with her aunts. Steff calls that sort of thing sexist. That's a new word she's got. Don't see why it bothers her. It's not like sometimes the women aren't talking the most interesting things.

For a while, I really thought we were going to make it through the evening without a fight. Stephanie came in, all rosy-faced and glowing from voting, then marching outside the poll all day. She'd left her protest signs in the garage, and she was wearing one of the good skirts and coats she took to school. When everyone said so, she laughed and went up to change into a workshirt and jeans.

"But you looked so pretty, just like a real college girl," her aunt told her.

"That was just window dressing," Stephanie said. "Can I help set the food out now? I'm famished."

She'd wolfed down about half a corned beef sandwich when the phone rang, and she flew up the stairs. "You're kidding. Massachusetts *already*? Oh wow! How's it look for Pennsylvania? I'm telling you, I think we're going to be lucky here, but I'm worried about the South..."

"You want another beer, Ron?" I asked my brother-in-law, who was turning red, pretending like he had swallowed something the wrong way and would choke if he didn't drink real fast. Personally, I think he voted for Wallace in the last election, but you can't pry the truth out of him about that with a crowbar.

We settled down to watch TV. Margaret and my sister Nance turned on the portable in the kitchen. I kind of hoped Stephanie would go in there, but she helped clear the table, then came in and sat beside me.

You could have knocked me over with a feather. Maybe the kids were right and people were sick of the bombings, the deaths, the feeling that Vietnam was going to hang around our necks till we choked on it. But state after state went to McGovern..."There goes Ohio! Straight on!" Stephanie shouted, raising a fist.

I don't know when all hell broke loose. One moment we were sitting watching John Chancellor cut to President Nixon's headquarters (and my daughter was doing this routine, like a Chatty Cathy doll, about Tricia Nixon). The next moment, she'd jumped up and was stamping one foot as she glared at her uncle.

"How *dare* you use that word?" she was saying to Ron, my brother-in-law. "They're *not* gooks. They're *Asians*. And it's their country, not ours, but we're destroying it for them. We've turned the kids into fugitives, the women into bar girls

...and they all had fathers, too, till we killed them! What kind of a racist pig..."

"Who you calling a racist, little Miss Steff & Nonsense?" asked Ron. By then, he'd probably had at least two beers too many and way too many of my daughter's yells of "straight on." "Why, when I was in the war, there was this Nee-grow sergeant..."

"It's 'black'!" she snapped. "You call them *black*! How, can you expect me to stay in the same house as this..."

She was out of the living room, and the front door slammed behind her before I could stop her.

"That little girl of yours is out of control," Ron told me. "That's what you get, sending her off to that snob school. OSU wasn't good enough, oh no. So what happens? She meets a bunch of radicals there and picks up all sorts of crazy ideas. Tell you, Joey, you better put a leash on that kid, or she'll get into real trouble."

I got up, and he shut up. Margaret came in from the kitchen. I shook my head at her: *everything under control.* I wanted to get a jacket or something. Stephanie had run out without her coat, and the evening was chilly.

"I'd teach her a good lesson, that's what I'd do," said Ron.

Damn! Hadn't I warned her, "I know you think it's funny calling your uncle Ronnie the Racist. But one of these days, it's going to slip out, and then there'll be hell to pay." But she'd said what I should have said. And that made me ashamed.

"She shouldn't have been rude to you," I said. "I'm going to tell her that. But you know how she feels about words like that. I don't much like them either. Besides, this is her house, too."

Ron was grumbling behind my back like an approaching thunderstorm, when I went into the front hall, took out a jacket from the closet, and went outside. Steffie was on the stoop, her face pressed against the cold brick. I put the jacket over her and closed my hands on hers. They were trembling. "Don't rub your face against the brick, baby. You could cut yourself."

She turned around and hugged me. I could feel she was crying with anger and trying hard not to. "I'm not going in there and apologizing," she told me.

"Not even for me?" I coaxed her. There'd been a time she'd do anything in the world for her old dad.

She tried to laugh and cry together, and sounded like the way she used to gurgle when she was a baby.

"I'll promise not to start any fights," she said. "But I won't promise to keep quiet if…"

"I told him you shouldn't have been rude to an elder and a guest…"

She hissed like the teenager she wasn't. Not anymore.

"I also told him this was your house and you had right to have your wishes respected, too. Now, will you come in and behave like a lady?"

"It's *woman*, daddy," she told me.

I hugged her. "You know what I mean. Lady or woman, you're still my little girl. You're supposed to be for peace. Can you try to keep it in your own home?"

She looked up, respect in her eyes. "Ooh, that was a *nice* one," she told me.

"Then remember, tantrums don't win any arguments. Now, you go in. Maybe your mother needs help with the dishes."

"He ought to help," she muttered. "You do. It wouldn't hurt."

"No, it wouldn't." To my surprise, I agreed. "But if we wait for him to get off his butt, your mother's going to be stuck with all of them."

The gift of her obedience hit me in the face like a cold wind when you've had too much to drink. My eyes watered, and the lights up and down Outlook Avenue flickered. Everyone was watching the returns. Some of them had promised to drop in later. The Passells' younger boy had gone to school with Steff. He was the only boy on the street still in school, studying accounting. The Carlsons' middle son, who'd played varsity football, but always took time to coach our Bear, had left OSU and was in the Army. So was the oldest Bentfield, who'd been our paperboy. Fine young men, all of them. And the girls had turned out good, too, even Reenie, who'd got married too young.

Just a one-block street, but you had everything on it. Even a black family had moved in. Maybe I'd had my worries to start off with, but I was real proud we'd all greeted them like neighbors. On some streets when that happened, the kids dumped garbage on the lawn or TP'ed the house.

It was a nice street, a good block, and we'd all lived on it a long time. Nothing fancy, but solid. I wished my father could have seen my house. We'd come back since he'd lost everything in the Depression. But that's the way of it. Each generation does a little bit better than the last one and makes things a little easier for the ones next in line.

We've been five generations in Youngstown. I like to think our name counts for something. Now, this is sort of embarrassing. I don't go to church much, but I looked out over that street and *hoped*, that's a better word for it, that my kids would make that name even more respected. My daughter, the whatever-she-wanted-to-be. A lawyer, maybe. And my son. Who knew? Maybe he'd come home and go back to school, and then this Ambassador—I couldn't see my Bear as a diplomat, but...

"How many beers did *you* have?" I asked the sky, gave myself a mental shake, and went back in in time to watch

President Nixon's concession speech. It wasn't, not really. You remember how close the race was against JFK. And the 1962 California election when he told the press, "You won't have Nixon to kick around any more."

I don't know. Man's a fighter, but he's not a good loser. I tell you, I don't know what a recount's going to do to this country just when we need a strong leader in place.

"Country's going to hell in a handbasket," Ron grumbled. "I'm going home. Hey, Nancy? You going to yak all night? C'mon!"

After he left, my wife and daughter came back into the living room. Margaret brought out a pot of coffee.

Stephanie sat down to watch McGovern's victory speech. She was holding her mother's hand.

"I admit I am distressed at this demand for a recount at just the time when our country needs to be united. But I am confident that the count will only reaffirm the judgment of the great American people as the bombing has gone on, pounding our hearts as well as a captive nation, that it is enough!

"Now, I have heard it said," the man went on with shining eyes, "that I do not care for honor. Say, rather, that I earn my honor where it may be found. Not in throwing lives after lives away in a war we should never have entered, but in admitting that we have gone as far as we may, and that now it is time for our friends the South Vietnamese to take their role as an independent people, not a client state. Accordingly, my first act as Commander in Chief will be…" his voice broke, "to bring them home. Our sons and brothers. The young fathers and husbands of America. Home."

Tears were pouring down the women's faces. I walked over to Margaret. All the years we've been married, she's never been one to show affection in front of the kids. Now she leaned her head against me. "Our boy's coming home!"

Stephanie's face glowed like the pictures of kids holding candles in church or the big protest marches. She could have been at McGovern headquarters; that school of hers has enough pull to put her that high, but she'd chosen to come home instead.

I put a hand on her hair. It was almost as silky as it had been when she was in diapers. Again, my hand curved around her head. It was so warm, just like when she'd been little. "Baby, it looks like you and your friends have won. I just hope you're right."

Something woke me early that morning. Not the house. Margaret's regular breathing was as always, and I could sense the presence of Stephanie, a now-unfamiliar blessing. I went downstairs, ran some water in the sink, and washed off the serving dishes Margaret had set to soak overnight. Nice surprise for her when she got up.

Of course, I wasn't surprised when the phone rang.

"Hey, Al," I greeted him. Drunk again. "What's the hurry? It's only six months, not five years between calls this time."

"How d'you like it, Joe?" he demanded. "Those little bastards pulled it off. They don't want to go, so, by God, they stop the war. Can you believe it? Not like us, was it. I tell you, ol' buddy, we were suckers. Go where we were told, hup two three four, following orders like goddam fools, and these kids change the rules on us and get away with it."

Maybe it would be better. Margaret and Steff had held hands and cried for joy. I had to believe it was better, that I wasn't just bitching because other men's sons wouldn't have to go through what I had. I started to talk Al down like I had in Korea, but my heart wasn't in it.

The sky was gray. All the houses on Outlook were dark. Soon it would be dawn and the streetlights would go out, regular as an army camp.

But what were those lights going on? I levered up from my chair—damn, my bones were creaking—and peered out. Lights on at Bentfield's? And, oh my God, Johnny Bentfield...no. Oh no. *Not my son, thank God!* Dammit, what kind of a man was I to thank God like that? Sometimes I make myself want to puke.

"Al!" I broke into his ramblings. "I gotta hang up *now*. Something's going on on the street."

"Probably a bunch of stoned kids, celebrating the new age. Well, they're welcome to it. Let 'em come running to me when it blows up in their faces. I'll laugh."

"Yeah, Al. Sure. But I gotta go."

Moving more quietly than I had since Korea, I slipped upstairs and slid open drawers for undershorts, slacks, a sports shirt. Very cautiously, listening to see if they'd wake up, I dressed in the bathroom, then left the house, moving as cautiously as if I were scouting out my own neighborhood. I sneaked over to Bentfield's and peered in the window. At least they didn't have a dog. If what I feared was true, they'd have more on their minds than listening for prowlers. And if I were wrong, please God, if I were wrong, they were good enough friends I could always make up something.

But they were in robes in the living room. Alma Bentfield sat hunched over, hands over her face, while Stan came in, gray-faced, with coffee. The two little girls clutched each other, too sleepy to feel yet how badly they were going to hurt.

God *damn*! Just a little longer, and we'd have brought Johnny home safe. Someone must have called from Vietnam. Unauthorized. Don't ask me how.

I slipped out of their yard and back home.

"What's wrong?" Margaret's voice was sharp and came from outside Stephanie's room. She must have heard what she thought was a prowler, found me gone, and run to see if our daughter needed help.

"Better get dressed," I told her. "There's a light on at Bentfield's. I've had a crazy feeling. I went over and looked. It's about as bad as it can get."

My wife's face twisted, and she clenched her hands.

"I'll wake Steff, too," she said. "She's grown up enough to help out."

I went upstairs to change into a suit. It was almost time to get dressed for work anyhow. But long after I should have left, I sat in the kitchen drinking coffee. Margaret was cooking something. A casserole to take over, maybe. A knife fell into the metal sink. We both jumped and she spilled the milk she was pouring.

"Shit!"

In twenty-five years of marriage, I don't think I'd ever heard her cuss like that.

She mopped up, and I poured myself another cup. I sat staring at the birds and butterflies on the wallpaper mural she took such care of. Different from birds in Southeast Asia, that was for sure: nice tame birds and pale colors. They call it a green hell there.

"It's time to go," she reminded me. I picked up the phone to call my office and tell my secretary I wouldn't be in just yet.

"Hope you're feeling all right," Mary-Lynn wished me, almost laughing.

"I'm fine," I almost snapped. No point taking it out on her. She'd gone to high school with my kids. I remember how old I felt the day I interviewed her—and found out that her mother had been my secretary when I'd started out in practice.

"That's good." She was almost singing. Guess she was relieved too about how the vote had gone. Her husband—the first one was no damn good, but this guy seems to be treating her okay—would be coming home. Vet or no vet, he damn well better be good to her. She's a nice kid, and besides, big as he is, I'll beat the crap out of him.

I drank my coffee and looked out at the street till the olive-drab Army car I was expecting pulled up outside Bentfield's and the long-legged uniformed men strode up the neat walk to the front door. It opened, so reluctantly. All over the street, doors opened, and the women started coming out. Each one carried a covered bowl or baking dish.

Margaret kissed me on the cheek. Her lips were cold. Then she and Stephanie went out. My daughter carried the casserole. She had on her good clothes again and lipstick the color of bubble gum. It looked fake against her pale face, and I wanted to tell her to wipe it off, but I didn't. Her legs, under the short, dark skirt, looked like a little girl's, heading into the doctor's office to get a shot. It was Johnny Bentfield who'd gotten shot.

My womenfolk went to Bentfield's and the door shut behind them.

All down the street, cars pulled out of the driveways like we were escaping.

When I got home that night, Steffie was in her jeans again, sitting in the living room.

"You shouldn't sit in the dark." I switched on some lights.

"Mom's upstairs with a headache. Took two Fiorinal." Margaret never took more than one.

I headed for the liquor cabinet and pulled out the Scotch.

"I'll do that," said my daughter. She mixed me a double the way I like them. To my surprise, she poured a stiff one for herself.

"I don't know, kitten," I began.

"I'm legal," she said flatly. "And I was there. You weren't. God!" She sat down too fast and lifted her glass. But she knows better than to belt down good Scotch.

"You did the right thing," I praised her. She'd done a

good job, the sort of thing nice women like the ones on our street do without even thinking about it.

She wrapped her arms about her shoulders and hunched in. In her jeans and workshirt, she looked like a veteran of some army I'd never seen before. A vet who'd lost a buddy.

Finally, she looked up. The big brown eyes under their floppy bangs held my attention. "They brought her a flag. It was for John, they said. She didn't want to take it, but they put it in her hands. Her knees caved in, but she had to take the flag. We all sat around her. All day. Even after the soldiers left. They had other houses to visit. God *damn*!"

"Don't swear, baby. It's not nice."

"Wasn't nice to be there. Or to have to be there. What if…"

"Don't think about it!"

What kind of a father was I, leaving her alone like that? But I couldn't help it. I got up and went outside to check the garage door. Saw a neighbor.

"You hear about Bentfield?" he asked. Carefully, he bent and broke a dead branch off the hedge that divides our property.

I nodded. "My daughter's pretty shook up."

"It's worse than that. Stan told me, and I'm not telling the family. It wasn't VC that got his boy. 'Friendly fire,' they call it. He was stationed in front of the regular troops and, well, someone screwed up."

That's what happens when you cut and run. You get stuck facing something even worse. I had to go in and face Steffie like nothing had happened. She wasn't crying, at least, but she'd turned the lights off again.

"You want dinner? Mom said to heat stuff up."

I shook my head.

"Me neither."

"Let's not tell her we skipped dinner. She'd get mad."

We sat in the dark for a long time. After a while, the house got chilly, and it was time to go to bed.

Well, Nixon had his recount. It was close. Even closer than when he'd lost against Kennedy. I don't know, if I'd have thought he'd be such a bad loser, maybe I wouldn't have voted for him the first time. And the grins on the faces of those guys who look like Ho Chi Minh's grandsons at the UN made me want to wipe them out with my fist.

"It's face, y'know," Al said. After all these years, he'd finally made it to Youngstown on a business trip. Some of us got together at his Holiday Inn. These days, Al sells steel pipe. Frankly, I think he drinks through them—the gut he's got on him now! "Now that we're pulling out, they don't respect us. Not that they ever did, all that much. Talk, about yellow... I know who's yellow, those little yellow..."

"Al." Father Klein picked his beer bottle out of his hand. "You've had enough. We've all had enough."

Al lurched onto his feet, his face red. Peanuts scattered across the table. I swept them back into the bowl. Didn't think Al would take on Father Klein. He was wearing his collar, for one thing. For another, he'd always been able to punch out anyone in our outfit.

"I wanted us to win," Al said. The fight drained out of him. "You know what happens when you retreat. Remember what we'd have got if they'd caught us in Korea? Tiger cages and bamboo under our fingernails. This isn't going to be a retreat. It's a goddamned rout. Who's holding the fort while everyone's pulling out? You mark my words, it's going to be a bloodbath."

"It's okay, Al," Father Klein said. "Joey and I'll walk you back to your room and you can stick your head in the john."

Pro-war or peacenik, we all went sort of crazy that spring. The atlas from our *Britannica* fell open at the mark of

Southeast Asia as I showed Margaret just where our men were pulling back from.

"It's so green. Can't they just jump out?" Our dining room is white and gold: formal, Margaret calls it. If she likes it, fine, I'm happy. It seemed weird to be talking about weapons and jungles as we sat at a table covered by a cloth, eating off real silver.

"McGovern won't let us burn off the jungle. It's a no-no. Like DDT. Damn! It's all tunnels underneath. The VC can pop out of a tunnel, strike from behind, then disappear. Or hide in a village. You can't tell VC from rice farmers. And there's no good aerial cover."

"I don't want to talk about this at dinner," she said, and closed the atlas. She didn't ever want to talk about it. Well, she wasn't a vet. God forbid we ever use our women like that, though those nurses...you've really got to hand it to them. They've got guts. Day after day, nurses flew out with their patients. The big, silent planes flew out too, with the flags and the coffins. But the news wasn't showing them much anymore.

McGovern called it peace with honor. Withdrawal with honor, someone had tried to call it at a press conference; the reporters had cracked up. They'd had to fade to black real fast. Besides, you couldn't say that around the kids. McGovern still had them in the palm of his hand. They had a lot of influence, and they wanted our boys out. McGovern always had a bunch of them following him around, as interns or admirers or something. They were beginning to look a little frantic.

It was Father Klein who called it the long defeat. We were fighting to lose. It reminded me of something. Once I had to help the Bear with his history homework, and I read this thing about a Children's Crusade. They wanted to do what their elders couldn't—free the Holy Land, miracles, that sort of thing. So they left home and went on Crusade. And none of 'em ever made it back.

Every time the phone rang, I dreaded it. Sometimes it was Steff. She'd turned expert, like all the kids. We talked over the withdrawal, and she said the exotic names in tones I hadn't heard for years. Sometimes it was relief operations. Everyone wanted a check. Once it was Steff's school—some lady from development assuring us that no, the school wasn't planning to close down as it had in 1970 so everyone could go do relief work. Oddly enough, I don't think I'd have minded if it had. Let the college kids do their share. But while she had me on the phone, could she possibly convince me to donate...

Yeah, sure.

Al never called. After a while that sort of worried me, I picked up the phone one evening at a decent hour and called him. Got his Mrs. and the cold shoulder, too, till I explained. Al was resting, she said. He'd been working too hard lately. No, he couldn't come to the phone.

Drying out, I thought. Not all the casualties of a war happen in combat.

Used to be, letters from the Bear were a surprise—a treat to top off a good deal or a reward to make up for a lousy one. Now, I started calling home about the time the mail usually came. "Any news?" I'd ask. Usually, there wasn't. If there was, Margaret would read Bear's letters to me. Steffie said he was still writing her, but she didn't offer.

Don't know when he had time. He said he was helping out when he was off-duty in one of the orphanages. Run by French nuns. Didn't know he'd learned some French, too. Maybe he wouldn't mind if his dad stuck his nose into his business when he came back and suggested going to college on a GI bill. There *had* to be a GI bill or something, didn't there? I mean, we owe those boys a lot.

Well, he always had been good with kids. He sent us one

snapshot. There he was, all spit and polish, with these cute little round-faced kids with their bright eyes crawling all over him, scuffing up those patent shoes.

At least he got to keep clean and dry. I remembered how your feet felt like they'd rot off if you couldn't get them out of those stinking boots. In the jungle, you get mold on everything, it's so damp. I didn't like it when the Bear would complain that he had it soft, compared to most of the men. I was scared he'd try to transfer out. But I guess someone talked to him, and he thought of what he owed to his mom and sister, because after a while, he didn't talk about that anymore.

And meanwhile, those goddamn VC were getting closer to Saigon. The whole fucking—sorry, I never swear like that, must be thinking back to my army days—country was falling apart. Hated to admit it, but Al was right. As long as we came on like Curtis LeMay and threatened, at least, to bomb 'em back to the Stone Age, they'd at least respected what we could do to them if we really set our minds to it. Now, "paper tiger" was the kindest name they had for us.

President McGovern began to look haunted. He'd be a one-term president, that was for sure. And when he came down with cardiac arrhythmia, some of us wondered if he'd even manage that. The kids who surrounded his staff looked pretty grim, too. Like the kids who get caught stealing cars and suddenly realize that things are not going to be much fun anymore.

The anchormen on the evening news sounded like preachers at a funeral. I'm not making this up; it happened at Da Nang. You saw a plane ready for takeoff. Three hundred people crowded in, trampling on women and children, they were so panicky. Then the crew wanted to close the doors and get out of there, but the people wouldn't get off the runway, clear the stairs. They pulled some off the wheels and took off anyway. And you could see little black specks as people fell off where they'd hung on to the rear stairway.

Did McGovern say anything? Sure. "We must put the past behind us. Tragic as these days are, they are the final throes of a war we never should have entered. In the hard days to come, I call upon the American people to emulate the discipline and courage of our fine servicemen who are withdrawing in good order from Vietnam."

I'd of spat, but Margaret was watching the news with me. We couldn't *not* watch. Funny, neither of us had ever liked horror films, but we had to watch the news.

Some people waded into the sea, the mothers holding their babies over their heads. They overloaded fishing boats, and the Navy found them floating. Or maybe the boats hadn't overloaded. Those people mostly hadn't much, but it wouldn't have been hard to take what they had, hit them on the head, and throw them overboard.

Refugees were flooding Saigon. The Bear's French orphanage was mobbed, and the grounds of all the embassies were full. Would the VC respect the embassies? How could they? Human life means nothing to them, or else they wouldn't treat their own people the way they do. And Cambodia's even worse, no matter what Steffie's poli-sci profs say.

In a letter I didn't show my wife, Barry told me he could hear the cluster bombs drop. The North Viets were at Xuanloc, thirty-five miles northwest of Saigon, on the way to Bien Hoa airfield, heading south, always heading south.

"If our allies had fought as well as they did at Xuanloc, maybe we wouldn't be in this fix, Dad," Barry wrote me. "It doesn't look good. Don't tell Mom. But the Navy's got ships standing offshore in the Gulf of Thailand and a fleet of choppers to fly us out to them. I hope..."

I crumpled the letter in my hand. Later, I smoothed it out

and made myself read it, though. My son was out in that green hell, and I was scared to read his letter? That wasn't how I'd want to greet him when the choppers finally brought him out. He'd be one of the last to leave, I knew that. Probably pushing the ambassador ahead of him.

I wrote I was proud of him. I didn't say the half of what I meant. I don't know if he got the letter.

Then one morning Mary-Lynn met me at the door of my office, and she'd been crying.

She wouldn't let me inside. "Mrs. Black called. You have to go home, she says. Right away. Oh, Mr. Black, I'm so sorry!" She wiped at her nose. I was in shock. I pulled my handkerchief from my suit jacket and handed it to her.

She put her hands out as if I was going to pass out. "There's a...there's a *car* out there..."

"Not..." I couldn't say the word. It would make it real. My boy. Never coming home? I couldn't make myself believe it.

"They've got a car there and Marines—oh, your wife says please, please come straight home..."

The spring sun hit my shoulders like something I'd never felt before. What right did the sun have to shine here? The trees in Crandall Park were fresh and green, and the gardens at the big corner house where they always spent a mint on flowers looked like something out of the first day of the world. How did they dare? My boy had been shot. Other men's sons had been shot in a green hell they should have burnt down to ash.

A voice broke in on the radio.

"...the American Embassy has closed its gates, and the Ambassador...Ambassador Bunker has refused evacuation..."

He'd have been there, my son. Firing into the enemy, not wanting to fire, I knew that, but there'd be a wall of Marines between the VC and the panicked crowd and the diplomats they had sworn to protect....

I had people to protect too. I put my foot hard on the gas, peeled round a slowpoke station wagon with three kids and their mom in it, and roared up Fifth Avenue.

"...We interrupt this program...there is a rumor that Ambassador Bunker has been shot....We repeat, this is a rumor, no one has seen his body..."

Sweet suffering Christ! Damn that red light, no one was around, so it wouldn't matter if I crashed it. Didn't want to smear myself all over the landscape before I got home; Margaret would never forgive me if I got myself killed coming home to her now, of all times.

*God*damn siren! I thought of giving the cop a run for his money, but you don't do that in Youngstown. Not ever, and especially not if you're a lawyer.

The man who got out of the car recognized me. "Hey, Counselor, what you think you're doing? You were going seventy and you crashed that light..." He sniffed at my breath, then pulled out his pad. "You know better than that. Now I wish I could let you off with a warning..."

A fist was squeezing my throat. Finally, it let up long enough for me to breathe. "It's my boy..." I said. Then I laid my head down on the steering wheel.

A hand came in over my shoulder and took the keys. "I'm driving you home. The way you're driving, you could get yourself...Come on, Counselor."

I made him let me off up the street. No telling what Margaret would have thought if she'd seen a cop car roll up to the door. The Marine car was in the drive. The men get out of the car and followed me. I made it up the front walk, feeling like I was walking off a three-day binge. Toni Carlson opened the door. She was crying, but Margaret wasn't. Sure enough, the living room and kitchen were full of women with their covered dishes.

"I called Steffie's school," Margaret said before I could even get to her. She had Barry's service photo out like they do in the newspapers. His face grinned under his hat. God, he was a good-looking boy. "Her plane gets in this afternoon."

"I'm going to pick her up," said a voice from behind me.

"Sir," began one of the Marines. A fine young man. I had...I have...a son like him.

He shook my hand and bravely said the things they're supposed to say. "Sir, the President of the United States and the Secretary of Defense have asked me to inform you that your son..." The boy's voice faltered, and he went on in his own words.

Missing. Presumed dead. My son was...is...a hero. But presumed dead. After Ambassador Bunker died (that wasn't supposed to get out yet, but he supposed I had a right to know), the surviving Marines were supposed to withdraw. But Barry gave his seat to a local woman and a child.

"Probably knew them from the orphanage," I muttered.

"No doubt, sir," said the Marine. It wasn't his business to comment. He'd be glad to get out, even if he had more families' hearts to break that day. Lord, I wished I could.

At least he didn't have a damn flag. As long as you don't get the flag, you can still hope.

Her school sent Steffie home, the way these schools do when there's been a death in the family. Pinkos they may be, but I've got to admit each of her professors and the college president wrote us nice letters. Take as much time as you need before coming back to class, they told Steff. Better than she got from some of her friends. Once or twice, when she thought I wasn't looking, I saw her throw out letters. And I heard her shouting on the phone at someone, then hang up with a bang. All she ever said was, "You never know who's really your friend."

I thought she'd do better to stick out the term, but she decided to take the semester off. Seeing how Margaret brightened at that news, I didn't insist she go back. And when my wife threw a major fit and screamed, "I can't bear to lose *both* the men in our family!" at the dinner table and practically *ordered* me to get an EKG, I kept the appointment with our doctor that she'd made.

Oddly enough, now that the worst had happened, I slept like a baby right through the next time the phone rang at 3:00 A.M.

Steffie came into our room. She spoke to Margaret. "It's from Frankfurt. West Germany."

Why would she be getting a call from West Germany of all places?

Margaret got up and threw on a robe. "It's in, then?"

My daughter nodded. I stared at both women. Beyond family resemblance, their faces wore the same expression: guilt, fear, and a weird kind of anticipation under the sorrow that had put circles under their eyes.

Like the damn fool husbands on TV, I waited for my womenfolk to explain what was going on. It didn't much matter. After all, when your country's lost a war and a son, what else can happen?

"We have to Talk," Margaret said in *that* tone of voice. "I'll make us some coffee."

So at three in the morning, we sat down to a family conference. Margaret poured coffee. To my surprise, she looked imploringly at Steffie.

"The call from Frankfurt came through on my line," she said.

That stupid Princess phone!

"That's where they evacuate the refugees and process them."

My hand closed on the spoon till it hurt. How did that rate a transatlantic phone call?

Stephanie took a deep, deep breath and drew herself up. For a moment, I thought I could see her brother, making up his mind at the Embassy to give up his place to a woman and a child.

Our eyes met. She'd been thinking of Barry too.

"You know that woman and kid Barry pushed onto the helicopter in his place?"

"The ones he knew from the orphanage?"

"Where'd you get that idea?" Margaret broke in.

"Mom, he *did* meet Nguyen at the orphanage."

"Now wait a damn minute, both of you. Maybe it's too early, but no one's making sense!"

Margaret set down her coffee cup. "Joe, please listen."

"Dad, about a year ago, Barry wrote me. He'd met a girl who worked at the French Embassy. She's from Saigon and her name is Nguyen."

I held up a hand. I wanted to be stupid. I wanted to be Ward Cleaver and have this episode end. Margaret would switch off the TV set, the show would be over, we could all go back to bed, and none of this, *none* of the whole past miserable year would have happened.

So my boy had sacrificed himself for a friend....

"She's his *wife,* Daddy. And the child..."

When you're on the front lines and you get hit bad, it doesn't hurt at first. You go into shock.

"You knew about this?" I asked Margaret. She looked down, ashamed.

"And didn't tell me?" Both women looked down.

"My son *married*—how do we know it's true?—he says he *married* this goddamn gook! Her people *killed* him, and you have the nerve to say..."

"If you say that word, I'll never speak to you again!" Stephanie was on her feet, her big flannel nightgown billowing in flowers and hearts about her. "Nguyen's not a bar girl. Barry said she's a lady. She worked at the French Embassy. She speaks French and Vietnamese...some English."

"They seem to have communicated just fine without it!" I snapped, hating myself.

They'd hidden this from me! Barry had written to Stephanie, and all those calls when she'd said, "I need to talk to Mom," they were talking about this unknown girl. This gook girl. Who my son had planned to bring home. I could just see Ronnie the Racist's face.

They'd hidden this from me.

"Oh Mom, I'm making such a mess of this!" Steffie cried. "I didn't really believe he'd take it like this..."

"Give him some time, darling," said my wife. "We were caught by surprise, too."

"*You* give him some time," my daughter burst into tears. "The only grandkid he may ever have, and all he can think of is to ask, 'Are they really married?' and call the mother a gook and a bar girl! I haven't got time for this! I have to pack and go to Washington to meet Nguyen, and then I have to go..."

I reached up and grasped my daughter's wrist.

"Just where do you think you're going?"

That little bit of a thing faced me down. "I'm joining the Red Cross relief effort." She laughed, shakily. "I wish I'd listened to you and become a nurse after all. It's a hell of a lot more useful than a poli-sci major for what I need to do. We're going over there."

"That hellhole's already swallowed one of my kids!"

"That's right. So I'm going over there to look for him."

I shook my head at her. Just one small girl in the middle of a war zone. What did she think she could do?

"Daddy, you know I've *always* looked after my brother. No matter how big he got. Except with this...this mess about the war. I did what I thought was right, and see how it worked out." She wiped at her eyes.

"Somehow, I have to make up for that. All of us do. So I'm going to look for him. And if I...when I find him...so help me, I am going to beat the crap out of him for scaring us this way!" She was sobbing noisily now, and when I held out my arms, she flung herself into them.

"Oh Daddy, I was wrong, it all went wrong and it got so fucked up!"

"Don't use words like that," I whispered, kissing my girl's hair. "Not in front of your mother."

"It's all right," said Margaret. "I feel the same way."

"Unless I find him, Nguyen and the little boy are all we've got of Barry. And we're all *they've* got. But all you can do is call them bad words and...and..."

I patted her back and met my wife's eyes. She nodded, and I knew we'd be having guests in the house. No, scratch that. We'd be having new family members come to live here. And if my sister's husband even *thought* of opening his big fat mouth, I'd shut it for him the way I'd wanted to for the past thirty years.

Stephanie pulled out of my arms and pushed her bangs out of her eyes. I sighed and picked my words. If I said things wrong, I was scared I'd lose her.

"We've been in this town for five generations," I began slowly. "I think our family has enough of a reputation so people will welcome...what did you say her name was?"

"Nguyen," Margaret whispered. Her eyes were very bright. "I'll brush up on my French." She used to teach it before we got married. "And the little boy—our grandson—is Barry, Jr. I can't imagine how that sounds in a Vietnamese accent, can you?"

A tiny woman in those floaty things Vietnamese women wore. A little lady. My son's wife...or widow. And one of those cute little black-eyed kids, unless he looked like Bear. Family. Just let anyone *dare* say anything.

"We can put them in Barry's room," I stammered. "I suppose."

"Nguyen can have mine," said Steffie. "I won't need it. Oh, Daddy, I was wrong about so many things. But I was right about you after all."

She kissed me, then ran upstairs, a whirlwind in a flowered nightgown. I could hear closets and drawers protesting and paper ripping.

"I wish she'd been right about all of them," I told Margaret. She took my hand.

"I'm going with Stephanie to pick up...Nguyen," my wife informed me.

It would get easier, I sensed, for both of us to think of her and the boy as family once we met them. My son's wife. My son's son. This wasn't how I'd thought that would be.

In a few minutes, once the shock wore off, I supposed I'd get to see the pictures. I knew there had to be pictures. But you don't live with a woman for this many years without knowing when she has more to say. And having a pretty good idea of what it is—most of the time.

This time, though, my guess was right. "Joe, I want you to come with us to Washington so we can all meet as a family. Nguyen must be terrified. She's lost everything and, and everyone."

Her voice trembled, but she forced it to calm. "It would mean a lot to her. Steff says the Vietnamese are Confucian. If the head of our family were there to greet her, she'd *know* she was welcome, she and the little one."

A smile flickered across her face. "I wonder where we can get a crib," she mused. "All our friends' children are grown and haven't started having babies yet. We'll be the first to have a grandchild."

I bent over and hugged her. "Did you make a third plane reservation?"

She smiled at me. "What do you think?"

"I'll carry your suitcase downstairs for you, baby," I told my daughter.

"Oh, Dad, you know I'll have to lug my own stuff once I go overseas..."

"As long as you're in *my house,* young lady—"

"It's on my bed." I went into her room to get it. She'd taken a cheap plaid fabric thing, not one of the good, big Samsonite cases she'd gotten for high school graduation. Her room wasn't just clean: it was sterile. She'd even torn down her posters and hung the crewelwork back up. I wondered what this strange new daughter-in-law of mine would make of the pretty blue and lilac room.

My foot sent something spinning and rolling. I bent to retrieve the thing, which promptly jagged my finger. One of Stephanie's protest buttons, hurled away as if in despair, poor girl. "Suppose they gave a war and nobody came?" it asked.

Suppose they did? It had never happened yet.

Suppose, instead, they gave a peace? That hadn't worked, either.

But I can always hope, can't I?

After all, I have a grandson to look out for.

Larry Niven

All the Myriad Ways

There were timelines branching and branching, a mega-universe of universes, millions more every minute. Billions? Trillions? Trimble didn't understand the theory, though God knows he'd tried. The universe split every time someone made a decision. Split, so that every decision ever made could go both ways. Every choice made by every man, woman and child on Earth was reversed in the universe next door. It was enough to confuse any citizen, let alone Detective-Lieutenant Gene Trimble, who had other problems.

Senseless suicides, senseless crimes. A city-wide epidemic. It had hit other cities too. Trimble suspected that it was worldwide, that other nations were simply keeping it quiet.

Trimble's sad eyes focused on the clock. Quitting time. He stood up to go home, and slowly sat down again. For he had his teeth in the problem, and he couldn't let go.

Not that he was really accomplishing anything.

But if he left now, he'd only have to take it up again tomorrow.

Go, or stay?

And the branchings began again. Gene Trimble thought of other universes parallel to this one, and a parallel Gene Trimble in each one. Some had left early. Many had left on time, and were now halfway home to dinner, out to a movie, watching a strip show, racing to the scene of another death. Streaming out of police headquarters in all their multitudes, leaving a multitude of Trimbles behind them. Each of these trying to deal, alone, with the city's endless, inexplicable parade of suicides.

Gene Trimble spread the morning paper on his desk. From the bottom drawer he took his gun-cleaning equipment, then his .45. He began to take the gun apart.

The gun was old but serviceable. He'd never fired it except on the target range, and never expected to. To Trimble, cleaning his gun was like knitting, a way to keep his hands busy while his mind wandered off. Turn the screws, don't lose them. Lay the parts out in order.

Through the closed door to his office came the sounds of men hurrying. Another emergency? The department couldn't handle it all. Too many suicides, too many casual murders, not enough men.

Gun oil. Oiled rag. Wipe each part. Put it back in place.

Why would a man like Ambrose Harmon go off a building?

In the early morning light he lay, more a stain than a man, thirty-six stories below the edge of his own penthouse roof. The pavement was splattered red for yards around him. The stairs were still wet. Harmon had landed on his face. He wore a bright silk dressing gown and a sleeping jacket with a sash.

Others would take samples of his blood, to learn if he had acted under the influence of alcohol or drugs. There was little to be learned from seeing him in his present condition.

"But why was he up so early?" Trimble wondered. For the call had come in at 8:03, just as Trimble arrived at headquarters.

"So late, you mean." Bentley had beaten him to the scene by twenty minutes. "We called some of his friends. He was at an all-night poker game. Broke up around six o'clock."

"Did Harmon lose?"

"Nope. He won almost five hundred bucks."

"That fits," Trimble said in disgust. "No suicide note?"

"Maybe they've found one. Shall we go up and see?"

"We won't find a note," Trimble predicted.

Even three months earlier Trimble would have thought, *How incredible!* or, *Who could have pushed him?* Now, riding up in the elevator, he thought only, *Reporters.* For Ambrose Harmon was news. Even among this past year's epidemic suicides, Ambrose Harmon's death would stand out like Lyndon Johnson in a lineup.

He was a prominent member of the community, a man of dead and wealthy grandparents. Perhaps the huge inheritance, four years ago, had gone to his head. He had invested tremendous sums to back harebrained, quixotic causes.

Now, because one of the harebrained causes had paid off, he was richer than ever. The Crosstime Corporation already held a score of patents on inventions imported from alternate time tracks. Already those inventions had started more than one industrial revolution. And Harmon was the money behind Crosstime. He would have been the world's next billionaire—had he not walked off his balcony.

They found a roomy, luxuriously furnished apartment in good order, and a bed turned down for the night. The only sign of disorder was the clothing—slacks, sweater, a silk turtleneck shirt, knee-length shoesocks, no underwear—piled on a chair in the bedroom. The toothbrush had been used.

He got ready for bed, Trimble thought. He brushed his teeth, and then he went out to look at the sunrise. A man who kept late hours like that, he wouldn't see the sunrise very often. He watched the sunrise, and when it was over he jumped.

Why?

They were all like that. Easy, spontaneous decisions. The victim/killers walked off bridges or stepped from their balconies or suddenly flung themselves in front of subway trains. They strolled halfway across a freeway, or swallowed a full bottle of laudanum. None of the methods showed previous planning. Whatever was used, the victim had had it all along; he never actually went out and *bought* a suicide weapon. The victim rarely dressed for the occasion, or used makeup, as an ordinary suicide would. Usually there was no note.

Harmon fit the pattern perfectly.

"Like Richard Cory," said Bentley.

"Who?"

"Richard Cory, the man who had everything. 'And Richard Cory, one calm summer night, went home and put a bullet through his head.' You know what I think?"

"If you've got an idea, let's have it."

"The suicides all started about a month after Crosstime got started. I think one of the Crosstime ships brought back a new bug from some alternate timeline."

"A suicide bug?"

Bentley nodded.

"You're out of your mind."

"I don't think so. Gene, do you know how many Crosstime pilots have killed themselves in the last year? More than twenty percent!"

"Oh?"

"Look at the records. Crosstime has about twenty vehicles in action now, but in the past year they've employed sixty-two pilots. Three disappeared. Fifteen are dead, and all but two died by suicide."

"I didn't know that." Trimble was shaken.

"It was bound to happen sometime. Look at the alternate worlds they've found so far. The Nazi world. The Red

Chinese world, half bombed to death. The ones that are so totally bombed, that Crosstime can't even find out who did it. The one with the Black Plague mutation, and no penicillin until Crosstime came along. Sooner or later—"

"Maybe, maybe. I don't buy your bug, though. If the suicides are a new kind of plague, what about the other crimes?"

"Same bug."

"Uh uh. But I think we'll check up on Crosstime."

Trimble's hands finished with the gun and laid it on the desk. He was hardly aware of it. Somewhere in the back of his mind was a prodding sensation: the *handle,* the piece he needed to solve the puzzle.

He'd spent most of the day studying Crosstime, Inc. News stories, official handouts, personal interviews. The incredible suicide rate among Crosstime pilots could not be coincidence. He wondered why nobody had noticed it before.

It was slow going. With Crosstime travel, as with relativity, you had to throw away reason and use only logic. Trimble had sweated it out. Even the day's murders had not distracted him.

They were typical, of a piece with the preceding eight months' crime wave. A man had shot his foreman with a gun bought an hour earlier, then strolled off toward police headquarters. A woman had moved through the back row of a dark theater, using an ice pick to stab members of the audience through the backs of their seats. She had chosen only young men. They had killed without heat, without concealment; they had surrendered without fear or bravado. Perhaps it was another kind of suicide.

Time for coffee, Trimble thought, responding unconsciously to dry throat plus a muzziness in the mouth plus slight fatigue. He set his hands to stand up, and—

The image came to him of an endless row of Trimbles, lined up like the repeated images in facing mirrors. But each image was slightly different. He would go get the coffee *and* he wouldn't *and* he would send somebody for it *and* someone was about to bring it without being asked. Some of the images were drinking coffee, a few had tea or milk, some were smoking, some were leaning too far back with their feet on the desks (and a handful of these were toppling helplessly backward), some were, like this present Trimble, introspecting with their elbows on the desk.

Damn Crosstime anyway.

He'd have had to check Harmon's business affairs, even without the Crosstime link. There might have been a motive there, for suicide or for murder, though it had never been likely.

In the first place, Harmon had cared nothing for money. The Crosstime group had been one of many. At the time that project had looked as harebrained as the rest: a handful of engineers and physicists and philosophers determined to prove that the theory of alternate time tracks was reality.

In the second place, Harmon had no business worries.

Quite the contrary.

Eleven months ago an experimental vehicle had touched one of the worlds of the Confederate States of America, and returned. The universes of alternate choice were within reach. And the pilot had brought back an artifact.

From that point on, Crosstime travel had more than financed itself. The Confederate world's "stapler," granted an immediate patent, had bought two more ships. A dozen miracles had originated in a single, technologically advanced timeline, one in which the catastrophic Cuba War had been no more than a wet firecracker. Lasers, oxygen-hydrogen rocket motors, computers, strange plastics—the list was still growing. And Crosstime held all the patents.

In those first months the vehicles had gone off practically at random. Now the pinpointing was better. Vehicles could select any branch they preferred. Imperial Russia, Amerindian America, the Catholic Empire, the dead worlds. Some of the dead worlds were hells of radioactive dust and intact but deadly artifacts. From these worlds Crosstime pilots brought strange and beautiful works of art which had to be stored behind leaded glass.

The latest vehicles could reach worlds so like this one that it took a week of research to find the difference. In theory they could get even closer. There was a phenomenon called "the broadening of the bands."...

And that had given Trimble the shivers.

When a vehicle left its own present, a signal went on in the hangar, a signal unique to that ship. When the pilot wanted to return, he simply cruised across the appropriate band of probabilities until he found the signal. The signal marked his own unique present.

Only it didn't. The pilot always returned to find a clump of signals, a broadened band. The longer he stayed away, the broader was the signal band. His own world had continued to divide after his departure, in a constant stream of decisions being made both ways.

Usually it didn't matter. Any signal the pilot chose represented the world he had left. And since the pilot himself had a choice, he naturally returned to them all. But—

There was a pilot by the name of Gary Wilcox. He had been using his vehicle for experiments, to see how close he could get to his own timeline and still leave it. Once, last month, he had returned twice.

Two Gary Wilcoxes, two vehicles. The vehicles had been wrecked: their hulls intersected. For the Wilcoxes it could have been sticky, for Wilcox had a wife and family. But one of the duplicates had chosen to die almost immediately.

Trimble had tried to call the other Gary Wilcox. He was too late. Wilcox had gone skydiving a week ago. He'd neglected to open his parachute.

Small wonder, thought Trimble. At least Wilcox had had motive. It was bad enough, knowing about the other Trimbles, the ones who had gone home, the ones drinking coffee, et cetera. But—suppose someone walked into the office right now, and it was Gene Trimble?

It could happen.

Convinced as he was that Crosstime was involved in the suicides, Trimble (some other Trimble) might easily have decided to take a trip in a Crosstime vehicle. A short trip. He could land *here*.

Trimble closed his eyes and rubbed at the corners with his fingertips. In some other timeline, very close, someone had thought to bring him coffee. Too bad this wasn't it.

It didn't do to think too much about these alternate timelines. There were too many of them. The close ones could drive you buggy, but the ones further off were just as bad.

Take the Cuba War. Atomics had been used, *here*, and now Cuba was uninhabited, and some American cities were gone, and some Russian. It could have been worse.

Why wasn't it? How did we luck out? Intelligent statesmen? Faulty bombs? A humane reluctance to kill indiscriminately?

No. There was no luck anywhere. Every decision was made both ways. For every wise choice you bled your heart out over, you made all the other choices too. And so it went, all through history.

Civil wars unfought on some worlds were won by either side on others. Elsewhen, another animal had first done murder with an antelope femur. Some worlds were still all nomad; civilization had lost out. If every choice was cancelled elsewhere, why make a decision at all?

Trimble opened his eyes and saw the gun.

That gun, too, was endlessly repeated on endless desks. Some of the images were dirty with years of neglect. Some smelled of gunpowder, fired recently, a few at living targets. Some were loaded. All were as real as this one.

A number of these were about to go off by accident.

A proportion of these were pointed, in deadly coincidence, at Gene Trimble.

See the endless rows of Gene Trimble, each at his desk. Some are bleeding and cursing as men run into the room following the sound of the gunshot. Many are already dead.

Was there a bullet in there? Nonsense.

He looked away. The gun was empty.

Trimble loaded it. At the base of his mind he felt the touch of the *handle*. He would find what he was seeking.

He put the gun back on his desk, pointing away from him, and he thought of Ambrose Harmon, coming home from a late night. Ambrose Harmon, who had won five hundred dollars at poker. Ambrose Harmon, exhausted, seeing the lightening sky as he prepared for bed. Going out to watch the dawn.

Ambrose Harmon, watching the slow dawn, remembering a two-thousand-dollar pot. He'd bluffed. In some other branching of time, he had lost.

Thinking that in some other branching of time that two thousand dollars included his last dime. It was certainly possible. If Crosstime hadn't paid off, he might have gone through the remains of his fortune in the past four years. He liked to gamble.

Watching the dawn, thinking of all the Ambrose Harmons on that roof. Some were penniless this night, and they had not come out to watch the dawn.

Well, why not? If he stepped over the edge, here and now, another Ambrose Harmon would only laugh and go inside.

If he laughed and went inside, other Ambrose Harmons would fall to their deaths. Some were already on their ways down. One changed his mind too late, another laughed as he fell....

Well, why not?...

Trimble thought of another man, a nonentity, passing a firearms store. Branching of timelines, he thinks, looking in, and he thinks of the man who took his foreman's job. Well, why not?...

Trimble thought of a lonely woman making herself a drink at three in the afternoon. She thinks of myriads of alter egos, with husbands, lovers, children, friends. Unbearable, to think that all the might-have-beens were as real as herself. As real as this ice pick in her hand. Well, why not?...

And she goes out to a movie, but she takes the ice pick.

And the honest citizen with a carefully submerged urge to commit rape, just once. Reading his newspaper at breakfast, and there's another story from Crosstime: they've found a world line in which Kennedy the First was assassinated. Strolling down a street, he thinks of world lines and infinite branchings, of alter egos already dead, or jailed, or President. A girl in a miniskirt passes, and she has nice legs. Well, why not?...

Casual murder, casual suicide, casual crime. Why not? If alternate universes are a reality, then cause and effect are an illusion. The law of averages is a fraud. You can do anything, and one of you will, or did.

Gene Trimble looked at the clean and loaded gun on his desk. Well, why not?...

And he ran out of the office shouting, "Bentley, listen, I've got the answer..."

And he stood up slowly and left the office shaking his

head. This was the answer, and it wasn't any good. The suicides, murders, casual crimes would continue....

And he suddenly laughed and stood up. Ridiculous! Nobody dies for a philosophical point!...

And he reached for the intercom and told the man who answered to bring him a sandwich and some coffee....

And picked the gun off the newspapers, looked at it for a long moment, then dropped it in the drawer. His hands began to shake. On a world line very close to this one...

And he picked the gun off the newspapers, put it to his head

and

fired. The hammer fell on an empty chamber.

fired. The gun jerked up and blasted a hole in the ceiling.

fired.

The bullet tore a furrow in his scalp.

took off the top of his head.

Pamela Sargent

The Sleeping Serpent

1

Yesuntai Noyan arrived in Yeke Geren in early winter, stumbling from his ship with the unsteady gait and the pallor of a man who had recently crossed the ocean. Because Yesuntai was a son of our Khan, our commander Michel Bahadur welcomed the young prince with speeches and feasts. Words of gratitude for our hospitality fell from Yesuntai's lips during these ceremonies, but his restless gaze betrayed his impatience. His mother, I had heard, was Frankish, and he had a Frank's height, but his sharp-boned face, dark slits of eyes, and sturdy frame were a Mongol's.

At the last of the feasts, Michel Bahadur seated me next to the Khan's son, an honor I had not expected. The commander, I supposed, had told Yesuntai a little about me, and would expect me to divert the young man with tales of my earlier life in the northern woods. As the men around us sang and shouted to servants for more wine, Yesuntai leaned toward me.

"I hear," he murmured, "that I can learn much from you, Jirandai Bahadur. Michel tells me that no man knows this land better than you."

"I am flattered by such praise." I made the sign of the cross over my wine, as I had grown used to doing in Yeke Geren. Yesuntai dipped his fingers into his cup, then sprin-

177

kled a blessing to the spirits. Apparently he followed our old faith, and not the cross; I found myself thinking a little more highly of him.

"I am also told," Yesuntai went on, "that you can tell many tales of a northern people called the Hiroquois."

"That is only the name our Franks use for all the nations of the Long House." I gulped down more wine. "Once, I saw my knowledge of that people as something that might guide us in our dealings with them. Now it is only fodder on which men seeking a night's entertainment feed."

The Noyan lifted his brows. "I will not ask you to share your stories with me here."

I nodded, relieved. "Perhaps we might hunt together sometime, Noyan. Two peregrines I have trained need testing, and you might enjoy a day with them."

He smiled. "Tomorrow," he said, "and preferably by ourselves, Bahadur. There is much I wish to ask you."

Yesuntai was soon speaking more freely with the other men, and even joined them in their songs. Michel would be pleased that I had lifted the Noyan's spirits, but by then I cared little for what that Bahadur thought. I drank and thought of other feasts shared inside long houses with my brothers in the northern forests.

Yesuntai came to my dwelling before dawn. I had expected an entourage, despite his words about hunting by ourselves, but the Khan's son was alone. He gulped down the broth my wife Elgigetei offered, clearly impatient to ride out from the settlement.

We saddled our horses quickly. The sky was almost as gray as the slate-colored wings of the falcons we carried on our wrists, but the clouds told me that snow would not fall before dusk. I could forget Yeke Geren and the life I had chosen for one day, until the shadows of evening fell.

We rode east, skirting the horses grazing in the land our settlers had cleared, then moved north. A small bird was flying toward a grove of trees; Yesuntai loosed his falcon. The peregrine soared, a streak against the gray sky, her dark wings scimitars, then suddenly plummeted toward her prey. The Noyan laughed as her yellow talons caught the bird.

Yesuntai galloped after the peregrine. I spied a rabbit darting across the frost-covered ground, and slipped the tether from my falcon; he streaked toward his game. I followed, pondering what I knew about Yesuntai. He had grown up in the ordus and great cities of our Frankish Khanate, been tutored by the learned men of Paris, and would have passed the rest of his time in drinking, dicing, card playing, and claiming those women who struck his fancy. His father, Sukegei Khan, numbered two grandsons of Genghis Khan among his ancestors, but I did not expect Yesuntai to show the vigor of those great forefathers. He was the Khan's son by one of his minor wives, and I had seen such men before in Yeke Geren, minor sons of Ejens or generals who came to this new land for loot and glory, but who settled for hunting along the great river to the north, trading with the nearer tribes, and occasionally raiding an Inglistani farm. Yesuntai would be no different; so I thought then.

He was intent on his sport that day. By afternoon, the carcasses of several birds and rabbits hung from our saddles. He had said little to me, and was silent as we tethered our birds, but I had felt him watching me. Perhaps he would ask me to guide him and some of his men on a hunt beyond this small island, before the worst of the winter weather came. The people living in the regions nearby would not trouble hunters. Our treaty with the Ganeagaono, the Eastern Gatekeepers of the Long House, protected us, and they had long since subdued the tribes to the south of their lands.

We trotted south. Some of the men watching the horse herds

were squatting around fires near their shelters of tree branches and hides. They greeted us as we passed, and congratulated us on our game. In the distance, the rounded bark houses of Yeke Geren were visible in the evening light, wooden bowls crowned by plumes of smoke rising from their roofs.

The Great Camp—the first of our people who had come to this land had given Yeke Geren its name. "We will build a great camp," Cheren Noyan had said when he stepped from his ship, and now circles of round wooden houses covered the southern part of the island the Long House people called Ganono, while our horses had pasturage in the north. Our dwellings were much like those of the Manhatan people who had lived here, who had greeted our ships, fed us, sheltered us, and then lost their island to us.

Yesuntai reined in his horse as we neared Yeke Geren; he seemed reluctant to return to the Great Camp. "This has been the most pleasant day I have passed here," he said.

"I have also enjoyed myself, Noyan." My horse halted at his side. "You would of course find better hunting away from this island. Perhaps—"

"I did not come here only to hunt, Bahadur. I have another purpose in mind. When I told Michel Bahadur of what I wish to do, he said that you were the man to advise me." He paused. "My father the Khan grows even more displeased with his enemies the Inglistanis. He fears that, weak as they are, they may grow stronger here. His spies in Inglistan tell him that more of them intend to cross the water and settle here."

I glanced at him. All of the Inglistani settlements, except for the port they called Plymouth, sat along the coast north of the long island that lay to the east of Yeke Geren. A few small towns, and some outlying farms—I could not see why our Khan would be so concerned with them. It was unfortunate that they were there, but our raids on their westernmost

farms had kept them from encroaching on our territory, and
if they tried to settle farther north, they would have to
contend with the native peoples there.

"If more come," I said, "then more of the wretches will
die during the winter. They would not have survived this
long without the aid of the tribes around them." Some of
those people had paid dearly for aiding the settlers, succumb-
ing to the pestilences the Inglistanis had brought with them.

"They will come with more soldiers and muskets. They
will pollute this land with their presence. The Khan my
father will conquer their wretched island, and the people of
Eire will aid us to rid themselves of the Inglistani yoke. My
father's victory will be tarnished if too many of the island
dogs find refuge here. They must be rooted out."

"So you wish to be rid of the Inglistani settlements." I
fingered the tether hanging from my falcon. "We do not have
the men for such a task."

"We do not," he admitted, "but the peoples of these lands
do."

He interested me. Perhaps there was some iron in his soul
after all. "Only the Hodenosaunee, the Long House nations,
can help you," I said, "and I do not know if they will. The
Inglistanis pose no threat to the power of the Long House."

"Michel told me we have a treaty with that people."

"We have an agreement with the Ganeagaono, who are
one of their five nations. Once the Long House People
fought among themselves, until their great chiefs Degana-
wida and Hayawatha united them. They are powerful
enough now to ignore the Inglistanis."

Yesuntai gazed at the bird that clutched his gauntleted
wrist. "What if they believed the Inglistanis might move
against them?"

"They might act," I replied. "The Hodenosaunee have no
treaties with that people. But they might think they have

something to gain from the Inglistani presence. We have never given firearms to the people here, but the Inglistanis do so when they think it's to their advantage. By making war on the Inglistani settlements, you might only drive them into an alliance with the Long House and its subject tribes, one that might threaten us."

"We must strike hard and exterminate the lot," Yesuntai muttered. "Then we must make certain that no more of the wretches ever set foot on these shores."

"You will need the Long House People to do it."

"I must do it, one way or another. The Khan my father has made his will known. I have his orders, marked with his seal. He will take Inglistan, and we will destroy its outposts here. There can be no peace with those who have not submitted to us—the Yasa commands it. Inglistan has not submitted, so it will be forced to bow."

I was thinking that Sukegei Khan worried too much over that pack of island-dwellers. Surely Hispania, even with a brother Khan ruling there, was more of a threat to him than Inglistan. I had heard many tales of the splendor of Suleiman Khan's court, of slaves and gold that streamed to Granada and Córdoba from the continent to our south, of lands taken by the Hispanic Khan's conquistadors. The Hispanians were as fervent in spreading their faith as in seizing loot. In little more than sixty years, it was said that as many mosques stood in the Aztec capital of Tenochtitlan as in Córdoba itself. Suleiman Khan, with African kings as vassals and conquests in this new world, dreamed of being the greatest of the European Khans. How easy it had been for him to allow us settlements in the north while he claimed the richer lands to the south.

But I was a Bahadur of Yeke Geren, who knew only what others told me of Europe. My Khanate was a land I barely remembered, and our ancient Mongol homeland no more than a setting for legends and tales told by travelers. The Ejens of the Altan Uruk, the descendants of Genghis Khan, still sent their tribute to Karakorum, but the bonds of our Yasa, the laws the greatest of men had given us, rested more lightly on their shoulders. They might bow to the Kha-Khan of our homeland, but many of the Khans ruled lands greater than his. A time might come when the Khans of the west would break their remaining ties to the east.

"Europe!" I cleared my throat. "Sometimes I wonder what our Khans will do when all their enemies are vanquished."

Yesuntai shook his head. "I will say this—my ancestor Genghis Khan would have wondered at what we are now. I have known Noyans who go no farther to hunt than the parks around their dwellings, and others who prefer brocades and perfumed lace to a sheepskin coat and felt boots. Europe has weakened us. Some think as I do, that we should become what we were, but there is little chance of that there."

Snow was sifting from the sky. I urged my horse on; Yesuntai kept near me.

By the time we reached my circle of houses, the falling snow had become a curtain veiling all but the nearest dwellings from our sight. Courtesy required that I offer Yesuntai a meal, and a place to sleep if the snow continued to fall. He accepted my hospitality readily; I suspected there was more he wanted to ask me.

We halted at the dwelling next to mine. Except for a horse-drawn wagon carrying a wine merchant's barrels, the winding roads were empty. I shouted to my servants; two boys hurried outside to take the peregrines and our game from us. A shadowy form stirred near the dwelling. I squinted, then recognized one of my Manhatan servants. He lay in the snow, his hands around a bottle.

Anger welled inside me. I told one of the boys to get the Manhatan to his house, then went after the wagon. The driver slowed to a stop as I reached him. I seized his collar and dragged him from his seat.

He cursed as he sprawled in the snow. "I warned you before," I said. "You are not to bring your wine here."

He struggled to his feet, clutching his hat. "To your Manhatans, Bahadur—that's what you said. I was passing by, and thought others among your households might have need of some refreshment. Is it my fault if your natives entreat me for—"

I raised my whip. "You had one warning," I said. "This is the last I shall give you."

"You have no reason—"

"Come back to my circle, Gérard, and I'll take this whip to you. If you are fortunate enough to survive that beating—"

"You cannot stop their cravings, Bahadur." He glared up at me with his pale eyes. "You cannot keep them from seeking me out elsewhere."

"I will not make it easier for them to poison themselves." I flourished the whip; he backed away from me. "Leave."

He waded through the snow to his wagon. I rode back to my dwelling. Yesuntai had tied his horse to a post; he was silent as I unsaddled my mount.

I led him inside. Elgigetei greeted us; she was alone, and my wife's glazed eyes and slurred speech told me that she had been drinking. Yesuntai and I sat on a bench in the back of the house, just beyond the hearth fire. Elgigetei brought us wine and fish soup. I waited for her to take food for herself and to join us, but she settled on the floor near our son's cradle to work at a hide. Her mother had been a Manhatan woman, and Elgigetei's brown face and thick black braids had reminded me of Dasiyu, the wife I had left among the Ganeagaono. I had thought her beautiful once, but Elgigetei had the weaknesses of the Manhatan people, the laziness, the craving for drink that had wasted so many of them. She scraped at her hide listlessly, then leaned over Ajiragha's cradle to murmur to our son in the Manhatan tongue. I had never bothered to learn the language. It was useless to master the speech of a people who would soon not exist.

"You are welcome to stay here tonight," I said to the Noyan.

"I am grateful for this snowstorm," he murmured. "It will give us more time to talk. I have much to ask you still about the Hiroquois." He leaned back against the wall. "In Khanbalik, there are scholars in the Khitan Khan's court who believe that the forefathers of the people in these lands came here long ago from the regions north of Khitai, perhaps even from our ancestral grounds. These scholars claim that once a land bridge far to the north linked this land to Sibir. So I was told by travelers who spoke to those learned men."

"It is an intriguing notion, Noyan."

"If such people carry the seed of our ancestors, there may be greatness in them."

I sipped my wine. "But of course there can be no people as great as we Mongols."

"Greatness may slip from our grasp. Koko Mongke Tengri meant for us to rule the world, yet we may lose the strength to hold it."

I made a sign as he invoked the name of our ancient God, then bowed my head. Yesuntai lifted his brows. "I thought you were a Christian."

"I was baptized," I said. "I have prayed in other ways since then. The Long House People call God Hawenneyu, the Great Spirit, but He is Tengri by another name. It matters not how a man prays."

"That is true, but many who follow the cross or the crescent believe otherwise." Yesuntai sighed. "Long ago, my ancestor Genghis Khan thought of making the world our pasturage, but then learned that he could not rule it without mastering the ways of the lands he had won. Now those ways are mastering us." He gazed at me with his restless dark eye. "When we have slaughtered the Inglistanis here, more of our people will come to settle these lands. In time, we may have to subdue those we call our friends. More will be claimed here for our Khanate and, if all goes well, my father's sons and grandsons will have more of the wealth this land offers. Our priests will come, itching to spread the word of Christ among the natives, and traders will bargain for what we do not take outright. Do you find this a pleasing prospect?"

"I must serve my Khan," I replied. His eyes narrowed, and I sensed that he say my true thoughts. There were still times when I dreamed of abandoning what I had here and vanishing into the northern forests.

He said, "An ocean lies between us and Europe. It may become easier for those who are here to forget the Khanate."

"Perhaps."

"I am told," Yesuntai said then, "that you lived for some time among the Long House People."

My throat tightened. "I dwelled with the Ganeagaono, the Owners of the Flint. Perhaps Michel Bahadur told you the story."

"Only that you lived among them."

"It is a long tale, but I will try to make it shorter. My father and I came to these shores soon after we found this island—we were in one of the ships that followed the first expedition. Cheren Noyan had secured Yeke Geren by then. I was nine when we arrived, my father's youngest son. We came alone, without my mother or his second wife—he was hoping to return to Calais a richer man." I recalled little of that journey, only that the sight of the vast white-capped sea terrified me whenever I was well enough to go up on deck to help the men watch for Inglistani pirates. Perhaps Yesuntai had also trembled at being adrift on that watery plain, but I did not wish to speak of my fear to him.

"A year after we got here," I went on, "Cheren Noyan sent an expedition upriver. Hendrick, one of our Dutch sailors, captained the ship. He was to map the river and see how far it ran, whether it might offer us a passageway west. My father was ordered to join the expedition, and brought me along. I was grateful for the chance to be with the men."

Yesuntai nodded. "As any boy would be."

"We went north until we came to the region the Ganeagaono call Skanechtade—Beyond the Openings—and anchored there. We knew that the Flint People were fierce warriors. The people to the south of their lands lived in terror of them, and have given them the name of Mohawk, the Eaters of Men's Flesh, but we had been told the Owners of the Flint would welcome strangers who came to them in peace. Hendrick thought it was wise to secure a treaty with them before going farther, and having an agreement with the Ganeagaono would also give us a bond with the other four nations of the Long House."

I swallowed more wine. Yesuntai was still, but his eyes kept searching me. He would want to know what sort of man I was before entrusting himself to me, but I still knew little about him. I felt somehow that he wanted more than allies in a campaign against the Inglistanis, but pushed that notion aside.

"Some of us," I said, "rowed to shore in our longboats. A few Ganeagaono warriors had spied us, and we made ourselves understood with hand gestures. They took us to their village. Everyone there greeted us warmly, and opened their houses to us. All might have gone well, but after we ate their food, our men offered them wine. We should have known better, after seeing what strong drink could do to the Manhatan. The Flint People have no head for wine, and our men would have done well to stay sober."

I stared at the earthen floor and was silent for a time. "I am not certain how it happened," I continued at last, "but our meeting ended in violence. A few of our men died with tomahawks in their heads. Most of the others fled to the boats. You may call them cowards for that, but to see a man of the Flint People in the throes of drunkenness would terrify the bravest of soldiers. They were wild—the wine is poison to them. They were not like the Manhatan, who grow sleepy and calmly trade even their own children for strong drink."

"Go on," Yesuntai said.

"My father and I were among those who did not escape. The Ganeagaono had lost men during the brawl, and now saw us as enemies. They began their tortures. They assailed my father and his comrades with fire and whips—they cut pieces of flesh from them, dining on them while their captives still lived, and tore the nails from their hands with hot pincers. My father bore his torment bravely, but the others did not behave as Mongols should, and their deaths were not glorious." I closed my eyes for a moment, remembering the sound of their shrieks when the children had thrown burning coals on their staked bodies. I had not known then whom I hated more, the men for losing their courage or the children for their cruelty.

"I am sorry to hear it," Yesuntai said.

"Only my father and I were left alive. They forced us to run through the village while rows of people struck at us with whips and heavy sticks. The men went at us first, then the women, and after them the children. I did not understand then that they were honoring us by doing this. My father's wounds robbed him of life, but I survived the beatings, and it was then that the Ganeagaono made me one of them. I was taken to a house, given to a woman who admired the courage my father had shown during the torture, and was made a member of their Deer Clan. My foster mother gave me the name of Senadondo."

"And after that?" he asked.

"Another ship came upriver not long after. We expected a war party, but Cheren Noyan was wise enough to send envoys out from the ship to seek peace. Because I knew the Ganeagaono tongue by then, I was useful as an interpreter. The envoys begged forgiveness, saying that their men were to blame for violating the hospitality of the Flint People, so all went well. In the years to follow, I often dealt with the traders who came to us offering cloth and iron for furs and beaver pelts—they did not make the mistake of bringing wine again. After a time, I saw that I might be of more use to both my own people and my adoptive brothers if I returned to Yeke Geren. The Ganeagaono said farewell to me and sent me back with many gifts."

Speaking of the past made me long for the northern woods, for the spirits that sang in the mountain pines, for the sight of long houses and fields of corn, for Dasiyu, who had refused to come with me or to let our son depart with me. The boy belonged to her Wolf Clan, not to mine; his destiny was linked to hers. It had always been that way among the Long House People. I had promised to return, and she had called my promise a lie. Her last words to me were a curse.

"I might almost think," Yesuntai said, "that you wish you were among those people now."

"Is that so strange, Noyan?"

"They killed your father, and brought you much suffering."

"We brought that fate upon ourselves. If my father's spirit had not flown from him, they would have let him live, and honored him as one of their own. I lost everything I knew, but from the time the Ganeagaono adopted me, they treated me only with kindness and respect. Do you understand?"

"I think I do. The children of many who fought against us now serve us. Yet you chose to return here, Jirandai."

"We had a treaty. The Flint People do not forget their treaties—they are marked with the strings of beads they call wampum, which their wise men always have in their keeping." Even as I spoke, I wondered if, in the end, my exile would prove useless.

How full of pride and hope I had been, thinking that my efforts would preserve the peace between this outpost of the Khanate and the people I had come to love. I would be, so I believed, the voice of the Ganeagaono in the Mongol councils. But my voice was often ignored, and I had finally seen what lay behind Cheren Noyan's offer of peace. A treaty would give his men time to learn more about the Long house, and any weaknesses that could later be exploited. Eventually, more soldiers would come to wrest more of these lands from the natives. Our Khan's minions might eventually settle the lands to the north, and make the Long House People as wretched as the Manhatans.

"I came back," I continued, "so that our Noyans and Bahadurs would remember the promises recorded on the belts we exchanged with the Owners of the Flint. We swore peace, and I am the pledge of that peace, for the Ganeagaono promised that they would be bound to us in friendship for as long as I remained both their brother and the Khan's servant. That promise lives here." I struck my chest. "But some of our people are not so mindful of our promises."

Yesuntai nodded. "It is the European influence, Bahadur. Our ancestors kept the oaths they swore, and despised liars, but the Europeans twist words and often call lies the truth." He took a breath. "I will speak freely to you, Jirandai

Bahadur. I have not come here only to rid this land of Inglistanis. Europe is filled with people who bow to the Khans and yet dream of escaping our yoke. I would hate to see them slip from their bonds on these shores. Destroying the Inglistani settlements will show others that they will find no refuge here."

"I can agree with such a mission," I said.

"And your forest brothers will be rid of a potential enemy."

"Yes."

"Will you lead me to them? Will you speak my words to them and ask them to join us in this war?"

"You may command me to do so, Noyan," I said.

He shifted his weight on the bench. "I would rather have your assent. I have always found that those who freely offer me their oaths serve me better than those pressed into service, and I imagine you have your own reasons for wishing to go north."

"I shall go with you, and willingly. You will need other men, Noyan. Some in Yeke Geren have lost their discipline and might not do well in the northern forests. They wallow in the few pleasures this place offers, and mutter that their Khan has forgotten them."

"Then I will leave it to you to find good men who lust for battle. I can trust those whom I brought with me."

I took out my pipe, tapped tobacco into it from my pouch, lit it, and held it out to Yesuntai. "Will you smoke a pipe with me? We should mark our coming expedition with some ceremony."

He accepted the pipe, drew in some smoke, then choked and gasped for air before composing himself. Outside, I heard a man, a sailor perhaps, and drunk from the sound of him, call out to another man in Frankish. What purpose could a man find here, waiting for yet another ship to arrive with news from the Khanate and baubles to trade with the natives for the pelts, birds, animals, and plants the Khan's court craved? I was not the only man who thought of deserting Yeke Geren.

"I look forward to our journey," Yesuntai said, "and to seeing what lies beyond this encampment." He smiled as he passed the pipe to me.

That spring, with forty of Yesuntai's soldiers and twenty more men I had chosen, we sailed upriver.

2

The Ganeagaono of Skanechtade welcomed us with food. They crowded around us as we went from house to house, never leaving us alone even when we went to relieve ourselves. Several men of my Deer Clan came to meet me, urging more of the game and dried fish their women had prepared upon me and my comrades. By the time we finished our feast, more people had arrived from the outlying houses of the village to listen to our words.

Yesuntai left it to me to urge the war we wanted. After I was empty of eloquence, we waited in the long house set aside for our men. If the men of Skanechtade chose the warpath, they would gather war parties and send runners to the other villages of the Ganeagaono to persuade more warriors to join us.

I had spoken the truth to the people of Skanechtade. Deceit was not possible with the Ganeagaono, and especially not for me. I was still their brother, even after all the years I thought of as my exile. The Ganeagaono would know I could not lie to them; this war would serve them as well as us. Whoever was not at peace with them was their enemy. In that, they were much like us. A people who might threaten their domain as well as ours would be banished from the shores of this land.

Yet my doubts had grown, not about our mission, but of what might come afterward. More of our people would cross the ocean, and the Bahadurs who followed us to Yeke Geren might dream of subduing the nations we now called our friends. There could be no peace with those who did not submit to us in the end, and I did not believe the Ganeagaono and the other nations of the Long House would ever swear an oath to our Khan.

I had dwelled on such thoughts as we sailed north, following the great river that led to Skanechtade. By the time we rowed away from the ship in our longboats, I had made my decision. I would do what I could to aid Yesuntai, but whatever the outcome of our mission, I would not return to Yeke Geren. My place was with the Ganeagaono, who had granted me my life.

"Jirandai," Yesuntai Noyan said softly. He sat in the back of the long house, his back against the wall, his face hidden in shadows; I had thought he was asleep. "What do you think they will do?"

"A few of the young chiefs want to join us. That I saw when I finished my speech." Some of our men glanced toward me; most were sleeping on the benches that lined the walls. "We will have a few bands, at least."

"A few bands are useless to me," Yesuntai muttered. "A raid would only provoke our enemies. I must have enough men to destroy them."

"I have done what I can," I replied. "We can only hope my words have moved them."

Among the Ganeagaono, those who wanted war had to convince others to follow them. The sachems who ruled their councils had no power to lead in war; I had explained that to Yesuntai. It was up to the chiefs and other warriors seeking glory to assemble war parties, but a sign that a sachem favored our enterprise might persuade many to join us. I had watched the sachems during my speech; my son was among them. His dark eyes had not betrayed any of his thoughts.

"I saw how you spoke, Jirandai," Yesuntai said, "and felt the power in your words, even if I did not understand them. I do not believe we will fail."

"May it be so, Noyan." I thought then of the time I had traveled west with my adoptive father along the great trail that runs to the lands of the Nundawaono. There, among the Western Gatekeepers of the Long House nations, I had first heard the tale of the great serpent brought down by the thunderbolts of Heno, spirit of storms and rain. In his death throes, the serpent had torn the land asunder and created the mighty falls into which the rapids of the Neahga River flowed. My foster father had doubts about the story's ending, although he did not say so to our hosts. He had stood on a cliff near the falls and seen a rainbow arching above the tumultuous waters; he had heard the steady sound of the torrent and felt the force of the wind that never died. He believed that the serpent was not dead, but only sleeping, and might rise to ravage the land again.

Something in Yesuntai made me think of that serpent. When he was still, his eyes darted restlessly, and when he slept, his body was tense, ready to rouse itself at the slightest disturbance. Something was coiled inside him, sleeping but ready to wake.

Voices murmured beyond the doorway to my right. Some of the Ganeagaono were still outside. A young man in a deerskin kilt and beaded belt entered, then gestured at me.

"You," he said, "he who is called Senadondo." I lifted my head at the sound of the name his people had given to me. "I ask you to come with me," he continued in his own tongue.

I got to my feet and turned to Yesuntai. "It seems someone wishes to speak to me."

He waved a hand. "Then you must go."

"Perhaps some of the men want to hear more of our plans."

"Or perhaps a family you left behind wishes to welcome you home."

I narrowed my eyes as I left. The Noyan had heard nothing from me about my wife and son, but he knew I had returned to Yeke Geren as a man. He might have guessed I had left a woman here.

The man who had come for me led me past clusters of houses. Although it was nearly midnight, with only a sliver of moon to light our way, people were still awake; I heard them murmuring beyond the open doors. A band of children trailed us. Whenever I slowed, they crowded around me to touch my long coat or to pull at my silk tunic.

We halted in front of a long house large enough for three families. The sign of the Wolf Clan was painted on the door. The man motioned to me to go inside, then led the children away.

At first, I thought the house was empty, then heard a whisper near the back. Three banked fires glowed in the central space between the house's bark partitions. I called out a greeting; as I passed the last partition, I turned to my right and saw who was waiting for me.

My son wore his headdress, a woven cap from which a single large eagle feather jutted from a cluster of smaller feathers. Braided bands with beads adorned his bare arms; rattles hung from his belt. My wife wore a deerskin cloak over a dress decorated with beads. Even in the shadows beyond the fire, I saw the strands of silver in her dark hair.

"Dasiyu," I whispered, then turned to my son. "Teyendanaga."

He shook his head slightly. "You forget—I am the sachem Sohaewahah now." He gestured at one of the blankets that covered the floor; I sat down.

"I hoped you would come back," Dasiyu said. "I wished for it, yet prayed that you would not."

"Mother," our son murmured. She pushed a bowl of hommony toward me, then sat back on her heels.

"I wanted to come to you right away," I said. "I did not know if you were here. When the men of my own clan greeted me, I feared what they might say if I asked about you, so kept silent. I searched the crowd for you when I was speaking."

"I was there," Dasiyu said, "sitting behind the sachems among the women. Your eyes are failing you."

I suspected that she had concealed herself behind others. "I thought you might have another husband by now."

"I have never divorced you." Her face was much the same, only lightly marked with lines. I thought of how I must look to her, leather-faced and broader in the belly, softened by the years in Yeke Geren. "I have never placed the few belongings you left with me outside my door. You are still my husband, Senadondo, but it is Sohaewahah who asked you to come to this house, not I."

My son held up his hand. "I knew you would return to us, my father. I saw it in my vision. It is of that vision that I wish to speak now."

That a vision might have come to him, I did not doubt. Many spirits lived in these lands, and the Ganeagaono, as do all wise men, trust their dreams. But evil spirits can deceive men, and even the wise can fail to understand what the spirits tell them.

"I would hear of your vision," I said.

"Two summers past, not long after I became Sohaewahah, I fell ill with a fever. My body fought it, but even after it passed, I could not rise from my bed. It was then, after the fever was gone, that I had my vision and knew it to be truth." He gazed directly at me, his eyes steady. "Beyond my doorway, I saw a great light, and then three men entered my dwelling. One carried a branch, another a red tomahawk, and the third bore the shorter bow and the firestick that are your people's weapons. The man holding the branch spoke, and I knew that Hawenneyu was speaking to me through him. He told me of a storm gathering in the east, over the Ojikhadagega, the great ocean your people crossed, and said that it threatened all the nations of the Long House. He told me that some of those who might offer us peace would bring only the peace of death. Yet his words did not frighten me, for he went on to say that my father would return to me, and bring a brother to my side."

He glanced at his mother, then looked back at me. "My father and the brother he brought to me," he continued, "would help us stand against the coming storm—this was the Great Spirit's promise. When my vision passed, I was able to rise. I left my house and went through the village, telling everyone of what I had been shown. Now you are here, and the people remember what my vision foretold, and yet I see no brother."

"You have a brother," I said, thinking of Ajiragha. "I left him in Yeke Geren."

"But he is not here at my side, as my vision promised."

"He is only an infant, and the Inglistanis are the storm that threatens you. More of them will cross the Great Salt Water."

"A war against them would cost us many men. We might trade with them, as we do with you. Peace is what we have always desired—war is only our way to prove our courage and to bring that peace about. You should know that, having been one of us."

"The Inglistanis will make false promises, and when more of them come, even the Long House may fall before their soldiers. You have no treaties with the Inglistanis, so you are in a state of war with them now. Two of the spirits who came to you bore weapons—the Great Spirit means for you to make war."

"But against whom?" Dasiyu asked. She leaned forward and shook her fist. "Perhaps those who are on your island of Ganono are the storm that will come upon us, after we are weakened by battle with the pale-faced people you hate."

"Foolish woman," I muttered, "I am one of you. Would I come here to betray you?" Despite my words, she reminded me of my own doubts.

"You should not have come back," she said. "Whenever I dreamed of your return, I saw you alone, not with others seeking to use us for their own purposes. Look at you—there is nothing of the Ganeagaono left in you. You speak our words, but your garments and your companions show where your true loyalty lies."

"You are wrong." I stared at her; she did not look away. "I have never forgotten my brothers here."

"You come to spy on us. When you have fought with our warriors in this battle, you will see our weaknesses more clearly, the ways in which we might be defeated, and we will not be able to use your pale-faced enemies against you."

"Is this what you have been saying to the other women? Have you gone before the men to speak against this war?"

Dasiyu drew in her breath; our son clutched her wrist. "You've said enough, Mother," he whispered. "I believe what he says. My vision told me he would come, and the spirits held the weapons of war. Perhaps my brother is meant to join me later." He got to his feet. "I go now to add my voice to the councils. It may be that I can persuade those who waver. If we are to follow the warpath now, I will set aside my office to fight with you."

He left us before I could speak. "You'll have your war," Dasiyu said. "The other sachems will listen to my son, and ask him to speak for them to the people. The wise old women will heed his words, because they chose him for his position."

"This war will serve you."

She scowled, then pushed the bowl of hommony toward me. "You insult me by leaving my food untouched."

I ate some of the dried corn, then set the bowl down. "Dasiyu, I did not come here only to speak of war. I swore an oath to myself that, when this campaign ends, I will live among you again."

"And am I to rejoice over that?"

"Cursed woman, anything I do would stoke your rage. I went back to speak for the Long House in our councils. I asked you to come with me, and you refused."

"I would have had to abandon my clan. My son would never have been chosen as a sachem then. You would not be promising to stay with us unless you believed you have failed as our voice."

Even after the years apart, she saw what lay inside me. "Whatever comes," I said, "my place is here."

She said nothing for a long time. The warmth inside the long house was growing oppressive. I opened my coat, then took off my headband to mop my brow.

"Look at you," she said, leaning toward me to touch the braids coiled behind my ears. Her hand brushed the top of my shaven head lightly. "You had such a fine scalplock—how could you have given it up?" She poked at my mustache. "I do not understand why a man would want hair over his lip." She fingered the fabric of my tunic. "And this—a woman might wear such a garment. I used to admire you so when I watched you dance. You were the shortest of the men, but no man here had such strong arms and broad shoulders, and now you hide them under these clothes."

I drew her to me. She was not as she had been, nor was I; once, every moment in her arms had only fed the flames inside me. Our fires were banked now, the fever gone, but her welcoming warmth remained.

"You have changed in another way, Senadondo," she said afterward. "You are not so nasty as you were."

"I am no longer a young man, Dasiyu. I must make the most of what moments I am given."

She pulled a blanket over us. I held her until she was asleep; she nestled against me as she once had, her cheek against my shoulder, a leg looped around mine. I did not know how to keep my promise to stay with her. Yesuntai might want a spy among the Flint People when this campaign was concluded; he might believe I was his man for the task.

I slept uneasily. A war whoop awakened me at dawn. I slipped away from my wife, pulled on my trousers, and went to the door.

A young chief was running through the village. Rattles were bound to his knees with leather bands, and he held a red tomahawk; beads of black wampum dangled from his weapon. He halted in front of the war post, lifted his arm, and embedded the tomahawk in the painted wood. He began to dance, and other men raced toward him, until it seemed most of the village's warriors had enlisted in the war.

They danced, bodies bent from the waist, arms lifting as if to strike enemies, hands out to ward off attack. Their feet beat against the ground as drums throbbed. I saw Yesuntai then; he walked toward them, his head thrown back, a bow in one hand. I stepped from the doorway, felt my heels drumming against the earth, and joined the dancers.

3

Yesuntai, a Khan's son, was used to absolute obedience. The Ganeagaono, following the custom of all the Long House People, would obey any war chiefs in whom they had confidence. I had warned Yesuntai that no chief could command the Flint People to join in this war, and that even the women were free to offer their opinions of the venture.

"So be it," the young Noyan had said to that. "Our own women were fierce and brave before they were softened by other ways, and my ancestor Bortai Khantun often advised her husband Genghis Khan, although even that great lady would not have dared to address a war kuriltai. If these women are as formidable as you say, then they must have bred brave sons." I was grateful for his tolerance.

But the people of Skanechtade had agreed to join us, and soon their messengers returned from other villages with word that chiefs in every Ganeagaono settlement had agreed to go on the warpath. My son had advised us to follow the custom of the Hodenosaunee when all of their nations fought in a common war, and to choose two supreme commanders so that there would be unanimity in all decisions. Yesuntai, it was agreed, would command, since he had proposed this war, and Aroniateka, a cousin of my son's, would be Yesuntai's equal. Aroniateka, happily, was a man avid to learn a new way of warfare.

This was essential to our purpose, since to have any chance against the Inglistanis, the Ganeagaono could not fight in their usual fashion. The Long House People were still new to organized campaigns with many warriors, and most of their battles had been little more than raids by small parties. Their men were used to war, which, along with the hunt, was their favorite pursuit, but this war would be more than a ritual test of valor.

The Flint People had acquired horses from us in trade, but had never used them in warfare. Their warriors moved so rapidly on foot through the forests that mounts would only slow their progress. We would have to travel on foot, and take any horses we might need later from the Inglistania. The men I had chosen in Yeke Geren had hunted and traded with the Hodenosaunee, and were used to their ways. Those Yesuntai had brought were veterans of European campaigns, but willing to adapt.

The whoops of Skanechtade's warriors echoed through the village as they danced. The women busied themselves making moccasins and preparing provisions for their men. Runners moved between villages with the orders of our two commanders and returned with promises that the other war parties would follow them. Yesuntai would have preferred more time for planning, to send out more scouts before we left Ganeagaono territory, but we had little time. War had been declared, and our allies were impatient to fight. We needed a swift victory over our enemy. If we did not defeat the Inglistanis by late autumn, the Ganeagaono, their honor satisfied by whatever they had won by then, might abandon us.

A chill remained in the early spring air, but most of the Ganeagaono men had shed the cloaks and blankets that covered their upper bodies in winter. Our Mongols followed their example and stripped to the waist, and I advised Yesuntai's men to trade their felt boots for moccasins. Dasiyu gave me a kilt and a pair of deerskin moccasins; I easily gave up my Mongol tunic and trousers for the garb I had once worn.

Eight days after we had come to Skanechtade, the warriors performed their last war dance. Men streamed from the village toward the river; Dasiyu followed me to the high wall that surrounded the long houses and handed me dried meat and a pouch of corn flour mixed with maple sugar.

"I will come back," I said, "when this war is over."

"If you have victory, I shall welcome you." She gripped my arms for a moment, then let go. "If you suffer defeat, if you and your chief lead our men only to ruin, your belongings will be outside my door."

"We will win," I said.

The lines around her lids deepened as she narrowed her eyes. "See that you do, Senadondo."

We crossed to the eastern side of the great river, then moved south. Some of our scouts had explored these oak covered hills, and Yesuntai had planned his campaign with the aid of Inglistani maps our soldiers had taken during a raid the year before. We would travel south, then move east through the Mahican lands, keeping to the north of the enemy settlements. Our forces would remain divided during the journey, so as not to alert the Inglistanis. Plymouth, the easternmost enemy settlement, overlooked an ocean bay. When Plymouth was taken, we would move south toward another great bay and the town called Newport. This settlement lay on an island at the mouth of the bay, and we would advance on it from the east. Any who escaped us would be forced to flee west toward Charlestown.

A wise commander always allows his enemy a retreat, since desperate defenders can cost a general many men, while a sweep by one wing of his force can pick off retreating soldiers. We would drive the Inglistanis west. When Charlestown fell, the survivors would have to run to the settlement they called New Haven. When New Haven was crushed, only New London, their westernmost town, would remain, and from there the Inglistanis could flee only to territory controlled by us.

At some point, the enemy was likely to sue for peace, but there could be no peace with the Inglistanis. Our allies and we were agreed; this would be a war of extermination.

These were our plans, but obstacles lay ahead. The Mahicans would present no problem; as payers of tribute to the Long House, they would allow us safe passage through their lands. But the Wampanoag people dwelled in the east, and the Pequots controlled the trails that would lead us south to Newport. Both groups feared the Flint People and had treaties with the Inglistanis. Our men would be more than a match for theirs if the Wampanoags and Pequots fought in defense of their pale-faced friends. But such a battle would cost us warriors, and a prolonged battle for Plymouth would endanger our entire strategy.

Our forces remained divided as we moved. Speed is one of a soldier's greatest allies, so we satisfied our hunger with our meager provisions and did not stop to hunt. At night, when we rested, Ganeagaono warriors marked the trees with a record of our numbers and movements, and we halted along the way to read the markings others had left for us. Yesuntai kept me at his side. I was teaching him the Ganeagaono tongue, but he still needed me to speak his words to his fellow commander Aroniateka.

In three days, we came to a Mahican settlement, and alerted the people there with war cries. Their chiefs welcomed us outside their stockade, met with us, and complained bitterly about the Inglistanis, who they believed had designs on their lands. They had refrained from raids, not wanting to provoke the settlers, but younger Mahicans had chided the chiefs for their caution. After we spoke of our intentions, several of their men offered to join us. We had expected safe passage, but to have warriors from among them lifted our spirits even higher.

We turned east, and markings on tree trunks told us of other Mahicans that had joined our forces. Yesuntai, with his bowcase, quiver, and sword hanging from his belt, and his musket over his shoulder, moved as easily through the woods as my son in his kilt and moccasins. A bond was forming between them, and often they communicated silently with looks and gestures, not needing my words. Wampanoag territory lay ahead, yet Yesuntai's confidence was not dampened, nor was my son's. The Great Spirit our Ganeagaono brethren called Hawenneyu, and that Yesuntai knew under the name of Tengri, would guide them; I saw their faith in their dark eyes when they lifted their heads to gaze through the arching tree limbs at the sky. God would give them victory.

4

God was with us. Our scouts went out, and returned with a Wampanoag boy, a wretched creature with a pinched face and tattered kilt. A Mahican with us knew the boy's tongue, and we soon heard of the grief that had come to his village. Inglistani soldiers had attacked without warning only a few days ago, striking in the night while his people slept. The boy guessed that nearly two hundred of his Wampanoag people had died, cut down by swords and firesticks. He did not know how many others had managed to escape.

We mourned with him. Inwardly, I rejoiced. Perhaps the Inglistanis would not have raided their allies if they had known we were coming against them, but their rash act served our purpose. The deed was proof of their evil intentions; they would slaughter even their friends to claim what they wanted. Wampanoags who might have fought against us now welcomed us as their deliverers. Yesuntai consulted with Aroniateka, then gave his orders. The left wing of our force would strike at Plymouth, using the Wampanoags as a shield as they advanced.

The Wampanoags had acquired muskets from the Inglistanis, and now turned those weapons against their false friends. By the time my companions and I heard the cries of gulls above Plymouth's rocky shore, the flames of the dying town lighted our way. Charred hulls and blackened masts were sinking beneath the gray waters; warriors had struck at the harbor first, approaching it during the night in canoes to burn the ships and cut off any escape to the sea. Women leaped from rocks and were swallowed by waves; other Inglistanis fled from the town's burning walls, only to be cut down by our forces. There was no need to issue a command to take no prisoners, for the betrayed Wampanoags were in no mood to show mercy. They drove their captives into houses and set the dwellings ablaze; children became targets for their arrows.

The Flint People do not leave the spirits of their dead to wander. We painted the bodies of our dead comrades, then buried them with their weapons and the food they would need for the long journey ahead. Above the burial mound, the Ganeagaono freed birds they had captured to help bear the spirits of the fallen to Heaven, and set a fire to light their way.

From the ruins of Plymouth, we salvaged provisions, bolts of cloth, and cannons. Much of the booty was given to the Wampanoags, since they had suffered most of the casualties. Having achieved the swift victory we needed, we loaded the cannons onto ox-drawn wagons, then moved south.

5

The center and left wings of our forces came together as we entered Pequot territory. The right wing would move toward Charlestown while we struck at Newport.

Parties of warriors fanned out to strike at the farms that lay in our path. We met little resistance from the Pequots, and they soon understood that our battle was with the Inglistanis, not with them. After hearing of how Inglistani soldiers had massacred helpless Wampanoags, many of their warriors joined us, and led us to the farms of those they had once called friends. The night was brightened by the fires of burning houses and crops, and the silence shattered by the screams of the dying. We took what we needed, and burned the rest.

A few farmers escaped us. The tracks of their horses ran south; Newport would be warned. The enemy was likely to think that only enraged Wampanoags and Pequots were moving against them, but would surely send a force to meet us. We were still four days' distance from the lowlands that surrounded Newport's great bay when we caught sight of Inglistani soldiers.

They were massed together along the trail that led through the forest, marching stiffly in rows, their muskets ready. The Wampanoags fired upon them from the trees, then swept toward them as the air was filled with the sharp cracks of muskets and the whistling of arrows. Volleys of our metal-tipped arrows and the flint-headed arrows of the Ganeagaono flew toward the Inglistanis; enemy soldiers fell, opening up breaks in their line. Men knelt to load their weapons as others fired at us from behind them, and soon the ground was covered with the bodies of Wampanoags and Pequot warriors.

The people of these lands had never faced such carnage in battle, but their courage did not fail them. They climbed over the bodies of dead and wounded comrades to fight the enemy hand-to-hand. The soldiers, unable to fire at such close range, used their muskets as clubs and slashed at our allies with swords; men drenched in blood shrieked as they swung their tomahawks. I expected the Inglistanis to retreat, but they held their ground until the last of their men had fallen.

We mourned our dead. The Wampanoags and the Pequots, who had lost so many men, might have withdrawn and let us fight on alone. Aroniateka consulted with their war chiefs, then gave us their answer. They would march with us against Newport, and share in that victory.

6

Swift, early successes hearten any warrior for the efforts that lie ahead. We advanced on Newport fueled by the victories we had already won. Summer was upon us as we approached the southeast end of the great bay. The island on which Newport stood lay to the west, across a narrow channel; the enemy had retreated behind the wooden walls of the town's stockade.

By day, we concealed ourselves amid the trees bordering the shore's wetlands. At night, the Ganeagaono cut down trees and collected rope we had gathered from Inglistani farms. Several of Yesuntai's older officers had experience in siege warfare; under their guidance, our allies quickly erected five catapults. In the early days of our greatness, we had possessed as little knowledge of sieges as the Flint People, but they seemed more than willing to master this new art. We did not want a long siege, but would be prepared for one if necessary. If Newport held out, we would leave a force behind and move on to our next objective.

When the moon showed her dark side to the earth, we brought out our catapults under cover of darkness and launched cannonballs at the five ships anchored in Newport's harbor, following them with missiles of rock packed with burning dried grass. The sails of the ships became torches, and more missiles caught enemy sailors as they leaped from the decks. The ships were sinking by the time we turned the catapults against the town's walls. The Inglistanis would have no escape by sea, and had lost the ships they might have used to bombard us.

We assaulted Newport for three days, until the Inglistani cannons fell silent. From the western side of the island, Inglistanis were soon fleeing in longboats toward Charlestown. There were many breaches in the stockade's walls, and few defenders left in the doomed town when we began to cross the channel in our canoes, but those who remained fought to the last man. Even after our men were inside the walls, Inglistanis shot at us from windows and roofs, and for every enemy we took there, two or three of our warriors were lost. We stripped enemy bodies, looted the buildings, then burned the town. Those hiding on the western side of the bay in Charlestown would see the great bonfire that would warn them of their fate.

The Wampanoags returned to their lands in the north. We left the Pequots to guard the bay and to see that no more Inglistani ships landed there. Our right wing would be advancing on Charlestown. We returned to the bay's eastern shore and went north, then turned west. A party of men bearing the weapons of war met us along one woodland trail, and led us to their chiefs. By then, the Narragansett people of the region had decided to throw in their lot with us.

7

Terror has always been a powerful weapon against enemies. Put enough fear into an enemy's heart, and victories can be won even before one meets him in the field. Thus it was during that summer of war. Charlestown fell, ten days after Newport. In spite of the surrender, we expected some of the survivors to hide in their houses and take their revenge when we entered the town. Instead, they gave up their weapons and waited passively for execution. Those I beheaded whispered prayers as they knelt and stretched their necks, unable to rouse themselves even to curse me. A few gathered enough courage to beg for their children's lives.

Yesuntai was merciful. He spared some women and children, those who looked most fearful, led them and a few old men to a longboat, and gave them a message in Frankish to deliver to those in New Haven. The message was much like the traditional one sent by Mongol Khans to their enemies: God has annihilated many of you for daring to stand against us. Submit to us, and serve us. When you see us massed against you, surrender and open your gates to us, for if you do not, God alone knows what will happen to you.

If was easy to imagine the effect this message would have on New Haven's defenders, if the Inglistanis we had spared survived their journey along the coast to deliver it. I did not believe that the Inglistanis would surrender immediately, but some among them would want to submit, and dissension would sap their spirit.

Most of our forces moved west, toward New Haven, followed by Inglistanis we had spared to carry canoes and haul cannons. Yesuntai had mastered enough of the Flint People's language to speak with Aroniateka, and left me with the rear guard. We would travel to the north of the main force. paralleling its path, and take the outlying farms.

Most of the farms we found were abandoned. We salvaged what we could and burned the rest. Days of searching empty farmhouses gave me time to reflect on how this campaign would affect my Ganeagaono brothers.

Their past battles had been for glory, to show their courage, to bring enemies to submission, and to capture prisoners who might, in the end, became brothers of the Long House. They had seen that unity among their Five Nations would make them stronger. Now we were teaching them that a victory over certain enemies was not enough, that sometimes only the extermination of that enemy would end the conflict, that total war might be necessary. Perhaps they would have learned that lesson without us, but their knowledge of this new art would change them, as surely as the serpent who beguiled the first man and woman changed man's nature. They might turn what they had learned against us.

Victories can hearten any soldier, but a respite from battle can also cause him to let down his guard. With a small party led by my son, I followed a rutted road toward one farm.

From the trees beyond the field, where the corn was still only tall enough to reach a man's waist, we spied a log dwelling, with smoke rising from its chimney. A white flag attached to a stick stood outside the door.

"They wish to surrender," I murmured to my son.

He shook his head. "The corn will hide us. We can get close enough to—"

"They are willing to give themselves up. Your men will have captives when they return to their homes. The Inglistanis have lost. Yesuntai will not object if we spare people willing to surrender without a fight."

My son said, "You are only weary of killing. My people say that a man weary of war is also weary of life."

"The people whose seed I carry have the same saying." He had spoken the truth. I was tiring of the war I had helped to bring about, thinking of what might follow it. "I shall speak to them."

"And we will guard your back," my son replied.

I left the trees and circled the field as the others crept through the corn. When I was several paces from the door, I held out my hands, palms up. "Come outside," I shouted in Frankish, hoping my words would be understood. "Show yourselves." I tensed, ready to fling myself to the ground if my son and his men suddenly attacked.

The door opened. A man with a graying beard left the house, followed by a young girl. A white cap hid her hair, but bright golden strands curled over her forehead. She gazed at me steadily with her blue eyes; I saw sorrow in her look, but no fear. A brave spirit, I thought, and felt a heaviness over my heart that might have been pity.

The man's Frankish was broken, but I was able to grasp his words. Whatever his people had done, he had always dealt fairly with the natives. He asked only to be left on his farm, to have his life and his family's spared.

"It cannot be," I told him. "You must leave this place. My brothers will decide your fate. That is all I can offer you, a chance for life away from here."

The man threw up an arm. The girl was darting toward the doorway when I saw a glint of metal beyond a window. A blow knocked the wind from me and threw me onto my back. I clutched at my ribs and felt blood seep from me as the air was filled with the sound of war whoops.

They had been lying in wait for us. Perhaps they would not have fired at me if I had granted the man his request; perhaps they had intended an ambush all along. I cursed myself for my weakness and pity. I would have another scar to remind me of Inglistani treachery and the cost of a moment's lack of vigilance, if I lived.

When I came to myself, the cabin was burning. A man knelt beside me, tending my wounds. Pain stabbed at me along my right side as I struggled to breathe. Two bodies in the gray clothes of Inglistani farmers lay outside the door. The Ganeagaono warriors danced as the flames leaped before them.

My son strode toward me, a scalp of long, golden hair dangling from his belt. "You cost me two men," he said. I moved my head from side to side, unable to speak. "I am sorry, Father. I think this war will be your last."

"I will live," I said.

"Yes, you will live, but I do not think you will fight again." He sighed. "Yet I must forgive you, for leading us to what your people call greatness." He lifted his head and cried out, echoing the war whoops of his men.

8

I was carried west on a wagon, my ribs covered with healing herbs and bound tightly with Inglistani cloth. A few men remained with me while the rest moved on toward New Haven. Every morning I woke expecting to find that they had abandoned me, only to find them seated around the fire.

A man's pride can be good medicine, and the disdain of others a goad. I was able to walk when Yesuntai sent a Bahadur to me with news of New Haven's surrender. Few soldiers were left in New Haven; most had fled to make a stand in New London. The young Noyan expected a fierce battle there, where the valor of the Inglistanis would be fired by desperation. He wanted me at his side as soon as possible.

The Bahadur had brought a spare horse for me. As we rode, he muttered of the difficulties Yesuntai now faced. Our Narragansett allies had remained behind in their territory, as we had expected, but the Mahicans, sated by glory, were already talking of returning to their lands. They thought they could wait until spring to continue the war; they did not understand. I wondered if the Ganeagaono had the stomach for a siege that might last the winter. They would be thinking of the coming Green Corn festival, of the need to lay in game for the colder weather and of the families that waited for them.

The oaks and maples gave way to more fields the Inglistanis had cleared and then abandoned. I smelled the salt of the ocean when we caught sight of Mongol and Mahican sentries outside a makeshift stockade. Yesuntai was camped to the east of New London, amid rows of Ganeagaono bark shelters. In the distance, behind a fog rolling in from the sea, I glimpsed the walls of the town.

Yesuntai and Aroniateka were outside one shelter, sitting at a fire with four other men. I heaved myself from my horse and walked toward them.

"Greetings, Jirandai," Yesuntai said in Mongol. "I am pleased to see you have recovered enough to take part in our final triumph."

I squatted by the fire and stretched out my hands. My

ribs still pained me; I suspected they always would. "This is likely to be our hardest battle," I said.

"Then our glory will be all the greater when we win it." Yesuntai accepted a pipe from Aroniateka and drew in the smoke. "We will take New London before the leaves begin to turn."

"You plan to take it by storm?" I asked. "That will cost us."

"I must have it, whatever it costs. My fellow commander Aroniateka is equally impatient for this campaign to end, as I suspect you are, Bahadur." His eyes held the same look I had seen in my son's outside the burning farmhouse, that expression of pity mingled with contempt for an old man tired of war.

I slept uneasily that night, plagued by aching muscles strained by my ride and the pain of my wounds. The sound of intermittent thunder over the ocean woke me before dawn. I crept from my shelter to find other men outside, shadows in the mists, and then knew what we were hearing. The sound was that of cannons being fired from ships. The Inglistanis would turn the weapons of their ships against us, whatever the risk to the town. They would drive us back from the shore and force us to withdraw.

Yesuntai had left his shelter. He paced, his arms swinging as if he longed to sweep the fog away. I went to him, knowing how difficult it would be to persuade him to give up now. A man shouted in the distance, and another answered him with a whoop. Yesuntai would have to order a retreat, or see men slaughtered to no purpose. I could still hear the sound of cannons over the water, and wondered why the Inglistanis had sailed no closer to us.

A Mongol and a Ganeagaono warrior were pushing their way through knots of men. "Noyan!" the Mongol called out to Yesuntai. "From the shore I saw three ships—they fly the blue and white banners of your father! They have turned their weapons against the Inglistanis!"

The men near us cheered. Yesuntai's face was taut, his eyes slits. He turned to me; his hands trembled as he clasped my shoulders.

"It seems," he said softly, "that we will have to share our triumph."

The ships had sailed to New London from Yeke Geren. They bombarded the town as we advanced from the north and east, driving our remaining Inglistani captives before us against the outer stockade. The sight of these wretches, crying out in Inglistani to their comrades and dying under the assault of their own people's weapons, soon brought New London's commander to send up white flags.

Michel Bahadur left his ship to accept the surrender. We learned from him that our Khan has at last begun his war against Inglistan that spring; a ship had brought Michel the news only recently. By now, he was certain, the Khanate's armies would be marching on London itself. Michel had quickly seen that his duty lay in aiding us, now that we were openly at war with the Inglistanis.

Michel Bahadur praised Yesuntai lavishly as they embraced in the square of the defeated town. He spoke of our courage, but in words that made it seem that only Michel could have given us this final triumph. I listened in silence, my mind filled with harsh thoughts about men who claimed the victories of others for their own.

We celebrated the fall of New London with a feast in the town hall. Several Inglistani women who had survived the ravages of Michel's men stood behind them to fill their cups. There were few beauties among those wan and narrow-faced creatures, but Michel had claimed a pretty dark-haired girl for himself.

He sat among his men, Yesuntai at his side, drinking to our victory. He offered only a grudging tribute to the Ganeagaono and the Mahicans and said, with the air of a man granting a great favor, that they would be given their share of captives. I had chosen to sit with the Ganeagaono chiefs, as did most of the Mongols who had fought with us. Michel's men laughed when three of the Mahican chiefs slid under tables, overcome by the wine and whiskey. My son, watching them, refused to drink from his cup.

"Comrades!" Michel bellowed in Frankish. I brooded over my wine, wondering what sort of speech he would make now. "Our enemies have been crushed! I say now that in this place, where we defeated the last of the Inglistani settlers, we will make a new outpost of our Khanate! New London will become another great camp!"

I stiffened in shock. The men around Michel fell silent as they watched us. Yesuntai glanced in my direction; his fingers tightened around his cup.

"New London was to burn," Yesuntai said at last. "It was to suffer the fate of the other settlements."

"It will stand," Michel said, "to serve your father our Khan. Surely you cannot object to that, Noyan."

Yesuntai seemed about to speak, then sank back in his seat. Our Narragansett and Wampanoag allies would feel betrayed when they learned of Michel's intentions. The Bahadur's round, crafty face reminded me of everything I despised in Europeans—their greed, their treachery, their lies.

My son motioned to me, obviously expecting me to translate Michel's words. I leaned toward him. "Listen to me," I said softly in the tongue of the Flint People, "and do nothing rash when you hear what I must say now. The war chief who sailed here to aid us means to camp in this place. His people will live in this town we have won."

His hand darted toward his tomahawk, then fell. "So this is why we fought. I should have listened to Mother when she first spoke against you."

"I did not know what Michel Bahadur meant to do, but what happens here will not trouble the Long House."

"Until your people choose to forget another promise."

"I am one of you," I said.

"You are only an old man who allowed himself to be deceived." He looked away from me. "I know where honor lies, even if your people do not. I will not shame you before your chief by showing what I think of him. I will not break our treaty in this place." He turned to Aroniateka and whispered to him. The chiefs near them were still; only their eyes revealed their rage.

I had fulfilled my duty to my Khan. All that remained was to keep my promise to myself, and to Dasiyu.

9

I walked along New London's main street, searching for Yesuntai. Warriors stumbled along the cobblestones, intoxicated by drink, blind to the contemptuous stares of our Frankish and Dutch sailors. The whiskey Michel's men had given them from the looted stores had made them forget their villages and the tasks that awaited them there.

I found Yesuntai with a party of Ganeagaono warriors and a few Inglistani captives. "These comrades are leaving us," Yesuntai said. "You must say an eloquent farewell for me. I still lack the words to do it properly."

One of the men pulled at his scalplock. "It is time for us to go," he said in his language. Five Mahicans clutching bottles of whiskey staggered past us. "To see brave men in such a state sickens me."

I nodded in agreement. "My chief Yesuntai will forever remember your valor. May Grandfather Heno water your fields, the Three Sisters give you a great harvest, and the winter be filled with tales of your victories."

The warriors led their captives away; two of the smaller children wept as they clung to their mothers' hands. They would forget their tears and learn to love the People of the Long House, as I had.

"The rest should go home as well," I said to Yesuntai. "There is nothing for them here now."

"Perhaps not."

"They will have stories to tell of this war for many generations. Perhaps the tales of their exploits can make them forget how they were treated here. I wish to speak to you, Noyan."

"Good. I have been hoping for a chance to speak to you."

I led him along a side street to the house where Aroniateka and my son were quartered with some of their men. All of them were inside, sitting on blankets near the fireplace. At least these men had resisted the lure of drink, and had refused the bright baubles Michel's men had thrown to our warriors while claiming the greater share of the booty for themselves. They greeted us with restraint, and did not ask us to join them.

We seated ourselves at a table in the back of the room. "I swore an oath to you, Yesuntai Noyan," I said, "and ask you to free me from it now." I rested my elbows on the table. "I wish to return to Skanechtade, to my Ganeagaono brothers."

He leaned forward. "I expected you to ask for that."

"As for my wife Elgigetei and my son Ajiragha, I ask only that you accept them into your household. My wife will not miss me greatly, and perhaps you can see that Ajiragha does not forget his father. You were my comrade in arms, and I will not sneak away from your side in the night. You do not need me now. Even my son will tell you that I am a man who has outlived his taste for battle. You will lose nothing by letting me go."

"And what will you do," he said, "if my people forsake their treaties?"

"I think you know the answer to that."

"You told me of the treaty's words, that we and the Flint People would be at peace for as long as you were both their brother and the Khan's servant. You will no longer be our servant if you go back to Skanechtade."

"So you are ready to seize on that. If the men of Yeke Geren fail to renew their promises, that will show their true intentions. I had hoped that you—"

"Listen to me."Yesuntai's fingers closed around my wrist. "I have found my brothers in your son and Aroniateka, and among the brave men who fought with us. They are my brothers, not the rabble who came here under Michel's command."

"Those men serve your father the Khan."

"They serve themselves," he whispered, "and forget what we once were."

I shook my arm free of his grasp. He was silent for a while, then said, "Koko Mongke Tengri, the Eternal Blue Sky that covers all the world, promised us dominion over Etugen, the Earth. I told you of the wise men in Khitai who believe that the ancestors of the peoples in these lands once roamed our ancient homeland. I know now that what those scholars say is true. The people here are our long-lost brothers—they are more truly Mongol than men whose blood has been thinned by the ways of Europe. For them to rule here is in keeping with our destiny. They could make an ulus here, a nation as great as any we have known, one that might someday be a match for our Khanates."

I said, "You are speaking treason."

"I am speaking the truth. I have had a vision, Jirandai. The spirits have spoken to me and shown me two arcs closing in a great circle, joining those who have been so long separated. When the peoples of this land are one ulus, when they achieve the unity our ancestors found under Genghis Khan, then perhaps they will be the ones to bring the rest of the world under their sway. If the Khans in our domains cannot accept them as brothers, they may be forced to bow to them as conquerors." Yesuntai paused. "Are we to sweep the Inglistanis from these lands only so that more of those we rule can flood these shores? They will forget the Khanate, as our people are forgetting their old homeland. They will use the peoples of this land against one another in their own disputes, when they have forgotten their Khan and fall to fighting among themselves. I see what must be done to prevent that. You see it, too. We have one more battle to fight before you go back to Skanechtade."

I knew what he wanted. "How do you plan to take Yeke Geren?" I asked.

"We must have Michel's ships. My Mongols can man them. We also need the Ganeagaono." He gazed past me at the men seated by the fire, "You will speak my words to your son and Aroniateka, and then we will act—and soon. Your brothers will be free of all their enemies."

Yesuntai spoke of warring tribes on the other side of the world, tribes that had wasted themselves in battles with one another until the greatest of men had united them under his standard. He talked of a time long before that, when other tribes had left the mountains, forests, and steppes of their ancient homeland to seek new herds and territories, and of the northern land bridge they had followed to a new world. He spoke of a great people's destiny, of how God meant them to rule the world, and of those who, in the aftermath of their glory, were forgetting their purpose. In the lands they had conquered, they would eventually fall out among themselves;

the great ulus of the Mongols would fracture into warring states. God would forsake them. Their brothers in this new world could reach for the realm that rightly belonged to them.

Aroniateka was the first to speak after I translated the Noyan's speech. "We have a treaty with your people," he said. "Do you ask us to break it?" "We ask that you serve the son of our Khan, who is rightful leader here," I replied. "Those who came here to claim our victory will take the lands we freed for themselves, and their greed will drive them north to yours. Michel Bahadur and the men of Yeke Gerenhave have already broken the treaty in their hearts."

"I am a sachem," my son said, "and will take up my duties again when I am home. I know what is recorded on the belts of wampum our wise men have in their keeping. Our treaty binds us as long as my father Senadondo is our brother and the servant of his former people, as long as he is our voice among them."

"I found that many grew deaf to my voice," I said. "I will not go back to live in Yeke Geren. I have told my chief Yesuntai that I will live among the Owners of the Flint until the end of my days."

My son met Yesuntai's gaze. How alike their eyes were, as cold and dark as those of a serpent. "My dream told me that my father would bring me a brother," my son said. "I see my brother now, sitting before me." I knew then that he would bring the other chiefs to agree to our plans.

We secured the ships easily. Yesuntai's soldiers rowed out to the vessels; the few sailors left on board, suspecting nothing, were quickly overcome. Most of Michel's men were quartered in the Inglistani commander's house and the three nearest it; they were sleepy with drink when we struck. Michel and his officers were given an honorable death by strangulation, and some of the Dutch and Frankish sailors

hastily offered their oaths to Yesuntai. The others were given
to the Ganeagaono, to be tortured and then burned at the
stake as we set New London ablaze.

I sailed with Yesuntai and his men. The Ganeagaono and
the Mahicans who had remained with us went west on foot
with their Inglistani captives. When we reached the narrow
strait that separated Yeke Geren from the long island of
Gawanasegeh, people gathered along the cliffs and the shore
to watch us sail south toward the harbor. The ships anchored
there had no chance to mount a resistance, and we lost only
one of our vessels in the battle. By then, the Ganeagaono and
Mahicans had crossed to the northern end of Yeke Geren in
canoes, under cover of night, and secured the pastures there.

They might have withstood our assault. They might have
waited us out, until our allies tired of the siege and the icy
winds of winter forced us to withdraw to provision our ships.
But too many in Yeke Geren had lost their fighting spirit, and
others thought it better to throw in their lot with Yesuntai.
They surrendered fourteen days later.

About half of the Mongol officers offered their oaths to
Yesuntai; the rest were beheaded. Some of the Mahicans
would remain in what was left of Yeke Geren, secure treaties
with the tribes of Gawanasegeh and the smaller island to our
southwest, and see that no more ships landed there. The
people of the settlement were herded into roped enclosures.
They would be distributed among the Ganeagaono and taken
north, where the Flint People would decide which of them
were worthy of adoption.

I searched among the captives for Elgigetei and Ajiragha.
At last an old man told me that they had been taken by a fever
only a few days before we attacked the harbor. I mourned for
them, but perhaps it was just as well. My son might not have
survived the journey north, and Dasiyu would never have

accepted a second wife. I had the consolation of knowing that my deeds had not carried their deaths to them.

Clouds of migrating birds were darkening the skies when I went with Yesuntai to our two remaining ships. A mound of heads, those of the officers we had executed, sat on the slope leading down to the harbor, a monument to our victory and a warning to any who tried to land there.

The Noyan's men were waiting by the shore with the surviving Frankish and Dutch sailors. The ships were provisioned with what we could spare, the sailors ready to board. Men of the sea would be useless in the northern forests, and men of uncertain loyalties who scorned the ways of the Flint People would not be welcomed there.

Yesuntai beckoned to a gray-haired captain. "This is my decree," he said. 'You will sail east, and carry this message to my father." He gestured with a scroll. "I shall recite the message for you now: I will make a Khanate of this land, but it will not be sullied by those who would bring the sins of Europe to its shores. When an ulus has risen here, it will be the mighty nation of our long-lost brothers. Only then will the circle close and all our brothers be joined, and only if all the Khans accept the men of this land as their equals. It is then that we will truly rule the world, and if my brother Khans do not willingly join this ulus of the world to come, only God knows what will befall them."

"We cannot go back with such a message," the captain said. "Those words will cost us our heads."

"You dishonor my father by saying that. You are my emissaries, and no Khan would stain his hands with the blood of ambassadors." Yesuntai handed the scroll to the old man. "These are my words, marked with my seal. My father the Khan will know that I have carried out his orders, that the people of Inglistan will not set foot here again. He will also know that there is no need for his men to come here, since it is I who will secure this new Khanate." He narrowed his eyes. "If you do not wish to claim the Khan's reward for this message, then sail where you will and find what refuge you can. The Khan my father, and those who follow him to his throne, will learn of my destiny in time."

We watched as the sailors boarded the longboats and rowed toward the ships. Yesuntai threw an arm over my shoulders as we turned away from the sea and climbed toward Yeke Geren. "Jirandai," he murmured, "or perhaps I should call you Senadondo now, as your Long House brothers do. You must guide me in my new life. You will show me what I must do to become a Khan among these people."

He would not be my Khan. I had served him for the sake of the Flint People, not to make him a Khan, but would allow him his dream for a little while. Part of his vision would come to pass; the Long House People would have a great realm, and Yesuntai might inspire them to even greater valor. But I did not believe that the Hodenosaunee, a people who allowed all to raise their voices in their councils, would ever bow to a Khan and offer him total obedience. My son would honor Yesuntai as a brother, but would never kneel to him. Yesuntai's sons would be Ganeagaono warriors, bound to their mother's clan, not a Mongol prince's heirs.

I did not say this to Yesuntai. He would learn it in time, or be forced to surrender his dream to other leaders who would make it their own. The serpent that had wakened to disturb the lands of the Long House would grow, and slip westward to meet his tail.

Catch That Zeppelin!

This year on a trip to New York City to visit my son who is a social historian at a leading municipal university there, I had a very unsettling experience. At black moments, of which at my age I have quite a few, it still makes me distrust profoundly those absolute boundaries in Space and Time which are our sole protection against Chaos, and fear that my mind—no, my entire individual existence—may at any moment at all and without any warning whatsoever be blown by a sudden gust of Cosmic Wind to an entirely different spot in a Universe of Infinite Possibilities. Or, rather, into another Universe altogether. And that my mind and individuality will be changed to fit.

But at other moments, which are still in the majority, I believe that my unsettling experience was only one of those remarkably vivid waking dreams to which old people become increasingly susceptible, generally waking dreams about the past in which at some crucial point one made an entirely different and braver choice than one actually did, or in which the whole world made such a decision with a completely different future resulting. Golden glowing might-have-beens nag increasingly at the minds of some older people.

In line with this interpretation I must admit that my whole unsettling experience was structured very much like a dream. It began with startling flashes of a changed world. It continued into a longer period when I completely accepted the changed world and delighted in it, and despite fleeting quivers of uneasiness, wished I could bask in its glow forever. And it ended in horrors, or nightmares, which I hate to mention, let alone discuss, until I must.

Opposing this dream notion, there are times when I am completely convinced that what happened to me in Manhattan and in a certain famous building there was no dream at all, but absolutely real, and that I did indeed visit another Time Stream.

Finally, I must point out that what I am about to tell you I am necessarily describing in retrospect, highly aware of several transitions involved and, whether I want to or not, commenting on them and making deductions that never once occurred to me at the time.

No, at the time it happened to me—and now at this moment of writing I am convinced that it did happen and was absolutely real—one instant simply succeeded another in the most natural way possible. I questioned nothing.

As to why it all happened to me, and what particular mechanism was involved, well, I am convinced that every man or woman has rare brief moments of extreme sensitivity, or rather vulnerability, when his mind and entire being may be blown by the Change Winds to Somewhere Else. And then, by what I call the Law of the Conservation of Reality, blown back again.

I was walking down Broadway somewhere near 34th Street. It was a chilly day, sunny despite the smog—a bracing day—and I suddenly began to stride along more briskly than is my cautious habit, throwing my feet ahead of me with a faint suggestion of the goose step. I also threw back my shoulders and took deep breaths, ignoring the fumes which tickled my nostrils. Beside me, traffic growled and snarled, rising at times to a machine-gun rata-tat-tat. While pedestrians were scuttling about with that desperate ratlike urgency characteristic of all big American cities, but which reaches its ultimate in New York, I cheerfully ignored that too. I even smiled at the sight of a ragged bum and a furcoated gray-haired society lady both independently dodging across the street through the hurtling traffic with a cool practiced skill one sees only in America's biggest metropolis.

Just then I noticed a dark, wide shadow athwart the street ahead of me. It could not be that of a cloud, for it did not move. I craned my neck sharply and looked straight up like the veriest yokel, a regular *Hans-Kopf-in-die-Luft* (Hans-Head-in-the-Air, a German figure of comedy).

My gaze had to climb up the giddy 102 stories of the tallest building in the world, the Empire State. My gaze was strangely accompanied by the vision of a gigantic, long-fanged ape making the same ascent with a beautiful girl in one paw—oh, yes, I was recollecting the charming American fantasy-film *King Kong,* or as they name it in Sweden, *Kong King.*

And then my gaze clambered higher still, up the 222-foot sturdy tower, to the top of which was moored the nose of the vast, breathtakingly beautiful, streamlined, silvery shape which was making the shadow.

Now here is the most important point. I was not at the time in the least startled by what I saw. I knew at once that it was simply the bow section of the German Zeppelin *Ostwald,* named for the great German pioneer of physical chemistry and electrochemistry, and queen of the mighty passenger and light-freight fleet of luxury airlines working out of Berlin, Baden-Baden, and Bremerhaven. That matchless Armada of Peace, each titanic airship named for a world-famous German scientist—the *Mach,* the *Nernst,* the *Humboldt,* the *Fritz Haber,* the French-named *Antoine Henry Becquerel,* the American-named *Edison,* the Polish-named *Sklodowska,* the American-Polish *T. Sklodowska Edison,* and even the Jewish-named *Einstein!* The great humanitarian navy in which I held a not unimportant position as international sales consultant and *Fachman*—I mean expert. My chest swelled with justified pride at this *edel*—noble—achievement of *der Vaterland*.

I knew also without any mind-searching surprise that the length of the *Ostwald* was more than one half the 1,472-foot height of the Empire State Building plus its mooring tower, thick enough to hold an elevator. And my heart swelled again with the thought that the Berlin *Zeppelinturm* (dirigible tower) was only a few meters less high. Germany, I told myself, need not strain for mere numerical records—her sweeping scientific and technical achievements speak for themselves to the entire planet.

All this literally took little more than a second, and I never broke my snappy stride. As my gaze descended, I cheerfully hummed under my breath *Deutschland, Deutschland uber Alles*.

The Broadway I saw was utterly transformed, though at the time this seemed every bit as natural as the serene presence of the *Ostwald* high overhead, vast ellipsoid held aloft by helium. Silvery electric trucks and buses and private cars innumerable purred along far more evenly and quietly, and almost as swiftly, as had the noisy, stenchful, jerky gasoline-powered vehicles only moments before, though to me now the latter were completely forgotten. About two blocks ahead, an occasional gleaming electric car smoothly swung into the wide silver arch of a quick-battery-change station, while others emerged from under the arch to rejoin the almost dreamlike stream of traffic.

The air I gratefully inhaled was fresh and clean, without trace of smog.

The somewhat fewer pedestrians around me still moved quite swiftly, but with a dignity and courtesy largely absent before, with the numerous blackamoors among them quite as well dressed and exuding the same quiet confidence as the Caucasians.

The only slightly jarring note was struck by a tall, pale, rather emaciated man in black dress and with unmistakably Hebraic features. His somber clothing was somewhat shabby, though well kept, and his thin shoulders were hunched. I got the impression he had been looking closely at me, and then instantly glanced away as my eyes sought his. For some reason I recalled what my son had told me about the City College of New York—CCNY—being referred to surreptitiously and jokingly as Christian College Now Yiddish. I couldn't help chuckling a bit at that witticism, though I am glad to say it was a genial little guffaw rather than a malicious snicker. Germany in her well-known tolerance and noble-mindedness has completely outgrown her old, disfiguring anti-Semitism—after all, we must admit in all fairness that perhaps a third of our great men are Jews or carry Jewish genes, Haber and Einstein among them—despite what dark and, yes, wicked memories may lurk in the subconscious minds of oldsters like myself and occasionally briefly surface into awareness like submarines bent on ship murder.

My happily self-satisfied mood immediately reasserted itself, and with a smart, almost military gesture I brushed to either side with a thumbnail the short, horizontal black mustache which decorates my upper lip, and I automatically swept back into place the thick comma of black hair (I confess I dye it) which tends to fall down across my forehead.

I stole another glance up at the *Ostwald,* which made me think of the matchless amenities of that wondrous deluxe airliner: the softly purring motors that powered its propellers—electric motors, naturally, energized by banks of lightweight TSE batteries and as safe as its helium; the Grand Corridor running the length of the passenger deck from the Bow Observatory to the stern's like-windowed Games Room, which become the Grand Ballroom at night; the other peerless rooms letting off that corridor—the *Gesellschaft-*

straum der Kapitan (Captain's Lounge) with its dark wood-
work, manly cigar smoke and *Damentische* (Tables for Ladies),
the Premier Dining Room with its linen napery and silver-
plated aluminum dining service, the Ladies' Retiring Room
always set out profusely with fresh flowers, the Schwartzwald
bar, the gambling casino with its roulette, baccarat, chemmy,
blackjack (*ving-et-un*), its tables for skat and bridge and
dominoes and sixty-six, its chess tables presided over by the
delightfully eccentric world's champion Nimzowitch, who
would defeat you blindfold, but always brilliantly, simultaneously or one at a time, in charmingly baroque brief
games for only two gold pieces per person per game (one gold
piece to nutsy Minzy, one to the DLG), and the supremely
luxurious staterooms with costly veneers of mahogany over
balsa; the hosts of attentive stewards, either as short and
skinny as jockeys or else actual dwarfs, both types chosen to
save weight; and the titanium elevator rising through the
countless bags of helium to the two-decked Zenith Observatory, the sun deck windscreened but roofless to let in the
ever-changing clouds, the mysterious fog, the rays of the stars
and good old Sol, and all the heavens. Ah, where else on land
or sea could you buy such high living?

I called to mind in detail the single cabin which was
always mine when I sailed on the *Ostwald—meine Stamm-
kabine*. I visualized the Grand Corridor thronged with
wealthy passengers in evening dress, the handsome officers,
the unobtrusive ever-attentive stewards, the gleam of white
shirt fronts, the glow of bare shoulders, the muted dazzle of
jewels, the music of conversations like string quartets, the
lilting low laughter that traveled along.

Exactly on time I did a neat *"Links, marschieren!"* ("To the
left, march!") and passed through the impressive portals of
the Empire State and across its towering lobby to the muted
silver-doored bank of elevators. On my way I noted the silver-

glowing date: 6 May 1937 and the time of day: 1:07 P.M. Good!—since the *Ostwald* did not cast off until the tick of three P.M., I would be left plenty of time for a leisurely lunch and good talk with my son, if he had remembered to meet me—and there was actually no doubt of that, since he is the most considerate and orderly minded of sons, a real German mentality, though I say it myself.

I headed for the express bank, enjoying my passage through the clusters of high-class people who thronged the lobby without any unseemly crowding, and placed myself before the doors designated "Dirigible Departure Lounge" and in briefer German *"Zum Zeppelin."*

The elevator hostess was an attractive Japanese girl in skirt of dull silver with the DLG, Double Eagle and Dirigible insignia of the German Airship Union emblazoned in small on the left breast of her mutedly silver jacket. I noted with unvoiced approval that she appeared to have an excellent command of both German and English and was uniformly courteous to the passengers in her smiling but unemotional Nipponese fashion, which is so like our German scientific precision of speech, though without the latter's warm underlying passion. How good that our two federations, at opposite sides of the globe, have strong commercial and behavioral ties!

My fellow passengers in the lift, chiefly Americans and Germans, were of the finest type, very well dressed—except that just as the doors were about to close, there pressed in my doleful Jew in black. He seemed ill at ease, perhaps because of his shabby clothing. I was surprised, but made a point of being particularly polite towards him, giving him a slight bow and brief but friendly smile, while flashing my eyes. Jews have as much right to the acme of luxury travel as any other people on the planet, if they have the money—and most of them do.

During our uninterrupted and infinitely smooth passage upward, I touched my outside left breast pocket to reassure myself that my ticket—first class on the *Ostwald*—and my papers were there. But actually I got far more reassurance and even secret joy from the feel and thought of the documents in my tightly zipperred inside left breast pocket: the signed preliminary agreements that would launch America herself into the manufacture of passenger zeppelins. Modern Germany is always generous in sharing her great technical achievements with responsible sister nations, supremely confident that the genius of her scientists and engineers will continue to keep her well ahead of all other lands; and after all, the genius of two Americans, father and son, had made vital though indirect contributions to the development of safe airship travel (and not forgetting the part played by the Polish-born wife of the one and mother of the other).

The obtaining of those documents had been the chief and official reason for my trip to New York City, though I had been able to combine it most pleasurably with a long overdue visit with my son, the social historian, and with his charming wife.

These happy reflections were cut short by the jarless arrival of our elevator at its lofty terminus on the 100th floor. The journey old love-smitten King Kong had made only after exhausting exertion we had accomplished effortlessly. The silvery doors spread wide. My fellow passengers hung back for a moment in awe and perhaps a little trepidation at the thought of the awesome journey ahead of them, and I— seasoned airship traveler that I am—was the first to step out, favoring with a smile and nod of approval my pert yet cool Japanese fellow employee of the lower echelons.

Hardly sparing a glance toward the great, fleckless window confronting the doors and showing a matchless view of Manhattan from an elevation of 1,250 feet minus two stories, I briskly turned, not right to the portals of the Departure Lounge and tower elevator, but left to those of the superb German restaurant *Krahenest* (Crow's Nest).

I passed between the flanking three-foot-high bronze statuettes of Thomas Edison and Marie Sklodowska Edison niched in one wall and those of Count von Zeppelin and Thomas Sklodowska Edison facing them from the other, and entered the select precincts of the finest German dining place outside the Fatherland. I paused while my eyes traveled searchingly around the room with its restful, dark wood paneling deeply carved with beautiful representations of the Black Forest and its grotesque supernatural denizens— kobolds, elves, gnomes, dryads (tastefully sexy) and the like. They interested me since I am what Americans call a Sunday painter, though almost my sole subject matter is zeppelins seen against blue sky and airy, soaring clouds.

The *Oberkellner* came hurrying toward me with menu tucked under his left elbow and saying, *"Mein Herr!* Charmed to see you once more! I have a perfect table-for-one with porthole looking out across the Hudson."

But just then a youthful figure rose springily from behind a table set against the far wall, and a dear and familiar voice rang out to me with *"Hier, Papa!"*

"Nein, Herr Ober," I smilingly told the head waiter as I walked past him, *"heute hab ich ein Gesellshafter. Mein Sohn."*

I confidently made my way between tables occupied by well-dressed folk, both white and black.

My son wrung my hand with fierce family affection, though we had last parted only that morning. He insisted that I take the wide, dark, leather-upholstered seat against the wall, which gave me a fine view of the entire restaurant, while he took the facing chair.

"Because during this meal I wish to look only on you, Papa." he assured me with manly tenderness. "And we have at least an hour and a half together, Papa—I have checked your luggage through, and it is likely already aboard the *Ostwald*." Thoughtful, dependable boy!

"And now, Papa, what shall it be?" he continued after we had settled ourselves. I see that today's special is *Sauerbraten mit Spatzel* and sweet-sour red cabbage. But there is also *Paprikahuhn* and—"

"Leave the chicken to flaunt her paprika in lonely red splendor today," I interrupted him. "Sauerbraten sounds fine."

Ordered by my Herr Ober, the aged wine waiter had already approached our table. I was about to give him directions when my son took upon himself that task with an authority and a hostfulness that warmed my heart. He scanned the wine menu rapidly but thoroughly.

"The Zinfandel 1933," he ordered with decision, though glancing my way to see if I concurred with his judgment. I smiled and nodded.

"And perhaps *ein Tropfchen Schnapps* to begin with?" he suggested.

"A brandy?—yes!" I replied. "And not just a drop, either. Make it a double. It is not every day I lunch with that distinguished scholar, my son."

"Oh, Papa," he protested, dropping his eyes and almost blushing. Then firmly to the bent-backed, white-haired wine waiter, "*Schnapps also. Doppel.*" The old waiter nodded his approval and hurried off.

We gazed fondly at each other for a few blissful seconds. Then I said, "Now tell me more fully about your achievements as a social historian on an exchange professorship in the New World. I know we have spoken about this several times, but only rather briefly and generally when various of your friends were present, or at least your lovely wife. Now I would like a more leisurely man-to-man account of your great work. Incidentally, do you find the scholarly apparatus— books, *und so weiter* (et cetera)—of the Municipal Universities of New York City adequate to your needs after having enjoyed those of Baden-Baden University and the institutions of high learning in the German Federation?"

"In some respects they are lacking," he admitted. "However, for my purposes they have proved completely adequate." Then once more he dropped his eyes and almost blushed. "But Papa, you praise my small efforts far too highly." He lowered his voice, "They do not compare with the victory for international industrial relations you yourself have won in a fortnight."

"All in a day's work for the DLG," I said self-deprecatingly, though once again lightly touching my left chest to establish contact with those important documents safely sewed in my inside left breast pocket. "But, now, no more polite fencing!" I went on briskly. "Tell me all about those 'small efforts,' as you modestly refer to them."

His eyes met mine. "Well, Papa," he began in suddenly matter-of-fact fashion, "all my work these last two years has been increasingly dominated by a firm awareness of the fragility of the underpinnings of the good world-society we enjoy today. If certain historically minute key-events, or cusps, in only the past one hundred years had been decided differently—if another course had been chosen than the one that was—then the whole world might now be plunged in wars and worse horrors then we ever dream of. It is a chilling insight, but it bulks continually larger in my entire work, my every paper."

I felt the thrilling touch of inspiration. At that moment the wine waiter arrived with our double brandies in small goblets of cut glass. I wove the interruption into the fabric of my inspiration. "Let us drink then to what you name your chilling insight," I said. "*Prosit!*"

The bite and spreading warmth of the excellent *schnapps* quickened my inspiration further. "I believe I understand exactly what you're getting at..." I told my son. I set down

my half-emptied goblet and pointed at something over my
son's shoulder.

He turned his head around, and after one glance back at
my pointing finger, which intentionally waggled a tiny bit from
side to side, he realized that I was not indicating the entry of
the *Krahenest,* but the four sizable bronze statuettes flanking it.

"For instance," I said, "if Thomas Edison and Marie
Sklodowska had not married, and especially if they had not
had their supergenius son, then Edison's knowledge of electricity and hers of radium and other radioactives might never
have been joined. There might never have been developed
the fabulous T.S. Edison battery, which is the prime mover of
all today's surface and air traffic. Those pioneering electric
trucks introduced by the *Saturday Evening Post* in Phila-
delphia might have remained an expensive freak. And the
gas helium might never have been produced industrially to
supplement earth's meager subterranean supply."

My sons's eyes brightened with the flame of pure scholarship. "Papa," he said eagerly, "you are a genius yourself! You
have precisely hit on what is perhaps the most important of
those cusp-events I referred to. I am at this moment finishing
the necessary research for a long paper on it. Do you know,
Papa, that I have firmly established by researching Parisian
records that there was in 1894 a close personal relationship
between Marie Sklodowska and her fellow radium researcher
Pierre Curie, and that she might well have become Madame
Curie—or perhaps, Madame Becquerel, for he too was in
that work—if the dashing and brilliant Edison had not most
opportunely arrived in Paris in December 1894 to sweep her
off her feet and carry her off to the New World to even
greater achievements?

"And just think, Papa," he went on, his eyes aflame, "what
might have happened if their son's battery had not been
invented—the most difficult technical achievement, hedged

by all sorts of seemingly scientific impossibilities, in the entire millennium-long history of industry. Why, Henry Ford might have manufactured automobiles powered by steam or by exploding natural gas or conceivably even vaporized liquid gasoline, rather than the mass-produced electric cars which have been such a boon to mankind everywhere—not our smokeless cars, but cars spouting all sorts of noxious fumes to pollute the environment."

Cars powered by the danger-fraught combustion of vaporized liquid gasoline!—it almost made me shudder and certainly it was a fantastic thought, yet not altogether beyond the bounds of possibility, I had to admit.

Just then I noticed my gloomy, black-clad Jew sitting only two tables away from us, though how he had got himself into the exclusive *Krahenest* was a wonder. Strange that I had missed his entry—probably immediately after my own, while I had eyes only for my son. His presence somehow threw a dark though only momentary shadow over my bright mood. Let him get some good German food inside him and some fine German wine, I thought generously—it will fill that empty belly of his and even put a bit of a good German smile in those sunken Yiddish cheeks! I combed my little mustache with my thumbnail and swept the errant lock of hair off my forehead.

Meanwhile my son was saying, "Also, Father, if electric transport had not been developed, and if during the last decade relations between Germany and the United States had not been so good, then we might never have gotten from the wells in Texas the supply of natural helium our Zeppelins desperately needed during the brief but vital period before we had put the artificial creation of helium onto an industrial footing. My researchers at Washington have revealed that there was a strong movement in the U.S. military to ban the sale of helium to any other nation, Germany in particular.

Only the powerful influence of Edison, Ford, and a few other key Americans, instantly brought to bear, prevented that stupid injunction. Yet if it had gone through, Germany might have been forced to use hydrogen instead of hellium to float her passenger dirigibles. That was another crucial cusp."

"A hydrogen-supported Zeppelin!—ridiculous! Such an airship would be a floating bomb, ready to be touched off by the slightest spark," I protested.

"Not ridiculous, Father," my son calmly contradicted me, shaking his head. "Pardon me for trespassing in your field, but there is an inescapable imperative about certain industrial developments. If there is not a safe road of advance, then a dangerous one will invariably be taken. You must admit, Father, that the development of commercial airships was in its early stages a most perilous venture. During the 1920's there were the dreadful wrecks of the American dirigibles *Roma, Shenandoah,* which broke in two, *Akron,* and *Macon,* the British *R-38,* which also broke apart in the air, and *R-101,* the French *Dixmude,* which disappeared in the Mediterranean, Mussolini's *Italia,* which crashed trying to reach the North Pole, and the Russian *Maxim Gorky,* struck down by a plane, with a total loss of no fewer than 340 crew members for the nine accidents. If that had been followed by the explosions of two or three hydrogen Zeppelins, world industry might well have abandoned forever the attempt to create passenger airships and turned instead to the development of large propeller-driven, heavier-than-air craft."

Monster airplanes, in danger every moment of crash from engine failure, competing with good old unsinkable Zeppelins?—impossible, at least at first thought. I shook my head, but not with as much conviction as I might have wished. My son's suggestion was really a valid one.

Besides, he had all his facts at his fingertips and was complete master of his subject, as I also had to allow. Those

nine fearful airship disasters he mentioned had indeed occurred, as I knew well, and might have topped the scale in
favor of long-distance passenger and troop-carrying airplanes, had it not been for helium, the T.S. Edison battery,
and German genius.

Fortunately I was able to dump from my mind these
uncomfortable speculations and immerse myself in admiration of my son's multisided scholarship. That boy was a
wonder!—a real chip off the old block, and, yes, a bit more.

"And now, Dolfy," he went on, using my nickname (I did
not mind), "may I turn to an entirely different topic? Or
rather to a very different example of my hypothesis of
historical cusps?"

I nodded mutely. My mouth was busily full with fine
Sauerbraten and those lovely, tiny German dumplings, while
my nostrils enjoyed the unique aroma of sweet-sour red
cabbage. I had been so engrossed in my son's revelations that
I had not consciously noted our luncheon being served. I
swallowed, took a slug of the good, red Zinfandel, and said,
"Please go on."

"It's about the consequences of the American Civil Way,
Father," he said surprisingly. "Did you know that in the
decade after that bloody conflict, there was a very real danger
that the whole cause of Negro freedom and rights—for
which the war was fought, whatever they say—might well
have been completely smashed? The fine work of Abraham
Lincoln, Thaddeus Stevens, Charles Sumner, the Freedmen's
Bureau, and the Union League Clubs put to naught? And
even the Ku Klux Klan underground allowed free reign
rather than being sternly repressed? Yes, Father, my thor-
oughgoing researchings have convinced me such things
might easily have happened, resulting in some sort of re-
enslavement of the Blacks, with the whole war to be refought
at an indefinite future date, or at any rate Reconstruction

brought to a dead halt for many decades—with what disas-
trous effects on the American character, turning its deep
simple faith in freedom to hypocrisy, it is impossible to
exaggerate. I have published a sizable paper on this subject in
the *Journal of Civil War Studies.*"

I nodded somberly. Quite a bit of this new subject matter
of his was *terra incognita* to me; yet I knew enough of
American history to realize he had made a cogent point.
More than ever before, I was impressed by his multifaceted
learning—he was indubitably a figure in the great tradition
of German scholarship, a profound thinker, broad and deep.
How fortunate to be his father. Not for the first time, but
perhaps with the greatest sincerity yet, I thanked God and
the Laws of Nature that I had early moved my family from
Braunau, Austria, where I had been born in 1889, to Baden-
Baden, where he had grown up in the ambience of the great
new university on the edge of the Black Forest and only 150
kilometers from Count Zeppelin's dirigible factory in Würt-
temberg, at Friedrichshafen on Lake Constance.

I raised my glass of *Kirschwasser* to him in a solemn, silent
toast—we had somehow got to that stage in our meal—and
downed a sip of the potent, fiery, white, cherry Brandy.

He leaned toward me and said, "I might as well tell you,
Dolf, that my big book, at once popular and scholarly, my
Meisterwerk, to be titled *If Things Had Gone Wrong,* or perhaps
If Things Had Turned for the Worse, will deal solely—though
illuminated by dozens of diverse examples—with my theory
of historical cusps, a highly speculative concept but firmly
footed in fact." He glanced at his wristwatch, muttered, "Yes,
there's still time for it. So now"—His face grew grave, his
voice clear though small—"I will venture to tell you about
one more cusp, the most disputable and yet most crucial of
them all." He paused. "I warn you, dear Dolf, that this cusp
may cause you pain."

"I doubt that," I gold him indulgently. "Anyhow, go ahead."

"Very well. In November of 1918, when the British had broken the Hindenburg Line and the weary German army was defiantly dug in along the Rhine, and just before the Allies, under Marshal Foch, launched the final crushing drive which would cut a bloody swath across the heartland to Berlin—"

I understood his warning at once. Memories flamed in my mind like the sudden blinding flares of the battlefield with their deafening thunder. The company I had commanded had been among the most desperately defiant of those he mentioned, heroically nerved for a last-ditch resistance. And then Foch had delivered that last vast blow, and we had fallen back and back and back before the overwhelming numbers of our enemies with their field guns and tanks and armored cars innumerable and above all their huge aerial armadas of De Haviland and Handley-Page and other big bombers escorted by insect-buzzing fleets of Spads and other fighters shooting to bits our last Fokkers and Pfalzes and visiting on Germany a destruction greater far than our Zeps had worked on England. Back, back, back, endlessly reeling and regrouping, across the devastated German countryside, a dozen times decimated yet still defiant until the end came at last amid the ruins of Berlin, and the most bold among us had to admit we were beaten and we surrendered unconditionally—

These vivid, fiery recollections came to me almost instantaneously.

I heard my son continuing. "At that cusp moment in November, 1918, Dolf, there existed a very strong possibility—I have established this beyond question—that an immediate armistice would be offered and signed, and the war ended inconclusively. President Wilson was wavering, the French were very tired, and so on.

"And if that had happened in actuality—harken closely to me now, Dolf—then the German temper entering the decade of the 1920's would have been entirely different. She would have felt she had not been really licked, and there would inevitably have been a secret recrudescence of pan-German militarism. German scientific humanism would not have won its total victory over the Germany of the—yes!—Huns.

"As for the Allies, self-tricked out of the complete victory which lay within their grasp, they would in the long run have treated Germany far less generously than they did after their lust for revenge had been sated by that last drive to Berlin. The League of Nations would not have become the strong instrument for world peace that it is today; it might well have been repudiated by America and certainly secretly detested by Germany. Old wounds would not have healed because, paradoxically, they would not have been deep enough.

"There, I've said my say. I hope it hasn't bothered you too badly, Dolf."

I let out a gusty sigh. Then my wincing frown was replaced by a brow serene. I said very deliberately, "Not one bit, my son, though you have certainly touched my own old wounds to the quick. Yet I feel in my bones that your interpretation is completely valid. Rumors of an armistice were indeed running like wildfire through our troops in that black autumn of 1918. And I know only too well that if there had been an armistice at that time, then officers like myself would have believed that the German soldier had never really been defeated, only betrayed by his leaders and by red incendiaries, and we would have begun to conspire endlessly for a resumption of the war under happier circumstances. My son, let us drink to your amazing cusps."

Our tiny glasses touched with a delicate ting, and the last drops went down of biting, faintly bitter *Kirschwasser*. I buttered a thin slice of pumpernickel and nibbled it—always good to finish off a meal with bread. I was suddenly filled with an immeasurable content. It was a golden moment, which I would have been happy to have go on forever, while I listened to my son's wise words and fed my satisfaction in him. Yes, indeed, it was a golden nugget of pause in the terrible rush of time—the enriching conversation, the peerless food and drink, the darkly pleasant surroundings—

At that moment I chanced to look at my discordant Jew two tables away. For some weird reason he was glaring at me with naked hate, though he instantly dropped his gaze—

But even that strange and disquieting event did not disrupt my mood of golden tranquility, which I sought to prolong by saying in summation, "My dear son, this has been the most exciting though eerie lunch I have ever enjoyed. Your remarkable cusps have opened to me a fabulous world in which I can nevertheless utterly believe. A horridly fascinating world of sizzling hydrogen Zeppelins, of countless evil-smelling gasoline cars built by Ford instead of his electrics, of re-enslaved American blackamoors, of Madame Becquerels or Curies, a world without the T.E. Edison battery and even T.S. himself, a world in which German scientists are sinister pariahs instead of tolerant, humanitarian, greatsouled leaders of world thought, a world in which a mateless old Edison tinkers forever at a powerful storage battery he cannot perfect, a world in which Woodrow Wilson doesn't insist on Germany being admitted at once to the League of Nations, a world of festering hatreds reeling toward a second and worse world war. Oh, altogether an incredible world, yet one in which you have momentarily made me believe, to the extent that I do actually have the fear that time will suddenly shift gears and we will be plunged into that bad dream world, and our real world will become a dream—"

I suddenly chanced to see the face of my watch—

At the same time my son looked at his own left wrist—

"Dolf," he said, springing up in agitation, "I do hope that with my stupid chatter I haven't made you miss—"

I had sprung up too—

"No, no, my son," I heard myself say in a fluttering voice, "but it's true I have little time in which to catch the *Ostwald*. *Auf Wiedersehn, mein Sohn, auf Wiedersehn!*"

And with that I was hastening, indeed almost running, or else sweeping through the air like a ghost—leaving him behind to settle our reckoning—across a room that seemed to waver with my feverish agitation, alternately darkening and brightening like an electric bulb with its fine tungsten filament about to fly to powder and wink out forever—

Inside my head a voice was saying in calm yet deathknell tones, "The lights of Europe are going out. I do not think they will be rekindled in my generation—"

Suddenly the only important thing in the world for me was to catch the *Ostwald*, get aboard her before she unmoored. That and only that would reassure me that I was in my rightful world. I would touch and feel the *Ostwald*, not just talk about her—

As I dashed between the four bronze figures, they seemed to hunch down and become deformed, while their faces became those of grotesque, aged witches—four evil kobolds leering up at me with a horrid knowledge bright in their eyes—

While behind me I glimpsed in pursuit a tall, black, white-faced figure, skeletally lean—

The strangely short corridor ahead of me had a blank end—the Departure Lounge wasn't there—

I instantly jerked open the narrow door to the stairs and darted nimbly up them as if I were a young man again and not 48 years old—

On the third sharp turn I risked a glance behind and down—

Hardly a flight behind me, taking great pursuing leaps, was my dreadful Jew—

I tore open the door to the 102nd floor. There at last, only a few feet away, was the silver door I sought of the final elevator and softly glowing above it the words, "*Zum Zeppelin.*" At last I would be shot aloft to the *Ostwald* and reality.

But the sign began to blink as the *Krahenest* had, while across the door was pasted askew a white cardboard sign which read, "Out of Order."

I threw myself at the door and scrabbled at it, squeezing my eyes several times to make my vision come clear. When I finally fully opened them, the cardboard sign was gone.

But the silver door was gone too, and the words above it forever. I was scrabbling at seamless pale plaster.

There was a touch on my elbow. I spun around.

"Excuse me, sir, but you seem troubled," my Jew said solicitously. "Is there anything I can do?"

I shook my head, but whether in negation or rejection or to clear it, I don't know. "I'm looking for the *Ostwald*," I gasped, only now realizing I'd winded myself on the stairs. "For the zeppelin," I explained when he looked puzzled.

I may be wrong, but it seemed to me that a look of secret glee flashed deep in his eyes, though his general sympathetic expression remained unchanged.

"Oh, the zeppelin," he said in a voice that seemed to me to have become sugary in its solicitude. "You must mean the *Hindenburg.*"

Hindenburg?—I asked myself. There was no zeppelin named *Hindenburg*. Or was there? Could it be that I was mistaken about such a simple and, one would think, immutable matter? My mind had been getting very foggy the last minute or two. Desperately I tried to assure myself that I was indeed myself and in my right world. My lips worked and I muttered to myself, *Bin Adolf Hitler, Zeppelin Fachman . . .*

"But the *Hindenburg* doesn't land here, in any case," my Jew was telling me, "though I think some vague intention once was voiced about topping the Empire State with a mooring mast for dirigibles. Perhaps you saw some news story and assumed—"

His face fell, or he made it seem to fall. The sugary solicitude in his voice became unendurable as he told me, "But apparently you can't have heard today's tragic news. Oh, I do hope you weren't seeking the *Hindenburg* so as to meet some beloved family member or close friend. Brace yourself, sir. Only hours ago, coming in for her landing at Lakehurst, New Jersey, the *Hindenburg* caught fire and burned up entirely in a matter of seconds. Thirty or forty at least of her passengers and crew were burned alive. Oh, steady yourself, sir."

"But the *Hindenburg*—I mean the *Ostwald!*—couldn't burn like that," I protested. "She's a helium zeppelin."

He shook his head. "Oh, no. I'm no scientist, but I know the *Hindenburg* was filled with hydrogen—a wholly typical bit of reckless German risk-running. At least we've never sold helium to the Nazis, thank God."

I stared at him, wavering my face from side to side in feeble denial. While he stared back at me with obviously a new thought in mind.

"Excuse me once again," he said, "but I believe I heard you start to say something about Adolf Hitler. I suppose you know that you bear a certain resemblance to that execrable dictator. If I were you, sir, I'd shave my mustache."

I felt a wave of fury at this inexplicable remark with all its baffling references, yet withal a remark delivered in the unmistakable tones of an insult. And then all my surrounding momentarily reddened and flickered and I felt a tremendous wrench in the inmost core of my being, the sort of wrench one might experience in transiting timelessly from one universe into another parallel to it. Briefly I became a man still named

Adolf Hitler, same as the Nazi dictator and almost the same age, a German-American born in Chicago, who had never visited Germany or spoken German, whose friends teased him about his chance resemblance to the other Hitler, and who used stubbornly to say, "No, I won't change my name! Let the *Fuehrer* bastard across the Atlantic change his! Ever hear about the British Winston Churchill writing the American Winston Churchill, who wrote *The Crisis* and other novels, and suggesting he change his name to avoid confusion, since the Englishman had done some writing too? The American wrote back it was a good idea, but since he was three years older, he was senior and so the Britisher should change *his* name. That's exactly how I feel about that son of a bitch Hitler."

The Jew still stared at me sneeringly. I started to tell him off, but then I was lost in a second weird, wrenching transition. The first had been directly from one parallel universe to the another. The second was also in time—I aged 14 or 15 years in a single infinite instant while transiting from 1937 (where I had been born in 1889 and was 48) to 1973 (where I had been born in 1910 and was 63). My name changed back to my truly own (but what is that?). And I no longer looked one bit like Adolf Hitler the Nazi dictator (or dirigible expert?), and I had a married son who was a sort of social historian in a New York City municipal university, and he had many brilliant theories, but none of historical cusps.

And the Jew—I mean the tall, thin man in black with possibly Semitic features—was gone. I looked around and around but there was no one there.

I touched my outside left breast pocket, then my hand darted tremblingly underneath. There was no zipper on the pocket inside and no precious documents, only a couple of grimy envelopes with notes I'd scribbled on them in pencil.

I don't know how I got out of the Empire State Building. Presumably by elevator. Though all my memory holds for that period is a persistent image of King Kong tumbling down from its top like a ridiculous yet poignantly pitiable giant teddy bear.

I do recollect walking in a sort of trance for what seemed hours through a Manhattan stinking with monoxide and carcinogens innumerable, half waking from time to time (usually while crossing streets that snarled, not purred) and then relapsing into trance. There were big dogs.

When I at last fully came to myself, I was walking down a twilit Hudson Street at the north end of Greenwich Village. My gaze was fixed on a distant and unremarkable pale-gray square of a building top. I guess it must be that of the World Trade Center, 1,350 feet tall.

And then it was blotted out by the grinning face of my son, the professor.

"Justin!" I said.

"Fritz!" he said. "We'd begun to worry a bit. Where did you get off to, anyhow? Not that it's a damn bit of my business. If you had an assignation with a go-go girl, you needn't tell me."

"Thanks," I said, "I do feel tired, I must admit, and somewhat cold. But no, I was just looking at some of my old stamping grounds," I told him, "and taking longer than I realized. Manhattan's changed during my years on the West Coast, but not all that much."

"It's getting chilly," he said. "Let's stop in at that place ahead with the black front. It's the White Horse. Dylan Thomas used to drink there. He's supposed to have scribbled a poem on the wall of the can, only they painted it over. But it has the authentic sawdust."

"Good," I said, "only we'll make mine coffee, not ale. Or if I can't get coffee, then cola."

I am not really a *Prosit!*-type person.

Greg Bear

Through Road No Whither

The long black Mercedes rumbled out of the fog on the road south from Dijon, moisture running in cold trickles across its windshield. Horst von Ranke moved the military pouch to one side and carefully read the maps spread on his lap, eyeglasses perched low on his nose, while Waffen Schutzstaffel Oberleutnant Albert Fischer drove. "Thirty-five kilometers," von Ranke said under his breath. "No more."

"We are lost," Fischer said. "We've already come thirty-six."

"Not quite that many. We should be there any minute now."

Fischer nodded and then shook his head. His high cheek-ones and long, sharp nose only accentuated the black uniform with silver death's heads on the high, tight collar. Von Ranke wore a broad-striped gray suit; he was an under-secretary in the Propaganda Ministry, now acting as a courier. They might have been brothers, yet one had grown up in Czechoslovakia, the other in the Ruhr; one was the son of a coal miner, the other of a brewer. They had met and become close friends in Paris, two years before.

"Wait," von Ranke said, peering through the drops on the side window. "Stop."

Fischer braked the car and looked in the direction of von Ranke's long finger. Near the roadside, beyond a copse of young trees, was a low thatch-roofed house with dirty gray walls, almost hidden by the fog.

"Looks empty," von Ranke said.

"It is occupied; look at the smoke," Fischer said. "Perhaps somebody can tell us where we are."

They pulled the car over and got out, von Ranke leading the way across a mud path littered with wet straw. The hut looked even dirtier close up. Smoke rose in a darker brown-gray twist from a hole in the peak of the thatch. Fischer nodded at his friend and they cautiously approached. Over the crude wooden door letters wobbled unevenly in some alphabet neither knew, and between them they spoke nine languages. "Could that be Rom?" von Ranke asked, frowning. "It does look familiar—Slavic Rom."

"Gypsies? Romany don't live in huts like this, and besides, I thought they were rounded up long ago."

"That's what it looks like," von Ranke said. "Still, maybe we can share some language, if only French."

He knocked on the door. After a long pause he knocked again, and the door opened before his knuckles made the final rap. A woman too old to be alive stuck her long, wood-colored nose through the crack and peered at them with one good eye. The other was wrapped in a sunken caul of flesh. The hand that gripped the door edge was filthy, its nails long and black. Her toothless mouth cracked into a wrinkled, round-lipped grin. "Good evening," she said in perfect, even elegant German. "What can I do for you?"

"We need to know if we are on the road to Dôle," von Ranke said, controlling his repulsion.

"Then you're asking the wrong guide," the old woman said. Her hand withdrew and the door started to close. Fischer kicked out and pushed her back. The door swung open and began to lean on worn-out leather hinges.

"You do not treat us with the proper respect," he said.

"What do you mean, 'the wrong guide'? What kind of guide are you?"

"So *strong*," the old woman crooned, wrapping her hands in front of her withered chest and backing away into the gloom. She wore colorless, ageless gray rags. Worn knit sleeves extended to her wrists.

"Answer me!" Fischer said, advancing despite the strong odor of urine and decay in the hut.

"The maps I know are not for this land," she sang, stopping before a cold and empty hearth.

"She's crazy," von Ranke said. "Let the local authorities take care of her later. Let's be off." But a wild look was in Fischer's eye. So much filth, so much disarray, and impudence as well; these things made him angry.

"What maps do you know, crazy woman?" he demanded.

"Maps in time," the old woman said. She let her hands fall to her side and lowered her head, as if, in admitting her specialty, she was suddenly humble.

"Then tell us where we are," Fischer sneered.

"Come, we have important business," von Ranke said, but he knew it was too late. There would be an end, but it would be on his friend's terms, and it might not be pleasant.

"You are on a through road no whither," the old woman said.

"What?" Fischer towered over her. She stared up as if at some prodigal son returned home, her gums shining spittle.

"If you wish a reading, sit," she said, indicating a low table and three battered wood chairs. Fischer glanced at her, than at the table.

"Very well," he said, suddenly and falsely obsequious. Another game, von Ranke realized. Cat and mouse.

Fischer pulled out a chair for his friend and sat across from the old woman. "Put your hands on the table, palms down, both of them, both of you," she said. They did so. She lay her ear to the table as if listening, eyes going to the beams of light coming through the thatch. "Arrogance," she said. Fischer did not react.

"A road going into fire and death," she said. "Your cities in flame, your women and children shriveling to black dolls in the heat of their burning homes. The death camps are found and you stand accused of hideous crimes. Many are tried and hanged. Your nation is disgraced, your cause abhorred." Now a peculiar light came into her eye. "And many years later, a comedian swaggers around on stage, in a movie, turning your Führer into a silly clown, singing a silly song. Only psychotics will believe you, the lowest of the low. Your nation will be divided among your enemies. All will be lost."

Fischer's smile did not waver. He pulled a coin from his pocket and threw it down before the woman, then pushed the chair back and stood. "Your maps are as crooked as your chin, hag," he said. "Let's go."

"I've been suggesting that," von Ranke said. Fischer made no move to leave. Von Ranke tugged on his arm but the SS Oberleutnant shrugged free of his friend's grip.

"Gypsies are few, now, hag," he said. "Soon to be fewer by one." Von Ranke managed to urge him just outside the door. The woman followed and shaded her eye against the misty light.

"I am no gypsy," she said. "You do not even recognize the words?" She pointed at the letters above the door.

Fischer squinted, and the light of recognition dawned in his eyes. "Yes," he said. "Yes, I do, now. A dead language."

"What are they?" von Ranke asked, uneasy.

"Hebrew, I think," Fischer said. "She is a Jewess."

"No!" the woman cackled. "I am no Jew."

Von Ranke thought the woman looked younger now, or at least stronger, and his unease deepened.

"I do not care what you are," Fischer said quietly. "I only wish we were in my father's time." He took a step toward her. She did not retreat. Her face became almost youthfully bland, and her bad eye seemed to fill in. "Then, there would be no regulations, no rules—I could take this pistol"—he tapped his holster—"and apply it to your filthy Kike head, and perhaps kill the last Jew in Europe." He unstrapped the holster. The woman straightened in the dark hut, as if drawing strength from Fischer's abusive tongue. Von Ranke feared for his friend. Rashness would get them in trouble.

"This is not our fathers' time," he reminded Fischer.

Fischer paused, the pistol half in his hand, his finger curling around the trigger. "Old woman"—though she did not look half as old, perhaps not even old at all, and certainly not bent and crippled—"you have had a very narrow shave this afternoon."

"You have no idea who I am," the woman half-sang, half-moaned.

"*Scheisse*," Fischer spat. "Now we will go, and report you and your hovel."

"I am the scourge," she breathed, and her breath smelled like burning stone even three strides away. She backed into the hut but her voice did not diminish. "I am the visible hand, the pillar of cloud by day and the pillar of fire by night."

Fischer's face hardened, and then he laughed. "You are right," he said to von Ranke, "she isn't worth our trouble." He turned and stomped out the door. Von Ranke followed, with one last glance over his shoulder into the gloom, the decay. *No one has lived in this hut for years*, he thought. Her shadow was gray and indefinite before the ancient stone hearth, behind the leaning, dust-covered table.

In the car von Ranke sighed. "You *do* tend toward arrogance, you know that?"

Fischer grinned and shook his head. "You drive, old

friend. *I'll* look at the maps." Von Ranke ramped up the Mercedes's turbine until its whine was high and steady and its exhaust cut a swirling hole in the fog behind. "No wonder we're lost," Fischer said. He shook out the Pan-Deutschland map peevishly. "This is five years old—1979."

"We'll find our way," von Ranke said. "I wouldn't miss old Krumnagel's face when we deliver the plans. He fought so long against the antipodal skip bombers.... And you delay us by fooling with an old woman."

"It is my way," Fischer said. "I hate disarray. Do you think he will try to veto the Pacific Northwest blitz?"

"He won't dare. He will know his place after he sees the declarations," von Ranke said. The Mercedes whined its way toward Dôle.

From the door of the hut the old woman watched, head bobbing. "I am not a Jew," she said, "but I loved them, too, oh, yes, I loved all my children." She raised her hand as the long black car roared into the fog.

"I will bring you to justice, whatever line you live upon, and all your children, and their children's children," she said. She dropped a twist of smoke from her elbow to the dirt floor and waggled her finger. The smoke danced and drew black figures in the dirt. "As you wished, into the time of your fathers." The fog grew thinner. She brought her arm down, and forth years melted away with the mist.

High above a deeper growl descended on the road. A wide-winged shadow passed over the hut, wings flashing stars, invasion stripes and cannon fire.

"Hungry bird," the shapeless figure said. "Time to feed."

Barry N. Malzberg

Ship Full of Jews

Cristoforo could hear the moaning from steerage, the Chassids were chanting again, moaning and raving in their strange and steeped tongue, the sounds of the Hebrew emerging cloudily from the deck of the *Pinta,* filling him with some mixture of dread and regard, religiosity and hope, the swells and pitching of the barren seas reminding him of the essential perilousness of his journey. Images of spices, fragrant bouquets from the sullen and mysterious East rose in his nostrils, taunting thoughts of the new and deadly continent opening up before him possessed him with a kind of graciousness. The sounds of the Chassids were overwhelming. Sometimes they would pray for hours, unstopping, one choir beginning when another paused, filling the moist air with imprecations and song, at other times they were silent, pitching and rolling in the deck, the queasiness of their condition doubtless the origin of this strange and necessary silence. Cristoforo did not understand any of it.

Of course the Chassids were not to understand, they were to transport. Isabella had pointed this out to him. "They are none of your concern," she had said, "they are being deported, will keep to themselves under guard, will pray and rave in their strange way, but have nothing to do with your journey." The excitable queen had gazed at him, her eyes full and penetrating in the darkness. There was something very special between her and Cristoforo; that had been his intima-

255

tion from the start, but of course under Ferdinand's cruel
gaze and with the happenstance of the Inquisition, it was
impossible to bring this strange and stunned accord to any
kind of realization. Cristoforo was a temporal man, his mind
was seized by the fragrance of spices, but his imagination
remained clear and pristine, somewhere to the side of fantasy. He had an assignment to commit, the Chassids were
only the most marginal part. Standing on the deck, swaying,
finding purchase on the thin and decaying boards of this
wretched ship that was, his great friend, the queen, had
insisted, the very best available to him, Cristoforo pondered
his fate, considered his condition, swung his keen and penetrating gaze toward *el Norte,* the hidden land beyond the dip
of the great horizon. *Santa María,* Cristoforo murmured, and
did not know if he was invoking that mother of passage or
merely repeating the name of that third and most eccentric
ship, filled with roustabouts and assassins, also deported
from Spain, a gang so cruel that he had taken Ferdinand's
instruction not to deal with that ship at all, even in his
capacity as overseer of the voyage. "You will really be much
better, my son," Ferdinand had said, "staying with your crew
and examining the route with compass and disjunction,
allowing the guards to control that hostile ship." Cristoforo
had shrugged. Who was he to argue with Ferdinand? A king's
reputation stood between him and all desire. Cristoforo
lusted hopelessly for the queen, but all proportion was
necessary within the arc of condition. Sometimes his
thoughts were metaphysical, sometimes they were practical,
and at all times the three ships rolled and sculled their way
toward the New World. Abolish all desire, Cristoforo
thought, and the spices of desire may someday soon by yours.

"Excuse me, master," his yeoman said, approaching with
downcast gaze and suitable humility. Everyone knew of
Cristoforo's special relationship with Isabella, also his terrible

temper and the secret instructions from the queen, which reportedly granted him the right to scuttle any who displeased him. Behind lay the specter of the Inquisition, only for the Jews so far, but who could tell; ahead lay the equally imponderable New World; but somewhere in the middle Cristoforo presided, and his word was terrible, his authority absolute. "The rabbi has requested permission to speak to you. He asked me to carry this message."

Rabbi? What Rabbi? Cristoforo could feel his consciousness swim as he slowly reoriented himself to the possession of a steerage filled not only with chanting but with hierarchy. There was a leader or several leaders of the Chassids, yes, and they obtained not only the spiritual but the temporal title *rebbe*, corrupted by the idiomatic language of his day to this less forbidding form. Jesus had been *rebbe*, too, Cristoforo noted, not a religious man, no longer possessed by any vision other than the spicy and nefarious East toward which they so perilously cruised, he recalled from his childhood pictures of the bearded Master, who had of course emerged from the Pharisees of his day and had been put to torture and death for daring to rival them in popularity. Or was that the story? He was not sure; the Inquisition of course was a final settling of accounts for this ancient injustice, but Cristoforo, concerned with matters of the sea as well as certain entanglements on shore, which even before Isabella had made his life colorful and difficult, had not paid much attention to this. "Master," the yeoman said, "I have brought the Rabbi to the deck. He is instant over there; he is asking for appearances."

Cristoforo shrugged. A shrug seemed to possess him head to toe, front to back, through all the specious and yet solid aspects of his frame; he had been shrugging, he sometimes thought, all his life. Shrug for the mean-spirited Barcelona of his day, which seemed obsessed with questions of reparation that could not concern a simple master of the seas. A shrug for Isabella, who, after all, was beyond him for all of her flirtatiousness and desirability and would have made much trouble in the possession, a trouble that he suspected, she would have found no less titillating than the specter of his murder. Shrug for the *Santa María* and its decks full of felons who would be the first to grapple with the savages of the New Land if the savages were to show any hostile intention. Shrug for the jewels and fragrances that Ferdinand had promised him if he were successful on this difficult mission. Shrug for this and shrug for that, meet the temper of the world with a certain calculated indifference and ignore the screams and concerns of the Inquisition which, after all, had absolutely nothing to do with him and which would go on its tortuous way whether or not he was present. "So, bring him here," Cristoforo said. "Let me discuss with you later the proper way to deal below deck, do you hear me?"

"Whatever you say, master," the yeoman said, and gestured. The rabbi, a huge bearded man wrapped in the vestments of his calling—but they *all* seemed to wear this strange and elaborate garb—shuffled toward him downcast, his eyes seeking the deck, then his head tilting upward, the strange, luminous, Israelic eyes locking with Cristoforo's in a way that induced strange sensations, perhaps due to the odors of steerage wafting from the rabbi and the vague screams across the water, which might have been emanating from the *Niña,* just barely visible, or the more distant *Santa María,* which, *Jesus Christo,* he could not and would not want to see in these conditions. "Well, well," he said to the Jew as the yeoman backed away, submission in all of his posture—if nothing else he had established deference in this crew, he had the weight of royalty behind him, and there were rumored special and terrible arrangements that the king could visit even at a distance upon mutineers, spies among the crew. "Tell me what brings you above deck? Yes, what do you want?"

The Jew, still staring at him in that curious and affecting way, said, "My name is Solomon. *Schelemo,* I come to ask you a favor."

"I am not interested in your name," Cristoforo said. "Your names, frankly, mean nothing to me."

"Yes, but—"

"If I wanted to establish special relations with Jews," Cristoforo said, "it would not be through the medium of names. I would request your presence in other ways. You are here, below the decks, on sufferance, through the mercy of Isabella and Ferdinand, our king and queen. I have nothing whatsoever to do with any of this, I am simply under orders."

"That is understood," the Jew said. "The conditions below are impossible. There are five hundred and fifty-two of us, and we are fainting. We are placed one upon another in tight racks and without fresh air, without even the possibility of air. There is much fainting and illness."

"This is not my account," Cristoforo said. "Conditions are difficult for all of us. This is a voyage of privation."

"I beg of you," Solomon said. "Permit us to come above decks. Not all together, but ten or twenty at a time, just to relieve ourselves of this torment, to take the air, to move—"

"Conditions are worse on the *Santa María,*" Cristoforo said. "It is a slave ship, filled with the darkest felons of our time. But they do not complain. They drift upon the waters to the New World uncomplainingly, and they hold against the day."

"I know nothing of that," Solomon said. "I know only the conditions below deck. We are perishing. Soon the disease will begin, then the slow and terrible wasting of flesh. Even our most fervent prayers will go unanswered."

Cristoforo shrugged. Another shrug. Shrug at this, turn away from that, consider the Marins, who, it was rumored, had renounced their Judaism to live in secret and had thus evaded the eye of the Inquisition while seeking penalties in other ways. Shrug at the sea, shrug at the New World itself. If it had been left to him, he would have been a merchant at the port of Barcelona and would have left conditions such as these to the more intrepid. How did this happen to him? How had he become the master of such a rude voyage? It was all that Cristoforo could do not to reach out and shake the rabbi, explain that there were many in agony here and that agony was not now only a matter of steerage. But he said nothing of course. The loneliness and fervency of command.

"I am sorry," he said, "I cannot help you. You will have to do what you can down there. It is so decreed. The conditions were made quite explicit to me, surely the same was done for you."

"But how long," Solomon said. "How long will this voyage be?"

Another shrug. Shrug at distance, at lust, at all the complications of empire and design. "I can't answer that," Cristoforo said. "It could be weeks, it could be a matter of days. We have been at sea for almost a month and we are in uncharted waters. When the New World looms over the horizon and not before, then the journey will end. The rest is in hands we cannot understand. Surely you know of imponderables, of fate."

"I know of nothing," Solomon said. "You misjudge us, all of us, clearly. We are not cattle. We are as you, and we are suffering. Men, women, and little children, some with pets smuggled aboard, all in pain, all of them with special and necessary grace. Do you understand any of this?"

"You are to return below deck at once," Cristoforo said, the dark lash of anger trailing through his bowels. "Now, before this continues. You are insolent and you are exceeding my patience. You were taken aboard by measure of the queen's generosity and because she took a sudden and unaccustomed pity upon you. I know of nothing else."

"They cry," Solomon said. "They pray, and in their prayers is their spirit and their torment." He gestured. "Can't you hear?" Indeed, the keening of the Jews to which Cristoforo had accommodated himself as he had to the stunning curvature of the water struck him suddenly, rose up within him now with the urgency if not the fragrance of those spices he sought. Words seemed to emerge dimly from the groans of insistence, then subsided. "*Adonai*," the Jews cried. "*Elohim, Brich hu omen*." "O countrymen," Solomon said, "my countrymen, my brother—"

"Enough," Cristoforo said. "I am the captain." He turned his back to signal that the interview was over, that the petition had been reviewed and denied, that, no less than Torquemada, he had been forced to obduracy as a means of containing these people. Behind him he could hear grunts, then whimpers as if Solomon were planning some desperate final assault. Cristoforo shook his head, folded his arm, stared grimly at the sea, which heaved from its greenish depths the small mysteries of flotsam, small pieces of debris that assumed vaguely organic shape, then were swallowed by the water. "*V'yisgadal. Shmeh rabo.*" The small and diminished sound of Solomon pattering away from him and then the chants rising from the spaces of Neptune, mingling with the sounds of the sea itself, swaddling Cristoforo in the dangerous and terrible sounds that signaled the slow turning of the earth, the emergence of the New World to the starboard. In the distance Cristoforo imagined that he could see mountains, could glimpse the tread of elephants, could see the bangles of princes as they contended with one another for the splendors of their new estate, but he knew the signs of delirium when from a great distance he let it signal him. He was a man of the sea. Cristoforo shrugged again, shrug for the Jews, for Torquemada's insistence, for Torquemada's descent. Shrug for the New World, shrug for the troubles and purchase of five hundred Jews below deck whom he would never see, could never grasp. More was to be done and later. He felt his body lighten as a sense of decision came upon him. This would only last to a certain point, then there would be another circumstance. He was sure of it. Shrug and step, step and shrug, a sudden disturbing intimation of Isabella's swollen and needful breast prodding at him as he signaled the yeoman to take over the helm, however momentarily.

On the *Santa María* Torquemada, enthused, gathered the desperadoes around him. Garbed as they, indistinguishable from them, far departed from the priestly robes of his magnificence, he had become their equal and therefore their superior. The plan was working. The cunning and ingenious plan—worked out in the most sacred places of the Church and then with the king and queen—was working. "O listen to me," Torquemada said. "O listen, friends and companions." They gathered around him, the most desperate men of Spain, men so desperate that on this voyage of desperadoes they had been segregated. Only Torquemada could control them, could understand and apprehend their spirit, and it was for this reason—*to test himself*—that he had embarked upon this exile. Behind him the Jews, who soon enough would be encountered. "The New World beckons," Torquemada said. "A place of justice, light, and peace. Attend to it! Can you not see it?" Unshaven and desperate heads turned, gleaning the new land through the spume of the sea. "Here we will begin afresh," Torquemada said. "That was the plan, the plan for all of us." They murmured in response. "Here," Torquemada said, "we will take the Jews and plant them, rid the world of Israel, depart then for new and better shores. But you must keep your courage up. Must not fail."

"Kill them," one of the men said. "We should go back to the master's ship and kill them now."

Torquemada smiled, thinking of how far he had taken them, how far all of them had come in this one sharp, difficult month of voyage. "Not just yet," he said. "It must be at the right time for the right purpose. Now it would be just slaughter. There was enough slaughter in Spain, here it will be of a different kind. We will seed the ground," Torquemada said. "We will expend their blood in the purposes of consecration, and it will be better."

"You talk like a priest," one of them said. "Are you a priest, then? Or are you one of us."

"I am one of this and one of the other," Torquemada said. "I make faith with you in these spaces as you make faith with me. Soon the mountains, the tablelands of the New World will be upon us and we will turn them holy under the gush of sacrificial blood. But for now," he said, "for now we must once again pray, we must place our knives and ordnance in protected places and pray for a good conclusion to this voyage. Do you hear me? *Ave María,*" Torquemada said, and continued with the familiar litany. They settled in with him, attentive as scholars to the rhythm of his words. *I had no choice,* Torquemada thought, looking at the high plumes of the water, the sails glinting against the turbulence. *It was difficult, but the only means to carry forth the Inquisition. One must constantly move outward in order to move inward. We had accomplished our sacred purposes in Madrid. Barcelona had become ours as well. Soon it would have turned within, and by losing everything we would have gone beyond risk. But here, here, by transporting the Jews, by moving forth even as we move back, we have encountered and made ripe the oldest possibilities of all.*

Or am I not sanctified? he thought, a man of doubt as well as of faith, just as the honored Savior himself had been. *Is it this or that? Is it one thing or the other? Is that shipful of Jews headed for the Jerusalem of the spirit that we will erect or, aligned in the sign of the cross, will they perish at the bottom of the seas? In Cristoforo's hands,* he thought, *but fortunately I can attend to the matters of transcendence, leave the temporal in the hands of Cristoforo.* "Thy will be done," Torquemada said. They looked at him intently. He raised his hands in the gesture of submission, feeling the terrible power of the water underneath.

In the racks Solomon said, "I did the best I could. I pleaded with him. I asked for air and light."

"But he said no," the three Davids said. "He said no," the Israelites said. "He would not have us," Judith and Rachel said, wiping the foreheads of the children who clustered. "He refused."

"That is right," Solomon said. "He refused. He said that we were steerage, garbage, at the behest of the queen but of no concern to him. I told him that we would die, and he turned away. There is nothing to be done."

"Cristoforo is not a man of mercy," Judith said. "He cares nothing for any of us."

"That is not so," Solomon said. "He is doing what he must, just as we are. He is in the control of larger forces. At least we are on the seas. We have been spared the Inquisition. Maybe it will be different for those of us who live. If they live. If we live. This damnable voyage…"

"Spared the Inquisition," Ruth said, taking Solomon's hand, "but not the Inquisitor. The Inquisitor is always with us. He comes in the night, he follows on the seas, he screams from the bowels of Neptune. I understand that now."

"Nothing to be done," Solomon said. "We are creatures of their mercy."

"I tell you," Rachel said, "that there is a judgment coming that is beyond all of us. They seek a New World, but it is eternally the old."

The steerage, silent when Solomon had returned, cast down to silence by hope or at least curiosity, resumed, broken fragments of prayers ascending only to the thin bulkheads that made them crouch against the racks, then dispersed. "It will not be long," Solomon said, "we cannot survive this. We are a shipful of Jews, not of mystics or explorers, and in our flight is our guilt and our culpability. Nevertheless—"

"Nevertheless," Judith said, as if she had taken his thought, pressing his hand, "nevertheless we have at least carried ourselves, carried a bit of testimony, moved to some different place through the designs of our own spirit. We are not Marins. We are not apostosaic. Our apostasy is of a different kind."

"All displacement is apostasy," Solomon said, the chanting murmuring about him, the disputation with Judith—*this woman,* to engage not only in prayers but Talmudic disputation with women was their peculiar but necessary fate in these conditions—continuing, all of their strange and strangely confluent anguish melding as the *Pinta* inexorably carried them toward a fate they could not determine, in all faith, in the faith of God, the one God of Israel whose Name was One and whose Oneness was indivisible in the heart of their exile.

Torquemada, seized by a sudden spirit of ecstasy and affirmation, struck as if by a bolt from the brow of the Holy Ghost, began to dance and heave upon the deck of the *Santa María,* incognizant of the stares of the felons, indifferent to the risks that this display of ecstasy might bring upon him, the steps of his dance carrying him from one side of the ship to the next while on the bosom of the ocean the craft lurched and spilled not only its provisions but its prayers in the sullen light of this journey.

And so, and so they came upon the New World then, the slave ship and the master's ship and the ship between, the shipful of Jews and the ship of the Inquisitor, caught their first glimpse of the New World through the mist and fog of their combined prayers, and in that moment, as Torquemada leapt, as the Jews chanted, as a grim and compliant Cristoforo set sextant and compass and shrugged toward this newest part of his destiny, in that moment it was as if all the centuries had slipped by and this strange and mismatched concatenation of spirits and flesh, voyagers and prisoners, repelled and necessitous, were gathered by that bolt that had struck Torquemada and that swept them from the bosom of the ocean to the bowels of the ship, then expelled them to all of the crevices of the twentieth century itself, myths of purgation and collision hastening their way toward the apostasies to come. The shipful of Jews, their captain, their keeper, and their inquisitor joined at last in that voyage of transcendence. Cristoforo dreamed it, dreamed it all, dreamed that he was in the enormous grasp of Isabella herself, her capacious sex absorbing and expelling him as would all of the centuries and scholars to come and the spray of his seed upon the ocean of the queen the plume to drag him past myth and toward that first terrible awareness of his destiny. Cristoforo the Jew. Cristoforo the keeper of souls *V'ysh ka'dash. Shmeh rabbo.*

Brich hu.

Omen.

Harry Turtledove

Archetypes

The knock on the door was tentative, the sort any secretary learns to make when he is not sure his superior wishes to be disturbed. But to Basil Argyros the interruption came as a relief. "Come in," he called, shoving papyrus scrolls and sheets of parchment to one side of his desk.

The magistrianos had been daydreaming anyhow, looking out from his office in the Praitorion toward the great brown stucco mass of the church of Hagia Sophia and, beyond it, softened by haze, the Asian coast across the Propontis from Constantinople.

The case he had been trying to ignore was an Egyptian land dispute, which meant it would not be settled in his lifetime no matter what he did, nor probably in his grandson's either. The insane litigiousness of the Egyptians had angered the Emperor Julian almost a thousand years before. They had only grown worse since, Argyros thought. As a good Christian, he condemned Julian the Apostate to Hell; as an official of the Roman Empire, he was convinced that dealing with Egyptians gave a foretaste of it.

And so he greeted his secretary with an effusiveness alien to his usually self-contained nature: "Good day, Anthimos! What can I do for you on this fine spring morning?"

Anthimos, a lean, stooped man whose fingers were always black with ink, eyed the magistrianos suspiciously; he wanted people to be as orderly and predictable as the numbers in his ledgers. At last he shrugged and said, "The Master of Offices is here to see you, sir."

"What?" Argyros' thick black eyebrows shot up in surprise. "Show him in, of course." George Lakhanodrakon headed the corps of magistrianoi, and was one of the few officials who reported directly to the Emperor.

The solid portliness of the Master of Offices seemed all the more imposing next to Anthimos, who fluttered about nervously until Argyros dismissed him. The magistrianos bowed low to Lakhanodrakon, waved him to a chair, offered wine. "Always a pleasure to see you, your illustriousness. What brings you here today? Not this wretched mess, I hope."

Lakhanodrakon rose, walked over to pick up one of the documents Argyros so described. He held it at arm's length; he was about fifty, a dozen or so years older than the magistrianos, and his sight was beginning to lengthen. He read for a moment. His strong, rather heavy features showed his distaste. "*Pcheris vs. Sarapion*, is it? I didn't know you were stuck with such drivel. No it's nothing to do with that, I promise."

"Then you're doubly welcome, sir," Argyros said sincerely. "I've been praying to St. Mouamet for a new assignment."

The patron of changes, eh?" Lakhanodrakon chuckled. Born a pagan in the Arabian desert, Mouamet had accepted Christianity on a trading journey to Syria, become a famed hymnographer, and ended his days as bishop of New Carthage in Ispania near the Pillars of Herakles. That was enough change to pack into any man's life.

The amusement fell from the Master of Offices' face. "Your prayers are about to be granted. Tell me what you make of this." He fumbled in the silk pouch that hung from his gold belt of rank, produced a rolled-up parchment, and handed it to Argyros.

The magistrianos slid off the ribbon that bound the parchment, skimmed through it. "It's bad Greek," he remarked.

"Keep going."

"Of course, sir." When he was done, Argyros said, "I take it this came from one of the cities in the East, Mesopotamia or perhaps Syria?"

"Mesopotamia—from Daras, to be exact."

The magistrianos nodded. "Yes, it has all the marks of a Persian piece: a polemic against the Orthodox faith, and an invitation to the Nestorians and hardcore Monophysites and other heretics to abandon their allegiance to the Empire and go over to the King of Kings. Preferably, I suppose, bringing the fortress of Daras with them."

"No doubt," Lakhanodrakon agreed dryly.

"Forgive me, sir," Argyros said, "but I've seen a great many handbills of this sort. Why bring this particular one to my attention?"

Instead of answering directly, the Master of Offices took another parchment from his beltpouch. "When you have examined this sheet, I trust you will understand—as well as I do, at any rate, which is not a great deal."

The magistrianos looked at Lakhanodrakon in puzzlement after reading the first few lines. "But this is just the same as the other—" His voice trailed away and his eyes snapped back to the parchment. He picked up the other sheet Lakhanodrakon had given him, held one in each hand. His jaw fell.

"You see it, then," the Master of Offices said. "Good. You are as quick as I thought you were."

"Thank you," Argyros said abstractedly. He was still

staring at the two pieces of parchment. They both said the same thing—exactly the same. It was not as if a scribe had copied out a message twice. Each line on both sheets had exactly the same words on it, written exactly the same size. The same word was misspelled in the third line of each sheet. A couple of lines later, the same incorrect verb form appeared in each, then an identical dative after a preposition where a genitive belonged. Near the end, the letter *pi* at the beginning of a word was half effaced on both handbills. They even shared the identical small smear of ink between two words.

The magistrianos put one sheet over the other, walked to the window. He held the parchments up to the sun, worked them until the left edges of the two messages were precisely aligned. Any differences would have been instantly apparent. There were none.

"Mother of God, help me!" Argyros exclaimed.

"May She protect the entire Empire," George Lakhanodrakon said soberly. "Not just these two, but hundreds of such sheets, have appeared in Daras, nailed to every wall big enough to hold one, it seems. They may well provoke the uprisings they seek—you know how touchy the East always is."

Argyros knew. Despite having been a part of the Roman Empire since before Christ's Incarnation, Syria and Mesopotamia were very different from its other regions. Latin was all but unknown there, and even Greek, the Empire's dominant tongue, was spoken only by a minority in the towns. Most people used Syriac or Arabic, as their ancestors had before them. Heresy flourished there as nowhere else.

And further east lay Persia, the Empire's eternal rival. The two great powers had been struggling for 1,400 years, each dreaming of vanquishing the other for good. The Persians always fostered unrest in the eastern provinces of the Empire. Worshipers of the sun and fire themselves, they gave Nestorians refuge and stirred up religious strife to occupy the Romans with internal troubles. But never on such a scale as this—

"How are they doing it?" Argyros said, as much to himself as to the Master of Offices.

"That is what I charge you with: to find out," Lakhanodrakon said. "Your success in ferreting out the secret of the Franco-Saxons' hellpowder last year made me think of you the moment those"—he jerked a thumb at the parchments Argyros was still holding—"came to my attention."

"You flatter me, your illustriousness."

"No, I need you," the Master of Offices said. Harsh lines of worry ran from his jutting nose to the corners of his mouth. "I tell you, I fear this worse than the hellpowder. That was only a threat against our borders; we have dealt with such before, a hundred times. But this could be a blow to the heart."

Argyros frowned. "Surely you exaggerate, sir."

"Do I? I've lain awake at night imagining the chaos these sheets could create. Suppose one said one thing, one another? They could fan faction against faction, heretic against Orthodox—"

His wave encompassed all of Constantinople. "Suppose a Persian agent smuggled even a donkeyload of these accursed things into the city!" Throughout the Empire, its capital was *the* city. "Men from every corner of the world live here—Jews, Egyptians, Armenians, Sklavenoi from the lands by the Ister, Franco-Saxons. Set them at each other's throats, and it could be the Nika riots come again!"

"You've seen farther than I have," Argyros admitted, shivering. It had been eight hundred years since Constantinople's mob, shouting *Nika*—Triumph—had almost toppled Justinian the Great from the Roman throne, but that was the standard against which all later urban uprisings were measured.

"Perhaps farther than the Persians, too, or they would not waste their time at the frontier," Lakhanodrakon said. "But they will not stay blind long, I fear. Beware of them, Basil. They are no rude barbarians to be befooled like the Franco-Saxons; they are as old in deceit as we."

"I shall remember," the magistrianos promised. He picked up the parchments Lakhanodrakon had given him, tucked them away. "The rest of this pile of trash I shall cheerfully consign to Anthimos. I'll leave for Daras in a day or two. As you know, I'm a widower; I have no great arrangements to make. But I would like to light a candle at church dedicated to St. Nicholas before I go."

"A good choice," the Master of Offices said.

"Yes—who better than the patron saint of thieves?"

"I've tried everything I can think of," the garrison commandant of Daras said, slamming a fist down on his desk in frustration. "Every incoming traveler has his baggage searched, and I keep patrols on the streets day and night. Yet the damned handbills keep showing up."

"I can't fault what you've done, Leontios," Argyros said, and the soldier leaned back in his chair with a sign of relief. He was a big, burly man, almost as tall as Argyros and thicker through the shoulders, but there was no question who dominated the conversation. Magistrianoi, roving agents with their commissions directly from the Master of Offices, could make or break even the leader of an outpost as important as Daras.

"More wine?" Leontios extended a pitcher.

"Er—no thanks," Argyros said, he hoped politely. The wine, like much of what was drunk in Mesopotamia, was made from dates. He found it sickeningly sweet. But he would have to work with Leontios, and did not want to hurt his feelings, so he held out his hand, remarking, "That's a handsome jug you have there. May I see it?"

"Oh, d'you like it? Seems ordinary enough to me."

"Hardly that. I'm not used to seeing reliefwork on pottery, and the depiction of our Lord driving the moneychangers from the Temple is well done, I think."

"If it pleases you so, take it and welcome," Leontios said at once, obviously afraid to antagonize the magistrianos in even a small way. "I'm sure you've seen much better, though, coming from the city."

"There's nothing to match it in Constantinople. The potters there decorate with glazes and drawings, not reliefs."

"Fancy that, us ahead of the capital!" Leontios said. He saw that Argyros did not want the winejug, and put it down. "The style's been all the rage in these parts—both sides of the border, come to that—the last five or ten years. I got this piece from old Abraham last summer. He's a damned Nestorian, but he does good work. His shop is only a block or so away, if you think you might find something you'd fancy."

"Perhaps I'll look him up." Argyros stood, fanned himself with his broad-brimmed hat of woven straw. It did not help much. "Is the heat always so bad?"

The garrison commander rolled his eyes. "My dear sir, this is only June—not even summer yet. If you're still in Daras in six weeks, you'll find out what heat is.

"Do you know that in the Franco-Saxon mountain country it sometimes snows in September? Last year that seemed the most hideous thing I could imagine. Now it strikes me as delightful."

Leontios ran a hairy, sweaty forearm across his face. "It strikes me as impossible. I wish you luck on this madness, more than I've had myself. If I can help in any way, you have only to ask."

"My thanks," Argyros said, and left. The commandant's office had been very warm, shielded though it was by thick walls from the worst Daras could do. The noonday heat outside was unbelievable, stupefying. The sun blazed down mercilessly from the blue enamel bowl of the sky.

The magistrianos squinted against the glare. He wished he could strip off his boots, trousers, and tunic (even if that was gauzy linen) and go naked under his hat. Some of the locals did, walking about in loincloth and sandals. More, though, covered their heads with white cotton cloths and swaddled themselves in great flowing robes, as if they were so many ambulatory tents.

The strange clothes only accented Argyros' feeling of being in an alien land. The houses and other buildings, save for the most splendid, were of whitewashed mud brick, not stone or timber. And the signs that advertised dyeshops or jewelers, taverns, and baths, were apt to be in three languages: angular Greek, the tight curlicues of Syriac, and the wild snakelike script the Arabs used. If any was missing, it was usually the Greek.

A couple of men talking in the street moved on when they saw the magistrianos approaching. They might not know him for an agent, but even if he spoke no word his outfit and his face—tanned but not swarthy—branded him as one loyal to Constantinople, and not to be trusted. He scowled. Such recognition was only going to make his job harder.

The shop across the street had to be the one Leontios had mentioned. There were dishes and jugs and cups in the window, and the Greek line of the signboard above them read FINE POTTERY BY ABRAAM: Greek, of course, could not show the sound of rough breathing in the middle of a word.

Abraam or Abraham stood in the doorway, crying his wares in guttural Syriac. Argyros watched as a smith came over from the foundry next door to bring him a flat, square iron plate. The two men eyed the magistrianos with the same distrust the street idlers had shown. He was getting used to that suspicious stare in Daras. He returned it imperturbably.

The smith, an enormous fellow baked brown as his leather apron by the sun, spat in the dirt roadway and ambled toward his own place of business, still glowering Argyros' way. Abraham the potter turned his back on the magistrianos with deliberate rudeness and went back into the darkness of his shop. Argyros saw him put the iron plate under a counter and talk briefly with a woman back there—whether wife, customer, or what, he did not know.

Operating out of Leontios' barracks would have made him altogether too conspicuous, so he went looking for an inn. He did not notice when the woman emerged from the pottery and hurried after him.

The first taverner he tried spoke only Arabic and catered to nomads out of the desert. As Argyros had but a few phrases of Arabic himself, he decided to go somewhere else.

Two men were waiting for him when he came outside to retrieve his horse. Something in their stance told him their breed at once: street toughs. He walked past them without a sideways glance, hoping his size would make them choose another victim.

But one grabbed at his arm. "Where you go to, you damned swaggering Melkite?" he said grinning, showing bad teeth. He used the eastern heretics' insulting name for one loyal to the dogmas of Constantinople: it meant "king's man."

"None of your concern," Argyros snapped, shaking off the man's hand and springing back. With a curse, the ruffian leaped at him, followed by his companion. The magistrianos kicked the first one where it did the most good. Two against one left no time for chivalry. The fellow went down with a wail, clutching at himself and spewing his last meal out in the dust.

The other tough had a short bludgeon. Argyros threw up

his left arm just in time to keep his head from being broken. He bared his teeth as pain shot through him from elbow to fingertips. His right hand darted to the knife at his belt. "Come on," he panted. "Even odds now."

The local was no coward. He waded in, swung again. Argyros ducked and slashed, coming up from below. The point of his dagger ripped through his enemy's sleeve. He felt the blade slice into flesh. The tough hissed. He was not through, though; he was ready for more fight.

Then a woman behind Argyros screamed something in Arabic. The magistrianos did not understand, but his opponent did. He whirled and fled. Argyros chased him, but he knew Daras' twisting alleyways as an outsider could not, and escaped.

Breathing hard and rubbing his arm, the magistrianos walked back to his horse. He saw what the woman's shout must have meant, for a squad of Leontios' soldiers had gathered round the good-for-naught he had leveled. They were prodding the wretch up, none too gently, with the butts of their spears.

Someone who had watched the brawl pointed at Argyros, which drew the squad-leader's attention. "You ruin this fellow here?" he demanded.

"Frankly, yes. I was set on for no reason and without warning. He had it coming." Anger made him careless with his words.

The squad-leader set his hands on his hips. "Talk like you're the Emperor, don't you? Anyone else see this little scramble?" He glanced at the swelling crowd.

Argyros' heart sank. He did not want to go back to Leontios and waste time on explanations, but he was sure the witnesses would side with a man of Daras rather than an obvious stranger. Unexpectedly, though, a woman spoke up for him: "It's as the tall man says. They attacked him first."

The squad-leader was as taken aback as the magistrianos. Seizing the initiative, Argyros took him aside and pressed a gold nomisma into his palm. along with some silver to keep his men happy. The trooper pocketed the bribe in a businesslike fashion. "Haul that scum out of here," he commanded, and his squad dragged the captive off; two men still had to support him. Onlookers began to drift away.

Argyros looked round to see if he could spot the woman who had come to his aid. She had been well back in the crowd, and he had not got a glimpse of her face. But he had no doubts, for she waited in the shadow of a building across the street instead of leaving with the rest of the spectators. Above a short veil filmy enough to be no more than token concealment, she looked saucily toward him.

"My thanks," the magistrianos said, walking over to her. Something besides mere gratitude put warmth in his voice. From tightly curled black hair to gilded sandals beneath henna-soled feet, she was a strikingly attractive woman. Her dark eyes were bright and lively, her mouth, half seen, full-lipped and inviting. The fitted ankle-length robe she wore displayed her figure to the best advantage; even in the shadow in which she stood, the red, gold, and green sequins at her bodice sparkled with each breath she took.

She said, "It would be wrong for so brave—and so mighty—a man to find himself in trouble he does not deserve." Her Greek had a slight throaty accent. That and her costume told Argyros she was of Persian origin. The border between the two empires went back and forth so often that such things were common on both sides.

"Thanks again," Argyros said; and then, not wanting the conversation to end as abruptly as that, he asked, "Would you happen to know of a decent inn?"

She burst out laughing. "It just so happens that I dance at the hostel of Shahin Bahram's son. It's clean enough and the food is good, if you don't mind eating Persian fare." When Argyros shook his head, she said, "Come on, then; I'll take you there. Bringing you in will make me money, too. I'm Mirrane, by the way."

The magistrianos gave his own name, but said that he had come from Constantinople as inspector of Daras' waterworks. The famous system of cisterns and drains and the dam across the nearby Cordes river added greatly to the strength of the town's fortifications.

"An important man," she murmured, moving closer to him. "Do you think your horse can carry two?"

"For a little way, certainly." He helped her mount in front of him; her waist was supple under his hands. When the horse started forward, she leaned back against him, and did not try to pull away. It made for an enjoyable ride.

Shahin's tavern was in the western part of Daras, not far from the church of the Apostle Bartholomew that Justinian had built when he renovated the town's works. Shahin folded Argyros into a bearhug and called him his lord, his master, his owner—none of which prevented a sharp haggle when it came to the price of a room.

At last Mirrane spoke in Persian: "Don't drive him away." Argyros had a hard time holding his face straight: no use letting the girl know he was fluent in her language, though he did not think there was anything more to this than her not wanting to lose her finder's fee. Shahin became more reasonable.

As was his custom when starting an investigation, the magistrianos wandered into the taproom to drink a little wine and soak up the local gossip. Shahin's place was good for that; it featured a mixed clientele, and talk came fast and furious in the three tongues of the imperial east and Persian as well. There was more chatter about doings in Ctesiphon, the Persian, capital, than over what was happening in Constantinople.

Naturally enough, the handbills were also a prominent subject, but not in a way that helped Argyros. The townsfolk seemed much less upset about them than George Lakhanodrakon or Leontios had been. One man, well in his cups, said with a shrug, "They're looking to break our nerve. I'll fret when I see a Persian army outside the walls, and not until."

The magistrianos tried to prompt him: "Don't you think that Nestorians might invite—" Several people shushed him, and he had to subside, for four musicians emerged from a back room to take their seats on low stools by the fireplace. One carried two vase-shaped drums and had a tambourine strapped to his calf, another brought a pair of flutes, a third a long trumpet, and the last a short-necked lute played with a bow, something Argyros had not seen at Constantinople.

At a nod from the lutanist, they began to play. The drummer's beat was more intricate than Argyros was used to, the tune lively but at the same time somehow languorous. Again he was conscious of the traditions older than the Roman Empire that lived on in the east.

Then Mirrane glided into the taproom, and the magistrianos worried about traditions no more. She wore only her veil and a few jeweled ornaments that sparkled in the torchlight; her smooth skin gleamed with oil. When she moved among the tables, it was as if she sought out a particular man to slay with lust. Sinuous as a serpent, she slid away from every arm that reached out to take hold of her.

"With a dance like that," Argyros whispered to the man at the table next to his, "why does she bother with the veil?"

The fellow was shocked enough to tear his burning gaze away from Mirrane. "It were a gross indecency, for a woman to show her face in public!"

"Oh."

Mirrane's eyes flashed as she recognized the magistrianos, and he knew she had chosen him for her victim.

Laughing, she waved to the musicians; the tune grew faster and more urgent. It would have taken a man of stone, which Argyros assuredly was not, to remain unstirred as she whirled in front of him. The oil on her skin was scented with musk; under it he caught the perfume of herself.

The music rose to a fiery crescendo. With a shout, Mirrane flung herself down on the seat by Argyros, cast her arms around his neck. With her warm length pressed against him, he hardly heard the storm of applause that filled the inn.

And later, when she went upstairs with him, he ignored with equal aplomb the jealous catcalls that followed them. Knowing what was important at any given moment, he told himself, was a virtue.

He woke the next morning feeling considerably rumpled but otherwise as well as he ever had in his life. The soft straw pallet was narrow for two; Mirrane's leg sprawled over his calf. He moved slowly and carefully, but woke her anyway as he got out of bed. "Sorry."

She smiled lazily up at him. "You have nothing to be sorry for."

"I'm glad of that." He politely turned his back to use the chamberpot, then splashed water on his face and rinsed his mouth from a ewer that stood next to the bed. He ran his fingers through his hair and beard, shook his head in mock dismay at the snarls he found. "You'd think the dogs dragged me in, the way I must look."

"Do you always worry so much?" she asked, rising and stretching luxuriously.

"As a matter of fact, yes." He went over to his saddlebags, which he had not yet unpacked, in search of a comb. Several jingling trinkets and her veil were draped over the leather sacks. She took them back from him while he rummaged.

He lifted out three or four small, tightly stoppered pots with bits of rag protruding from holes drilled through their corks. "What on earth are those?" Mirrane asked; they were not the sort of thing travelers usually carried.

Argyros thought fast. "They're filled with clay," he said. "I filter water from the cisterns through them; from the amount and type of sediment left behind, I can judge how pure the water is."

"Ah," she nodded, not revealing much interest in anything so mundane as the tools of his alleged trade.

All the same, he was relieved when he finally found his bone comb and stowed the pots away. They were filled, not with clay, but with the Franco-Saxon compound of charcoal, sulfur, and saltpeter that the armorers of Constantinople had dubbed hellpowder. Argyros had no intention of advertising its existence without dire need.

He combed out his tangled whiskers. "That's—ouch— better." When he was done dressing, he said, "I know what I do seems dull, but Daras may need all the water it can find to hold out against a Persian attack if these parchments I've heard about stir up the rebellion they're after!"

Mirrane's costume made a simple shrug worth looking at. "I've heard of them too, but there haven't been many here round Shahin's place." She hesitated. "Are you thinking we may be disloyal because we're of Persian blood? Shahin's grandfather converted to Christianity—Orthodox, not Nestorian— and he worships every week at Bartholomew's church."

He believed her. There was no point in lying about something of that sort; it was too easy to check. "I wasn't thinking any such thing," he said. "I'd rather not get stuck in a siege, though, especially in a city that may run dry. And," he added a moment later, "it would be sinful to risk you."

Since he had used the story he did, he thought it was actually wise to examine some of Daras' waterworks. One major cistern stood close to the church of the Apostle Bartholomew. He poked at the brickwork as if to check its soundness, then climbed the stairs to the top of the great tank and peered into it to see what the water level was.

One of the faces he noticed while he was puttering about seemed familiar. After a while he realized that the hawk-faced fellow lounging against a wall and munching a pomegranate was the flute-player at Shahin's tavern. The man was gone by the time he got down from the cistern, which left Argyros uncertain whether his presence was coincidental or the magistrianos' cover had satisfied him.

Leontios greeted him cordially when, having had enough play-acting, he went over to the garrison commander's head-quarters. "Any progress?"

"Not really," Argyros said. "I have more new questions than answers. First, are you sure your men have Daras sealed off from getting these handbills from outside?"

"I told you so yesterday. Oh, I'll not deny they'd take the gold to let some things through, but not that poison. We've lived through too many religious riots to want more."

"Fair enough. Next question: where can I find the best map of the city?"

Leontios tugged at his beard as he thought. "That would be in the eparch's office, not here. He collects the head-tax and the hearth-tax, so he has to keep track of every property in the city. My own charts are years out of date—the main streets don't change much, and they're mainly what I'm concerned with as a military man."

"No blame on you," Argyros assured him. "Now—third one pays for all. Do you keep note of where in Daras your troopers have pulled down parchments?"

He waited tensely. Many soldiers would not have both-ered with such minutiae. But the Roman bureaucratic tradi-tion was strong, even in the Army, and there was a chance—

Leontios' relieved grin told him he had won the gamble. "I have them," the garrison commander said. "I warn you, though, not all are in Greek. Do you read Arabic?"

"Not a word of it. But surely some bright young clerk in the eparch's chancery will. I shall go there now; when you gather your troopers' reports, please be so good as to send them after me."

"With pleasure." Leontios cocked an eyebrow at the magistrianos. "If I dared say no, I suppose you'd set upon me, as you did on those two hoodlums yesterday."

"Oh, that." Argyros had almost forgotten the incident. Doubting he would hear anything worthwhile, he asked, "What did you learn from the one your men took?"

"Ravings, I'm certain—what's the point of torturing a man who's just been kicked in the crotch? He keeps babbling of a woman who paid him and his partner to assault you. He's been eating poppy-juice, if you ask me. Anyone out to hire killers would pick a better pair than those sorry sods, don't you think?"

"I'd hope so," Argyros said, but the news disturbed him. The woman, he felt sure, was Mirrane, but he could not see the game she was playing. Had the attack been set up to make him grateful to her? If so, why was the hired tough still around to speak of it? "Perhaps I'll have a word with the fellow myself, after I'm done at the eparch's."

"Feel free. Meanwhile, I'll hunt up those notes and get them over there for you."

The chief map in the eparch's office was several feet square, an updated papyrus facsimile of the master map of Daras inscribed on a bronze tablet in the imperial chancery at Constantinople. At Argyros's request, the eparch—a plump, fussy little man named Mammianos—provided him with a small copy on a single sheet of parchment.

As the magistrianos had predicted, several of Mammianos' secretaries were fluent in Arabic. "One has to have them here, sir," the eparch said, "if one is transact the business necessary to the fisc." He assigned Argyros a clerk named Harun, which the magistrianos guessed to be a corruption of the perfectly good Biblical name Aaron.

After that there was nothing to do but wait for Leontios' messenger, who arrived an hour or so later with an armload of papyri, parchments, and ostraca. He dumped them in front of Argyros and departed.

The magistrianos sorted out the notes in Greek, which he could handle himself. "'In front of the shop of Peter son of Damian, on the Street of the Tailors,'" he read. "Where's that, Harun?" The clerk pointed with a stylus. Argyros made a mark on his map.

It was nearly sunset when the last dot went into its proper place. "Many thanks," Argyros said. He gave a nomisma to the secretary, who had proven a model of patience and competence, and waved off his stammered protests. "Go on, take it—you've earned it. I couldn't have done any of this without you. Mammianos is well served."

Leontios was on the point of going home when the magistrianos came back to his headquarters. "I'd about given up on you. What did you find? That the handbills are thickest in the parts of town where the most Nestorians live?"

"That's just what I expected," Argyros said, admiring the officer's quick wits. "But it isn't so. Here; see for yourself. Each dot shows where a parchment was found."

"The damn things are everywhere!" Leontios grunted after a quick look at the map.

"Not quite." Argyros bent over the parchment, pointed. "See, here's a patch where there isn't any."

"Isn't that big square building the barracks here? No wonder the filthy rabblerousers stayed away. They're bastards, but they're not fools, worse luck."

"So it is. Odd, though, wouldn't you say, that your strongpoint is on the edge of the empty area instead of at the center. And what of this other blank stretch?"

"Over in the west? Ah, but look, there's the church of St. Bartholomew in it. The priests would be as likely to raise the alarm as my soldiers. Likelier, maybe; not all my men are Orthodox."

"But again," Argyros pointed out, "the church is at the edge of the clear space, not in the middle. And look, here is the Great Church, in the very center of town, with a handbill nailed to one of its gates. The agitators aren't afraid of priests, it seems."

"So it does," Leontios said reluctantly. "What then?"

"I wish I knew. What puzzles me most, though, is this third empty area, close to the northern wall. From what Mammianos' clerk said, it's a solidly Nestorian district, and yet there are no parchments up in it."

"Where is that? Let me see. Aye, the fellow's right; that's the worst part of town, probably because of the stink. Dyers and butchers and gluemakers and tanners and such work there. To say nothing of thieves, that is—the one who went for you hailed from that section."

"Oh yes, him. He almost slipped my mind again. As I said, I'd like to ask him a few questions of my own."

Leontios looked embarrassed. "There's a harsher judge than you questioning him now, I'm afraid. He died a couple of hours ago."

"Died? How?" Argyros exclaimed.

"From what the gaoler says, pain in the belly, and I don't mean on account of your foot. If I had to guess, I'd think the fish-sauce went over; you know how hard it is to keep in this climate."

"I suppose so," the magistrianos said, but the ruffian's death struck him as altogether too pat. He stared down at the map on Leontios' desk, trying by sheer force of will to extract meaning from the cryptic pattern there. It refused to yield. Grumbling in annoyance, he rolled up the map and walked back to Shahin's tavern. A copper twenty-follis piece bought the services of a torchboy to light his way through the black maze of nighttime Daras.

The taproom was jammed when he got to the inn, and for good reason: Mirrane was already dancing. Her eyes lit up when she saw him standing against the back wall drinking a mug of wine (real grape wine, and correspondingly expensive) and chewing on unleavened pocketbread stuffed with lentils, mutton, and onions.

Later that night she said petulantly, "If your things were not still in your room, I would have thought you'd gone away and left me. Are your precious cisterns so much more interesting that I am?"

"Hardly," he said, caressing her. She purred and snuggled closer. "I find you fascinating." That was true, but he hoped she did not realize in how many senses of the word he meant it.

The magistrianos visited the northern part of the city on the following day. He noted that his shadow was back. He doubted the fellow was enjoying himself much, or learning much either. All of Argyros' actions were perfectly consistent with what he would have done had he been a genuine cistern-inspector.

The second of Daras' two major water-storage was easy to examine, for Justinian's engineer Chryses had diverted the Cordes river to flow between the town's outworks and its main wall, thereby also serving as a moat and offering extra protection against attack. To check the level of the water, all Argyros had to do was climb to the top of the wall and look down over the battlements.

Not much of Daras' masonry still dated from Justinian's time. The city had fallen to the Persians in the reign of his successor, and again less than half a century later when the madman Phokas almost brought the Empire to ruin, and two or three more times in the years since. Once or twice it had had to stand Roman siege while in Persian hands. Just the same, the ancient fortifications had been designed well, and all later military architects used them as their model.

The wall, then, was of stone, about forty feet high and ten thick. Arrow-slits and a runway halfway up gave defenders a second level from which to shoot at foes outside. The slits, though, were not wide enough for Argyros to stick his head through, and in any case he wanted the view from the top of the wall, so he climbed the whole long stairway. The man following him loitered at the base, and bought some hot chick-peas.

The magistrianos was a little jealous; in Daras' heat, the trudge had made his heart pound. In another way, though, Argyros had the better of it, for he was above the smell. As Leontios had said, northern Daras stank. It reeked of terrified animals and the excrement from the butchers' shops; of stale, sour urine from the dyers'; of that same vile odor and the sharper tang of tanbark from the tanneries; and of a nameless but unpleasant stench from cauldrons that bubbled behind every gluemaker's establishment. Added to the usual city stink of overcrowded, unwashed humanity, it made for a savage assault on the nose. The faint breeze that blew off the Cordes carried the scent of manure from the fields outside of town, but was ambrosial by comparison.

Argyros walked along the track atop the wall, peering down into Daras. It was the broadest view he could gain of the northern district. Searching there street by street would have been fruitless, especially since he was not sure what he was looking for.

With such gloomy reflections as that, he paced back and forth for a couple of hours. The sentries at the battlements came to ignore him; down below, the musician from Shahin's inn grew bored, and fell asleep sitting against the wall, his headcloth pulled low to shield his face from the sun.

The magistrianos could not have said what drew his attention to the donkey making its slow way down an alley, its driver beside it. Perhaps it was that the beast carried a couple of pots of glue along with several larger, roughly square packages, and he found it odd for an animal to be bearing burdens for two different shops. He certainly could not think of anything a gluemaker turned out that would go in those neatly wrapped bundles. They were about the size of—

His boots thumping on stone, he dashed down the steps and past his dozing shadow. Then, careless of the hard looks and angry shouts that he drew, he hurled himself into traffic, shoving past evil-tempered camels that bared their teeth at him and pushing merchants out of the way. As he trotted along, he panted out prayers that he could remember about where he had seen that donkey, and that he could find the spot now that he was at ground level.

It was somewhere near the three-story whitewashed building with the narrow windows, of that much he was sure. Just where, though, was another matter. And of course the donkey, though it was only ambling, would have gone some distance by the time he got to where he had seen it. Staring wildly down one lanelet after another, Argyros thought of Zeno's paradox about Achilles and the tortoise, and wondered if he would ever catch up.

There the beast was, about to turn into Daras' main north-south avenue, called the Middle Street after Constantinople's Mese. Imitating Leontios' gesture of a few days before, Argyros wiped sweat from his forehead with his sleeve and took a minute or two to let his breathing slow. He needed to seem natural.

A brisk walk let him come up behind the donkey's driver. "Excuse me," he said. "Do you speak Greek?"

The man spread his hands. "Little bit."

"Ah, good." As casually as he could, Argyros asked, "Tell me, are those parchments your donkey is carrying?"

He was tense as a strung bow. If the answer to that was yes, he half expected to be attacked on the spot. But the driver only nodded. "So they are. What about it?"

"Er—" For a moment, the magistrianos' usually facile tongue stumbled. Then he rallied: "May I buy one? I, uh, forgot to write out a receipt for several tenants of mine, and seeing you passing by with your bundles here reminded me of it."

How much of the explanation the local understood was not clear, but he knew what they word "buy" meant. After some brisk bargaining, they settled on half a silver miliaresion as a fair price. The donkey-driver undid one of his packages. Again Argyros got ready for action, thinking that the man did not know what he was carrying and that the subversive handbills would now be revealed.

But the parchment the driver handed him was blank. "Is all right?"

"Hmm? Oh, yes, fine, thank you," he said, distracted. As if he were an expert testing the quality of the goods, he riffled the corners of the stacked sheets—maybe the first few were empty to conceal the rest. But none had anything on it. He gave up. "You have a very fine stock here. Whatever scribe it's going to will enjoy writing on it."

"Thank you, sir." The donkey-driver pocketed his coin and tied up the package again. "Is not to any scribe going, though."

"Really?" the magistrianos said, not much interested. "To whom, then?"

The driver grinned, as if about to tell a funny story he did not think his listener would believe. "To Abraham the potter, of all peoples. He the glue wants, too."

"Really?" Argyros' tone of voice was entirely different this time. "What on earth does he need with a thousand sheets of parchment and enough glue to stick half of Daras down?"

"For all I know, he crazy," the man shrugged. "My master Yesuyab, he work on this order the last month. And when he get it ready to go, Musa the gluemaker next door, he tell me he gots for Abraham too, so would I take along? Why not, I say. My donkey strong."

"Yes, of course. Well, thank you again." Argyros let the fellow go, then stood staring after him until a man leading three packhorses yelled at him to get out of the way. He stepped aside, still scratching his head.

Something else occurred to him. He went back to the chancery. With Harun's capable help, he soon added two marks to his map of Daras, then a third, and, as an afterthought, a fourth. He studied the pattern they made. "Well, well," he said. "How interesting."

Mesopotamian night fell with dramatic suddenness. No sooner was the sun gone from the sky, it seemed, than full darkness came. Last night that had been a nuisance; now Argyros intended to take advantage of it. He had returned to Shahin's inn during the late afternoon, grumbling of having to go right back to the chancery, probably for hours. He had to stop himself from nodding at his crestfallen shadow, who looked up from a mug of beer in surprise and relief when he arrived.

The wretch trailed him again, of course, but he really did revisit Mammianos' headquarters. The scribes and secretaries eyed him curiously as he waited around doing nothing until his tracker grew bored and mooched off, convinced he was there for the evening as he had feared. The staff departed just before sunset, leaving the place to Argyros.

The magistrianos prowled through the black streets of Daras like a burglar, without any light to give away his presence. He slunk into a doorway when a squad of Leontios' troopers came tramping by. Soon he might need to call on the garrison commander for aid, but not yet.

The smithy next to Abraham's pottery shop made it easy to find, for which Argyros was grateful. As he had thought, the windows were shuttered and the place barred and locked, both front and back. Nothing surprising there—anyone in his right mind would have done the same.

He considered the lock that held the back door closed: a standard type. A hole had been drilled from top to bottom near one end of the door bar. There was a similar hole bored part of the way into the bottom board of the frame into which the bar was slid. Before Abraham had gone home, he had dropped a cylindrical metal pin down through the barhole so that half of it was in the frame and the rest above it, holding the bar in place.

The top of the metal cylinder was still lower than the level of the upper surface of the bar, so no passerby could hope to pull it out. Abraham, no doubt, had a key with hooks or catches fitted to those of the boltpin to let him draw it out again.

There were, however, other ways. Argyros reached into his beltpouch and took out a pair of long-snouted pincers, rather like the ones physicians used to clamp bleeding blood vessels. His set, though, instead of having flat inner surfaces, was curved within.

He slipped them into the bolthole. After some jiggling, he felt them slide down past the top of the pin. When he tightened them, it was easy to lift the bolt out of its socket.

The magistrianos left the door ajar to let a little light into the shop and give him the chance to find a lamp. He worked flint and steel until he got the wick going, then closed the door after him. The shuttered windows would keep the lamp's pale illumination from showing on the street out front.

He prowled about the inside of the cramped little shop. At first everything seemed quite ordinary. Here were two kilns, their fires out for the evening but still warm to the touch. A foot-powered wheel stood between them. There lay great lumps of refined clay, and jugs of water next to them to soften them. Abraham had molds in the shape of a hand, a fish, a bunch of grapes, and other things, as well as a set of what looked like sculptors' tools to create the reliefwork popular in Daras. Pots that were ready to sell filled shelves in the front of the store.

After a snarl of frustration, Argyros began to use his head. If anything here was not as it should be, it would be connected with the parchments Yesuyab had sent Abraham. Where were they? The magistrianos held the lamp high. He made a disgusted noise deep in his throat. He'd walked right past them—they were stacked by a table just to the left of the back door.

Excitement flared in the magistrianos as he saw the gluepots sitting on top of the table. Beside them were a couple of smaller vessels that proved full of ink, along with the square iron plate the smith had given to Abraham. A low iron frame had been put in place around it. The only other thing on the table was a large paintbrush.

The frustration returned. Here were parchment and ink, right enough, but Argyros could not see how the rest of the strange array contributed to making handbills. It would take a score of scribes to turn out as many as Abraham had parchments, and in that case they would be far from identical with one another.

There were four shelves over the table, each with a dozen small clay jars on it (except for the topmost, which had thirteen). Only because they were close to the parchments and glue, Argyros lifted down one of them. He turned it around in his hand, and almost dropped it—on the side turned to the wall was written a large majuscule delta: Δ.

He tore the stopper off, held the lamp over it, and peered in. At first he saw nothing that looked like a delta. The jar held a number of small rectangular blocks of clay, each about as long as the last joint of his middle finger but not nearly so thick. He picked one up. Sure enough, there was a raised letter at one end. It was still black with ink. He lifted out another clay block. It also had a delta on it. So did the next, and the next.

No wonder Abraham was involved in the plot, Argyros thought. The potter was used to creating reliefwork of all kinds; letters would come as no challenge to him. And Leontios had said he was a Nestorian. He had reason to be hostile to Constantinople, which forced religious unity to go with the political unity it brought.

Whistling tunelessly, the magistrianos put the jar back and chose another one from a couple of shelves higher up. This one was identified by a minuscule beta: β.

Like the first, it was filled with those little blocks of fired clay. Argyros took one out, confidently expecting to find a beta on one end of it. And so, in a way, he did, but reversed: ꟼ.

He thought a few uncharitable thoughts about the wits of anyone incompetent enough to make his letters backwards. Certain it was a mistake, he removed several more clay blocks from the jar. They were all the same, and all reversed.

He frowned. That was going to a lot of effort to perpetuate an error. He poured all but one of the little clay lumps back into their jar, turned the last one over and over as he thought. He held it so close to his face that he had to look at it crosseyed. It was still backwards.

He squeezed it between his thumb and index finger, as if trying to wring the answer from it by brute force. Naturally, and annoyingly, such treatment harmed the clay block not at all. It was harder on him. There was a square indentation in the meaty pad of his thumb from the base of the block. And on his forefinger—

He stared at the perfect, unreversed beta pressed into his flesh. "Of course!" he exclaimed, startled into speaking aloud. "It's like a signet ring, where everything has to be done backwards to show up the right way in the wax." The delta, he thought, had misled him because it was symmetrical.

He dipped the backwards beta into an inkpot, stamped it down on the tabletop, and grinned to see the letter appear right-side-to. He stamped it again, and again. Each impression, inevitably, was just like all the rest. "This is how it's done, all right," he breathed.

He discovered that the jars on the top two shelves contained minuscule letters (they were arranged in alphabetical order, to make finding each one easy), while their counterparts on the lower shelves all held majuscules. The extra jar on the highest board proved to have slightly smaller blocks of clay without any characters on them. They puzzled Argyros until he realized they had to be used to mark the spaces between words—because they were lower than their fellows, the ink that got on them would not appear on the parchment.

Like a child with a new toy, he decided to spell out his own name. One by one, he selected the letters that went into it and set them on the iron plate, leaning them against the edge of the iron frame for security. Even so, they kept falling over. And that, he decided, was probably what the glue was for: spread over the surface of the plate, it would hold the blocks in place.

He inked the brush, painted the tops of the letters, then

pressed a sheet of parchment over them. The result made him burst into startled laughter. There on the parchment, rather raggedly aligned, were the nonsense words *sorygrA lisaB*.

He thumped his forehead with the heel of his hand, muttering "Idiot!" under his breath. He quickly rearranged the clay blocks; naturally, if the letters themselves were backwards, their order had to be that way too, in order to appear correctly on the sheet. He felt like cheering when the second try rewarded him with a smeary *Basil Argyros*.

He wondered what to compose next. Almost without conscious thought, the first words of the Gospel according to John came into his mind: "In the beginning was the Word, and the Word was with God, and the Word was God."

A letter at a time, the evangelist's famous sentence took shape. Argyros suddenly stopped, halfway through, as the magnitude of what he was doing begin to sink in. The Persians, with their petty subversion in Daras, were only pikers, and George Lakhanodrakon's fear of the same at Constantinople seemed just as trivial.

Of course John had been speaking of the divine Logos, Christ Himself, but his words rang with eerie aptness. These simple little blocks of clay could spell *anything*, and make as many copies of it as one wanted. What power was more godlike than that?

The magistrianos was so struck with awe that he did not pay any attention to the approaching footfalls in the alley behind Abraham's shop. But the soft cry of alarm one of the newcomers raised on seeing the bar down from the door tore Argyros from his reverie. He cursed himself for his stupidity—the only reason all these dangerous paraphernalia were so openly displayed had to be that the Persians were going to reproduce another handbill tonight.

There were three stout iron hooks-and-eyes screwed into

the inside of the door panels and the doorframe. Abraham, evidently, was the sort of man who tied double knots in his sandal straps—and in his sandals, Argyros would have done the same. The potter's caution was the only thing that saved him. He had just hooked the last closure when someone large heaved an ungently shoulder against the door. It groaned, but held.

Familiar, throaty laughter came from the alleyway. "Is that you, dear Basil?" Mirrane called mockingly. "Where will you run now?"

It was an excellent question. The pottery's front door was barred on the outside, just as the back had been. So were the stout wooden shutters, which—damn Abraham anyway!— had locks both inside and out.

Mirrane let Argyros stew just long enough, then said, "Well, it seems we shan't raise Daras yet. A pity—but then, bagging one of the Emperor's precious magistrianoi (oh yes, I know who you are!) is not the smallest prize either."

"*You're* behind this!" he blurted. He had thought she was merely a pleasant distraction thrown his way by the real plotter—Shahin maybe, or Abraham, of Yesuyab whom he had never seen.

She might have been reading his thoughts. Bitterness edged her voice as she answered, "Aye, by the God Ormazd, I am! Did you think I lacked the wit or will because I am a woman? You'll not be the first to pay for that mistake, nor the last." She shifted from Greek to Persian, spoke to one of her henchmen: "I'll waste no more time on this Roman. Burn the place down!"

Someone let out a harsh protest in Arabic.

"Don't be a donkey, Abraham," Mirrane snapped. "The noise of breaking in the door might bring the watch—we're too close to the barracks to risk it. The King of Kings will pay you more than you would earn from this miserable hovel in the next fifty years. Come on, Bahram, set the torch. The bigger the blaze, the more likely it is to destroy everything we need out of the way, Argyros included."

"...Isn't that right, Basil?" she added through the door.

The magistrianos did not answer, but could not argue with her tactics. A very accomplished young woman indeed, he thought ruefully—and in such unexpected ways. He had no doubt several armed men would be waiting when smoke and flames drove him to try bursting out through the door. He could see Bahram's torchflame flickering, hot and yellow, under the doorjamb.

But Mirrane, for all her ruthless efficiency, did not know everything. Along with his burglar's pincers, Argyros had fetched a couple of the tightly corked clay pots he had passed off to her as sediment testers. Stooping, he set them at the base of the back door.

His lamp was beginning to gutter, but it still held enough oil for his need. He touched the flame to the rags that ran through the stoppers. Those were soaked in fat themselves, and caught at once.

As soon as the magistrianos saw they were burning, he put down the lamp and dove behind Abraham's counter. He clapped his hands over his ears.

It was not a moment too soon. The hellpowder bombs went off, the explosion of the first touching off the second. The blast was like the end of the world. Shattered bits of pottery flew round the shop, deadly as slingers' bullets. The double charge of the explosive mix the Franco-Saxons had discovered flung the door off its hinges, hurling it outward at Mirrane and her companions.

Dagger in had, Argyros scrambled to his feet. His head was ringing, but at least he knew where the thunderbolt had come from. To Mirrane and her friends in the alleyway, it was a complete and hideous surprise.

The magistrianos charged through the cloud of thick, brimstone-smelling smoke that hung in the shattered doorway. He discovered one of Mirrane's henchmen at once, by almost tripping over him. The fellow was down and writhing, his hands clutched round a long splinter of wood driven into his groin. He was no danger, and would not last long.

Several other men pelted down the alley as fast as they could run. Through half-deafened ears, Argyros heard their shouts of terror: "Devils!" "Demons!" "Mother of God, protect me from Satan!" "It's Ahriman, come to earth!" That last had to come from a Persian: Ahriman was Ormazd's wicked foe in their dualist faith.

One of the nearby shadows moved. Argyros whirled. "A trick I did not know about, it seems," Mirrane said quietly. Her self-possession was absolute; she might have been talking of the weather. She went on, "The game is yours this time, after all."

"And you with it!" he cried, springing toward her.

"Sorry, no." As he spoke, she opened the door behind her, stepped through, and slammed it in Argyros' face. The bar locked it just as he crashed into it. He rebounded, dazed at the impact. Mirrane said, "We'll meet again, you and I." He heard her beat a rapid retreat.

Only then did he think of anything beyond the predicament from which he had just escaped. As Mirrane had said, Abraham's pottery was only a block from the main barracks of Daras. Already Argyros could hear cries of alarm, and then the disciplined pound of a squadron running his way.

"here!" he shouted.

The squad-leader came puffing up, torch held high. He gaped at the wrecked doorway to Abraham's shop. "What's all this about?"

"No time to explain," the magistrianos snapped. He gave the underofficer his rank; the man stiffened to attention.

"Have some of your troopers break down that door," Argyros ordered, pointing to the one through which Mirrane had escaped. He quickly described her, then sent the rest of the squad round the corner to where the front entrance of the house or store or whatever it was let out.

They returned emptyhanded. At Argyros' urging, Leontios sealed the gates of Daras within the hour, and for the next two days the garrison forces searched the town from top to bottom. They caught Abraham hiding with Yesuyab the tailor, but of Mirrane no sign whatever turned up.

Argyros was disappointed, but somehow not surprised.

"Very clever, Basil, your use of the map to ferret out the nest of spies," George Lakhanodrakon said.

"Thank you, sir." Argyros' office chair creaked as he leaned back in it. "I'm only annoyed it took me as long as it did. I should have seen that the Persians deliberately avoided putting their parchments in certain parts of Daras so as to give Leontios no reason to search in them. But it wasn't until I found out that Yesuyab's tanning-works (and the gluemaker's next to it), Abraham's pottery, and Shahin's tavern were all in the exact centers of the empty areas that things began to make sense."

"A pretty piece of reasoning, no matter how you reached it." The Master of Offices hesitated, cleared his throat, went on, "All the same, I'm not entirely sure the situation you left behind satisfies me."

"I'm not certain what else I could have done, your illustriousness," the magistrianos said politely. "No more inflammatory handbills are appearing in Daras, the town was calm when I left it, and I discovered the means by which the Persians were producing so many copies of the same text." Excitement put warmth in his voice. "A means, I might add, which could be used to—"

"Yes, yes," the Master of Offices interrupted. "I don't intend to slight you, my boy, not at all. As I said, you did splendidly. But all the same, there is no final resolution of the problem underlying this particular spot of trouble. It could crop up again anywhere in the east, in Kirkesion or Amida or Martyropolis, the more so as the tricksy Persian baggage in charge of the scheme slipped through your net."

"There you speak truly, sir," Argyros said. Mirrane's getaway still rankled. Also, it piqued him that the enjoyment she showed in his arms had probably been assumed to lull him. It had seemed very real at the time. He hoped her parting warning would come true; one way or another, he wanted to test himself against her again.

He went on, "In any case, a second outbreak is not likely to be as serious as the first was. Now that we know how the thing is done, local officials should be able to search out clandestine letterers on their own. And if the government issues them sets of clay archetypes of their own, they can easily counter any lies the Persians try spreading."

"Issue them archetypes of their own?" Lakhanodrakon spread his hands in something approaching horror. "Don't you think this is a secret as dangerous as hellpower? It should be restricted in the same way, and the production of documents written with it limited to the imperial chancery here in the city."

"I'd like to believe I could convince you that this new way of lettering has more applications than simply the political."

The Master of Offices' scowl was like a stormcloud. "My concern is for the safety of the state. You'd need a powerful demonstration to alter my opinion here."

"I suppose so," Argyros said with a sigh. He seemed to change the subject: "Will you still be giving another reading next week, sir?"

Lakhanodrakon's scowl vanished. He was composing an

epic on Constans II's triumph over the Lombards in Italia, in iambic trimeters modeled after those George of Pisidia had used in his poems celebrating Herakleios' victories. "Yes, from the third book," he said. "I hope you'll be there?"

"I'm looking forward to it. I only wonder how many of your guests will be familiar with what you've already written."

"To some degree, a fair number, I suppose. Many will have been at the earlier readings last year and this past winter, and of course the manuscript will have circulated somewhat. I intend to summarize what's gone before, anyhow."

"No need for that," Argyros opened a desk drawer, handed a pile of thin papyrus codices to Lakhanodrakon.

"What on earth are these?"

"Books one and two of your *Italiad*, sir," Argyros said innocently. "I've given you thirty-five copies, which I believe will be enough for you to pass one on to everyone who is coming. If not, I still have the letters in their frames. I would be happy to make as many more as you need."

A couple of days ago Argyros would have sung a different tune. He did not fret about the cost of seven hundred sheets of papyrus. The stuff was cheap in Constantinople, because the government used so much of it. And finding a potter from Mesopotamia who could be made to understand how to make the clay archetypes had not been difficult for one who knew the city as the magistrianos did.

But Argyros was still squinting from the unaccustomed effort of putting twenty pages of poetry into frames a letter at a time—backwards. Anthimos had helped, some, but he never did get the hang of it, and the magistrianos spent almost as much time fixing his secretary's mistakes as he did making progress of his own. After a while, he had excused the hapless scribe. And then, halfway through page eighteen, he had run out of omegas, and had to rush back to the potter to get more.

It was all worth it now, though, watching the astonishment on the Master of Offices' face turn to delight. "Thirty-five copies?" Lakhanodrakon whispered in wonder. "Why, saving the Bible and Homer, I don't know of thirty-five copies of any work here in the capital. Perhaps Thucydides or Plato or St. John Chrysostom—and me. I feel ashamed to join the company you've put me in, Basil."

"It's a very good poem, sir," the magistrianos said loyally. "Don't you see now? With this new lettering, we can make so many copies of all our authors that they'll never again risk being lost because mice ate the last remaining one three days before it was due to be redone. Not just literature, either—how much better would our armies fare if every officer carried his own copy of Maurice's *Strategikon*? And lawyers and churchmen could be sure their texts matched one another, for all would come from the same original. Ship-captains would be able to take charts and sailing-guides from port to port—"

At last the Master of Offices was beginning to catch some of the younger man's enthusiasm. "The Virgin protect me, you may be right after all! I can see how this invention could prove a great boon for government. Imperial rescripts would become much easier to produce. And—oh, think of it! We could make endless copies of the same standard forms and send them throughout the Empire. And it might not even be too much labor to have other forms, on which we could keep track of whether the first ones had been properly dispatched. I can fairly see the scheme now, can't you?"

Argyros could, only too well. He wondered if he would be able to change his boss's mind back again.

Gregory Benford

We Could Do Worse

Everybody in the bar noticed us when we came in. You could see their faces tighten up.

The bartender reached over and put the cover on the free-lunch jar. I caught that even though I was watching the people in the booths.

They knew who we were. You could see the caution come into their eyes. I'm big enough that nobody just glances at me once. You get used to that after a while and then you start to liking it.

"Beer," I said when we got to the mahogany bar. The bartender drew it, looking at me. He let some suds slop over and wiped the glass and stood holding it until I put down a quarter.

"Two," I said. The bartender put the glass in front of me and I pushed it toward Phillips. He let some of the second beer slop out too because he was busy watching my hands. I took the glass with my right and with my left I lifted the cover off the free-lunch jar.

"No," he said.

I took a sandwich out.

"I'm gonna make like I didn't hear that," I said and bit into the sandwich. It was cheese with some mayonnaise and hadn't been made today.

I tossed the sandwich aside. "Got anything better?"

"Not for you," the bartender said.

"You got your license out where I can read it?"

"You guys is federal. Got no call to want my liquor license."

"Lawyer, huh?" Phillips asked slow and steady. He doesn't say much but people always listen.

The bartender was in pretty good shape, a middle-sized guy with big arm muscles, but he made a mistake then. His hand slid under the bar, watching us both, and I reached over and grabbed his wrist. I yanked his hand up and there was a pistol in it. The hammer was already cocked. Phillips got his fingers between the revolver's hammer and the firing pin. We pulled it out of the bartender's hand easy and I tapped him a light one in the snoot, hardly getting off my stool. He staggered back and Phillips put away the revolver in a coat pocket.

"Guys like you shouldn't have guns," Phillips said. "Get hurt that way."

"You just stand there and look pretty," I said.

"It's Garrett, isn't it?"

"Now don't never you mind," Phillips said.

The rest of the bar was quiet and I turned and gave them a look. "What do you expect?" I said loud enough so they could all hear. "Man pulls a gun on you, you take care of him."

A peroxide blond in a back booth called out, "You bastards!"

"There a back alley here?" I asked the whole room.

Their faces were tight and they didn't know whether to tell me the truth or not.

"Hey, yeah," Phillips said. "Sure there's a back door. You 'member, the briefing said so."

He's not too bright. So I used a different way to open them up. "Blondie, you want we ask you some questions? Maybe out in that alley?"

Peroxide looked steady at me for a moment and then

looked away. She knew what we'd do to her out there if she made any more noise. Women know those things without your saying.

I turned my back to them and said, "My nickel."

The bartender had stopped his nose from bleeding but he wasn't thinking very well. He just blinked at me.

"Change for the beers," I said. "You can turn on that TV, too."

He fumbled getting the nickel. When the last of The Milton Berle Hour came on the bar filled with enough sound so anybody coming from the street wouldn't notice that nobody was talking. They were just watching Phillips and me.

I sipped my beer. Part of our job is to let folks know we're not fooling around anymore. Show the flag, kind of.

The Berle show went off and you could smell the tense sweat in the bar. I acted casual, like I didn't care. The government news bulletins were coming on and the bartender started to change the channel and I waved him off.

"Time for Lucy," he said. He had gotten some backbone into his voice again.

I smiled at him. "I guess I know what time it is. Let's inform these citizens a li'l."

There was a Schlitz ad with dancing and singing bottles, the king of beers, and then more news. They mentioned the new directives about the state of emergency, but nothing I didn't already know two days ago. Good. No surprises.

"Let's have Lucy!" somebody yelled behind me.

I turned around but nobody said anything more. "You'd maybe like watchin' the convention?" I said.

Nobody spoke. So I grinned and said, "Maybe you patriots could learn somethin' that way."

I laughed a little and gestured to the bartender. He spun the dial and there was the Republican convention, warming up. Cronkite talking over the background noise.

"Somethin', huh?" I said to Phillips. "Not like four years ago."

"Don't matter that much," Phillips said. He watched the door while I kept an eye on the crowd.

"You kiddin'? Why, that goddamn Eisenhower almost took the nomination away from Taft last time. Hadn't been for Nixon deliverin' the California delegation to old man Taft, that pinko general coulda won."

"So?" Phillips sipped his beer. A station break came and I could hear tires hissing by outside in the light rain. My jacket smelled damp. I never wear a raincoat on a job like this. They get in your way. The street lights threw stretched shapes against the bar windows. Phillips watched the passing shadows, waiting calm as anything for one of them to turn and come in the door.

I said, "You think Eisenhower, with that Kraut name, woulda picked our guy for the second spot?"

"Mighta."

"Hell no. Even if he had, Eisenhower didn't drop dead a year later."

"You're right there," Phillips said to humor me. He's not a man for theory.

"I tell you, Taft winnin' and then dyin', it was a godsend. Gave us the man we shoulda had. Never coulda elected him. The Commies, they'd never have let him get in power."

Phillips stiffened. I thought it was what I'd said, but then a guy came through the doors in a slick black raincoat. He was pale and I saw it was our man. Cheering at the convention came up then and he didn't notice anything funny, not until he got a few steps in and saw the faces.

Garrett's eyes widened as I came to him. He pulled his hands up like he was reaching for something under his coat, or maybe just to protect himself.

I didn't care which. I hit him once in the stomach to take

the wind out of him and then gave him two quick overhand punches in the jaw. He went down nice and solid and wasn't going to get back up in a hurry.

Phillips searched him. There was no gun after all. The bar was dead quiet.

A guy in a porkpie hat came up to me all hot and bothered, like he hadn't been paying attention before, and said, "You can't just attack a, a member of the Congress! That's Congressman Garrett there! I don't care—"

The big talk went right out of him when I slammed a fist into his gut. Porkpie was another lawyer, no real fight in him.

I walked back to the bar and drained my beer. The '56 convention was rolling on, nominations just starting, but you knew that was all bull. Only one man was possible, and when the election came there'd by plenty guys like me to fix it so he won.

Just then they put on some footage of the president and I stood there a second, just watching him. There was a knot in my throat when I looked at him, a real American. There were damn few of us, even now. We'd gotten in by accident, maybe, but now we were going to make every day count. Clean up the country. And hell, if the work wasn't done by the time his second term ended in 1961, we might have to diddle the Constitution a little, keep him in power until things worked okay.

Cronkite come on then, babbling about letting Adlai Stevenson out of house arrest, and I went to help Phillips get Garrett to his feet. I sure didn't want to have to haul the guy out to our car.

We got him up with his raincoat all twisted around him. Then the porkpie hat guy was there again, but this time with about a dozen of them behind him. They looked mad and jittery. A bunch like that can be trouble. I wondered if this was such a good idea, taking Garrett in his neighborhood bar.

But the chief said we had to show these types we'd go anywhere, anytime.

Porkpie said, "You got no warrant."

"Sure I do." I showed them the paper. These types always think paper is God.

"Sit down," Phillips said, being civil. "You people all sit down."

"That's a congressman you got there. We—"

"Traitor, is what you mean," I said.

Peroxide came up then, screeching. "You think you can just take anybody, you lousy sonsabitches—"

Porkpie took a poke at me then. I caught it and gave him a right cross, pretty as you please. He staggered back. Still, I saw we could really get in a fix here if they all came at us.

Peroxide called out, "Come on, we can—"

She stopped when I pulled out the gun. It's a big steel automatic, just about the right size for a guy like me. Some guys use silencers with them, but me, I like the noise.

They all looked at it awhile and their faces changed, closing up, each one of them alone with their thoughts, and then I knew they wouldn't do anything.

"Come on," I said. We carried the traitor out into the night. I was so pumped up he felt light.

Even a year before, we'd have had big trouble bringing in a Commie network type like Garrett. He was a big deal on the House Internal Security Committee and had been giving us a lot of grief. Now nailing him was easy. And all because of one man at the top with real courage.

We don't bother with the formalities anymore. Phillips opened the trunk of the Pontiac and I dumped Garrett in. Easier and faster than cramming him into the front, and I wanted to get out of there.

Garrett was barely conscious and just blinked at me as I slammed down the trunk. They'd wake him up plenty later.

As I came around to get in the driver's side I looked through the window of the bar. Cronkite was interviewing the president now. Ol' Joe looked like he was in good shape, real statesmanlike, but tough, you could see that.

Cronkite was probably asking him why he'd chosen Nixon for the VP spot, like there was no other choice. Like I'd tried to tell Phillips, Nixon's delivering California on the delegate issue in '52 had paved the way for the Taft ticket. And old Bob Taft, rest his soul, knew what the country needed when the vice presidency nomination came up.

Just like now. Joe, he doesn't forget a debt. So Dick Nixon was a shoo-in. McCarthy and Nixon—good ticket, regional balance, solid anti-Commie values. We could do worse. A lot worse.

I got in and gunned the motor a little, feeling good. The rain had stopped. The meat in the trunk was as good as dead, but we'd deliver it fresh anyway. We took off with a roar into the darkness.

Nicholas A. DiChario

The Winterberry

May, 1971

It was Uncle Teddy who taught me how to read and write. I think it took a long time but I'm not sure. I heard him arguing with Mother about it one night a few years ago when I wasn't supposed to be out of my room, but I was very excited with the next day being my birthday and I couldn't sleep.

"He can do it," Uncle Teddy had said.

And Mother said, "He doesn't care whether he reads or writes. It's you who cares. Why do you torture yourself? Let him be."

"He's fifty-four years old," Uncle Teddy said.

"*Let him be!*" Mother sounded very angry.

I listened to Uncle Teddy walk across the room. "If you feel that way," he said, "why didn't you just let him die?"

There was a long silence before Mother said, "I don't know," and another long silence after that.

Something in their voices frightened me so I returned to my room. I became very ill, and for several weeks Dr. Armbruster came to see me every day but he wouldn't let anyone else come in because he said I was too weak to have visitors.

But sometime after, when I was much better, Uncle Teddy came to visit and he brought a picture book with him which made me remember his talk with Mother. I'm glad

310

Uncle Teddy got his way because now I read and write a lot even though I throw most of my writing away. I hide some of it though and keep it just for myself, and it's not because I'm being sneaky, it's more because some of the things I write are my own personal secrets and I don't want to tell anyone, just like people don't want to tell me things sometimes when I ask them questions.

December, 1977

I am very excited about Christmas almost being here. I am looking forward to Uncle Teddy's stay because he always has something fun in mind. Yesterday after he arrived he walked me through the house and showed me all of the decorations—wreaths and flowers and a huge Christmas tree near the front hall, strung with tinsel and candles. He brought with him several boxes full of gifts, all shapes and sizes, wrapped in bright colors—red and green and blue and silver with bows and ribbons—and I knew they were all for me because he put them under my tree upstairs.

Our house is very large. Mother calls it a mansion. She doesn't allow me to go anywhere except the room on my floor. She says I have everything I need right here.

That's why sometimes at night I'll walk around when everything is dark and everyone is asleep or in their rooms for the night. I don't think I'm being sneaky, it's just that I am very curious and if I ask about things no one tells me what I want to know. I've come to know this house very well. There are many hidden passageways behind the walls and I know them all by heart. I will hear things every once in a while that mother would not like me to hear.

There was a big happening in the house last night and the servants were very busy, although it did not look to be a planned thing because everyone appeared disorganized and Mother didn't come to lock me in my room.

I went through one of my passageways that led to the main entrance of the house and I peeked through a tiny opening in the wall and saw a very beautiful woman with dark hair standing inside the door. She was so beautiful that I held my breath. It must have been very cold outside because she was wearing a long black winter coat and there were flakes of snow on her hair. When she spoke, it was the most soft and delicate voice I had ever heard. She said, "Merry Christmas."

I wanted to stay and watch the woman forever but I knew Mother would be up to check on me so I ran back to my room and pretended to be asleep. Mother came in and kissed my head and said, "Sleep well, child," like she did every night. I listened very closely for a long time hoping to hear the voice of the woman again, but next thing I knew it was morning, and she was gone.

October, 1982
I heard Mother and Dr. Armbruster arguing yesterday. They were just talking pleasantly for a while and I was listening in my passageway to the low, pleasant sound of their voices. The doctor was saying things I did not understand about sickness and diets and so on, when all of a sudden he said, "But John is doing fine," and Mother just about exploded with anger.

"His name is not John, do you understand me? Don't you ever call him by that name again! John is dead! My John is dead!" I had never heart Mother get so angry except for that one time with Uncle Teddy. She made the doctor leave right away and told him he could be replaced, but I hoped that she wouldn't do that because I sort of liked Dr. Armbruster.

I don't know who John is, but I felt very bad for Mother. I had never really thought about my own name before. Uncle Teddy and everyone calls me Sonny because it's short for Sonny Boy, and that's good enough for me. But it made me wonder how someone could get a name like John. Uncle

Teddy was probably named after a teddy bear. Mother was just Mother.

May, 1987
Today was a very special day. It was my seventieth birthday. Uncle Teddy came to visit and I was very excited because I hadn't seen him in such a long time. We had a big cake and a lot of food and we played checkers for an hour. Then Uncle Teddy took me outside for a walk!

I'll never forget it as long as I live. I think Mother was not happy about it because she did not want to let me go at first, but Uncle Teddy talked her into it and we went outside surrounded by men in black suits and ties and shoes. Uncle Teddy asked me if I minded if his friends went with us, and of course I didn't care. They came to my party and they had a right to have fun. In fact, I told them that if they smiled more they might have a nicer time all around, but Uncle Teddy said they were usually very serious people and were happy that way.

It was a sunny day. The wind blew in my face and stung my eyes at first, but if felt good. Uncle Teddy took me all around the yard and into the garden where I smelled the roses and touched the bushes and the vines. I listened to the birds calling and the insects buzzing. I never dreamed they would sound so loud and so near.

I touched the winterberry hollies which were very special to me because I could always see their bright red berries from my window, even during the cold cold winters.

After a short time I caught a chill and had to go inside, and I was weak for the rest of the day. But I didn't care—I had such fun! I'll always remember it.

August, 1996
One night I entered a storage room through my passageway where there were a lot of tools and brooms and rags and

buckets and things. I rummaged around in the dark and my hands found a flashlight. I thought this would be a wonderful thing to have so I took it with me hoping that no one would miss it. Now I can sit in bed at night and read and write as long as I like and not have to worry about someone seeing my light.

I have not seen Mother in a very long time. I wondered if she was angry with me even though I didn't think she knew about my passageways or my late-night writing. Mother would have yelled at me if she knew.

I've been seeing more and more of Uncle Teddy, so I asked him about Mother today and he said that she went away on a very long trip and I wouldn't be seeing her for a while.

I asked him how long that might be and he said not long, he said soon we'd all be seeing her and then maybe we'd find out whether we did the right thing, whether the choices we'd made over the years had been the proper ones. He looked very sad when he said this, and then he said, "I think there is such a place, Sonny Boy, a place where we learn why everything is the way it is."

I asked him if Dr. Armbruster had gone with Mother since I hadn't seem him in so long and I was seeing Dr. Morelande almost every day now, and Uncle Teddy told me yes.

I thought about how lucky Mother was to visit this place, a place where every time you asked a question you got an answer, and I could not blame her if she didn't want to come back for a while. I told Uncle Teddy so, and he seemed to cheer up. We played cards for the rest of the afternoon.

May, 1997
Today was my eightieth birthday. I had been very sick and I was afraid that I might not be able to have my party, but Dr. Morelande said it was OK so we had cake and games with

Uncle Teddy and I had a very nice time even though I had to stay in bed.

It was after my party that I had a scare. I was very weak, and I probably should have just gone to sleep, but being so excited all day and not being allowed to get up, I turned restless after dark, so I decided to take a short walk through my passageways.

I followed a path that led to the back of a closet in Uncle Teddy's room, and I saw some light coming through the darkness so I went up to it. That's all I was going to do—peek and go away—until I saw Uncle Teddy crying. I'd never seen Uncle Teddy cry before. He was in bed. He had a large, green book on his lap, and every so often he would turn a page and cry some more.

I watched him for a while, waiting for him to be all right, but he didn't stop crying and I couldn't stand to watch him any longer, so I did a foolish thing and I entered his room through the closet.

"Sonny Boy," he said, "what are you doing here?"

I thought he might be angry with me so I wanted to say that I saw him crying, and that I only wanted to help him and be a friend, but before I could say anything he said, "So you know about the passages," and he didn't seem to be upset at all.

"Come over here, Sonny," he said.

I went and sat on the edge of his bed. He was looking at a photo album. Mother had shown me some photo albums years ago, and I thought they were interesting and we had a lot of fun even though I didn't recognize any of the faces. I don't ever remember crying over them. But Uncle Teddy's album was different. There were newspaper pictures, and headlines, and articles.

Uncle Teddy was looking at a picture of a man and a woman. The man seemed very serious-looking, and his right hand was raised like an Indian chief's, but he had on a suit and tie and no headdress. The man's eyes were closed.

The woman had short black hair with long bangs, and she was looking down.

And then all of a sudden I just about screamed. I knew that woman. I remembered her from...from somewhere.

Uncle Teddy said, "You know her, don't you? Think, Sonny Boy, think very hard. What do you remember?"

I did think very hard, and then I remembered where I had seen her. She was the beautiful black-haired woman I had seen at Christmastime in the main entrance of the house years ago.

But then there was more. As I looked at the woman in the picture something very strange came into my head. I had a passing thought of this same woman in a pretty white gown, with a white veil over her face. It was just a piece of a thought that I could not keep in my mind for very long, but I'll never forget it. I reached out and touched the picture.

"Always grand," Uncle Teddy said. "She was wearing a very dignified, raspberry-colored suit that day."

But that's not what I had seen. I had seen the white gown. I had seen something that happened before my room and my house and my passageways and Mother and Uncle Teddy. Was there anything before them? Yes, I think there was. It was more than a passing thought—it was a *memory*.

"Was I married, Uncle Teddy?" I asked him.

He smiled. "Yes, you were. You proposed to her by telegram, you know, from Paris."

I thought this was interesting, but nothing more than that. Uncle Teddy started to cry again.

"Please, don't cry," I said.

He held my hand then. "I'm sorry we couldn't tell her you were alive. We couldn't tell your children, not anyone, not even Father because we couldn't be sure of his reaction.

Mother was adamant about that. No one could know. Just Bobby and Mother and myself—and the doctors, of course. Now there's just me.

"It was for the good of the country. Those were critical times. The eyes of the world were watching us. We could not afford hesitancy. We felt you would have wanted it that way. Do you understand?"

I didn't, but I nodded anyway to stop Uncle Teddy from crying. He was clutching my arm very hard.

He traced the newspaper picture with his finger. "She was a strong woman, Sonny Boy. You would have been proud of her. I remember her standing right next to Lyndon, solid as a rock, little more than hour after you were pronounced dead."

I was very confused about Uncle Teddy calling me dead, and about what the woman in the picture had to do with any of it, so I closed the book and placed it on the floor. I remembered what Mother used to do to make me feel better, so I thought that maybe the same thing might help Uncle Teddy feel better too.

I pulled his bed covers up to his chin, brushed back his hair, kissed him on the forehead, and turned out his light. "Sleep well, child," I said, and then I went back to my room. I was sure Uncle Teddy would be just fine in the morning. It had always worked for me.

December, 2008

Dr. Morelande is the only one who comes to see me anymore. He says that Uncle Teddy is so busy he can't find time to stop by. But I don't think that's exactly true. I think Uncle Teddy went on vacation with Mother and Dr. Armbruster, and he is having so much fun that he is not coming back at all.

Dr. Morelande has tried very hard to make this a good Christmas, but I am sorry to say I am not very happy. I am tired all of the time, and I can't even move out of bed. Dr.

Morelande asked me if I wanted anything for Christmas, but if I couldn't have Mother or Uncle Teddy, then there was nothing to ask for.

But then I thought about it and thought about it for a long time, and I remembered the pictures Uncle Teddy had shown me many years ago. I told Dr. Morelande about the green photo album in Uncle Teddy's room and asked him if he could find it for me. A little while later Dr. Morelande returned with the book.

Together we went through the pictures, and when we got to the one Uncle Teddy had shown me, the one with the man and the beautiful dark-haired woman, I made him stop.

"There *is* something I want for Christmas," I told him. "There is something I want very much."

I decided to tell Dr. Morelande about the passageways then. I didn't think that I would get in trouble. I made him put me in my wheelchair and take me for a walk behind the walls. He argued with me at first, but I refused to be put off.

I told him exactly which path to follow. He wheeled me all the way down to the wall at the main entrance. I looked through the small opening. I was sure that the beautiful dark-haired woman would be standing at the door in her winter coat. I was disappointed that she wasn't there. I thought that if I waited long enough she would certainly show up—she would come back like the winterberry, bright and strong even in the cold cold winter. There would be snowflakes in her hair, and she would say "Merry Christmas" in her lovely voice. So we waited.

Finally Dr. Morelande said that if I agreed to go to bed, he would wait for the woman, and bring her directly to me as soon as she arrived. I thought that this would be a good idea since I was so tired.

When she arrives, we will have many things to discuss. I have decided to make her my new friend. I think I will show her my book of writings. I think I will ask her about the white gown to show her that I have not forgotten, and then I'll ask her about the children Uncle Teddy mentioned. I won't tell her about the vacation place where everyone has gone without me, and not because I'm being sneaky, but only because I am very lonely and I would like her to stay with me for a while.

Kim Stanley Robinson

The Lucky Strike

War breeds strange pastimes. In July of 1945 on Tinian Island in the North Pacific, Captain Frank January had taken to piling pebble cairns on the crown of Mount Lasso—one pebble for each B-29 takeoff, one cairn for each mission. The largest cairn had four hundred stones in it. It was a mindless pastime, but so was poker. The men of the 509th had played a million hands of poker, sitting in the shade of a palm around an upturned crate sweating in their skivvies, swearing and betting all their pay and cigarettes, playing hand after hand after hand, until the cards got so soft and dog-eared you could have used them for toilet paper. Captain January had gotten sick of it, and after he lit out for the hilltop a few times some of his crewmates started trailing him. When their pilot Jim Fitch joined them it became an official pastime, like throwing flares into the compound or going hunting for stray Japs. What Captain January thought of the development he didn't say. The others grouped near Captain Fitch, who passed around his battered flask. "Hey, January," Fitch called. "Come have a shot."

January wandered over and took the flask. Fitch laughed at his pebble. "Practicing your bombing up here, eh, Professor?"

"Yah," January said sullenly. Anyone who read more than the funnies was Professor to Fitch. Thirstily January knocked back some rum. He could drink it any way he pleased up here, out from under the eye of the group psychiatrist. He passed the flask on to Lieutenant Matthews, their navigator.

"That's why he's the best," Matthews joked. "Always practicing."

Fitch laughed. "He's best because I make him be best, right, Professor?"

January frowned. Fitch was a bulky youth, thick-featured, pig-eyed—a thug, in January's opinion. The rest of the crew were all in their mid-twenties like Fitch, and they liked the captain's bossy roughhouse style. January, who was thirty-seven, didn't go for it. He wandered away, back to the cairn he had been building. From Mount Lasso they had an overview of the whole island, from the harbor at Wall Street to the north field in Harlem. January had observed hundreds of B-29s roar off the four parallel runways of the north field and head for Japan. The last quartet of this particular mission buzzed across the width of the island, and January dropped four more pebbles, aiming for crevices in the pile. One of them stuck nicely.

"There they are!" said Matthews. "They're on the taxiing strip."

January located the 509th's first plane. Today, the first of August, there was something more interesting to watch than the usual Superfortress parade. Word was out that General Le May wanted to take the 509th's mission away from it. Their commander Colonel Tibbets had gone and bitched to Le May in person, and the general had agreed the mission was theirs, but on one condition: one of the general's men was to make a test flight with the 509th, to make sure they were fit for combat over Japan. The general's man had arrived, and now he was down there in the strike plane, with Tibbets and the whole first team. January sidled back to his mates to view the takeoff with them.

"Why don't the strike plane have a name, though?" Haddock was saying.

Fitch said, "Lewis won't give it a name because it's not his plane, and he knows it." The others laughed. Lewis and his crew were naturally unpopular, being Tibbets' favorites.

"What do you think he'll do to the general's man?" Matthews asked.

The others laughed at the very idea. "He'll kill an engine at takeoff, I bet you anything," Fitch said. He pointed at the wrecked B-29s that marked the end of every runway, planes whose engines had given out on takeoff. "He'll want to show that he wouldn't go down if it happened to him."

" 'Course he wouldn't!" Matthews said.

"You hope," January said under his breath.

"They let those Wright engines out too soon," Haddock said seriously. "They keep busting under the takeoff load."

"Won't matter to the old bull," Matthews said. Then they all started in about Tibbets' flying ability, even Fitch. They all thought Tibbets was the greatest. January, on the other hand, liked Tibbets even less than he liked Fitch. That had started right after he was assigned to the 509th. He had been told he was part of the most important group in the war, and then given a leave. In Vicksburg a couple of fliers just back from England had bought him a lot of whiskies, and since January had spent several months stationed near London they had talked for a good long time and gotten pretty drunk. The two were really curious about what January was up to now, but he had stayed vague on it and kept returning the talk to the blitz. He had been seeing an English nurse, for instance, whose flat had been bombed, family and neighbors killed.... But they had really wanted to know. So he had told them he was onto something special, and they had flipped out their badges and told him they were Army Intelligence, and that if he ever broke security like that again he'd be transferred to Alaska. It was a dirty trick. January had gone back to Wendover and told Tibbets so to his face, and Tibbets had turned red and threatened him some more. January despised him for that. The upshot was that January was effectively out of the war, because Tibbets really played his favorites. January wasn't sure he really minded, but during their year's training he had bombed better than ever, as a way of showing the old bull he was wrong to write January off. Every time their eyes had met it was clear what was going on. But Tibbets never backed off no matter how precise January's bombing got. Just thinking about it was enough to cause January to line up a pebble over an ant and drop it.

"Will you cut that out?" Fitch complained. "I swear you must hang from the ceiling when you take a shit so you can practice aiming for the toilet." The men laughed.

"Don't I bunk over you?" January asked. Then he pointed."They're going."

Tibbets' plane had taxied to runway Baker. Fitch passed the flask around again. The tropical sun beat on them, and the ocean surrounding the island blazed white. January put up a sweaty hand to aid the bill of his baseball cap.

The four props cut in hard, and the sleek Superfortress quickly trundled up to speed and roared down Baker. Three-quarters of the way down the strip the outside right prop feathered.

"Yow!" Fitch crowed. "I told you he'd do it!"

The plane nosed off the ground and slewed right, then pulled back on course to cheers from the four young men around January. January pointed again. "He's cut number three, too."

The inside right prop feathered, and now the plane was pulled up by the left wing only, while the two right props windmilled uselessly. "Holy smoke!" Haddock cried. "Ain't the old bull something?"

They whooped to see the plane's power, and Tibbets' nervy arrogance.

"By God, Le May's man will remember this flight," Fitch hooted. "Why, look at that! He's banking!"

Apparently taking off on two engines wasn't enough for Tibbets; he banked the plane right until it was standing on its dead wing, and it curved back toward Tinian.

Then the inside left engine feathered.

War tears at the imagination. For three years Frank January had kept his imagination trapped, refusing to give it any play whatsoever. The dangers threatening him, the effects of the bombs, the fate of the other participants in the war, he had refused to think about any of it. But the war tore at his control. That English nurse's flat. The missions over the Ruhr. The bomber just below him blown apart by flak. And then there had been a year in Utah, and the viselike grip that he had once kept on his imagination had slipped away.

So when he saw the number two prop feather, his heart gave a little jump against his sternum and helplessly he was up there with Ferebee, the first team bombardier. He would be looking over the pilots' shoulders....

"Only one engine?" Fitch said.

"That one's for real," January said harshly. Despite himself he *saw* panic in the cockpit, the frantic rush to power the two right engines. The plane was dropping fast and Tibbets leveled it off, leaving them on a course back toward the island. The two right props spun, blurred to a shimmer. January held his breath. They needed more lift; Tibbets was trying to pull it over the island. Maybe he was trying for the short runway on the south half of the island.

But Tinian was too tall, the plane too heavy. It roared

right into the jungle above the beach, where 42nd Street met their East River. It exploded in a bloom of fire. By the time the sound of the explosion struck them they knew no one in the plane had survived.

Black smoke towered into white sky. In the shocked silence on Mount Lasso insects buzzed and creaked. The air left January's lungs with a gulp. He had been with Ferebee there at the end, he had heard the desperate shouts, seen the last green rush, been stunned by the dentist-drill-all-over pain of the impact.

"Oh my God," Fitch was saying. "Oh my God." Matthews was sitting. January picked up the flask, tossed it at Fitch.

"C-come on," he stuttered. He hadn't stuttered since he was sixteen. He led the others in a rush down the hill. When they got to Broadway a jeep careened toward them and skidded to a halt. It was Colonel Scholes, the old bull's exec. "What happened?"

Fitch told him.

"Those damned Wrights," Scholes said as the men piled in. This time one had failed at just the wrong moment; some welder stateside had kept flame to metal a second less than usual—or something equally minor, equally trivial—and that had made all the difference.

They left the jeep at 42nd and Broadway and hiked east over a narrow track to the shore. A fairly large circle of trees was burning. The fire trucks were already there.

Scholes stood beside January, his expression bleak. "That was the whole first team," he said.

"I know," said January. He was still in shock, in imagination crushed, incinerated, destroyed. Once as a kid he had tied sheets to his arms and waist, jumped off the roof and landed right on his chest; this felt like that had. He had no way of knowing what would come of this crash, but he had a suspicion that he had indeed smacked into something hard.

Scholes shook his head. A half hour had passed, the fire was nearly out. January's four mates were over chattering with the Seabees. "He was going to name the plane after his mother," Scholes said to the ground. "He told me that just this morning. He was going to call it *Enola Gay*."

At night the jungle breathed, and its hot wet breath washed over the 509th's compound. January stood in the doorway of his Quonset barracks hoping for a real breeze. No poker tonight. Voices were hushed, faces solemn. Some of the men had helped box up the dead crew's gear. Now most lay on their bunks. January gave up on the breeze, climbed onto his top bunk to stare at the ceiling.

He observed the corrugated arch over him. Cricketsong sawed through his thoughts. Below him a rapid conversation was being carried on in guilty undertones, Fitch at its center.

"January is the best bombardier left," he said. "And I'm as good as Lewis was."

"But so is Sweeney," Matthews said. "And he's in with Scholes."

They were figuring out who would take over the strike. January scowled. Tibbets and the rest were less than twelve hours dead, and they were squabbling over who would replace them.

January grabbed a shirt, rolled off his bunk, put the shirt on.

"Hey, Professor," Fitch said. "Where you going?"

"Out."

Though midnight was near it was still sweltering. Crickets shut up as he walked by, started again behind him. He lit a cigarette. In the dark the MPs patrolling their fenced-in compound were like pairs of walking armbands. The 509th, prisoners in their own army. Fliers from other groups had taken to throwing rocks over the fence. Forcefully

January expelled smoke, as if he could expel his disgust with it. They were only kids, he told himself. Their minds had been shaped in the war, by the war, and for the war. They knew you couldn't mourn the dead for long; carry around a load like that and your own engines might fail. That was all right with January. It was an attitude that Tibbets had helped to form, so it was what he deserved. Tibbets would *want* to be forgotten in favor of the mission, all he had lived for was to drop the gimmick on the Japs, he was oblivious to anything else, men, wife, family, anything.

So it wasn't the lack of feeling in his mates that bothered January. And it was natural of them to want to fly the strike they had been training a year for. Natural, that is, if you were a kid with a mind shaped by fanatics like Tibbets, shaped to take orders and never imagine consequences. But January was not a kid, and he wasn't going to let men like Tibbets do a thing to his mind. And the gimmick...the gimmick was not natural. A chemical bomb of some sort, he guessed. Against the Geneva Convention. He stubbed his cigarette against the sole of his sneaker, tossed the butt over the fence. The tropical night breathed over him. He had a headache.

For months now he had been sure he would never fly a strike. The dislike Tibbets and he had exchanged in their looks (January was acutely aware of looks) had been real and strong. Tibbets had understood that January's record of pinpoint accuracy in the runs over the Salton Sea had been a way of showing contempt, a way of saying *you can't get rid of me even though you hate me and I hate you*. The record had forced Tibbets to keep January on one of the four second-string teams, but with the fuss they were making over the gimmick January had figured that would be far enough down the ladder to keep him out of things.

Now he wasn't so sure. Tibbets was dead. He lit another cigarette, found his hand shaking. The Camel tasted bitter.

He threw it over the fence at a receding armband, and regretted it instantly. A waste. He went back inside.

Before climbing onto his bunk he got a paperback out of his footlocker. "Hey, Professor, what you reading now?" Fitch said, grinning.

January showed him the blue cover. *Winter's Tales*, by an Isak Dinesen. Fitch examined the little wartime edition. "Pretty racy, eh?"

"You bet," January said heavily. "This guy puts sex on every page." He climbed onto his bunk, opened the book. The stories were strange, hard to follow. The voices below bothered him. He concentrated harder.

As a boy on the farm in Arkansas, January had read everything he could lay his hands on. On Saturday afternoons he would race his father down the muddy lane to the mailbox (his father was a reader too), grab the *Saturday Evening Post* and run off to devour every word of it. That meant he had another week with nothing new to read, but he couldn't help it. His favorites were the Hornblower stories, but anything would do. It was a way off the farm, a way into the world. He had become a man who could slip between the covers of a book whenever he chose.

But not on this night.

The next day the chaplain gave a memorial service, and on the morning after that Colonel Scholes looked in the door of their hut right after mess. "Briefing at eleven," he announced. His face was haggard. "Be there early," He looked at Fitch with bloodshot eyes, crooked a finger. "Fitch, January, Matthews—come with me."

January put on his shoes. The rest of the men sat on their bunks and watched them wordlessly. January followed Fitch and Matthews out of the hut.

"I've spent most of the night on the radio with General Le

May," Scholes said. He looked them each in the eye. "We've decided you're to be the first crew to make a strike."

Fitch was nodding, as if he had expected it.

"Think you can do it?" Scholes said.

"Of course," Fitch replied. Watching him January understood why they had chosen him to replace Tibbets: Fitch was like the old bull, he had that same ruthlessness. The young bull.

"Yes, sir," Matthews said.

Scholes was looking at him. "Sure," January said, not wanting to think about it. "Sure." His heart was pounding directly on his sternum. But Fitch and Matthews looked serious as owls, so he wasn't going to stick out by looking odd. It was big news, after all; anyone would be taken aback by it. Nevertheless, January made an effort to nod.

"Okay," Scholes said. "McDonald will be flying with you as copilot." Fitch frowned. "I've got to go tell those British officers that Le May doesn't want them on the strike with you. See you at the briefing."

"Yes, sir."

As soon as Scholes was around the corner Fitch swung a fist at the sky. "Yow!" Matthews cried. He and Fitch shook hands. "We did it!" Matthews took January's hand and wrung it, his face plastered with a goofy grin. "We did it!"

"Somebody did it, anyway," January said.

"Ah, Frank," Matthews said. "Show some spunk. You're always so cool."

"Old Professor Stoneface," Fitch said, glancing at January with a trace of amused contempt. "Come on, let's get to the briefing."

The briefing hut, one of the longer Quonsets, was completely surrounded by MPs holding carbines. "Gosh," Matthews said, subdued by the sight. Inside it was already smoky. The walls were covered by the usual maps of Japan.

Two blackboards at the front were draped with sheets. Captain Shepard, the naval officer who worked with the scientists on the gimmick, was in back with his assistant Lieutenant Stone, winding a reel of film onto a projector. Dr. Nelson, the group psychiatrist, was already seated on a front bench near the wall. Tibbets had recently sicced the psychiatrist on the group—another one of his great ideas, like the spies in the bar. The man's questions had struck January as stupid. He hadn't even been able to figure out that Easterly was a flake, something that was clear to anybody who flew with him, or even played him in a single round of poker. January slid onto a bench beside his mates.

The two Brits entered, looking furious in their stiff-upper-lip way. They sat on the bench behind January. Sweeney's and Easterly's crews filed in, followed by the other men, and soon the room was full. Fitch and the rest pulled out Lucky Strikes and lit up; since they had named the plane only January had stuck with Camels.

Scholes came in with several men January didn't recognize, and went to the front. The chatter died, and all the smoke plumes ribboned steadily into the air.

Scholes nodded, and two intelligence officers took the sheets off the blackboards, revealing aerial reconnaissance photos.

"Men," Scholes said, "these are the target cities."

Someone cleared his throat.

"In order of priority they are Hiroshima, Kokura, and Nagasaki. There will be three weather scouts: *Straight Flush* to Hiroshima, *Strange Cargo* to Kokura, and *Full House* to Nagasaki. *The Great Artiste* and *Number 91* will be accompanying the mission to take photos. And *Lucky Strike* will fly the bomb."

There were rustles, coughs. Men turned to look at January and his mates, and they all sat up straight. Sweeney stretched back to shake Fitch's hand, and there were some quick laughs. Fitch grinned.

"Now listen up," Scholes went on. "The weapon we are going to deliver was successfully tested stateside a couple of weeks ago. And now we've got orders to drop it on the enemy." He paused to let that sink in. "I'll let Captain Shepard tell you more."

Shepard walked to the blackboard slowly, savoring his entrance. His forehead was shiny with sweat, and January realized he was excited or nervous. He wondered what the psychiatrist would make of that.

"I'm going to come right to the point," Shepard said. "The bomb you are going to drop is something new in history. We think it will knock out everything within four miles."

Now the room was completely still. January noticed that he could see a great deal of his nose, eyebrows, and cheeks; it was as if he were receding back into his body, like a fox into its hole. He kept his gaze rigidly on Shepard, steadfastly ignoring the feeling. Shepard pulled a sheet back over a blackboard while someone else turned down the lights.

"This is a film of the only test we have made," Shepard said. The film started, caught, started again. A wavery cone of bright cigarette smoke speared the length of the room, and on the sheet sprang a dead gray landscape: a lot of sky, a smooth desert floor, hills in the distance. The projector went *click-click-click-click, click-click-click-click.* "The bomb is on top of the tower," Shepard said, and January focused on the pinlike object sticking out of the desert floor, off against the hills. It was between eight and ten miles from the camera, he judged; he had gotten good at calculating distances. He was still distracted by his face.

Click-click-click-click, click—then the screen went white for a second, filling even their room with light. When the picture returned the desert floor was filled with a white bloom of fire. The fireball coalesced and then quite suddenly it leaped off the earth all the way into the *stratosphere*, by God, like a tracer bullet leaving a machine gun, trailing a whitish pillar of smoke behind it. The pillar gushed up and a growing ball of smoke billowed outward, capping the pillar. January calculated the size of the cloud, but was sure he got it wrong. There it stood. The picture flickered, and then the screen went white again, as if the camera had melted or that part of the world had come apart. But the flapping from the projector told them it was the end of the film.

January felt the air suck in and out of his open mouth. The lights came on in the smoky room and for a second he panicked, he struggled to shove his features into an accepted pattern, the psychiatrist would be looking around at them all—and then he glanced around and realized he needn't have worried, that he wasn't alone. Faces were bloodless, eyes were blinky or bug-eyed with shock, mouths hung open or were clamped whitely shut. For a few moments they all had to acknowledge what they were doing. January, scaring himself, felt an urge to say, "Play it again, will you?" Fitch was pulling his curled black hair off his thug's forehead uneasily. Beyond him January saw that one of the Limeys had already reconsidered how mad he was about missing the flight. Now he looked sick. Someone let out a long *whew*, another whistled. January looked to the front again, where the psychiatrist watched them, undisturbed.

Shepard said, "It's big, all right. And no one knows what will happen when it's dropped from the air. But the mushroom cloud you saw will go to at least thirty thousand feet, probably sixty. And the flash you saw at the beginning was hotter than the sun."

Hotter than the sun. More licked lips, hard swallows, readjusted baseball caps. One of the intelligence officers passed out tinted goggles like welder's glasses. January took his and twiddled the opacity dial.

Scholes said, "You're the hottest thing in the armed forces, now. So no talking, even among yourselves." He took a deep breath. "Let's do it the way Colonel Tibbets would have wanted us to. He picked every one of you because you were the best, and now's the time to show he was right. So—so let's make the old man proud."

The briefing was over. Men filed out into the sudden sunlight. Into the heat and glare. Captain Shepard approached Fitch. "Stone and I will be flying with you to take care of the bomb," he said.

Fitch nodded. "Do you know how many strikes we'll fly?"

"As many as it takes to make them quit." Shepard stared hard at all of them. "But it will only take one."

War breeds strange dreams. That night January writhed over his sheets in the hot wet vegetable darkness, in that frightening half sleep when you sometimes know you are dreaming but can do nothing about it, and he dreamed he was walking...

...*walking through the streets when suddenly the sun swoops down, the sun touches down and everything is instantly darkness and smoke and silence, a deaf roaring. Walls of fire. His head hurts and in the middle of his vision is a bluewhite blur as if God's camera went off in his face. Ah—the sun fell, he thinks. His arm is burned. Blinking is painful. People stumbling by, mouths open, horribly burned—*

He is a priest, he can feel the clerical collar, and the wounded ask him for help. He points to his ears, tries to touch them but can't. Pall of black smoke over everything, the city has fallen into the streets. Ah, it's the end of the world. In a park he finds shade and cleared ground. People crouch under bushes like frightened animals. Where the park meets the river red and black figures crowd into steaming water. A figure gestures from a copse of bamboo. He enters it, finds five or six faceless soldiers huddling. Their eyes have melted, their mouths are holes. Deafness spares him their words. The sighted soldier mimes drinking. The soldiers are thirsty. He nods and goes down to the river in search of a container. Bodies float downstream.

Hours pass as he hunts fruitlessly for a bucket. He pulls people from the rubble. He hears a bird screeching and he realizes that his deafness is the roar of the city burning, a roar like the blood in his ears but he is not deaf, he only thought he was deaf because there are no human cries. The people are suffering in silence. Through the dusky night he stumbles back to the river, pain crashing through his head. In a field men are pulling potatoes out of the ground that have been baked well enough to eat. He shares one with them. At the river everyone is dead—

—and he struggled out of the nightmare drenched in rank sweat, the taste of dirt in his mouth, his stomach knotted with horror. He sat up and the wet rough sheet clung to his skin. His heart felt crushed between lungs desperate for air. The flowery rotting jungle smell filled him and images from the dream flashed before him so vividly that in the dim hut he saw nothing else. He grabbed his cigarettes and jumped off the bunk, hurried out into the compound. Trembling he lit up, starting pacing around. For a moment he worried that the idiot psychiatrist might see him, but then he dismissed the idea. Nelson would be asleep. They were all asleep. He shook his head, looked down at his right arm and almost dropped his cigarette—but it was just his stove scar, an old scar, he'd had it most of his life, since the day he'd pulled the frypan off the stove and onto his arm, burning it with oil. He could still remember the round O of fear that his mother's mouth had made as she rushed in to see what was wrong. Just an old burn scar, he thought, let's not go overboard here. He pulled his sleeve down.

For the rest of the night he tried to walk it off, cigarette after cigarette. The dome of the sky lightened until all the compound and the jungle beyond it was visible. He was forced by the light of day to walk back into his hut and lie down as if nothing had happened.

Two days later Scholes ordered them to take one of Le May's men over Rota for a test run. This new lieutenant colonel ordered Fitch not to play with the engines on takeoff. They flew a perfect run. January put the dummy gimmick right on the aiming point just as he had so often in the Salton Sea, and Fitch powered the plane down into the violent bank that started their 150-degree turn and flight for safety. Back on Tinian the lieutenant colonel congratulated them and shook each of their hands. January smiled with the rest, palms cool, heart steady. It was as if his body were a shell, something he could manipulate from without, like a bomb-sight. He ate well, he chatted as much as he ever had, and when the psychiatrist ran him to earth for some questions he was friendly and seemed open.

"Hello, doc."

"How do you feel about all this, Frank?"

"Just like I always have, sir. Fine."

"Eating well?"

"Better than ever."

"Sleeping well?"

"As well as I can in this humidity. I got used to Utah, I'm afraid." Dr. Nelson laughed. Actually January had hardly slept since his dream. He was afraid of sleep. Couldn't the man see that?

"And how do you feel about being part of the crew chosen to make the first strike?"

"Well, it was the right choice, I reckon. We're the b—the best crew left."

"Do you feel sorry about Tibbets' crew's accident?"

"Yes, sir, I do." You better believe it.

After the jokes and firm handshakes that ended the interview January walked out into the blaze of the tropical noon and lit a cigarette. He allowed himself to feel how much he despised the psychiatrist and his blind profession at the same time he was waving good-bye to the man. Ounce brain. Why couldn't he have seen? Whatever happened it would be his fault.... With a rush of smoke out of him January realized how painfully easy it was to fool someone if you wanted to. All action was no more than a mask that could be perfectly manipulated from somewhere else. And all the while in that somewhere else January lived in a *click-click-click* of film, in the silent roaring of a dream, struggling against images he couldn't dispel. The heat of the tropical sun—ninety-three million miles away, wasn't it?—pulsed painfully on the back of his neck.

As he watched the psychiatrist collar their tail-gunner Kochenski, he thought of walking up to the man and saying *I quit. I don't want to do this.* In imagination he saw the look that would form in the man's eye, in Fitch's eye, in Tibbets' eye, and his mind recoiled from the idea. He felt too much contempt for them. He wouldn't for anything give them a means to despise him, a reason to call him coward. Stubbornly he banished the whole complex of thought. Easier to go along with it.

And so a couple of disjointed days later, just after midnight of August 9th, he found himself preparing for the strike. Around him Fitch and Matthews and Haddock were doing the same. How odd were the everyday motions of getting dressed when you were off to demolish a city, to end a hundred thousand lives! January found himself examining his hands, his boots, the cracks in the linoleum. He put on his survival vest, checked the pockets abstractedly for fishhooks, water kit, first aid package, emergency rations. Then the parachute harness, and his coveralls over it all. Tying his bootlaces took minutes; he couldn't do it when watching his fingers so closely.

"Come on, Professor!" Fitch's voice was tight. "The big day is here."

He followed the others into the night. A cool wind was blowing. The chaplain said a prayer for them. They took jeeps down Broadway to runway Able. *Lucky Strike* stood in a circle of spotlights and men, half of them with cameras, the rest with reporter's pads. They surrounded the crew; it reminded January of a Hollywood premiere. Eventually he escaped up the hatch and into the plane. Others followed. Half an hour passed before Fitch joined them, grinning like a movie star. They started the engines, and January was thankful for their vibrating, thought-smothering roar. They taxied away from the Hollywood scene and January felt relief for a moment until he remembered where they were going. On runway Able the engines pitched up to their twenty-three hundred rpm whine, and looking out the clear windscreen he saw the runway paint-marks move by ever faster. Fitch kept them on the runway till Tinian had run out from under them, then quickly pulled up. They were on their way.

When they got to altitude January climbed past Fitch and McDonald to the bombardier's seat and placed his parachute on it. He leaned back. The roar of the four engines packed around him like cotton batting. He was on the flight, nothing to be done about it now. The heavy vibration was a comfort, he liked the feel of it there in the nose of the plane. A drowsy, sad acceptance hummed through him.

Against his closed eyelids flashed a black eyeless face and he jerked awake, heart racing. He was on the flight, no way out. Now he realized how easy it would have been to get out of it. He could have just said he didn't want to. The simplicity of it appalled him. Who gave a damn what the psychiatrist or

Tibbets or anyone else thought, compared to this? Now there was no way out. It was a comfort, in a way. Now he could stop worrying, stop thinking he had any choice.

Sitting there with his knees bracketing the bombsight January dozed, and as he dozed he daydreamed his way out. He could climb the step to Fitch and McDonald and declare he had been secretly promoted to major and ordered to redirect the mission. They were to go to Tokyo and drop the bomb in the bay. The Jap War Cabinet had been told to watch this demonstration of the new weapon, and when they saw that fireball boil the bay and bounce into heaven they'd run and sign surrender papers as fast as they could write, kamikazes or not. They weren't crazy, after all. No need to murder a whole city. It was such a good plan that the generals back home were no doubt changing the mission at this very minute, desperately radioing their instructions to Tinian, only to find out it was too late...so that when they returned to Tinian January would become a hero for guessing what the generals really wanted, and for risking all to do it. It would be like one of the Hornblower stories in the *Saturday Evening Post*.

Once again January jerked awake. The drowsy pleasure of the fantasy was replaced with desperate scorn. There wasn't a chance in hell that he could convince Fitch and the rest that he had secret orders superseding theirs. And he couldn't go up there and wave his pistol around and *order* them to drop the bomb in Tokyo Bay, because he was the one who had to actually drop it, and he couldn't be down in front dropping the bomb and up ordering the others around at the same time. Pipe dreams.

Time swept on, slow as a second hand. January's thoughts, however, matched the spin of the props; desperately they cast about, now this way now that, like an animal caught by the leg in a trap. The crew was silent. The clouds below were a white scree on the black ocean. January's knee vibrated against the squat stand of the bombsight. He was the one who had to drop the bomb. No matter where his thoughts lunged they were brought up short by that. He was the one, not Fitch or the crew, not Le May, not the generals and scientists back home, not Truman and his advisors. Truman—suddenly January hated him. Roosevelt would have done it differently. If only Roosevelt had lived! The grief that had filled January when he learned of Roosevelt's death reverberated through him again, more strongly than ever. It was unfair to have worked so hard and then not see the war's end. And FDR would have ended it differently. Back at the start of it all he had declared that civilian centers were never to be bombed, and if he had lived, if, if, if. But he hadn't. And now it was smiling bastard Harry Truman, ordering *him*, Frank January, to drop the sun on two hundred thousand women and children. Once his father had taken him to be see the Browns play before twenty thousand, a giant crowd— "I never voted for you," January whispered viciously, and jerked to realize he had spoken aloud. Luckily his microphone was off. But Roosevelt would have done it differently, he *would have.*

The bombsight rose before him, spearing the black sky and blocking some of the hundreds of little cruciform stars. *Lucky Strike* ground on toward Iwo Jima, minute by minute flying four miles closer to their target. January leaned forward and put his face in the cool headrest of the bombsight, hoping that its grasp might hold his thoughts as well as his forehead. It worked surprisingly well.

His earphones crackled and he sat up. "Captain January." It was Shepard. "We're going to arm the bomb now, want to watch?"

"Sure thing." He shook his head, surprised at his own duplicity. Stepping up between the pilots, he moved stiffly to the roomy cabin behind the cockpit. Matthews was at his desk taking a navigational fix on the radio signals from Iwo Jima and Okinawa, and Haddock stood beside him. At the back of the compartment was a small circular hatch, below the larger tunnel leading to the rear of the plane. January opened it, sat down and swung himself feet first through the hole.

The bomb bay was unheated, and the cold air felt good. He stood facing the bomb. Stone was sitting on the floor of the bay; Shepard was laid out under the bomb, reaching into it. On a rubber pad next to Stone were tools, plates, several cylindrical blocks. Shepard pulled back, sat up, sucked a scraped knuckle. He shook his head ruefully: "I don't dare wear gloves with this one."

"I'd be just as happy myself if you didn't let something slip," January joked nervously. The two men laughed.

"Nothing can blow till I change those green wires to the red ones," Stone said.

"Give me the wrench," Shepard said. Stone handed it to him, and he stretched under the bomb again. After some awkward wrenching inside it he lifted out a cylindrical plug. "Breech plug," he said, and set it on the mat.

January found his skin goose-pimpling in the cold air. Stone handed Shepard one of the blocks. Shepard extended under the bomb again. "Red ends toward the breech." "I know." Watching them January was reminded of auto mechanics on the oily floor of a garage, working under a car. He had spent a few years doing that himself, after his family moved to Vicksburg. Hiroshima was a river town. One time a flatbed truck carrying bags of cement powder down Fourth Street hill had lost its brakes and careened into the intersection with the River Road, where despite the driver's efforts to turn it smashed into a passing car. Frank had been out in the yard playing, had heard the crash and saw the cement dust rising. He had been one of the first there. The woman and child in the passenger seat of the Model T had been killed. The woman driving was okay. They were from Chicago. A group of folks subdued the driver of the truck, who kept trying to help at the Model T, though he had a bad cut on his head and was covered with white dust.

"Okay, let's tighten the breech plug." Stone gave Shepard the wrench. "Sixteen turns exactly," Shepard said. He was sweating even in the bay's chill, and he paused to wipe his forehead. "Let's hope we don't get hit by lightning." He put the wrench down and shifted onto his knees, picked up a circular plate. Hubcap, January thought. Stone connected wires, then helped Shepard install two more plates. Good old American know-how, January thought, goose pimples rippling across his skin like cat's paws over water. There was Shepard, a scientist, putting together a bomb like he was an auto mechanic changing oil and plugs. January felt a tight rush of rage at the scientists who had designed the bomb. They had worked on it for over a year down there in New Mexico; had none of them in all that time ever stopped to think what they were doing?

But none of them had to drop it. January turned to hide his face from Shepard, stepped down the bay. The bomb looked like a big long trash can, with fins at one end and little antennae at the other. Just a bomb, he thought, damn it, it's just another bomb.

Shepard stood and patted the bomb gently. "We've got a live one now." Never a thought about what it would do. January hurried by the man, afraid that hatred would crack his shell and give him away. The pistol strapped to his belt caught on the hatchway and he imagined shooting Shepard—shooting Fitch and McDonald and plunging the controls forward so that *Lucky Strike* tilted and spun down into the sea like a spent tracer bullet, like a plane broken by flak, following the arc of all human ambition. Nobody would ever know what had happened to them, and their trash can would be dumped at the bottom of the Pacific where it belonged. He could even shoot everyone and parachute out, and perhaps be rescued by one of the Superdumbos following them....

The thought passed and remembering it January squinted with disgust. But another part of him agreed that it was a possibility. It could be done. It would solve his problem. His fingers explored his holster snap.

"Want some coffee?" Matthews asked.

"Sure," January said, and took his hand from the gun to reach for the cup. He sipped: hot. He watched Matthews and Benton tune the loran equipment. As the beeps came in Matthews took a straightedge and drew lines from Okinawa and Iwo Jima on his map table. He tapped a finger on the intersection. "They've taken the art out of navigation," he said to January. "They might as well stop making the navigator's dome," thumbing up at the little Plexiglas bubble over them.

"Good old American know-how," January said.

Matthews nodded. With two fingers he measured the distance between their position and Iwo Jima. Benton measured with a ruler.

"Rendezvous at five thirty-five, eh?" Matthews said. They were to rendezvous with the two trailing planes over Iwo.

Benton disagreed: "I'd say five-fifty."

"What? Check again, guy, we're not in no tugboat here."

"The wind—"

"Yah, the wind. Frank, you want to add a bet to the pool?"

"Five thirty-six," January said promptly.

They laughed. "See, he's got more confidence in me," Matthews said with a dopey grin.

January recalled his plan to shoot the crew and tip the plane into the sea, and he pursed his lips, repelled. Not for anything would he be able to shoot these men, who, if not friends, were at least companions. They passed for friends. They meant no harm.

Shepard and Stone climbed into the cabin. Matthews offered them coffee. "The gimmick's ready to kick their ass, eh?" Shepard nodded and drank.

January moved forward, past Haddock's console. Another plan that wouldn't work. What to do? All the flight engineer's dials and gauges showed conditions were normal. Maybe he could sabotage something? Cut a line somewhere?

Fitch looked back at him and said, "When are we due over Iwo?"

"Five-forty, Matthews says."

"He better be right."

A thug. In peacetime Fitch would be hanging around a pool table giving the cops trouble. He was perfect for war. Tibbets had chosen his men well—most of them, anyway. Moving back past Haddock, January stopped to stare at the group of men in the navigation cabin. They joked, drank coffee. They were all a bit like Fitch: young toughs, capable and thoughtless. They were having a good time, an adventure. That was January's dominant impression of his companions in the 509th; despite all the bitching and the occasional moments of overmastering fear, they were having a good time. His mind spun forward and he saw what these young men would grow up to be like as clearly as if they stood before him in businessmen's suits, prosperous and balding. They would be tough and capable and thoughtless, and as the years passed and the great war receded in time they would look back on it with ever-increasing nostalgia, for they would be the survivors and not the dead. Every year of this war would feel like ten in their memories, so that the war would always remain the central experience of their lives—a time when history lay palpable in their hands, when each of their daily acts affected it, when moral issues were simple, and others told them what to do—so that as more years passed and the survivors aged, bodies falling apart, lives in one rut or another, they would unconsciously push harder and harder to thrust the world into war again, thinking somewhere inside themselves that if they could only return to world war then they would magically be again as they were in the last one—young, and free, and happy. And by that time they would hold the positions of power, they would be capable of doing it.

So there would be more wars, January saw. He heard it in Matthews' laughter, saw it in their excited eyes. "There's Iwo, and it's five thirty-one. Pay up! I win!" And in future wars they'd have more bombs like the gimmick, hundreds of them no doubt. He saw more planes, more young crews like this one, flying to Moscow no doubt or to wherever, fireballs in every capital, why not? And to what end? To what end? So that the old men could hope to become magically young again. Nothing more sane than that.

They were over Iwo Jima. Three more hours to Japan. Voices from *The Great Artiste* and *Number 91* crackled on the radio. Rendezvous accomplished, the three planes flew northwest, toward Shikoku, the first Japanese island in their path. January went aft to use the toilet. "You okay, Frank?" Matthews asked. "Sure. Terrible coffee, though." "Ain't it always." January tugged at his baseball cap and hurried away. Kochenski and the other gunners were playing poker. When he was done he returned forward. Matthews sat on the stool before his maps, readying his equipment for the constant monitoring of drift that would now be required. Haddock and Benton were also busy at their stations. January maneuvered between the pilots down into the nose. "Good shooting," Matthews called after him.

Forward it seemed quieter. January got settled, put his

headphones on and leaned forward to look out the ribbed Plexiglas.

Dawn had turned the whole vault of the sky pink. Slowly the radiant shade shifted through lavender to blue, pulse by pulse a different color. The ocean below was a glittering blue plane, marbled by a pattern of puffy pink cloud. The sky above was a vast dome, darker above than on the horizon. January had always thought that dawn was the time when you could see most clearly how big the earth was, and how high above it they flew. It seemed they flew at the very upper edge of the atmosphere, and January saw how thin it was, how it was just a skin of air really, so that even if you flew up to its top the earth still extended away infinitely in every direction. The coffee had warmed January, he was sweating. Sunlight blinked off the Plexiglas. His watch said six. Plane and hemisphere of blue were split down the middle by the bombsight. His earphones crackled and he listened in to the reports from the lead planes flying over the target cities. Kokura, Nagasaki, Hiroshima, all of them had six-tenths cloud cover. Maybe they would have to cancel the whole mission because of weather. "We'll look at Hiroshima first," Fitch said. January peered down at the fields of miniature clouds with renewed interest. His parachute slipped under him. Readjusting it he imagined putting it on, sneaking back to the central escape hatch under the navigator's cabin, opening the hatch...he could be out of the plane and gone before anyone noticed. Leave it up to them. They could bomb or not but it wouldn't be January's doing. He could float down onto the world like a puff of dandelion, feel cool air rush around him, watch the silk canopy dome hang over him like a miniature sky, a private world.

An eyeless black face. January shuddered; it was as though the nightmare could return any time. If he jumped nothing would change, the bomb would still fall—would he feel any better, floating on his Inland Sea? Sure, one part of him shouted; maybe, another conceded; the rest of him saw that face. . . .

Earphones crackled. Shepard said, "Lieutenant Stone has now armed the bomb, and I can tell you all what we are carrying. Aboard with us is the world's first atomic bomb."

Not exactly, January thought. Whistles squeaked in his earphones. The first one went off in New Mexico. Splitting atoms: January had heard the term before. Tremendous energy in every atom, Einstein had said. Break one, and—he had seen the result on film. Shepard was talking about radiation, which brought back more to January. Energy released in the form of X rays. Killed by X rays! It would be against the Geneva Convention if they had thought of it.

Fitch cut in. "When the bomb is dropped Lieutenant Benton will record our reaction to what we see. This recording is being made for history, so watch your language." Watch your language! January choked back a laugh. Don't curse or blaspheme God at the sight of the first atomic bomb incinerating a city and all its inhabitants with X rays!

Six-twenty. January found his hands clenched together on the headrest of the bombsight. He felt as if he had a fever. In the harsh wash of morning light the skin on the backs of his hands appeared slightly translucent. The whorls in the skin looked like the delicate patterning of waves on the sea's surface. His hands were made of atoms. Atoms were the smallest building block of matter, it took billions of them to make those tense, trembling hands. Split one atom and you had the fireball. That meant that the energy contained in even one hand. . . he turned up a palm to look at the lines and the mottled flesh under the transparent skin. A person was a bomb that could blow up the world. January felt that latent power stir in him, pulsing with every hard heart-knock. What beings they were, and in what a blue expanse of a world!—

And here they spun on to drop a bomb and kill a hundred thousand of these astonishing beings.

When a fox or raccoon is caught by the leg in a trap, it lunges until the leg is frayed, twisted, perhaps broken, and only then does the animal's pain and exhaustion force it to quit. Now in the same way January wanted to quit. His mind hurt. His plans to escape were so much crap—stupid, useless. Better to quit. He tried to stop thinking, but it was hopeless. How could he stop? As long as he was conscious he would be thinking. The mind struggles longer in its traps than any fox.

Lucky Strike tilted up and began the long climb to bombing altitude. On the horizon the clouds lay over a green island. Japan. Surely it had gotten hotter, the heater must be broken, he thought. Don't think. Every few minutes Matthews gave Fitch small course adjustments. "Two seventy-five, now. That's it." To escape the moment January recalled his childhood. Following a mule and plow. Moving to Vicksburg (rivers). For a while there in Vicksburg, since his stutter made it hard to gain friends, he had played a game with himself. He had passed the time by imagining that everything he did was vitally important and determined the fate of the world. If he crossed a road in front of a certain car, for instance, then the car wouldn't make it through the next intersection before a truck hit it, and so the man driving would be killed and wouldn't be able to invent the flying boat that would save President Wilson from kidnappers—so he had to wait for that car because everything afterward depended on it. Oh damn it, he thought, damn it, think of something *different*. The last Hornblower story he had read—how would *he* get out of this? The round O of his mother's face as she ran in and saw his arm—The Mississippi, mud-brown behind its levees— Abruptly he shook his head, face twisted in frustration and despair, aware at last that no possible avenue of memory would serve as an escape for him now, for now there was no part of his life that did not apply to the situation he was in, and no matter where he cast his mind it was going to shore up against the hour facing him.

Less than an hour. They were at thirty thousand feet, bombing altitude. Fitch gave him altimeter readings to dial into the bombsight. Matthews gave him windspeeds. Sweat got in his eye and he blinked furiously. The sun rose behind them like an atomic bomb, glinting off every corner and edge of the Plexiglas, illuminating his bubble compartment with a fierce glare. Broken plans jumbled together in his mind, his breath was short, his throat dry. Uselessly and repeatedly he damned the scientists, damned Truman. Damned the Japanese for causing the whole mess in the first place, damned yellow killers, they had brought this on themselves. Remember Pearl. American men had died under bombs when no war had been declared; they had started it and now it was coming back to them with a vengeance. And they deserved it. And an invasion of Japan would take years, cost millions of lives— end it now, end it, they deserved it, they deserved it steaming river full of charcoal people silently dying damned stubborn race of maniacs!

"There's Honshu," Fitch said, and January returned to the world of the plane. They were over the Inland Sea. Soon they would pass the secondary target, Kokura, a bit to the south. Seven-thirty. The island was draped more heavily than the sea by clouds, and again January's heart leaped with the idea that weather would cancel the mission. But they did deserve it. It was a mission like any other mission. He had dropped bombs on Africa, Sicily, Italy, all Germany....He leaned forward to take a look through the sight. Under the X of the crosshairs was the sea, but at the lead edge of the sight was land. Honshu. At two hundred and thirty miles an hour that gave them about a half hour to Hiroshima. Maybe less. He wondered if his heart could beat so hard for that long.

Fitch said, "Matthews, I'm giving over guidance to you. Just tell us what to do."

"Bear south two degrees," was all Matthews said. At last their voices had taken on a touch of awareness, even fear.

"January, are you ready?" Fitch asked.

"I'm just waiting," January said. He sat up, so Fitch could see the back of his head. The bombsight stood between his legs. A switch on its side would start the bombing sequence; the bomb would not leave the plane immediately upon the flick of the switch, but would drop after a fifteen-second radio tone warned the following planes. The sight was adjusted accordingly.

"Adjust to a heading of two sixty-five," Matthews said. "We're coming in directly upwind." This was to make any side-drift adjustments for the bomb unnecessary. "January, dial it down to two hundred and thirty-one miles per hour."

"Two thirty-one."

Fitch said, "Everyone but January and Matthews, get your goggles on."

January took the darkened goggles from the floor. One needed to protect one's eyes or they might melt. He put them on, put his forehead on the headrest. They were in the way. He took them off. When he looked through the sight again there was land under the crosshairs. He checked his watch. Eight o'clock. Up and reading the papers, drinking tea.

"Ten minutes to AP," Matthews said. The aiming point was Aioi Bridge, a T-shaped bridge in the middle of the delta-straddling city. Easy to recognize.

"There's a lot of cloud down there," Fitch nodded. "Are you going to be able to see?"

"I won't be sure until we try it," January said.

"We can make another pass and use radar if we need to," Matthews said.

Fitch said. "Don't drop it unless you're sure, January."

"Yes, sir."

Through the sight a grouping of rooftops and gray roads was just visible between broken clouds. Around it green forest. "All right," Matthews exclaimed, "here we go! Keep it right on this heading, Captain! January, we'll stay at two thirty-one."

"And same heading," Fitch said. "January, she's all yours. Everyone make sure your goggles are on. And be ready for the turn."

January's world contracted to the view through the bombsight. A stippled field of cloud and forest. Over a small range of hills and into Hiroshima's watershed. The broad river was mud brown, the land pale hazy green, the growing network of roads flat gray. Now the tiny rectangular shapes of buildings covered almost all the land, and swimming into the sight came the city proper, narrow islands thrusting into a dark blue bay. Under the crosshairs the city moved island by island, cloud by cloud. January had stopped breathing, his fingers were rigid as stone on the switch. And there was Aioi Bridge. It slid right under the crosshairs, a tiny T right in a gap of clouds. January's fingers crushed the switch. Deliberately he took a breath, held it. Clouds swam under the crosshairs, then the next island. "Almost there," he said calmly into his microphone. "Steady," Now that he was committed his heart was humming like the Wrights. He counted to ten. Now flowing under the crosshairs were clouds alternating with green forest, leaden roads. "I've turned the switch, but I'm not getting a tone!" he croaked into the mike. His right hand held the switch firmly in place. Fitch was shouting something—Matthews' voice cracked across it— "Flipping it b-back and forth," January shouted, shielding the bombsight with his body from the eyes of the pilots. "But *still*—wait a second—"

He pushed the switch down. A low hum filled his ears. "That's it! It started!"

"But where will it land?" Matthews cried.

"Hold steady!" January shouted.

Lucky Strike shuddered and lofted up ten or twenty feet. January twisted to look down and there was the bomb, flying just below the plane. Then with a wobble it fell away.

The plane banked right and dove so hard that the centrifugal force threw January against the Plexiglas. Several thousand feet lower Fitch leveled it out and they hurtled north.

"Do you see anything?" Fitch cried.

From the tailgun Kochenski gasped "Nothing." January struggled upright. He reached for the welder's goggles, but they were no longer on his head. He couldn't find them. "How long has it been?" he said.

"Thirty seconds," Matthews replied.

January clamped his eyes shut.

The blood in his eyelids lit up red, then white.

On the earphones a clutter of voices: "Oh my God. Oh my God." The plane bounced and tumbled, metallically shrieking. January pressed himself off the Plexiglas. "Nother shockwave!" Kochenski yelled. The plane rocked again, bounced out of control, this is it, January thought, end of the world, I guess that solves my problem.

He opened his eyes and found he could still see. The engines still roared, the props spun. "Those were the shockwaves from the bomb," Fitch called. "We're okay now. Look at that! Will you look at that sonofabitch go!"

January looked. The cloud layer below had burst apart, and a black column of smoke billowed up from a core of red fire. Already the top of the column was at their height. Exclamations of shock clattered painfully in January's ears.

He stared at the fiery base of the cloud, at the scores of fires feeding into it. Suddenly he could see past the cloud, and his fingernails cut into his palms. Through a gap in the clouds he saw it clearly, the delta, the six rivers, there off to the left of the tower of smoke: the city of Hiroshima, untouched.

"We missed!" Kochenski yelled. "We missed it!"

January turned to hide his face from the pilots; on it was a grin like a rictus. He sat back in his seat and let the relief fill him.

Then it was back to it. "God damn it!" Fitch shouted down at him. McDonald was trying to restrain him. "January, get up here!"

"Yes, sir." Now there was a new set of problems.

January stood and turned, legs weak. His right fingertips throbbed painfully. The men were crowded forward to look out the Plexiglas. January looked with them.

The mushroom cloud was forming. It roiled out as if it might continue to extend forever, fed by the inferno and the black stalk below it. It looked about two miles wide, and a half mile tall, and it extended well above the height they flew at, dwarfing their plane entirely. "Do you think we'll all be sterile?" Matthews said.

"I can taste the radiation," McDonald declared. "Can you? It tastes like lead."

Bursts of flame sot up into the cloud from below, giving a purplish tint to the stalk. There it stood: lifelike, malignant, sixty thousand feet tall. One bomb. January shoved past the pilots into the navigation cabin, overwhelmed.

"Should I start recording everyone's reaction, Captain?" asked Benton.

"To hell with that," Fitch said, following January back. But Shepard got there first, descending quickly from the navigation dome. He rushed across the cabin, caught January on the shoulder, "You bastard!" he screamed as January stumbled back. "You lost your nerve, coward!"

January went for Shepard, happy to have a target at last, but Fitch cut in and grabbed him by the collar, pulled him around until they were face to face—

"Is that right?" Fitch cried, as angry as Shepard."Did you screw up on purpose?"

"No," January grunted, and knocked Fitch's hands away from his neck. He swung and smacked Fitch on the mouth, caught him solid. Fitch staggered back, recovered, and no doubt would have beaten January up, but Matthews and Benton and Stone leaped in and held him back, shouting for order. "Shut up! Shut up!" McDonald screamed from the cockpit, and for a moment it was bedlam, but Fitch let himself be restrained, and soon only McDonald's shouts for quiet were heard. January retreated to between the pilot seats, right hand on his pistol holster.

"The city was in the crosshairs when I flipped the switch," he said. "But the first couple of times I flipped it nothing happened—"

"That's a lie!" Shepard shouted. "There was nothing wrong with the switch, I checked it myself. Besides, the bomb exploded *miles* beyond Hiroshima, look for yourself! That's *minutes*." He wiped spit from his chin and pointed at January. "You did it."

"You don't know that," January said. But he could see the men had been convinced by Shepard, and he took a step back. "You just get me to a board of inquiry, quick. And leave me alone till then. If you touch me again," glaring venomously at Fitch and then Shepard, "I'll shoot you." He turned and hopped down to his seat, feeling exposed and vulnerable, like a treed raccoon.

"They'll shoot *you* for this," Shepard screamed after him.

"Disobeying orders—treason—" Matthews and Stone were shutting him up.

"Let's get out of here," he heard McDonald say. "I can taste the lead, can't you?"

January looked out the Plexiglas. The giant cloud still burned and roiled. One atom...Well, they had really done it to that forest. He almost laughed but stopped himself, afraid of hysteria. Through a break in the clouds he got a clear view of Hiroshima for the first time. It lay spread over its islands like a map, unharmed. Well, that was that. The inferno at the base of the mushroom cloud was eight or ten miles around the shore of the bay and a mile or two inland. A certain patch of forest would be gone, destroyed—utterly blasted from the face of the earth. The Japs would be able to go out and investigate the damage. And if they were told it was a demonstration, a warning—and if they acted fast—well, they had their chance. Maybe it would work.

The release of tension made January feel sick. Then he recalled Shepard's words and he knew that whether his plan worked or not he was still in trouble, In trouble! It was worse than that. Bitterly he cursed the Japanese, he even wished for a moment that he *had* dropped it on them. Wearily he let his despair empty him.

A long while later he sat up straight. Once again he was a trapped animal. He began lunging for escape, casting about for plans. One alternative after another. All during the long grim flight home he considered it, mind spinning at the speed of the props and beyond. And when they came down on Tinian he had a plan. It was a long shot, he reckoned, but it was the best he could do.

The briefing hut was surrounded by MPs again. January stumbled from the truck with the rest and walked inside. He was more than ever aware of the looks given him, and they were hard, accusatory. He was too tired to care. He hadn't slept in more than thirty-six hours, and had slept very little since the last time he had been in the hut, a week before. Now the room quivered with the lack of engineer vibration to stabilize it, and the silence roared. It was all he could do to hold on to the bare essentials of his plan. The glares of Fitch and Shepard, the hurt incomprehension of Matthews, they had to be thrust out of his focus. Thankfully he lit a cigarette.

In a clamor of question and argument the others described the strike. Then the haggard Scholes and an intelligence officer led them through the bombing run. January's plan made it necessary to hold to his story: "...and when the AP was under the crosshairs I pushed down the switch, but got no signal. I flipped it up and down repeatedly until the tone kicked in. At that point there was still fifteen seconds to the release."

"Was there anything that may have caused the tone to start when it did?"

"Not that I noticed immediately, but—"

"It's impossible," Shepard interrupted, face red. "I checked the switch before we flew and there was nothing wrong with it. Besides, the drop occurred over a minute—"

"Captain Shepard," Scholes said. "We'll hear from you presently."

"But he's obviously lying—"

"Captain Shepard! It's not at all obvious. Don't speak unless questioned."

"Anyway," January said, hoping to shift the questions away from the issue of the long delay, "I noticed something about the bomb when it was falling that could explain why it stuck. I need to discuss it with one of the scientists familiar with the bomb's design."

"What was that?" Scholes asked suspiciously.

January hesitated. "There's going to be an inquiry, right?"

Scholes frowned. "This is the inquiry, Captain January. Tell us what you saw."

"But there will be some proceeding beyond this one?"

"It looks like there's going to be a court-martial, yes, Captain."

"That's what I thought. I don't want to talk to anyone but my counsel, and some scientist familiar with the bomb."

"*I'm* a scientist familiar with the bomb," Shepard burst out. "You could tell me if you really had anything, you—"

"I said I need a scientist!" January exclaimed, rising to face the scarlet Shepard across the table. "Not a G-God damned mechanic." Shepard started to shout, others joined in and the room rang with argument. While Scholes restored order January sat down, and he refused to be drawn out again.

"I'll see you're assigned counsel, and initiate the court-martial," Scholes said, clearly at a loss. "Meanwhile you are under arrest, on suspicion of disobeying orders in combat." January nodded, and Scholes gave him over to the MPs.

"One last thing," January said, fighting exhaustion. "Tell General Le May that if the Japs are told this drop was a warning, it might have the same effect as—"

"I told you!" Shepard shouted. "I told you he did it on purpose!"

Men around Shepard restrained him. But he had convinced most of them, and even Matthews stared at him with surprised anger.

January shook his head wearily. He had the dull feeling that his plan, while it had succeeded so far, was ultimately not a good one. "Just trying to make the best of it." It took all of his remaining will to force his legs to carry him in a dignified manner out of the hut.

* * *

His cell was an empty NCO's office. MPs brought his meals. For the first couple of days he did little but sleep. On the third day he glanced out the office's barred window, and saw a tractor pulling a tarpaulin-draped trolley out of the compound, followed by jeeps filled with MPs. It looked like a military funeral. January rushed to the door and banged on it until one of the young MPs came.

"What's that they're doing out there?" January demanded.

Eyes cold and mouth twisted, the MP said, "They're making another strike. They're going to do it right this time."

"No!" January cried. "No!" He rushed the MP, who knocked him back and locked the door. *"No!"* He beat the door until his hands hurt, cursing wildly. "You don't *need* to do it, it isn't *necessary*." Shell shattered at last, he collapsed on the bed and wept. Now everything he had done would be rendered meaningless. He had sacrificed himself for nothing.

A day or two after that the MPs led in a colonel, an iron-haired man who stood stiffly and crushed January's hand when he shook it. His eyes were a pale, icy blue.

"I am Colonel Dray," he said. "I have been ordered to defend you in court-martial." January could feel the dislike pouring from the man. "To do that I'm going to need every fact you have, so let's get started."

"I'm not talking to anybody until I've seen an atomic scientist."

"I am your *defense* counsel—"

"I don't care who you are," January said. "Your defense of me depends on you getting one of the scientists *here*. The higher up he is, the better. And I want to speak to him alone."

"I will have to be present."

So he would do it. But now January's lawyer, too, was an enemy.

"Naturally," January said. "You're my lawyer. But no one else. Our atomic secrecy may depend on it."

"You saw evidence of sabotage?"

"Not one word more until that scientist is here."

Angrily the colonel nodded and left.

Late the next day the colonel returned with another man. "This is Dr. Forest."

"I helped develop the bomb," Forest said. He had a crew cut and dressed in fatigues, and to January he looked more Army than the colonel. Suspiciously he stared back and forth at the two men.

"You'll vouch for this man's identity on your word as an officer?" he asked Dray.

"Of course," the colonel said stiffly, offended.

"So," Dr. Forest said. "You had some trouble getting it off when you wanted to. Tell me what you saw."

"I saw nothing," January said harshly. He took a deep breath; it was time to commit himself. "I want you to take a message back to the scientists. You folks have been working on this thing for years, and you must have had time to consider how the bomb should have been used. You know we could have convinced the Japs to surrender by showing them a demonstration—"

"Wait a minute," Forest said. "You're saying you didn't see anything? There wasn't a malfunction?"

"That's right," January said, and cleared his throat. "It wasn't *necessary*, do you understand?"

Forest was looking at Colonel Dray. Dray gave him a disgusted shrug. "He told me he saw evidence of sabotage."

"I want you to go back and ask the scientists to intercede for me," January said, raising his voice to get the man's attention. "I haven't got a chance in that court-martial. But if the scientists defend me then maybe they'll let me live, see? I don't want to get shot for doing something every one of you scientists would have done."

Dr. Forest had backed away. Color rising, he said, "What makes you think that's what we would have done? Don't you think we considered it? Don't you think men better qualified than you made the decision?" He waved a hand. "God damn it—what made you think you were competent to decide something as important as that!"

January was appalled at the man's reaction; in his plan it had gone differently. Angrily he jabbed a finger at Forest. "Because *I* was the man doing it, *Doctor* Forest. You take even one step back from that and suddenly you can pretend it's not your doing. Fine for you, but *I was there.*"

At every word the man's color was rising. It looked like he might pop a vein in his neck. January tried once more. "Have you ever tried to imagine what one of your bombs would do to a city full of people?"

"I've had enough!" the man exploded. He turned to Dray. "I'm under no obligation to keep what I've heard here confidential. You can be sure it will be used as evidence in Captain January's court-martial." He turned and gave January a look of such blazing hatred that January understood it. For these men to admit he was right would mean admitting that they were wrong—that every one of them was responsible for his part in the construction of the weapon January had refused to use. Understanding that, January knew he was doomed.

The bang of Dr. Forest's departure still shook the little office. January sat on his cot, got out a smoke. Under Colonel Dray's cold gaze he lit one shakily, took a drag. He looked up at the colonel, shrugged. "It was my best chance," he explained. That did something—for the first and only time the cold disdain in the colonel's eyes shifted to a little, hard, lawyerly gleam of respect.

The court-martial lasted two days. The verdict was guilty of disobeying orders in combat and of giving aid and comfort to the enemy. The sentence was death by firing squad.

For most of his remaining days January rarely spoke, drawing ever further behind he mask that had hidden him for so long. A clergyman came to see him, but it was the 509th's chaplain, the one who had said the prayer blessing the *Lucky Strike's* mission before they took off. Angrily January sent him packing.

Later, however, a young Catholic priest dropped by. His name was Patrick Getty. He was a little pudgy man, bespectacled and, it seemed, somewhat afraid of January. January let the man talk to him. When he returned the next day January talked back a bit, and on the day after that he talked some more. It became a habit.

Usually January talked about his childhood. He talked of plowing mucky black bottom land behind a mule. Of running down the lane to the mailbox. Of reading books by the light of the moon after he had been ordered to sleep, and of being beaten by his mother for it with a high-heeled shoe. He told the priest the story of the time his arm had been burnt, and about the car crash at the bottom of Fourth Street. "It's the truck driver's face I remember, do you see, Father?"

"Yes," the young priest said. "Yes."

And he told him about the game he had played in which every action he took tipped the balance of world affairs. "When I remembered that game I thought it was dumb. Step on a sidewalk crack and cause an earthquake—you know, it's stupid. Kids are like that." The priest nodded. "But now I've been thinking that if everybody were to live their whole lives like that, thinking that every move they made really was important, then...it might make a difference." He waved a hand vaguely, expelled cigarette smoke. "You're accountable for what you do."

"Yes," the priest said. "Yes, you are."

"And if you're given orders to do something wrong, you're still accountable, right? The orders don't change it."

"That's right."

"Hmph." January smoked a while. "So they say, anyway. But look what happens." He waved at the office. "I'm like the guy in a story I read—he thought everything in books was true, and after reading a bunch of westerns he tried to rob a train. They tossed him in jail." He laughed shortly. "Books are full of crap."

"Not all of them," the priest said. "Besides, you weren't trying to rob a train."

They laughed at the notion. "Did you read that story?"

"No."

"It was the strangest book—there were two stories in it, and they alternated chapter by chapter, but they didn't have a thing to do with each other! I didn't get it."

"...Maybe the writer was trying to say that everything connects to everything else."

"Maybe. But it's a funny way to say it."

"I like it."

And so they passed the time, talking.

So it was the priest who was the one to come by and tell January that his request for a Presidential pardon had been refused. Getty said awkwardly, "It seems the President approves the sentence."

"That bastard," January said weakly. He sat on his cot.

Time passed. It was another hot, humid day.

"Well," the priest said. "Let me give you some better news. Given your situation I don't think telling you matters, though I've been told not to. The second mission—you know there was a second strike?"

"Yes."

"Well, they missed too."

"What?" January cried, and bounced to his feet. "You're kidding!"

"No. They flew to Kokura, but found it covered by clouds. It was the same over Nagasaki and Hiroshima, so they flew back to Kokura and tried to drop the bomb using radar to guide it, but apparently there was a—a genuine equipment failure this time, and the bomb fell on an island."

January was hopping up and down, mouth hanging open, "So we n-never—"

"We never dropped an atom bomb on a Japanese city. That's right." Getty grinned. "And get this—I heard this from my superior—they sent a message to the Japanese government telling them that the two explosions were warnings, and that if they didn't surrender by September first we would drop bombs on Kyoto and Tokyo, and then wherever else we had to. Word is that the Emperor went to Hiroshima to survey the damage, and when he saw it he ordered the Cabinet to surrender. So..."

"So it worked," January said. He hopped around, "It worked, it worked!"

"Yes."

"Just like I said it would!" he cried, and hopping before the priest he laughed.

Getty was jumping around a little too, and the sight of the priest bouncing was too much for January. He sat on his cot and laughed till the tears ran down his cheeks.

"So—" he sobered quickly. "So Truman's going to shoot me anyway, eh?"

"Yes," the priest said unhappily. "I guess that's right."

This time January's laugh was bitter. "He's a bastard, all right. And proud of being a bastard, which makes it worse." He shook his head. "If Roosevelt had lived..."

"It would have been different, " Getty finished. "Yes.

Maybe so. But he didn't." He sat beside January. "Cigarette?" He held out a pack, and January noticed the white wartime wrapper. He frowned.

"Oh. Sorry."

"Oh well. That's all right." January took one of the Lucky Strikes, lit up. "That's awfully good news." He breathed out. "I never believed Truman would pardon me anyway, so mostly you've brought good news. Ha. They *missed*. You have no idea how much better that makes me feel."

"I think I do."

January smoked the cigarette.

"...So I'm a good American after all. I *am* a good American," he insisted, "no matter what Truman says."

"Yes," Getty replied, and coughed. "You're better than Truman any day."

"Better watch what you say, Father." He looked into the eyes behind the glasses, and the expression he saw there gave him pause. Since the drop every look directed at him had been filled with contempt. He'd seen it so often during the court-martial that he'd learned to stop looking; and now he had to teach himself to see again. The priest looked at him as if he were...as if he were some kind of hero. That wasn't exactly right. But seeing it...

January would not live to see the years that followed, so he would never know what came of his action. He had given up casting his mind forward and imagining possibilities, because there was no point to it. His planning was ended. In any case he would not have been able to imagine the course of the post-war years. That the world would quickly become an armed camp pitched on the edge of atomic war, he might have predicted. But he never would have guessed that so many people would join a January Society. He would never know of the effect the Society had on Dewey during the Korean crisis, never know of the Society's successful campaign for the test ban treaty, and never learn that thanks in part to the Society and its allies, a treaty would be signed by the great powers that would reduce the number of atomic bombs year by year, until there were none left.

Frank January would never know any of that. But in that moment on his cot looking into the eyes of young Patrick Getty, he guessed an inkling of it—he felt, just for an instant, the impact on history.

And with that he relaxed. In his last week everyone who met him carried away the same impression, that of a calm, quiet man, angry at Truman and others, but in a withdrawn, matter-of-fact way. Patrick Getty, a strong force in the January Society ever after, said January was talkative for some time after he learned of the missed attack on Kokura. Then he became quieter and quieter, as the day approached. On the morning that they woke him at dawn to march him out to a hastily constructed execution shed, his MPs shook his hand. The priest was with him as he smoked a final cigarette, and they prepared to put the hood over his head. January looked at him calmly. "They load one of the guns with a blank cartridge, right?"

"Yes," Getty said.

"So each man in the squad can imagine he may not have shot me?"

"Yes. That's right."

A tight, unhumorous smile was January's last expression. He threw down the cigarette, ground it out, poked the priest in the arm. "But I *know*." Then the mask slipped back into place for good, making the hood redundant, and with a firm step January went to the wall. One might have said he was at peace.

Permissions

"Lion Time in Timbuctoo" by Robert Silverberg. Copyright © 1990 by Robert Silverberg. First appeared in *Isaac Asimov's Science-Fiction Magazine*. Reprinted by permission of the author.

"Ike at the Mike" by Howard Waldrop. Copyright © 1982 *Omni* Publications International Ltd. First appeared in *Omni*. Reprinted by permission of the author.

"Over There" by Mike Resnick. Copyright © 1991 by Mike Resnick. Reprinted by permission of the author.

"Suppose They Gave a Peace..." by Susan Shwartz. Copyright © 1991 by Susan Shwartz. Reprinted by permission of the author.

"All the Myriad Ways" by Larry Niven. Copyright © 1968 by Galaxy Publishing Corp., 1971 by Larry Niven. First appeared in *Galaxy*. Reprinted by permission of the author and his agent, Eleanor Wood.

"The Sleeping Serpent" by Pamela Sargent. Copyright © 1992 by Pamela Sargent. First appeared in *Amazing Stories*, January 1992. Reprinted by permission of the author and her agents, Richard Curtis Associates, Inc.

"Catch That Zeppelin!" by Fritz Leiber. Copyright © 1975 Mercury Press. First appeared in *The Magazine of Fantasy & Science Fiction*. Reprinted by permission of the author's agent, Richard Curtis.

"Through Road No Whither" by Greg Bear. Copyright © 1985 by Greg Bear. Reprinted by permission of the author.

"Ship Full of Jews" by Barry N. Malzberg. Copyright © 1992 by Omni Publications, Inc. First appeared in *Omni*. Reprinted by permission of the author.

"Archetypes" by Harry Turtledove. Copyright © 1985 by Harry Turtledove. First appeared in *Amazing Science Fiction Stories*. Reprinted by permission of the author.

"We Could Do Worse" by Gregory Benford. Copyright © 1988 by Abbenford Associates, Inc. Reprinted by permission of the author.

"The Winterberry" by Nicholas DiChario. Copyright © 1992 by Nicholas DiChario. Reprinted by permission of the author.

"The Lucky Strike" by Kim Stanley Robinson. Copyright © 1984 by Kim Stanley Robinson. Reprinted by permission of the author.